KU-303-490

Praise for *Say Her Name*

'A beautiful act of remembrance, love, and understanding. An essential, unforgettable love story and a living testament to an extraordinary woman.'
—Gary Shteyngart

'The madness of love, of death, of loss, of literature—*Say Her Name* is madness knit up into magnificence. We can only suspect that Francisco Goldman is an alchemist, or a magician, or a Faust, or a Job, or all of these things, for with no breathing equipment, he has mined a pearl from the ocean's darkest depths. This book is fabulous in every sense of the word.'—Rivka Galchen

'*Say Her Name* must be the only book about love ever written. It's certainly the only one I'll ever need to read. Francisco Goldman has alchemised grief into joy, death into life, and the act of reading into one of resurrection. His book is a miracle.'—Susan Choi

'Francisco Goldman tells us that in "descending into memory like Orpheus" he hopes he might "bring Aura out alive for a moment." But in the act of writing, Goldman transcends the contraints of myth, and achieves nothing short of the impossible. Page by page, by the breath of his own words, *Say Her Name* restores Aura from shade to flesh, and returns her, unforgettably and permanently, to our world.'—Jhumpa Lahiri

'It doesn't matter what's "truth" and what's "fiction," for the story is inherently moving and tragic, and it focuses on loss and lament—universal themes whether they derive from memoir or from an author's imagination . . . Appropriately, in this novel of death and dying, Goldman writes gorgeous, h

BARKING & DAGENHAM

906 000 000 45852

'The feeling, the memorial incarnation that this book creates, is monumental. Essential . . . This book about tragic death is a gift for the living.'
—*Library Journal*, starred review

'There is beautiful writing in this book—beautiful, perceptive descriptions of places, beautifully turned assaults on the citadel of loss, on the firmament of love and passion, indelible glimpses of the self as bedlam. And thank goodness it's so, because it is such a sad story that only beauty could possibly redeem it.'—Richard Ford

'Enrapturing . . . Vivid . . . Goldman has entwined fact and fiction in his previous novels, but never so daringly or so poignantly. . . . Tender, candid, sorrowful, and funny, this ravishing novel embodies the relentless power of the sea, as hearts are exposed like a beach at low tide only to be battered by a resurgent, obliterating force, like the wave that claims Aura's life on the Oaxaca coast. Out of crushing loss and despair, Goldman has forged a radiant and transcendent masterpiece.'—*Booklist*, starred review

Say Her Name

Award-winning writer Francisco Goldman is the author of three novels, *The Divine Husband*, *The Long Night of White Chickens* and *The Ordinary Seaman*, and one work of non-fiction, *The Art of Political Murder: Who Killed the Bishop?* Goldman has been a contributing editor for *Harper's* magazine and his fiction, journalism and essays have appeared in *The New Yorker*, *The New York Review of Books*, *Esquire* and *The New York Times Magazine*. He currently directs the Premio Auro Estrada/Aura Estrada Prize and lives in Brooklyn and Mexico City.

ALSO BY FRANCISCO GOLDMAN

The Art of Political Murder

The Divine Husband

The Ordinary Seaman

The Long Night of White Chickens

LB OF BARKING & DAGENHAM LIBRARIES	
90600000045852	
Bertrams	30/03/2012
AF	£8.99
GEN	

Say Her Name

Francisco Goldman

Grove Press UK

First published in Great Britain in 2011 by Grove Press UK, an imprint of Grove/Atlantic Inc.

This paperback edition published in 2012

First published in the United States of America in 2011 by Grove/Atlantic Inc.

Copyright © Francisco Goldman, 2011

For their support during the writing of this book, my gratitude to the American Academy of Berlin and the von der Heyden Family Foundation; the Ucross Foundation; and Beatrice Monti and the Santa Maddalenna Foundation. Also my deepest thanks to N.G. in Mexico City and K.R. in New York—you helped me through the worst of it.—F. G.

The moral right of Francisco Goldman to be identified as the author of this work has been asserted by him in accordance with the Copyright, Designs and Patents Act of 1988.

All rights reserved. No part of this publication may be reproduced, stored in a retrieval system, or transmitted in any form or by any means, electronic, mechanical, photocopying, recording, or otherwise, without the prior permission of both the copyright owner and the above publisher of this book.

Every effort has been made to trace or contact all copyright-holders. The publishers will be pleased to make good any omissions or rectify any mistakes brought to their attention at the earliest opportunity.

"If You Find Yourself Caught In Love," written by Bob Kildea, Christopher Geddes, Michael Cooke, Richard Colburn, Sarah Martin, Stephen Jackson, and Stuart Murdoch. Copyright © 2003 Sony/ATV Music Publishing UK Limited. All rights administered by Sony/ATV Music Publishing LLC, 8 Music Square West, Nashville, TN 37203. All rights reserved. Used by permission.

"Little Red Cap" from the book The World's Wife by Carol Ann Duffy. Copyright © 1999 by Carol Ann Duffy. Originally published by Picador, an imprint Pan Macmillan, London. All rights reserved. Used by permission.

"Stephanie Says," written by Lou Reed. Copyright © Metal Machine Music. US and Canadian Rights for Metal Machine Music controlled and administered by Spirit One Music (BMI). World excluding US and Canadian Rights controlled and administered by EMI Music Publishing, Ltd. International Copyright Secured. Used by Permission. All Rights Reserved.

1 3 5 7 9 8 6 4 2

A CIP record for this book is available from the British Library.

Paperback ISBN 978 1 61185 594 4

Printed in Great Britain by
Grove Press UK
Ormond House
26–27 Boswell Street
LondonWC1N 3JZ

www.groveatlantic.com

Vladimir: Suppose we repented ...
Estragon: Our being born?
                    —*Waiting for Godot,* Samuel Beckett

It isn't simply death—it's always the death of someone.
                    —Serge Leclaire

Dear Losse! since thy untimely fate
My task hath beene to meditate
On Thee, on Thee; Thou art the Book,
The Library whereon I look,
Though almost blind.
                    —"Exequy on his Wife," Henry King,
                              Bishop of Chichester

I wouldn't want to be faster
or greener than now if you were with me O you
were the best of all my days
                    —"Animals," Frank O'Hara

... and perhaps you will find out when you go to
heaven, after your gig with the Shanghai Bureau. And
perhaps you will find your bear costume in a closet in
heaven.
                    —"My Shanghai Days," Aura Estrada

Say
Her
Name

1

Aura died on July 25, 2007. I went back to Mexico for the first anniversary because I wanted to be where it had happened, at that beach on the Pacific coast. Now, for the second time in a year, I'd come home again to Brooklyn without her.

Three months before she died, April 24, Aura had turned thirty. We'd been married twenty-six days shy of two years.

Aura's mother and uncle accused me of being responsible for her death. It's not as if I consider myself not guilty. If I were Juanita, I know I would have wanted to put me in prison, too. Though not for the reasons she and her brother gave.

From now on, if you have anything to say to me, put it in writing—that's what Leopoldo, Aura's uncle, said on the telephone when he told me that he was acting as Aura's mother's attorney in the case against me. We haven't spoken since.

Aura.

Aura and me

Aura and her mother

Her mother and me

A love-hate triangle, or, I don't know

Mi amor, is this really happening?

Où sont les axolotls?

Whenever Aura took leave of her mother, whether at the Mexico City airport or if she was just leaving her mother's apartment at night, or even when they were parting after a meal in a restaurant, her mother would lift her hand to make the sign of the cross over her and whisper a little prayer asking the Virgin of Guadalupe to protect her daughter.

Axolotls are a species of salamander that never metamorphose out
of the larval state, something like pollywogs that never become
frogs. They used to be abundant in the lakes around the ancient city
of Mexico, and were a favorite food of the Aztecs. Until recently,
axolotls were said to be still living in the brackish canals of Xochi-
milco; in reality they're practically extinct even there. They survive
in aquariums, laboratories, and zoos.

   Aura loved the Julio Cortázar short story about a man who
becomes so mesmerized by the axolotls in the Jardin des Plantes
in Paris that he turns into an axolotl. Every day, sometimes even
three times a day, the nameless man in that story visits the Jardin
des Plantes to stare at the strange little animals in their cramped
aquarium, at their translucent milky bodies and delicate lizard's tails,
their pink flat triangular Aztec faces and tiny feet with nearly human-
like fingers, the odd reddish sprigs that sprout from their gills, the
golden glow of their eyes, the way they hardly ever move, only now
and then twitching their gills, or abruptly swimming with a single
undulation of their bodies. They seem so alien that he becomes
convinced they're not just animals, that they bear some mysterious
relation to him, are mutely enslaved inside their bodies yet somehow,
with their pulsing golden eyes, are begging him to save them. One
day the man is staring at the axolotls as usual, his face close to the
outside of the tank, but in the middle of that same sentence, the "I"
is now on the inside of the tank, staring through the glass at the
man, the transition happens just like that. The story ends with the
axolotl hoping that he's succeeded in communicating something to
the man, in bridging their silent solitudes, and that the reason the
man no longer visits the aquarium is because he's off somewhere
writing a story about what it is to be an axolotl.

   The first time Aura and I went to Paris together, about five
months after she'd moved in with me, she wanted to go to the Jardin des Plantes to see Cortázar's axolotls more than she wanted to
do anything else. She'd been to Paris before, but had only recently

discovered Cortázar's story. You would have thought that the only reason we'd flown to Paris was to see the axolotls, though actually Aura had an interview at the Sorbonne, because she was considering transferring from Columbia. Our very first afternoon, we went to the Jardin des Plantes, and paid to enter its small nineteenth-century zoo. In front of the entrance to the amphibian house, or vivarium, there was a mounted poster with information in French about amphibians and endangered species, illustrated with an image of a red-gilled axolotl in profile, its happy extraterrestrial's face and albino monkey arms and hands. Inside, the tanks ran in a row around the room, smallish illuminated rectangles set into the wall, each framing a somewhat different humid habitat: moss, ferns, rocks, tree branches, pools of water. We went from tank to tank, reading the placards: various species of salamanders, newts, frogs, but no axolotls. We circled the room again, in case we'd somehow missed them. Finally Aura went up to the guard, a middle-aged man in uniform, and asked where the axolotls were. He didn't know anything about the axolotls, but something in Aura's expression seemed to give him pause, and he asked her to wait; he left the room and a moment later came back with a woman, somewhat younger than him, wearing a blue lab coat. She and Aura spoke quietly, in French, so I couldn't understand what they were saying, but the woman's expression was lively and kind. When we went outside, Aura stood there for a moment with a quietly stunned expression. Then she told me that the woman remembered the axolotls; she'd even said that she missed them. But they'd been taken away a few years before and were now in some university laboratory. Aura was in her charcoal gray woolen coat, a whitish wool scarf wrapped around her neck, strands of her straight black hair mussed around her soft round cheeks, which were flushed as if burning with cold, though it wasn't particularly cold. Tears, just a few, not a flood, warm salty tears overflowed from Aura's brimming eyes and slid down her cheeks.

Who cries over something like that? I remember thinking. I kissed the tears, breathing in that briny Aura warmth. Whatever it was that so got to Aura about the axolotls not being there seemed part of the same mystery that the axolotl at the end of Cortázar's story hopes the man will reveal by writing a story. I always wished that I could know what it was like to be Aura.

Où sont les axolotls? she wrote in her notebook. Where are they?

Aura moved in with me in Brooklyn about six weeks after she'd arrived in New York from Mexico City with her multiple scholarships, including a Fulbright and another from the Mexican government, to begin studying for a PhD in Spanish-language literature at Columbia. We lived together almost four years. At Columbia she shared her university housing with another foreign student, a Korean girl, a botanist of some highly specialized kind. I saw that apartment only two or three times before I moved Aura's things to my place. It was a railroad flat, with a long narrow hallway, two bedrooms, a living room at the front. A student apartment, filled with student things: her Ikea bookcase, a set of charcoal-hued nonstick pots and pans and utensils, a red beanbag chair, a stereo unit, a small toolbox, from Ikea too, still sealed in its clear plastic wrapper. Her mattress on the floor, clothing heaped all over it. That apartment made me feel nostalgic as hell—for college days, youth. I was dying to make love to her then and there, in the sumptuous mess of that bed, but she was nervous about her roommate coming in, so we didn't.

I took her away from that apartment, leaving her roommate, whom Aura got along with fine, on her own. But a month or so later, once she felt sure that she was going to stay with me, Aura found another student to take her share, a Russian girl who seemed like someone the Korean girl would like.

Up there, on Amsterdam Avenue and 119th Street, Aura lived at the edge of campus. In Brooklyn, she had to ride the subway at least one hour each way to get to Columbia, usually during rush hour, and she went almost every day. She could take the F train, transfer at Fourteenth Street and make her way through a maze of stairways and long tunnels, grim and freezing in winter, to the 2 and 3 express trains, and switch to the local at Ninety-sixth Street. Or she could walk twenty-five minutes from our apartment to Borough Hall and catch the 2 or 3 there. Eventually she decided she preferred the second option, and that was what she did almost every day. In winter the trek could be brutally cold, especially in the thin wool coats she wore, until finally I convinced her to let me buy her one of those hooded North Face down coats, swaddling her from the top of the head to below the knees in goose down–puffed blue nylon. No, mi amor, it doesn't make you look *fat*, not you in particular, everybody looks like a walking sleeping bag in one of those, and who cares anyway? Isn't it better to be snug and warm? When she wore the coat with the hood up, collar closed under her chin, with her gleaming black eyes, she looked like a little Iroquois girl walking around inside her own papoose, and she hardly ever went out into the cold without it.

Another complication of the long commute was that she regularly got lost. She'd absentmindedly miss her stop or else take the train in the wrong direction and, engrossed in her book, her thoughts, her iPod, wouldn't notice until she was deep into Brooklyn. Then she'd call from a pay phone in some subway station I'd never heard of, Hola, mi amor, well, here I am in the Beverly Road Station, I went the wrong way again—her voice determinedly matter-of-fact, no big deal, just another overscheduled New Yorker coping with a routine dilemma of city life, but sounding a touch defeated anyhow. She didn't like being teased about going the wrong way on the subway, or getting lost even when she was walking in our own neighborhood, but sometimes I couldn't help it.

From Aura's first day in our Brooklyn apartment to nearly her last, I walked her to the subway stop every morning—except on those mornings when she rode her bicycle to Borough Hall and left it locked there, though that routine didn't last long because the homeless drunks and junkies of downtown Brooklyn kept stealing her bike seat, or when it was raining or when she was just running so behind that she took a taxi to Borough Hall, or on the rare occasion when she flew out the door like a furious little tornado because it was getting late and I was still stuck on the can yelling for her to wait, and the two or three times when she was just so pissed off at me about something or other that she absolutely didn't want me to walk with her.

Usually though, I walked her to the F train stop on Bergen,

or I walked her to Borough Hall, though eventually we agreed that
when she was headed to Borough Hall I would go only as far as the
French guy's deli on Verandah Place—I had work to do and couldn't
just lose nearly an hour every day going to the station and back—
though she would try to coax me farther, to Atlantic Avenue, or to
Borough Hall after all, or even up to Columbia. Then I'd spend the
day in Butler Library—a few semesters previous I'd taught a writing
workshop at Columbia and I still had my ID card—reading or writing or trying to write in a notebook, or I'd sit at one of the library
computers checking e-mail or killing time with online newspapers,
routinely starting with the *Boston Globe* sports section (I grew up
in Boston). Usually we'd have lunch at Ollie's, then go and blow
money on DVDs and CDs at Kim's, or browse in Labyrinth Books,
coming out carrying heavy bags of books neither of us had the extra
time to read. On days when she hadn't convinced me to accompany
her to Columbia in the morning, she'd sometimes phone and ask
me to come all the way up there just to have lunch with her, and
as often as not, I'd go. Aura would say,

Francisco, I didn't get married to eat lunch by myself. I didn't
get married to spend time by myself.

On those morning walks to the subway, Aura always did most
or even all of the talking, about her classes, professors, other students, about some new idea for a short story or novel, or about her
mother. Even when she was being especially *neuras*, going on about
her regular anxieties, I'd try to come up with new encouragements
or else rephrase or repeat prior ones. But I especially loved it when
she was in the mood to stop every few steps and kiss and nip at my
lips like a baby tiger, and her mimed silent laughter after my *ouch*,
and the way she'd complain, *¿Ya no me quieres, verdad?* if I wasn't
holding her hand or didn't have my arm around her the instant she
wanted me to. I loved our ritual except when I didn't really love it,
when I'd worry, How am I ever going to get another damned book
written with this woman who makes me walk her to the subway
every morning and cajoles me into coming up to Columbia to have
lunch with her?

I still regularly imagine that Aura is beside me on the sidewalk. Sometimes I imagine I'm holding her hand, and walk with my arm held out by my side a little. Nobody is surprised to see people talking to themselves in the street anymore, assuming that they must be speaking into some Bluetooth device. But people do stare when they notice that your eyes are red and wet, your lips twisted into a sobbing grimace. I wonder what they think they are seeing and what they imagine has caused the weeping. On the surface, a window has briefly, alarmingly, opened.

One day that first fall after Aura's death, in Brooklyn, on the corner of Smith and Union, I noticed an old lady standing on the opposite corner, waiting to cross the street, a normal-looking old lady from the neighborhood, neat gray hair, a little hunched, a sweet jowly expression on her pale face, looking as if she were enjoying the sunlight and October weather as she waited patiently for the light to change. The thought was like a silent bomb: Aura will never find out about being old, she'll never get to look back on her own long life. That was all it took, thinking about the unfairness of that and about the lovely and accomplished old lady Aura had surely been destined to become.

Destined. Was I destined to have come into Aura's life when I did, or did I intrude where I didn't belong and disrupt its predestined path? Was Aura supposed to have married someone else, maybe some other Columbia student, that guy studying a few seats away from her in Butler Library or the one in the Hungarian Pastry Shop who couldn't stop shyly peeking at her? How can anything other than what happened be accurately described as destined? What about her own free will, her own responsibility for her choices? When the light changed and I crossed Smith Street, did that old lady notice my face as we passed? I don't know. My blurred gaze was fixed on the pavement and I wanted to be back inside our apartment. Aura was more present there than she was anywhere else.

The apartment, which I'd been renting for eight years by then, was the parlor floor of a four-story brownstone. Back when the

Rizzitanos, the Italian family that still owned the building, used to live there, occupying all four floors, the parlor would have been their living room. But it was our bedroom. It had such tall ceilings that to change a lightbulb in the hanging lamp I'd climb a five-foot stepladder, stand on tiptoes atop its rickety pinnacle and reach up as high as I could, though still end up bent over, arms flapping, fighting for balance—Aura, watching from her desk in the corner, said, You look like an amateur bird. Around the tops of the walls ran a plaster cornice, whitewashed like the walls, a neoclassical row of repeating rosettes atop a wider one of curled fronds. Two long windows, with deep sills and curtains, faced the street, and between the windows, rising from floor to ceiling like a chimney, was the apartment's gaudiest feature: an immense mirror in a baroque, gold-painted wooden frame. Now Aura's wedding dress partly covered the mirror, hung from a clothes hanger and butcher twine that I'd tied around gilded curlicues on opposite sides at the top. And on the marble shelf at the foot of the mirror was an altar made up of some of Aura's belongings.

When I came back from Mexico that first time, six weeks after Aura's death, Valentina, who studied with Aura at Columbia, and their friend Adele Ramírez, who was visiting from Mexico and staying with Valentina, came to pick me up at Newark Airport in Valentina's investment-banker husband's BMW station wagon. I had five suitcases: two of my own and three filled with Aura's things, not just her clothes—I'd refused to throw or give away almost anything of hers—but also some of her books and photos, and a short lifetime's worth of her diaries, notebooks, and loose papers. I'm sure that if that day some of my guy friends had come for me at the airport instead, and we'd walked into our apartment, it would have been much different, probably we would have taken a disbelieving look around and said, Let's go to a bar. But I'd hardly finished bringing in the suitcases before Valentina and Adele went to work building the altar. They dashed around the apartment as if they knew where everything was better than I did, choosing and carrying treasures back, occasionally asking for my opinion or suggestion. Adele, a visual artist, crouched over the marble shelf at the foot of the mirror, arranging: the denim hat with a cloth flower stitched onto it that Aura bought during our trip to Hong Kong; the green canvas satchel she brought to the beach that last day, with everything inside it just as she'd left it, her wallet, her sunglasses, and the two slender books she was reading (Bruno Schulz and Silvina Ocampo); her hairbrush, long strands of black hair snagged in the bristles; the cardboard tube of Chinese pick-up sticks she bought in the mall near our apartment in Mexico City and took into the T.G.I. Fridays there, where we sat drinking tequila and playing pick-up sticks two weeks before she died; a copy of the *Boston Review,* where her last published essay in English had appeared early that last summer; her favorite (and only) pair of Marc Jacobs shoes; her little turquoise drinking flask; a few other trinkets, souvenirs, adornments; photographs; candles; and standing empty on the floor at the foot of the altar, her shiny mod black-and-white-striped rubber rain boots with the hot pink soles. Valentina, standing before the towering mirror, announced: I know! Where's Aura's wedding dress? I went and got the wedding dress out of the closet, and the stepladder.

It was just the kind of thing Aura and I made fun of: a folkloric Mexican altar in a grad student's apartment as a manifestation of corny identity politics. But it felt like the right thing to do now, and throughout that first year of Aura's death and after, the wedding dress remained. I regularly bought flowers to put in the vase on the floor, and lit candles, and bought new candles to replace the burned-out ones.

The wedding dress was made for Aura by a Mexican fashion designer who owned a boutique on Smith Street. We'd become friendly with the owner, Zoila, who was originally from Mexicali. In her store we'd talk about the authentic taco stand we were going to open someday to make money off the drunk, hungry, young people pouring out of the Smith Street bars at night, all three of us pretending that we were really serious about joining in this promising business venture. Then Aura discovered that Zoila's custom-tailored bridal dresses were recommended on the

Web site Daily Candy as a thrifty alternative to the likes of Vera Wang. Aura went to Zoila's studio, in a loft in downtown Brooklyn, for three or four fittings, and she came home from each feeling more anxious than before. She was, at first, after she went to pick up the finished dress, disappointed in it, finding it more simple than she'd imagined it was going to be, and not much different from some of the ordinary dresses Zoila sold in her store for a quarter of the price. It was an almost minimalist version of a Mexican country girl's dress, made of fine white cotton, with simple embellishments of silk and lace embroidery, and it widened into ruffles at the bottom.

But in the end, Aura decided that she liked the dress. Maybe it just needed to be in its rightful habitat, the near-desert setting of the Catholic shrine village of Atotonilco, amid an old mission church and cactus and scrub and the green oasis grounds of the restored hacienda that we'd rented for the wedding, beneath the vivid blue and then yellow-gray immensity of the Mexican sky and the turbulent cloud herds coming and going across it. Maybe that was the genius of Zoila's design for Aura's dress. A sort of freeze-dried dress, seemingly plain as tissue paper, that shimmered to life in the charged thin air of the high plains of central Mexico. A perfect dress for a Mexican country wedding in August, a girlhood dream of a wedding dress after all. Now the dress was slightly yellowed, the shoulder straps darkened by salty perspiration, and one of the bands of lace running around the dress lower down, above where it widened out, was partly ripped from the fabric, a tear like a bullet hole, and the hem was discolored and torn from having been dragged through mud and danced on and stepped on during the long night into dawn of our wedding party, when Aura had taken off her wedding shoes and slipped into the dancing shoes we'd bought at a bridal shop in Mexico City, which were like a cross between white nurse shoes and seventies disco platform sneakers. A delicate relic, that wedding dress. At night, backed by the mirror's illusion of depth and the reflected glow of candles and lamps, the baroque frame like a golden corona around it, the dress looks like it's floating.

* * *

Despite the altar, or maybe partly because of it, our cleaning lady quit. Flor, from Oaxaca, now raising three children in Spanish Harlem, who came to clean once every two weeks, said it made her too sad to be in our apartment. The one time Flor did come, I watched her kneel to pray at the altar, watched her pick up photographs of Aura and press them to her lips, smudging them with her emphatic kisses and tears. She imitated Aura's reliable words of praise for her work, the happy pitch of her voice: Oh Flor, it's as if you work miracles! Ay, señor, said Flor. She was always so happy, so full of life, so young, so good, she always asked after my children. How could she do her job now, in that way that had always so pleased Aura, Flor pleadingly asked me, if she couldn't stop crying? Then she'd taken her sadness and tears home with her, home to her children, she explained later when she phoned, and that wasn't right, no señor, she couldn't do it anymore, she was sorry but she had to quit. I didn't bother to look for a new cleaning lady. I suppose I thought she would feel sorry for me and come back. I tried phoning, finally, to beg her to come back, and got a recorded message that the number was no longer in service. Then, months after she'd quit, incredibly, she repented and did phone and leave her new telephone number—apparently, she'd moved—on the answering machine. But when I phoned back, it was the wrong number. Probably I'd written it down wrong, I'm a touch dyslexic anyway.

Now, fifteen months after Aura's death, coming home without her again—no one to meet me at the airport this time—I found the apartment exactly as I'd left it in July. The bed was unmade. The first thing I did was open all the windows, letting in the cool, damp October air.

Aura's MacBook was still there, on her desk. I'd be able to pick up where I'd left off, working on, organizing, trying to piece together her stories, essays, poems, her just begun novel, and her unfinished writings, the thousands of fragments, really, that she left in her computer, in her labyrinthine and scattered manner of storing files and documents. I thought I felt ready to immerse myself in that task.

In the bedroom there were old dead rose petals, darker than blood, on the floor around the vase in front of the altar, but the vase was empty. In the kitchen, Aura's plants, despite not having been watered in three months, were still alive. I stuck my finger in the soil of one pot and found it moist.

Then I remembered that I'd left a key with the upstairs neighbors, asking them to water Aura's plants while I was away. I'd only intended to go to Mexico for the first anniversary and stay a month, but I'd stayed three, and they'd kept it up all that time. They'd thrown out the dead roses, which must have begun to rot and smell. And they'd collected my mail in a shopping bag that they had put next to the couch, just inside the apartment door.

On the beach we—I and some of the swimmers who saw or heard my cries for help—pulled Aura out of the water and set her down in the almost ditchlike incline gouged by the waves, and then we picked her up again and carried her to where it was level and laid her on the hot sand. As she fought for air, closing and opening her mouth, whispering only the word "*aire*" when she needed me to press my lips to hers again, Aura said something that I don't actually remember hearing, just as I remember so little of what happened, but her cousin Fabiola, before she took off looking for an ambulance, heard it and later told me. What Aura said, one of the last things she ever said to me, was:

Quiéreme mucho, mi amor.

Love me a lot, my love.

No quiero morir. I don't want to die. That may have been the last full sentence she ever spoke, maybe her very last words.

Did that sound self-exculpating? Is this the kind of statement I should prohibit myself from making? Sure, Aura's plea and invocation of love would play well on any jury's emotions and sympathies, but I'm not in a courtroom. I need to stand nakedly before the facts; there's no way to fool this jury that I am facing. It all matters, and it's all evidence.

2

Is this really happening, mi amor? Am I really back in Brooklyn again without you? Throughout your first year of death and now, out on the streets at night, *pounding the pavement,* up one side of the block, down the other, lingering at steamy windows looking at menus that I know by heart, what take-out food should I choose, what cheap restaurant should I eat in tonight, what bar will I stop into for a drink or two or three or five where I won't feel so jarringly alone—but where don't I feel jarringly alone?

The five or so years before I met Aura were the loneliest I'd ever known. The year plus months since her death were much lonelier. But what about the four years in between? Was I a different man than I was before those four years, an improved man, because of the love and happiness that I experienced? Because of what Aura gave to me? Or was I just the same old me who, for four years, was inexplicably lucky? Four years—are those too few years to hold such significance in a grown man's life? Or can four years mean so much that they will forever outweigh all the others put together?

After she died, for the first month or so, I didn't dream about Aura, though in Mexico City I felt her presence everywhere. Then, in the fall, when she should have been starting her classes, I had my first dream, one in which it was urgent that I buy a cell phone. In the middle of a lush green field with a silvery stream running through it, I found a wooden hut that was a cell phone store, and I went inside. I was desperate to phone Wendy, another classmate and friend of Aura's. I wanted to ask Wendy if Aura missed me. I wanted to ask Wendy, in these exact words, *Does she miss our domestic routines?* I carried the new cell phone, silvery with sapphire keys, out of the hut, into the field, toward the stream, but I couldn't get it to work. Frustrated, I hurled the phone away.

Do you miss our domestic routines, mi amor?

Can this really be happening to us?

Degraw Street, where we lived, supposedly marks the border between Carroll Gardens and Cobble Hill. Our apartment was on the Carroll Gardens side of the street, Cobble Hill on the other side. When I first moved there, about four years before I met Aura, Carroll Gardens still seemed like the classic Brooklyn Italian neighborhood, old-fashioned Italian restaurants where mobsters and politicians used to eat, lawn statues of the Virgin, old men playing bocce ball in the playground; especially on summer nights, with so many loud tough-guy types milling around, I'd always feel a little menaced walking through there. Cobble Hill was where Winston Churchill's mother was born and still looked the part, with its landmark Episcopalian church that had a Tiffany interior, quaint carriage house mews, and park. Both neighborhoods had pretty much blended together now, overtaken mostly by prosperous young white people. 9/11 had accelerated the process—nice and quiet, family-seeming neighborhood across the Brooklyn Bridge. Now, by day, you wove through long crooked trains of baby carriages on the Court Street sidewalks, and ate lunch or went for coffee in places filled with young moms, au pairs, and an embarrassing number of writers. The Italian men's social clubs had become hipster cocktail bars. On every street brownstones converted into apartments years ago were being renovated back into single-family homes. A few blocks away, just across the BQE is Red Hook, the harbor and port; at night you can hear ships' foghorns, Aura loved that; with a swimmer's little wriggle she'd nestle closer in bed and hold still, as if the long mournful blasts were about to float past us like manta rays in the dark.

This was Aura's yoga studio; here's the spa she'd go to for a massage when she was stressed; here was her favorite clothing boutique, and there, her second favorite; our fish store; this is where she bought those cool eyeglasses with yellow-tinted lenses; our late-night burger and drinks place; our brunch place; "the-restaurant-we-always-fight-in"—that's what walking these streets had become now, a silent chanting of the stations. The neighborhood has an abundance of Italian pizza parlors and brick-oven places, and a single small antiseptic Domino's Pizza on the corner of Smith and Bergen, by the subway exit, its customers mostly residents of the Hoyt Street housing projects and black and Latino teenagers from a nearby high school. One night we were coming home late from drinking with friends when, without saying anything, Aura darted through the Domino's glass doors and stood at the counter no more than a minute, I swear, before she came back out with a giant pizza box in her hands and a look-what-I-just-won grin. All the upscale pizza places were closed by that hour, but I bet at that moment none could have satisfied Aura's hungry impulse like Domino's. Where she grew up in Mexico City, amid the residential complexes of the city's south, every evening an army of helmeted delivery boys on motorbikes, thousands upon thousands, buzzed and zoomed like bees through the clogged expressways and streets, speeding fast food pizza to the apartments and families of working and single mothers like Aura's. Now I never walk past that Domino's without seeing her coming out the door with the pizza and that smile.

The long-defunct mud-hued Catholic church across the street from our apartment was being converted into a condo building (the developers, Orthodox Jews, and the work crew, Mexican); Aura would have been happy about the new Trader Joe's down at Atlantic and Court; on Smith Street, the taco place we were going to open with Zoila opened but Zoila's boutique closed last year and I still don't know where she's gone to. Around the corner is the grungy but popular Wi-Fi café that Aura often liked to study and work in when she wasn't up at Columbia. She found it easier to concentrate there than at home. No me bugging her for attention or sex or noisily typing away in the next room, no mother phoning from Mexico. I'd come in and see her sitting at one of the tables against the brick wall, half-eaten bagel atop its wax-paper bag, mug of coffee, hair pushed back by a barrette or a red band or tied back to keep it out of her face as she leaned over her laptop, headphones on, that determined, locked-in look, lightly biting her lower lip, and I'd stand and watch her or pretend I'd never seen her before and wait for her to lift her eyes and see me. I used to come to this café to work, too. She didn't mind. We'd share a table, have lunch or split a bagel or a cookie. Now I only come in for morning take-out coffee. Waiting in the inevitable line, I stare at the row of tables, the long blue bench against the wall, strangers sitting there with their computers.

I hadn't thrown away or moved out any of Aura's clothes, they were still in her chest of drawers and in the walk-in closet. Her cold weather coats and jackets, including the down one, hung from a peg by the front door. At least once a day I'd open a drawer and hold a pile of her clothes to my nose, frustrated that they smelled more of the drawer's wood than of Aura, and sometimes I emptied out a drawer on the bed and lay facedown in her clothes. I knew that eventually I should give these things away—her clothes, at least—that there was somebody out there who could not afford a down coat and whose life would be made more bearable by it, maybe even saved. I pictured an illegal immigrant woman or girl in some brutally cold place, a meatpacking plant town in Wisconsin, a Chicago tenement without heat. But I wasn't ready to let go of anything. It wasn't even an argument I had with myself—though I did discuss it with some of Aura's friends. At first they had seemed fixated on the idea that, for my own good, I needed to get rid of some of her things. Nobody suggested I had to get rid of everything. Why couldn't I do it a little at a time, donate some of her coats to the city's winter coat drive, for starters? In the end, of course, I should keep a few special things, such as her wedding dress, "to remember her by." During those first months, I drifted away from most of my male friends and shut myself off from my family—my mother and siblings—and only wanted to be around women: Aura's friends but also a few women I'd been close to since long before Aura.

With the exception of the table that I wrote at in the corner of the middle room—the one between the kitchen and the parlor room where we slept—and some of the old bookshelves, Aura and I had slowly gotten rid of and replaced all the furniture from my slovenly bachelor years. It frustrated Aura that we hadn't moved into a new apartment, free of traces and reminders of my past without her, a place she could make wholly ours, though she did completely transform the apartment we had. Sometimes I'd come home and find her pushing even the heaviest furniture around, changing the crowded layout in a way that had never occurred to me or even seemed possible, as if the apartment were some kind of complicated puzzle that could only be solved by pushing furniture around and that she'd become obsessed with, or else maybe it could never be solved, but she always made the place look better.

The last piece of furniture we bought, at a secondhand store about five blocks away, was a fifties-style kitchen table, its inlaid Formica top patterned in cerulean blue and pearly white, cheery as a child's painting of a sunny sky and clouds. In the kitchen, also, was the evergreen-painted kitchen hutch that we'd bought at an antique store in a small rural town in the Catskills during a weekend when we were visiting Valentina and Jim at their country house; about two months after we bought it, the store's exasperated owner phoned—it wasn't her first call—to tell us that if we didn't come for the hutch soon, she'd put it up for sale again, no money back. That kitchen hutch was no bargain. Farmhouse hutches of just that kind could be found for the same price in our neighborhood antique stores and on Atlantic Avenue. But we rented an SUV in Brooklyn to go and fetch ours, and spent the weekend at a sort of Italian-American hunting lodge, a Plexiglas Jacuzzi with shiny brass fixtures and an artificial gas fireplace in our cabin, where we holed up with books, wine, a football game on TV with the sound off, laughing our heads off when we tried to fuck in the ridiculous Jacuzzi, and whenever we were hungry we'd go into the restaurant, which was decorated with several generations' worth of autographed photos of New York Yankees, to dig back into the perpetual all-you-can-eat buffet, spaghetti with giant meatballs, sausage lasagna, and the like. In the end, that hutch ended up costing us about four times what we would have paid to buy one in Brooklyn.

In our kitchen, along with the hutch, were all our other culinary things—utensils, pots and pans—mostly untouched since last touched by Aura. Her Hello Kitty toaster that branded every piece of toast with the Hello Kitty logo—I did still use that toaster, smiling away at Aura's girly nerdiness whenever I spread butter over the kitty face. The Cuisinart ice-cream maker Aura bought just so that she could make dulce de leche ice cream for her birth-day party when she turned thirty, the ice-cream maker's metallic freezing cylinder still sitting in the freezer. The long dining table from ABC Carpet and Home that we paid for with wedding gift money, and that with its extensions at both ends provided enough space for the twenty-plus friends who came to that party, sitting jammed in around it. We made cochinita pibil, soft pork oozing citrus-and-achiote spiced juices inside a wrapping of banana leaves roasted parchment dry, and rajas con crema, and arroz verde, and Valentina came early and prepared her meatballs in chipotle sauce in our kitchen, and there was a gorgeously garish birthday cake from a Mexican bakery in Sunset Park—white, orange, and pink frosting, fruit slices in a glazed ring on top—served with Aura's ice cream. Her birthday present that year was two long rustic benches for seating at the table. She wanted us to have lots of dinner parties.

It isn't true that to be happy in New York City you have to be rich. I'm not saying that another twenty, thirty, fifty grand a year wouldn't have improved our circumstances and maybe made us even happier. But few people who'd known me or Aura before we got together would have guessed either of us had any talent for domestic life.

Aura's three simultaneous scholarships added up to a startling salary, for a full-time student anyway. As I never asked her to pay rent, or for much of anything else, she'd had money to spend and to save. She'd wanted to use her savings to help us buy a house or an apartment one day, if I ever managed to save enough money of my own, which I was determined to do. When I finally went and closed Aura's account, I was astonished at how much was there. Now I was pretty much living off those savings, money from the scholarships but also what she'd been saving since her adolescence. I'd already used up the insurance reimbursement money that was meant to pay off the credit cards I'd used for Aura's medical, hospital, and ambulance bills in Mexico. I'd paid only about half of those charges, digging myself still deeper into debt. So I was in debt. And so what? Because I had only a part-time position in the English department at the small Connecticut college where I was teaching, I hadn't been entitled to paid bereavement leave. But I couldn't bear to teach that semester after Aura's death, so I'd resigned. I knew that soon I would have to get a job. What kind of job? No idea. But I couldn't see myself teaching again. I had my reasons. The enthusiasm and willed energy of a committed performer that somebody like me, not a trained literary scholar, is going to need to hold the attention of a classroom of easily bored twenty-year-olds, that was gone. In love with Aura, married, unabashedly happy, I'd been a good and entertaining literature clown.

The plants Aura had kept out on the fire escape had been dead since last winter and were now just plastic and clay pots filled with dirt and plant rubble, gray stems, and crinkly leaves. But her plastic folding chair was still out there, dirty-urban-weather-streaked but otherwise untouched by any human since the last time she sat in it, along with the glass ashtray at its foot, washed out by more than a year of rain. Sometimes squirrels jumped onto the seat from the fire escape's railing, drank from the rain or melted snow pooled in its slight concavity. In nice weather Aura liked to sit out there on the fire escape, in that little rusted cage, feet propped on the stairs leading to the landing above, surrounded by her plants, reading, writing on her laptop, smoking a little. She wasn't a heavy smoker. Some days she'd smoke a few cigarettes; other days, none. Occasionally, she smoked pot, usually when someone at school gave her some. I still had her last, almost empty, bag of pot in the drawer of our kitchen hutch. To Aura it was as if the fire escape was no less a garden than our downstairs neighbors' actual backyard garden that she sat perched above. I'd tease her that she was like Kramer from the *Seinfeld* show who did things like that, celebrating the Fourth of July by setting a lawn chair in front of his apartment door, pretending the hallway was a backyard in the suburbs, and sitting there with beer, cigar, and a hot dog.

One morning I found myself standing in the kitchen looking through the window at the chair on the fire escape as if I'd never seen it before. That's when I thought to name it Aura's Journey Chair. I imagined her descending slowly down a long shaft of yellow-pink translucent light, in a sitting position, holding a book open in her hands, landing softly in the chair, returned from her long, mysterious journey. She glances up from her book, notices me watching through the kitchen window, and says, like always, in her cheerful, hoarse-sounding voice, Hola, mi amor.

Hola, mi amor. But where did you go? Why were you away so long? I know you didn't get married just to go off by yourself like that and leave me alone here!

The weekend before we left for Mexico at the end of June, Valentina and Jim had invited us to their country house again. We were headed back to the city late on Sunday afternoon when Aura and Valentina said that they wanted to stop at a shop in town that we'd visited the day before. Jim and I and their smelly dog, Daisy, waited in the car and minutes later I saw Aura coming out of the shop with a new purchase clasped in her arms, a Joseph's multicolored dream coat of a quilt, in a clear plastic casing, that she told me had cost only $150. A good price, I agreed, for such a beautiful quilt, and brand-new, too, no musty grandma relic. An affixed brochure told about the American artist who'd spent years traveling through foreign lands studying textiles and who now designed these quilts that were then hand stitched by seamstresses at her workshop in India.

A few days later, as we were packing, Aura came out from the closet carrying the folded quilt in both arms and laid it into the open suitcase on the floor. So she wanted to bring the quilt to the apartment in Mexico. And then she wanted to bring it back to Brooklyn in the fall? Así es, mi querido Francisco, she answered, with that lightly sarcastic formality that indicated she'd anticipated my skepticism. I rarely opposed Aura's wishes, with the exception, I admit, of her wanting to move to a bigger apartment, or one with a garden where we could have a dog, because we really couldn't afford to do that just yet. But this time I did oppose her. It doesn't make sense, I said, to bring the quilt to Mexico and back with us in September. Look, it takes up almost the whole suitcase by itself. And don't we already have a nice duvet on the bed in Mexico? But the quilt is so beautiful, Aura insisted. And we just bought it. Why should the subletter get to enjoy it before we do? Maybe we should just keep the quilt in Mexico, she said; at least we *own* that apartment. (It was her mother's, actually; she'd bought it for Aura before Aura had even met me, though we'd taken over the mortgage payments.) We don't have to leave the quilt out for the subletter, I argued. You can just put it away in the closet, and we can inaugurate it in the fall when we get back. Imagine how much we'll miss the quilt this winter if we leave it behind in Mexico.

Without another word, Aura pulled the quilt out of the suitcase and carried it into the closet. She came back into the bedroom and resumed her packing in stony silence. For the next few minutes, she hated me. I was her worst enemy ever. I had to bite the inside of my cheek to keep from laughing.

After Aura's death, Valentina told me that the quilt hadn't really cost $150; it had cost $600. Aura had been afraid to tell me.

But it wasn't just the money, I knew. It was that she didn't

want me to think of her as the *kind of woman* who would drop so
much money on a quilt—even though I knew she was—in the same
way that she'd get upset whenever I noticed that she was perusing
celebrity gossip or fashion Web sites on her laptop while we read
or worked in bed before going to sleep at night. She'd sit with the
computer balanced on her knees, the screen turned away from me,
emitting staccato spurts of typing, jumping from window to window.
It didn't bother me that she liked celebrity and fashion Web sites.
Though that is exactly what would have bugged her, catching this
glimpse of herself through my eyes, me supposedly loving it that my
brainy superliterary grad student young wife could have the same
enjoyments as any frivolous housewifey girl who never read anything deeper than *People*. That I could love that, that I presumably
found that cute and sexy, that she could satisfy that *cursi* macho
voyeurism—how embarrassing! At the end of a long day, she liked
losing herself in those Web sites; ¿y qué? It had no significance. Even
my noticing it at all was already a distortion or an exaggeration of
who she *really* was. Why couldn't I just keep my eyes on my own
book or laptop? My defense was that I was entranced by almost
everything she did and could hardly ever take my eyes off her. Really,
I was just waiting for her to put the computer away and tumble into
my arms under the covers. She knew that, too.

When I came back to Brooklyn alone from Mexico that first
time after Aura's death it was mid-September, hot and steamy. It
seemed, that fall of 2007, as if summer refused to end, hanging over
the city like a punishment. I ran the air conditioner night and day.
But finally, with the first dip in temperature, I went to the closet
and, just like I'd promised Aura, took the quilt out of its plastic case
and laid it over the bed. The quilt was made up of thin horizontal
strips of miscellaneous fabrics—every conceivable hue of bright
color seemed represented, reds slightly predominating—arranged
in parallel rows running lengthwise. It really did seem to vibrate
before my eyes. The quilt added to the strikingly feminine aspect
of what was now my widower's bedroom. Stuffed animals and toy
robots; a miniature ruby slipper dangling from a lamp shade; a big

chocolate heart from Valentine's Day a few years before, still in its cellophane wrapper and ribbon. Plush love seat in a corner, piled with big colorful cushions, next to the television. Wedding dress over the mirror. The carved, painted winged angel from Taxco with its scarlet-lipped white face of a lewd adolescent cherub, hanging from the pronged lamp over the bed, very slowly and perpetually spinning at the end of its nylon cord, fixing its wooden stare on me alone in bed just as it used to stare at Aura and I together, and slowly turning away.

Often in the mornings, when Aura had just woken up, she would turn to me in bed and say, Ay, mi amor, que feo eres. ¿Por qué me casé contigo?, her voice sweet and impish. Oh my love, how ugly you are. Why did I marry you?

¿Soy feo? I would ask sadly. This was one of our routines.

Sí, mi amor, she'd say, eres feo, pobrecito. And she'd kiss me, and we'd laugh. A laugh, I can say for myself, that began deep in my belly and rumbled up through me, spreading that giddy smile on my face that you see in photographs of me from those years, that goofy grin that didn't leave my face even when I was reciting my wedding vows—Aura's expression, meanwhile, appropriately emotional and solemn, if a little stunned—which made our wedding pictures kind of embarrassing to look at.

Aura put her quilt away in the closet and came back into the bedroom and finished packing for her death, three weeks and one day away.

3

That first day back in the apartment with Valentina and Adele Ramírez, it was like stepping into an absolute emptiness, outside of time—after I'd brought the suitcases in and we'd hung the wedding dress and built the altar, I said, I wonder where Aura kept her engagement ring? (Or did I say, I wonder where she keeps her engagement ring?) She hadn't brought the ring to Mexico, not wanting to risk having it stolen. She'd never worn it regularly, anyway. It was too ostentatious to wear to school, she'd decided. She worried about giving the other grad students the impression that she was a bourgeois rich girl from the Mexican upper class, hypocritically playing at the austere life of a grad student of literature so that she could return home someday wearing her Ivy League doctorate as just another expensive bauble. Aura believed, or rather had painfully discovered, that she often gave people, American academics especially, that totally false impression.

I used to worry that Aura had lost her engagement ring and was afraid to tell me. She lost things all the time—so did I—and I'd already settled with myself that if she'd lost it, I wasn't going to let it bother me. Why should it bother me? Whenever I decided that she really had lost the ring, because I hadn't seen it on her finger in such a long while, I'd also decide to not even mention it, to let its disappearance pass in silence as if there'd never been a ring in the first place. It was silly, probably even wrong, to have spent so much on a tidbit of a diamond, one that had maybe been mined in Africa in some unethical and even murderous way but that even I could see, when compared to its rivals for purchase on the diamond dealer's tray, seemed to be waving minuscule twinkle hands in the air to call attention to its own happy radiance. It's not like diamond engagement rings are the only enduring rite or institution on the planet with a possible connection to conveniently overlooked criminal and bloody doings. Once the momentous, life-changing invitation had been made and accepted, wasn't the money well and joyously spent? Once I'd slipped the ring on Aura's finger and she'd said yes and we'd kissed—I proposed in Puerto Escondido—maybe the most satisfying act would have been to throw the ring away into the ocean right after, cleaving our moment and our memories of it from this expensive trifle you always had to worry about losing. Or maybe she could have taken the ring back to Mexico City, shown it off to her mother, to her tío Leopoldo, and to her friends, and then we could have thrown it off some highway overpass, where some street kid might eventually find it, altering his life for the better or the terrible. That way I never would have wasted a second wondering whether she'd lost the ring and was keeping it a secret.

Then we'd be out for dinner at her favorite restaurant for her birthday, or our wedding anniversary or Valentine's Day, or for whatever occasion we'd decided merited an expensive New York City night out, and there it would be, sparkling away on her finger. That diamond came and went like a wandering star in the night sky, visible from earth only two or three times a year.

But I knew how much she cared about the ring because of the one time she did almost lose it, when we were in Austin, Texas, for a book fair. Aura had studied at the University of Texas during the two years that a student strike shut down the National Autonomous University of Mexico, where she was majoring in English literature. Her mother, Juanita, an administrator at the university, wasn't going to let her daughter just languish at home or waste her days roaming the vast, nearly abandoned, apocalyptic city that was the UNAM campus during the strike years, lying around with her friends in the grass, smoking pot in *el aeropuerto*—as students called the tree-shaded stretch of lawn where they met to get high—or hanging out with rock-star strikers in the graffiti-coated, barricaded buildings. Bored with being out of school, Aura had totally turned against both strike and strikers anyway. Juanita and two of Aura's professors, who were also her godparents, pulled some strings with some old Mexican colleagues who were now professors at the University of Texas to get her admitted there on a foreign student scholarship.

In Austin at UT, Aura lived in a dorm at first, and then shared the floor of a house with three other foreign students: two Panamanian girls and Irina, from Romania via Israel, a long-limbed, waifish beauty, a local kickboxing champ and a drummer in a rock band as well as a poetry-writing literature student. Smart young women with strong accents who learned to look after themselves and each other, and who didn't care that the gringa college and sorority girls never included them in anything from day one. Harder to deal with were the predatory preconceptions of white boys who believed all brown females must be just like the ones selling dirty sex so cheaply across the border, or that it was practically obligatory, a sort of reversed chivalry, to treat them that way. But this was my way of talking, not Aura's—she didn't use words like "white boys," and thought it pretty ridiculous whenever I did. She would refer to gringos or los blancos, never sneeringly, though sometimes indignantly. Here's a poem Aura wrote in one of her notebooks during her Austin days:

> Me vuelvo sucio
> Y leo Bukowski aunque lo odie
> Parece quisiera ser hombre
> Para quitar a las mujeres del camino
> Que nadie se escandalice
> Esto es privado
> Esto es mentira
> La poesía es ficticia y no salva a nadie[1]

Nevertheless, those were wild times. There's hardly a photograph of Aura and her housemates where they aren't holding

---

[1] I'm turning slutty / And I read Bukowski though I hate it / It seems that I'd like to be a man / And pick up all the women who cross my path / Nobody be scandalized / This is private / This is a lie / Poetry is fiction and doesn't save anybody

beers, or looking totally stoned, or like they've been up all night: muss-haired, girl grimy, and pretty delicious. But Aura studied hard, wrote a paper in English on Raymond Carver that her professor read out to the class, and worked relentlessly on what she would submit as her baccalaureate thesis at the UNAM when the strike was over, on W. H. Auden. And for all the supposed craziness, she had only one boyfriend there, a Jewish kid originally from Houston, a musician in the Austin country-rock-hippy mode. One of the Panamanian girls, green-eyed Belinda who was three or four years younger than the other three, told me it was Aura who kept her out of trouble in Austin, guiding her through several crises; she said that Aura was like a surrogate mother to her. But Aura had a surrogate mother of her own in Texas, Irina. Though actually Irina was more like an antimother. She used to encourage and even intoxicate Aura with the idea that she should defy her mother's expectations that she pursue an academic career, which Aura would at least seem to go on dutifully fulfilling for nearly the rest of her life. But some of Irina's style and daring rubbed off on Aura, at least as a kind of ideal. In New York, Aura took kickboxing lessons for a few months at a gym near Penn Station, traveling the subways between Columbia and Brooklyn with scarlet boxing gloves dangling from her backpack. Later, Irina would be one of Aura's three bridesmaids at our wedding, along with Valentina and Fabiola, who came to the beach with us that last summer. The book fair in Austin, where I gave the usual sparsely attended reading, was a reunion weekend for Irina and Aura, a chance for them to girl talk for hours like old times and catch up on everything, including the surprise news of our engagement.

When the weekend was over, Irina came to our hotel to drive us to the airport, and we were almost there when Aura realized that she wasn't wearing her ring. She was sure she'd left it at the hotel. We had to go back for it. At the front desk they gave us another key card. There was no sign that anyone had been in the room since we'd left. The tray piled with our dirty breakfast plates was still on the floor by the unmade bed. We looked everywhere.

Aura began to resemble a mediocre mime on barbiturates as she bumbled about the room, her repertoire of searching motions depleted. I said that we'd better get going back to the airport so that we wouldn't lose our flight, too. It doesn't matter, mi amor, I said, I'll buy you a new one. But I couldn't have afforded another ring like that one, and I silently sulked over Aura having taken the ring and what it had cost for granted. But she hadn't asked for or required an expensive engagement ring, I argued with myself, and if I'd decided to go further into debt to buy it, that was 100 percent my problem.

The ring was lost: Aura's helpless, stricken expression told me this was so. She sat cross-legged on the floor, slumped forward, her head in her hands, and sobbed. Though many things could make Aura cry, these were the bereft sobs that erupted only at moments of sorrow or terror or hurt or extreme humiliation or some combination of these, and that as the minutes passed, instead of subsiding, only seemed to mount in hysteria and grief and could actually make you feel afraid for her or for her sanity. How could so much strong emotion and so many tears fit into this one little body, I'd think, helplessly looking on, stunned, or bending to embrace her—me who practically never cried, who felt like I was having a romantic poet's epiphany of feeling if my eyes got a little humid at a movie and then I'd try to call Aura's attention to it, like a cat showing off its hunting prowess by dropping a mauled mouse at its master's feet, exaggeratedly blinking my eyes, grabbing her fingers and raising them to the debatable teary moistness under my lashes, mira mi amor, I'm crying! At my father's funeral I did weep, for about five minutes. Little did I suspect what could come pouring out of me, that I would ever learn what it was like to feel swallowed up by my own sobbing, grief sucking me like marrow from a bone. Aura sat on the hotel room floor, alongside the tray of breakfast plates, crying over having lost her engagement ring. Irina was kneeling in front of her, holding one of Aura's hands in both of hers and raising it to her lips, and I was crouched on her other side, and we were both calling her sweetheart, both of us saying things like, Oh dear sweet Aura, oh my baby, it's okay, it's not the end of the world, it's just a ring, forget it, let's get going, let's go to the airport. Then Aura moved her hand toward the breakfast tray and just bumped one of the plates aside—and there it was, glinting away, it had been hiding under the rim of that yolk-smeared plate. Screams of astonishment and joy!

In Brooklyn that day, it occurred to me that maybe I'd never see the ring again. It was such a tiny thing, and God knows where Aura had hidden it, if in fact she hadn't lost it. If I find it, I should probably sell it, I thought. I have a lot of debt.

I bet I'll never find it, I told Valentina and Adele.

Wait, let me think, said Valentina. I'm good at figuring things like this out. Anyway, women tend to use the same logic when they hide their jewelry.

She stood in the middle of the bedroom, one arm crossed under her breasts and the back of her hand propping her other arm's elbow, chin resting on her fist, sunglasses dangling by one stem between two fingers, slowly swiveling her head. Hmmm, she said. Where. Wherewherewhere . . . Valentina walked directly to Aura's chest of drawers, pulled open a lower one, parted the sweaters and shirts folded and balled-up in there so that she could reach toward the back, and, as if she'd hidden it there herself, retrieved a Mexican trinket box of lacquered painted wood and opened it. Inside that box was the little dark velvet box; she snapped the lid open, and there was that familiar happy sparkle.

I guess I would have found it eventually.

About a week after Aura's death, at one of the little jewelry stores on the Zócalo, I'd bought a sturdy silver chain to wear around my neck and strung our wedding rings onto it there at the counter. (The horrible alacrity with which I'd set out on my daily mourning errands during those first weeks, as if furnishing a new home and life for my new sweetheart: getting prints made of digital photographs, searching out grief books in English and Spanish on the Internet and in bookstores, shopping for dark clothes, hiring a tailor to make me a mourning suit, trying out religions, sitting in churches, reading the Kaddish, going to meditation at the Centro Budista in Colonia Nápoles.) The jeweler used some tools, including a diminutive saw, to alter the clasp so that it couldn't be opened with just your hands. Our rings were platinum bands, engraved on their insides with our names and the date of our wedding: Paco & Aura 20/8/2005. In Brooklyn, after Valentina found the engagement ring, I decided to add it to the chain along with the wedding bands. I pulled the silver chain off over my head—it was the first time I'd taken it off. At the kitchen table, I inserted a nail into the tiny hole in the clasp, jostled it around, probing for some tiny catch, and tapped on it with a hammer. The clasp opened. I added the diamond ring to the chain, then closed the clasp and pulled against the chain with both hands until I was satisfied that it would hold.

I wore the diamond around my neck for a few days. Why did I think that doing that would make me feel better, or that my mourning chain now had more significance, or a new magic, because I'd added that ring to it? I didn't feel any better, I woke up every morning to the same sadness and grim stupor of disbelief, to which was now added the anxiety that that ring always seemed to awaken in me. What if one day I was robbed and the chain was stolen and I lost the engagement ring along with both wedding bands? It wasn't the value of the ring that stressed me, though it was worth enough to buy a Subaru if that was what I wanted. I thought, Then I'll be left without anything. Left without anything? They're just *things*! But I took the diamond ring off the chain and put it back where Aura had kept it.

I still had the shampoo Aura had brought with her to the beach. Tea-tree mint treatment shampoo in a little Sanborns bag. Whenever I was faced with some event or errand that seemed like it was going to be especially trying, I'd take the blue bottle into the shower and use just a small dollop of Aura's shampoo. I dreaded the day when the bottle would be empty, as if then I would have used up all that was left of the protective power of Aura's love too, which led to some tense inner debates—while the water in the shower warmed, or over morning coffee—about whether or not an occasion really merited using up more of the shampoo. She'd left two jars of face scrub in the shower, too. The first time I opened the pinkish jar, the larger of the two, I found the indentations of Aura's scooping fingers like fossils in the scrub's slushy, coconut-hued surface; I screwed the lid back on and put it away on the top shelf of the shower trolley—sometimes, though rarely, and only when the shower wasn't running, I opened it to stare at the imprints of her fingers again. And sometimes, in the shower, I dabbed face scrub from the smaller jar onto my skin, the gritty lemony paste bringing back the soapy-citrusy morning smell of those cheeks I'd pressed my lips to.

I know now what a shrink might say: that I was grasping for external replacements for the internal Lost Object, and for that part of me lost along with the autonomous Lost Object. That via shampoo and face scrub voodoo, I was trying to bring back being loved by and loving Aura, along with everything else that, with her death, had been lost and couldn't be a part of me anymore. Such is life in the shadow of the Lost Object. But I would never say that leaving the shampoo behind in Mexico would have been better. When the shampoo finally ran out, life would just become that much bleaker, that's all—and why shouldn't it become bleaker with every day that distanced me from Aura?

Here was an event that justified a bit of Aura's shampoo: the first day, nine months after her death, when I finally found the resolve to ride the subway all the way up to Columbia. I ate alone in Ollie's. Went and looked at CDs and DVDs at Kim's. I stood on the corner where we always said good-bye before she walked down the block to Casa Hispánica, where her department was housed. Casa Pánica, as she and Valentina used to call it. She hardly ever let me kiss her good-bye on that corner. She was self-conscious about our age difference, for one thing, and didn't want to give her professors or the other students anything to gossip about. I went into Butler Library and sat sipping a cup of coffee in a free chair against the bulletin-board-brown wall in the crowded cafeteria, which was where I often waited for Aura when I was lucky enough to find a table or even just a chair. I watched the students coming and going, watched them sitting, talking, studying, wearing their fashions, and thought about how, when I was with Aura, I was still connected through her to the global empire of youth, and that now I wasn't. (When will I ever again spend an hour and a half trailing anyone around in a Sephora or an Urban Outfitters—a seemingly trivial example, except that I almost certainly will never do *anything like that* again.) I walked down the corridor to the men's room and, for the first time in nine months, took a piss at one of its big old marble urinals, and even doing this felt ghostly. I went into the lobby and stood at one of the computers and wrote an e-mail to Aura telling her that I was back in Butler Library for the first time without her and how much I missed her. I went out the door into the quad. On Broadway I bought a *New York Times* for the subway ride home and, as always, when I turned to the obituary page and read, in the headings, dead at 90 ... 88 ... 73 ... 96 ... I felt that simmering acid rage. Whenever I did find an obituary for somebody even in his or her forties, I felt momentarily *better*; I felt a horrible satisfaction. See, you're not the only one who fucking died young, I'd think. But the daily listings in the *Times* of American casualties in Iraq, most even younger than Aura and more than a few of them women, even adolescent girls, made for a more perplexing juxtaposition, as if it was all happening in some other casino where they played a different game of fate, with different rules and odds, or else it was the same casino, just different gaming tables and a different metaphor for fate. Not that there weren't also bouts of nausea over the waste of those lives, too, and attempted subway telepathic communications: Hello Colorado, from the Brooklyn-bound F train, my name is Francisco ... you can call me Frank ... like your PFC Ramona, my Aura died very young ... my most heartfelt ... we know each other's sorrow, so we know each other ... maybe you would like to join my telepathic bereavement group. . . . The Iraqi dead aren't listed by name, but in an article on the same page I read, *20 civilian cars coming north from Basra with coffins strapped to their roofs, heading to bury their dead in the Shiite cemetery in the holy city of Najaf,* and I thought, At least one of those coffins holds a young wife who was adored by her husband; he rides in the car beneath her coffin. We know each other's sorrow, and each other's shame. We know each other.

What difference does it finally make, whether you visit the haunted places or stay away? It felt the same, either way, just the same.

I finally went up to Columbia, but fifteen months later I still hadn't gone back to Café le Roy, the neighborhood restaurant Aura and I went to most often, especially on weekends for brunch. Aura was sure the name must be a reference to the Triste-le-Roy of the Borges story "Death and the Compass," but no, it turned out the owner's name was Leroy. The waiters and managers there were mostly young Mexicans, and always so friendly to us, no matter how crowded the restaurant was or how impatient the people waiting for tables. They took our orders in Spanish, and spoke English to everybody else; they eagerly interrogated us about our lives, and we asked about theirs. Now, passing Café le Roy on my way to the subway, I crossed to the other side of the sidewalk. But they must have seen me, and I'd tell myself, I bet they think Aura has left me.

Whenever the Ecuadorian checkout girl at the supermarket on our corner, a cheerful chubby girl with acne scars and Coke-bottle glasses, asked, ¿Y tu esposa, señor? I'd tell her that my wife was fine. And she'd laughingly tease, Ohhh, she makes you do all the shopping now. ¡Que bueno!

Nor had I been back to the fish store. I was no longer that guy who went with his wife or came in alone twice a week to buy wild Alaskan salmon, always fillets for two, a bit of a splurge but it was what Aura liked, and often one or the other of the two friendly guys who worked there would lift a big glistening tangerine-hued slab of salmon off the bed of ice and start cutting as soon as either of us walked into the store.

No longer *him*. No longer a husband. No longer a man who goes to the fish store to buy dinner for himself and his wife. In less than a year I would be *no longer a husband* longer than I was a husband. But we'd lived together two more years than that. But then will come the day when I will have been *no longer with Aura* longer than I was with Aura.

Sometimes I would wake with the sense that I'd dreamed about Aura but I wouldn't remember the dream. One morning, though, a few weeks after I was back in Brooklyn that first time, I had a dream that I remembered when I woke up. I was in a chilly, austere room with walls of yellowish stone and understood I was inside a tomb. A brown-and-cream-striped wool blanket with a motionless human shape beneath it lay atop a rectangular stone slab. I knew that it was Aura under the blanket, because it was the same scratchy Guatemalan wool blanket we had at home, but now it was ragged and torn, like a blanket you'd see wrapped around a homeless person on the subway. I climbed onto the slab and stretched out beside her. Then there was movement under the blanket, and I realized she was slowly turning toward me. One end of the tattered blanket lifted as her two arms reached out, and I pulled the so familiar body close against mine, just as the top of her head emerged from underneath, her black hair (so like a Japanese girl's hair), its morning unruliness and baked fragrance tucked under my chin, like it always was in the mornings. Her arms around my neck, Aura tightly embraced me, embraced me like she used to embrace me.

I woke and sat up. I wasn't frightened, because it wasn't really a nightmare. I stared blankly around the room. Then I burrowed back under the multicolored quilt and concentrated on remembering the details of the dream. It was the first time I'd felt a loving embrace in months—since the last time I'd dreamed that Aura was embracing me, a few nights after her death. I actually whispered, Gracias, mi amor. Te amo. And stayed in bed until about noon.

*   *   *

No day ever felt better than the one before it. Emptiness, guilt, shame, and dread, on an endless loop. I felt worse for Aura— thinking about all that she lost was the quickest way to make me want to drop, moaning, to my knees. Often I would think, But it's even worse to lose a child, to lose your only child, your daughter . . . a single mother who has lost her only child! *Even worse.*

Before Aura went away to the University of Texas, she and her mother had hardly ever been apart for more than a few weeks. When she was thirteen she'd gone to summer camp in Cuba for three weeks; as a teenager she'd traveled through part of Europe on a package tour with her stepsister; later, two or three times, Juanita had sent her to Europe for summer school, to Paris and to Cambridge, England. Juanita paid for all of this on a university administrator's salary, often filling two posts simultaneously, and sometimes even taking a third part-time job.

But Juanita and I had had no communication. I didn't even know what she'd done with Aura's ashes.

I thought I could live a few more months on the money Aura had left in her savings account, and also the insurance money from Columbia University that I'd received as her closest surviving relative—I was the one who'd done the paperwork and claimed it.

Who should rightly be regarded as the closest surviving relative, the widowed husband or the orphaned mother?

For all I knew, Juanita had already spread Aura's ashes in some place she'd chosen for reasons entirely her own, and intended never to tell me where.

Juanita and her brother, or the university lawyers who were advising them, had wanted to have me arrested and sent to prison, even as they were waiting for investigators to turn up evidence against me—or maybe to fabricate evidence, that was a danger. A year later the risk of that happening seemed to have passed but my lawyer told me that if I was going back to the

coast for the first anniversary of Aura's death, I should stop in
to the district prosecutor's office there and give the necessary
declaration to close the case file; it was just a formality, he said,
but a prudent one. Go and tell your story. An open case, he said,
is like a live animal.

4

Like in that José José song, "Gavilán o Paloma," where he sings that he was pulled toward her like a wave, *una ola*, and he went up to her and said, *hola*, that's how it happened.

When I got to the King Juan Carlos Center at NYU, José Borgini's *presentación de libro* was just getting under way. An Argentine professor was giving the usual introductory remarks from the podium, and I launched myself into a late arrival pantomime of contrite hurry, practically breaking into a run as I pulled my wheeled suitcase down the auditorium aisle, yanked off coat, hat, and scarf and dumped them in an empty seat in front, and then I "bounded" up the side stairs to the stage, stumbled a bit against the top step, "strode" across the stage, and took my seat at the table next to Borgini. There were giggles in the audience and I saw the skunk-bearded professor looking over at me from the podium, his eyeglasses opaque glares in the stage lights. Señorrr Paaaco Gohhhldman, I presume—his Argentine accent was strong, and he had a high-pitched voice, almost a shriek. I lifted my hand and nodded, and when I reached for the bottle of Poland Spring water I knocked it over and it rolled to the front of the table but I caught it before it went off the edge. I was definitely cutting a dorky enough figure. That was Aura's first impression of me—she was in the audience—and she always laughed delightedly whenever she recounted it. *Pulling his suitcase behind him*, she liked to say with a low cackle, as if that was the *funny* part, imitating my trot down the aisle by rapidly bobbing her head and pertly holding her fist out as if clutching a suitcase handle. It was my yearly teaching semester at Wadley College, in Connecticut, and I used to stay over on campus one or two nights a week. I'd had an afternoon class there, and then caught the Metro North train to Grand Central right after.

I knew Borgini a little from Mexico City, though he was about ten years younger, in his thirties. I hadn't seen him since his last novel had won a big prize in Spain. Now that the book was coming out in English, he'd invited me to take part in his New York presentación, which is the way they do book launches in Mexico, other writers talking about the book instead of the author giving a reading. Borgini had flown over from Berlin, where he'd recently been named cultural attaché at the Mexican embassy. The other presenter was the Mexican novelist Gabriela Castresana, who'd moved from Mexico to Brooklyn some years before, to a duplex apartment that she owned only blocks from me and where she now lived with her two teenaged children. Gabriela, a charismatic flamboyant beauty in her forties, was the sort of socially agile writer who, wherever she went, seemed to make friends with everybody in the literary world, famous or not. That night, after the event, she was giving a dinner for Borgini in her apartment and supposedly Salman Rushdie was coming. When she told me on the phone I couldn't help cracking, What about Saul Bellow, doesn't he want to meet José Borgini, too? After the presentación, Borgini stayed in his seat signing books, Gabriela stood at the edge of the stage holding court with her fans, and I made for the wine table at the back of the auditorium. There was only one other person already there, a slight, pretty young woman, black hair in a chic pixie cut and gleaming black eyes—an elfin prettiness, a slim and lovely build, vivid lips, red lipstick. She smiled at me with that smile and I must have smiled back as if I couldn't believe my luck.

Hola! I said, and holding her plastic cup of red wine, looking at me in a way that anticipated a conversation, she responded, Hola.

(Hello! Meet your death.

Hello, my death.)

She had a gap between her top teeth and a beauty mark beneath the right side of her bottom lip. She was wearing a trim light-gray sweater, a pleated black wool dress, dark tights, and leather boots. An NYU grad student, is what I guessed. But she looked young enough to be an undergrad. My Latin American dream girl, ten years too late. I asked her if she'd liked the presentación, and she said, Sí, por supuesto, estaba muy bien, punctuated by an abrupt little nod that, along with her polite praise, seemed to say that of course the presentación had been the usual nonsense and hot air, not that she was blaming me, or anybody, or even cared, because it was the rare presentación that wasn't. Her voice was incredibly charming, husky and raspy, a little bit nasal, somewhat like a cartoon character's, with youth and good nature thrumming through it. Aura's smile and voice were always the first things people noticed about her. Also, her intelligence, her sweetness, and an otherworldly quality. (Many of the condolence messages had phrases like: Aura had an otherworldly quality . . . Aura reminded me of an enchanted forest creature, her eyes and her smile, and the funny things she used to say . . .) I was bowled over, and full of excited curiosity. I really was the kind of person who believed that this was the way it happened: at the most unexpected moment you met somebody, there was a magical connection, an instant complicity, and your life changed. Despite the contrary evidence of so many false alarms, I'd faithfully been waiting for such a moment for years. Another voice inside me warned, Fool, are you kidding? Look at her, she's *way* too young.

It turned out that she didn't study at NYU or even live in New York. She was at Brown. She'd come all the way from Providence.

You mean you came all the way to New York just for José Borgini's book presentación?

Yes, she said. She looked as if she wanted to say more. Finally she added, Well, not just for that. She said excuse me and turned back to the table for another cup of wine. I steeled myself against what I knew was coming: a friendly wave good-bye over her shoulder, and then she was going to walk back into the milling crowd, probably to rejoin whoever she'd come with, and in a few minutes I'd see her and her friends with their coats on, headed toward the exit, or maybe she'd leave with a boyfriend, though so far there'd been no sign of one. Either way I'd never get to speak to her again, or ever see that smile again. Surely she hadn't come from Providence, just for Borgini's book presentación, *all by herself*.

But she came back, and her expression was a bit anxious now, her smile more demure. Her nose was large, and speckled with light freckles or small beauty marks, but the funny thing about it was that from the front her nose actually looked small, or normal sized, roundish and a little turned up. Like everything else in her face, even her nose looked friendly and full of personality.

You came from Providence with friends? I asked.

No, not really, she said. I came by bus, the *Bonanza* bus, to the *Port Authority*. She smiled shyly, as if to say, I really like pronouncing those names.

But what did that mean, that she hadn't *really* come with friends?

What do you study at Brown? I asked, and she told me that she had a postgrad research scholarship in Latin American literature. So that explained it. She'd come to New York because of an academic interest in José Borgini's novels.

Well, he's my friend, she said.

How could I not have foreseen that? And I said, Ohhh, okay, you're José's friend. Great. So you're coming to dinner at Gabriela's?

Noooo, she said ruefully, I'm not. She'd pursed her lips and was looking at me intently, as if trying to make up her mind whether or not to explain. I swear my heart leapt and I thought, I'll take you to dinner, I'll skip Gabriela's and we'll go somewhere else, but before I could say that, she said, José says that it's a private dinner. He says he tried really hard to get me invited, but no. It's a dinner *petit comité*, for him to meet Salman Rushdie.

Petit comité?

Yes, she said.

That's what he said? *Petit comité?*

Yeah, she said. I don't really know what that's supposed to mean, that it's a dinner *petit comité*. Are they going to negotiate a big problem in world literature and save us? Then, making her voice go low, as if imitating a deep paternal voice that didn't seem to have much to do with soft-spoken Borgini, she said, *You know how these things are, Aura. It's Salman Rushdie.*

The funny deep voice, her forlorn smile and shrug, made me laugh out loud. I see, I said. And while we're at the *petit comité,* what are you supposed to do?

Oh, just go back to the hotel and wait, she said.

I was baffled. How could Borgini be involved with her if he wasn't even bringing her to dinner? Then why should she go back to his hotel—to his room?—to wait? Wait for what? Why hadn't he invited her to dinner?

That's crazy, I said. Everybody in New York gets to have dinner with Salman Rushdie sooner or later. (Not that I ever had.) Of course you can come with us. And if you can't, I'll have dinner with you somewhere else.

Oh no, you don't have to do that—with a burst of wheezily pealing laughter, the first time I ever heard that laugh.

Seconds later, Gabriela walked by on her way to the wine table, and I touched her arm. Gabriela, I said, this is Aura. A friend of José Borgini. She can come to dinner, right?

Gabriela glanced at Aura, and back at me, widening her enormous eyes as if adjusting to an intrusion of bright light. ¿Por qué no? she said. Yes, she can come.

At dinner, Borgini sat wedged between Gabriela and Salman Rushdie—the famous, heavy-lidded, narrowed eyes, and a surprisingly cherubic face beneath the balding Pnin-like dome; a complicated expression, like someone in a gentle-jolly mood and a dangerously mordant one at the same time. Borgini, with the much larger male body on his left speaking across him to the also larger, expansive-gestured female on his right, looked like the Dormouse. Salman Rushdie didn't speak Spanish and made it clear right off that it wasn't going to be a night for practicing diplomat French. But Borgini's English wasn't good enough for him to keep up. Gabriela, like a school crossing guard, occasionally halted the conversation to give Borgini a chance to speak, coaxing him with a question, helping with his English. I'd guess that Rushdie probably doesn't even remember meeting Borgini that night, and I'd bet the bank he has no memory of having sat opposite me, or that he ever learned my name. I wonder if he even remembers Aura. I thought it was all great—Aura and I left to ourselves at a corner of the table—the best thing that could have happened. I hardly recall even glancing over at Mt. Rushdie, and I wasn't feeling at all self-conscious about being in the presence of such an important world figure, as I probably would have if I hadn't been sitting next to Aura. To the background score of Salman Rushdie's burnished, clipped English voice and boyish titter, I was falling in love with Aura. (Do you remember us, Mr. Rushdie? Could you tell, peering at us through your famous falcon eyes, with your great novelist's noticing power, that we were falling in love, or that at least I was? Anything else? The faintest shadow of a hideous fate? Star-crossed, did you think? Am I going to survive this? Do I deserve to?) My attention was on Aura. If Borgini was looking across the table at her with a baleful or annoyed or any other kind of expression, she seemed oblivious. We sat close together at a corner of the table, knees touching, drinking wine, talking and laughing. She'd say something, I'd laugh, I'd say something, she'd laugh. A way of conversing with each other was established that was going to be *our* way of conversing. We liked to be comedians for each other, always. It didn't matter if what we were saying was actually funny or not. I wish I could remember everything we talked about at dinner that night, but of course I can't. I discovered that she was only twenty-five (damn!). Her study scholarship at Brown would be over in April. She was doing research there for her UNAM master's thesis in comparative literature, which was about the influence on Borges of such English writers as Hazlitt,

Lamb, and Stevenson. She was applying to PhD programs in the States and Europe. Recently the house in Providence where she was renting a room had caught fire and she'd had to move; luckily the flames hadn't reached her room, so she'd been able to save most of her possessions, though water from the firemen's hoses had soaked through the floor and ruined some of her books and the bedding. She said that all her clothes, even what she'd dry-cleaned, smelled of smoke now, and she raised her forearm so that I could smell her sweater. I took her fingers in mine and lifted her hand a bit while I lowered my nose to her sleeve and inhaled, and maybe there was a just discernible scent of wood smoke, of cigarette, too, and faint perfume, and that fragrance of bodily warmth as if baked into the wool that I could still find in her sweaters more than a year after her death. I looked up into her eyes and said, Yes, smoke, I can smell it. Anyway, she said, she didn't own that much, and she'd left her computer and most important books in her study carrel at the library. She told me about her friends in Providence, Mauricio, a gay lit student, also from Mexico, and Frances, a chubby black girl, her housemate in the fire-destroyed house, an art student at RISD. But the professor who was directing her studies at Brown, an eminent Chilean professor of comparative literature, Professor T__, who'd doted on her, had suddenly turned against her. Meeting with her in his office, Professor T__ had told Aura that she was never going to succeed as a literary scholar because she lacked seriousness. She was a frivolous rich girl, he told her, who thought the university's primary purpose was to entertain her. Is he handsome? I asked. Uy no, she shuddered, está *muy feo*. Also about sixty, divorced, ridiculously vain. Fox-red hair and beard, obviously dyed. Something wrong with one of his eyes, the pupil straying off to the side, like a little black fish, she said, that's always bumping against the same side of its bowl. Aura's smile could make anybody feel welcomed into her life, but it also left her vulnerable to grubby miscalculation. I said, Sounds like a case of unrequited crush, at least, which is understandable, though it sure doesn't excuse his speaking to you like that. I'm not a rich girl, said Aura, but sometimes I give people that impression.

I don't know why. Well, it's not necessarily an insult, I said. What did you say to him after he said that to you? Nothing, she said. I was so humiliated and sad, I went back to my room and cried. And I phoned my mom. She said "mom," in English. When she told her mother what Professor T__ had said, her mother was even more upset than Aura. She'd threatened to get on a plane from Mexico and come up there and punch him in the face. Well, he would have deserved it, I said. Yeah, said Aura, what a fucking asshole; that *asshole*. Though she'd probably learned to talk like that in Texas, she spoke English with something like an old-fashioned Brooklyn accent, like a hoarse cartoon chipmunk with a Brooklyn accent. She'd been avoiding Professor T__ ever since. She was spending all her time in the library working on her thesis on Borges and the English writers, and in the gym. She especially liked going to the gym at three in the morning, she told me, to work out on the elliptical machine. During exam weeks, the gym never closed.

Until recently, at Brown, Aura had worn dyed purple highlights in her hair. But I didn't find that out until after Aura was dead, when Mauricio, her friend at Brown, recalled it in a condolence e-mail. *When I first met Aura*, he wrote, *she had purple dye in her hair. Before we became friends, I thought of her as that girl with purple hair. Somehow, it really suited her. Suddenly, one day her hair was all black, and so it remained. For a while, after her hair was no longer purple, I felt a little sad whenever I saw her, as if some criminal had stolen it from her in a robbery and we all knew there was no way to get it back.*

That night we switched back and forth between English and Spanish. You could tell that Aura was proud of her English—it was better than my Spanish, though I never admitted that to her. Most of the Mexico City girls I knew spoke English with a soft, melodic lilt, as if they wanted to sound like Parisian girls trying to speak English, but not Aura.

How come when you speak English, I asked her, you sound like a New York Jew? We'd left Gabriela's and were walking on the sidewalk, with Borgini, whom we were ignoring. Salman Rushdie had vanished—inside a floating bubble, or else in a taxi.

Ha ha. She had an explanation for that. Because her mother was always working, when she was a child she'd spent many hours alone in their apartment watching television, and she'd taught herself English by watching television, *Seinfeld*, especially. They had cable, and *Seinfeld* was her and her mother's favorite show.

That night Aura told me a little bit about her mother. For most of Aura's life, her mother had worked as a secretary, mainly in the psychology department, and as an administrator at the UNAM. During her free hours, though, she'd been a student, too, taking classes in psychology and finally completing the college degree that she'd nearly finished at the university in Guanajuato before Aura was born. Then she'd begun enrolling in graduate classes, one a semester. Now she only needed to deliver her thesis to graduate with a doctorate in psychology.

We ended up in Zombie Hut, on Smith Street, for a nightcap. At the dinner party we'd drunk wine, but now we switched to vodka. A nightcap became one more, another, and probably another, though Borgini made his one vodka tonic last as long as all of our drinks. I was struck by how intimidated he looked. He stood facing Aura, holding on to his drink like it was a subway pole on a careening train, as if he couldn't find the composure he needed just to lift the glass to his lips in one motion, as if he couldn't even quite swallow. I'm sure that Zombie Hut was the last place Borgini wanted to be, with me tagging along—what a clamoring fool he must have thought me, openly hitting on Aura after bringing her into the *"petit comité"* from which he'd deviously or pusillanimously or just mystifyingly excluded her. But he didn't dare complain. He was, like they say, *so busted*. Yet, there in Zombie Hut, Aura couldn't have seemed more nonchalant about whatever his not inviting her to the dinner party had exposed about him. By then I'd half convinced myself that there couldn't be anything between them anyway. They must be just friends. Was Borgini gay?

I struck the board and cried, No more, I will abroad!

Aura was reciting poetry, in English, slowly moving her fist up and down. She could have been a (drunken) schoolgirl declaiming in a classroom. Her lovely lips seemed to form every word as if in Claymation, as if her lips and the words of the poem were made of the same malleable substance, and the words took shape in the air, solid and bright—chewable, kissable.

What!?! Shall I ever . . . sigh and pi-i-i-ne?

Sometimes her voice went up:

My life and lines are freeee . . .

And then went down, into her comical baritone:

free as the road [*rowww'd*]

And lower still, with bowed head, on the poem's end:

And I replied, My LORD.

It was a pretty long poem! I'd never memorized a poem that long. She said it was "The Collar," by George Herbert. A Mexico City girl standing in a Brooklyn bar reciting seventeenth-century English religious poetry. In the history of the borough, had that ever happened before?

I know that I shall meet my fate
Somewhere among the clouds above—

After basking in my incredulity over the Herbert recitation and taking a drink of her vodka, Aura had set her glass back down on the bar and launched into the Yeats poem.

Those that I fight I do not hate
Those that I guard I do not lo-o-o-o-ve

How that voice would echo inside me over the coming months, as it still does now.

> *A lonely impulse of delight*
> *Drove to this tumult in the clouds*
> *. . . seemed waste of breath,*
> *A waste of breath . . .*

One day I would realize that once Aura passed her threshold of a certain number of alcoholic drinks, usually three, or even two, if she was feeling happy, happy and loved, or else when she just wanted to show off, she'd recite poetry, almost always these two poems, and often each more than once, like a jukebox where someone has punched in the same two songs to play over and over.

> *I struck the board and cried, No more! I will abroad . . .*

In Zombie Hut, she was off again, round two.

> *I know that I shall meet my fate . . .*

Then Aura's mood changed. She forgot about me and became interested in Borgini again. That night, she never turned her attention back to me. They left the bar soon after. It all happened so fast. We were out on the sidewalk, saying good-bye, I kissed her cheek in the same way I would have if at dinner we'd only exchanged superficial pleasantries. I'd actually believed, in some part of my drunken, love-starved self, that I was going to be the one taking her home. Aura dove into the back of the taxi as if in pursuit of something rolling away from her, and he got in after and shut the door. For a moment she was a shadowy figure sitting up in the backseat of a taxi and I was never going to see her again. The taxi drove off down Smith Street. As if this were the end of a Babel story, I stood under the streetlight watching the taxi recede down the long street, revealed to myself as deluded, pathetic, and doomed to unhappiness.

But we'd exchanged addresses and telephone numbers. Like I'd promised, I sent her a copy of my most recent novel, published four years before. The weeks and months went by, and I received no reply. I told myself, She must have hated my book. But that's all right, she's way too young. You really have to forget about her.

Aura had first hooked up with Borgini the previous spring, at a literary conference at Brown in honor of the fortieth anniversary of the publication of Carlos Fuentes's magical realist ghost story, *Aura*, cohosted by her nemesis professor, who wasn't yet her nemesis. "Here we are, honoring *Aura*," ad-libbed Borgini, during his talk at the conference, "and I have found my own Aura." That created something of a sensation; Professor T__ may even have felt that the conference had been somehow hijacked by this too public romance between the glamorous young writer and the cute grad student with purple in her hair. Of course, he took it out on Aura. That's probably what turned him against her. Even five years later, all you had to do was mention Professor T__ in Aura's mother's presence and her anger would reignite. Furiously, she'd recall how she'd wanted to fly up to Providence to confront and even assault him. Juanita was a good-looking woman, but in her wrath her face was almost unbearably vivid, as if her features were being reflected and magnified in a smashed mirror's swept-up shards. She liked giving this kind of performance, taunting and slurring like a Mexican street thug, displaying the protective ferocity of her love for her daughter. And it wasn't just an act. Juanita regarded Aura's accomplishments—her success in school, her scholarships to U.S. universities—as her own accomplishments, too. She'd worked hard, double-time, triple-time, year after year, so that her daughter could have the same educational opportunities as any girl born into the Mexican upper class. When Professor T__ called her daughter a frivolous rich girl, he was uttering a blasphemous negation of Juanita's entire life—that's how Juanita took it, rather than as she might have, as a backhanded recognition of how well she'd succeeded.

Juanita wasn't a reader of fiction, but Fuentes's *Aura*—that story's beautiful young Aura is the mystical ghost of her hundred-year-old aunt who, succubus-like, inhabits her niece's body for sex—was a touchstone book for her generation in Mexico.

"My mother named me for your book, Maestro Fuentes," Aura told Carlos Fuentes at the conference. Aura had him autograph a copy for Juanita. She and Borgini posed for a picture with him.

In the diary Aura kept when she was at Brown from April to December, she mentioned only once, briefly, though in a tone of regret, the apparent end of her relationship with Borgini—JB, she called him there; almost everybody in her diary writings was referred to with initials, as if out of considerate discretion. She wrote very sketchily about her trip to New York, not even mentioning Borgini's book event or her dinner with Salman Rushdie, nor did she even allude to having met me, or to the book I'd sent her—there is no suggestion in that diary that our meeting made any impression on her. She cryptically recorded another visit, later that same fall, from another boyfriend from Mexico, who she referred to as "P."

On several pages she described the quiet and boredom of Providence, which she felt suited her for the time being—she liked the long days of cold autumn rain spent holed up in her room with her books, or in the library. In one entry, she criticized herself for finding it so easy to write out of introspection while never having trained herself to be able to describe with precision how, on a sunny, windy day, Providence's grid of streets filled and swirled with yellow, orange, red leaves. "Have spent much of this day thinking about my mother"—there was more than one entry like that. "Am worried about Ma." "I miss my mother." She wrote about the progress of her thesis with anxiety, but also with growing excitement and pride. She wanted that thesis to make her stand out, to provide proof of a destiny. She wanted it to show Professor T__ how wrong he'd been about her. She described the reliable sense of lonely refuge she found in her reading and in her books:

... those lands are the only ones, it seems, that I can visit without ruining. But maybe that will help me, someday, to find a way to escape from this little piece of land that I've already ruined. I was born ruined, by a past I know nothing about.

That might sound like a pretty typical expression of postadolescent angst and self-absorption. It sure was typical of Aura. Her insecurities and fears, her obsession with the mysteries of her early childhood and of her birth father's abandonment of her and her mother when she was four fill so many pages of her notebooks and diaries that it's impossible to read through them without feeling distressed for her, and puzzled over how relentlessly she punished herself. Was she really so unhappy and lonely, or was it just the exaggerated diary rhetoric of a young woman to whom, as she herself had observed, this kind of writing came too easily?

In an entry later in the diary, dated April 24, the day she turned twenty-six, she wrote that her father had phoned her to wish her a happy birthday for the first time in more than twenty years. The conversation was brief, she tersely reported, and he'd sounded nervous.

That was the last time Aura ever spoke to her father.

5

Every so often, I dream of a picture taken of me at age 5. I'm sitting on the edge of a wooden fence. Behind, a humungous tree gives me shadow from a sun that can't be seen.

That's the entire content of a document, written in English, saved as Toexist.doc in Aura's computer. Every day I found something in her computer that I'd never read before. It was moving to discover that she used to dream about that photograph because it haunted me, too; I'd already switched it from her desk to mine. In the picture, five-year-old Aura is wearing wrinkled denim overalls and a pink T-shirt. Her black hair, shining glossily with light from that sun you can't see, is cut in ragamuffin bowl style, jagged bangs falling over her eyebrows, and the lower halves of her ears stick out. Aura had big ears; I do, too. Our child was definitely going to have "humongous" ears. The fence is tall enough so that to have crawled up and settled onto her perch atop it must have felt like a small triumph, at least. So the look on her face, the close-lipped smile, the direct gaze toward the camera, could be one of quiet satisfaction. But her expression also seems so sweetly trusting and unknowing that you can't help but reflect on the little girl's solitude and vulnerability, a mood amplified by the darkened mass of foliage and thick snaking branches above her.

It seems like just another unfairness to Aura to analyze her every childhood photograph for signs and portents of doom. But even when she was alive, every time I looked at that picture, I felt a new surge of protective feeling for her. I'd imitate the tight little smile that made her cheeks bulge, the blankly trusting gaze. I'd tell her she still looked like that.

How do I look? she'd sometimes ask, and I'd imitate that look, and she'd say, Noooo, I don't, and we'd crack up.

I found another paragraph saved as Elsueñodemimadre.doc:

My Mother's Dream

My mother's dream, which growing up I made sure to gradually and systematically crumble, was to see me installed as a French Academic. The fact that my origins were in the Mexican Bajío and that I lacked all dexterity with the language of my great-grandfather never gave her any pause. Because of that, when I told her that I wanted to go to New York City to pursue a degree in the department of Hispanic languages, the glass of red Bordeaux wine she was sipping from went crooked in her hand and she made a scandal in the restaurant we were in, dining on crepes filled with four cheeses.

6

I'm an air balloon, circling the earth, hardly ever touching down, and nobody ever takes hold of my rope to pull on it and draw me close. It's hard for me, listen, it's so hard, it costs me everything, to touch down on earth. Sometimes I think it has to do with eating so little. At Brown I met a girl who told me that she'd been diagnosed as anorexic—she told me all about herself, and I realized she was like my double.

I'm back in Mexico. In my mother's new apartment. A difficult year awaits me. Uncertain in more than one respect.

Aura had returned to Mexico City at the beginning of December, after her final semester at Brown, when she wrote that in her diary. She was lonely, feeling a little lost and fearful of the future. Up there in Brooklyn, I wasn't exactly thrilled about my life; it had been five years since I'd last had a girlfriend or any even briefly steady lover. In Aura's diary I can follow her innocent trek across that stretch of months, from when we first met in New York right up to where, turning the page, you'd expect to find us falling in love, except that's where it ends, as if not even she could believe what happened next and abandoned her diary like a novel with a too far-fetched plot. During the years we were together, Aura didn't keep a regular diary, so that notebook was the last of the dozens of diaries Aura had kept from the time she was six or seven, back when she used to write in her diary at all hours of the night, often under the covers with a flashlight while her stepsister Katia slept in her nearby bed.

In a few hours we're leaving for Guanajuato for Christmas.

It's still dark out, but down below on the Periférico, the all-day traffic jam is already underway, sounding like squawking plastic trumpets, pounding drums, and crazed roars in a crowded fútbol stadium buried under the earth.

Juanita's new condominium apartment was on the ninth floor of a building abutting the Periférico, the intracity north-south expressway. It must have been about five in the morning. Aura's bed was the foldout couch in the study. She was probably sitting up, floppy leather-bound notebook pressed against her upraised thighs, sleep-tousled hair, the soft pucker of her mouth, the twitching pen in her fist, eyes fixed on the page with a liquid stillness of concentration, like perfectly aligned bubbles in a carpenter's level. In the future, Aura and I would spend more than a few nights on that same couch, though if her stepfather Rodrigo was away when we visited, which he frequently was, I'd sleep there alone while Aura slept with her mother. Aura, when speaking or writing about her stepfather, tended to refer to him only as "the husband." And Juanita rarely held herself back from belittling her husband with her famous sarcasm, whether about money (his lack of), politics (left-wing), ambition (missing), or even intelligence (lower than mother's and daughter's). Rodrigo was famous for taking it: a disciplined rocklike impassivity, though often seething inside and capable of eruption. But I could tell that he loved Aura, that he was proud of her, and he was always kind to me. We often talked about American football. He was a big Colts fan, for some reason. One Sunday we watched a Colts-Patriots play-off game at the Hooters on Insurgentes, where Aura and Juanita joined us later for burgers and beers, the two of them bemusedly observing the agile young waitresses in hot pants Rollerblading around the restaurant with loaded trays balanced on their shoulders beneath the luminous football-filled big screens, and that launched Juanita into a reminiscence about what a Rollerblading dervish Aura had been as a girl; she described her twirling and jumping around the

Copilco parking lot like an Olympic star—what I remember is just the deeply contented sense of belonging to an ordinary family that I had that afternoon, a feeling I'd hardly ever known in my life.

But I wasn't on the scene yet that predawn morning, days before Christmas, when Aura, just home from Brown, was in bed writing in her diary. Outside her window the invisibly smoldering air over the Valley of Mexico was like a vast nighttime harbor, the illuminated tops of isolated tall buildings anchored in it like futuristic Chinese junks, television and radio towers like lit-up masts and cranes; on the horizon were the ink black mountains of the Sierra del Ajusco. For the next half hour or so, she watched those mountains slowly emerge from the starless dark, the uneven row of pointy peaks outlined by a silver glow, raspberry smears seeping into the sky just above; the dawn light gradually infusing the slopes like a blue phosphorescent dye, bringing into relief pine forests, winding strips of road, and mottled terrains. Aura carefully described all of that in her notebook. All her life, she reflected, in the DF, in Guanajuato and Taxco—maybe in San José Tacuaya, too, though she couldn't remember—she'd woken to views of mountains outside her window. Then came the steamrolled Austin horizon, the cupcake hills of Providence. What would the next year bring? Hopefully, the skyscrapers and bridges of New York City. While she was at Brown she'd visited New York three times, including once with her mother, and each visit had left her more convinced that New York was where she wanted to be. She would live, she wrote in her diary, in one of those apartments that was like a nest perched high above a spectacular avenue. As soon as she stepped out onto any Manhattan sidewalk she felt swept up in the infinite city's powerful and purposeful current—somehow Mexico City, also infinite, seemed as much New York's reverse as the swarm of dangling threads on the underside of a tightly woven rug. The city of Auden, Bob Dylan, Woody Allen, of the tragic other Dylan whose poems she'd also memorized in her English poetry classes at the UNAM, of Seinfeld and Elaine. (Aura had a rarely confided conviction that she could have been a successful comedienne. She'd imagined herself a film director, too; during her last year at the Colegio Guernica she kept a notebook in which she pasted newspaper cuttings and wrote about every movie she saw at the Cineteca Nacional. She even asked her mother for permission to apply to the Centro Nacional de las Artes to study acting and film. Juanita forbade it, but she had profound reasons for dreading that profession. Her father had acted in some of Mexico's most iconic movies, playing opposite such stars as María Félix and Dolores del Río—he was the debonair young husband shot dead within the first five minutes of the movie, the flirtatious mailman who turns up at the door in the nick of time, eyes and teeth sparkling, to deliver the climactic love letter. But Juanita's father was also a drunk, a morphine addict, a philanderer, and a gambler, and died at thirty-two, when she was an infant. Juanita possessed no memory of him.) Aura grew up watching videocassettes of Woody Allen movies, often at night in bed with her mother, the same movies over and over, especially the New York City romance and hyperneurotic comedies. She loved the screwball comedies, too, and as a little girl would act out routines from *Sleeper* in the shower, from Cantinflas and Tin-Tan movies, too. Juanita had practically installed Woody Allen as a household tutelary saint, his framed photograph hanging on her bedroom wall. Yet once Aura revealed her wish to go to grad school at Columbia, her mother hardly ever again passed up a chance to say something negative about New York.

But wouldn't any normal mother anywhere have worried if her only child, in the fall of 2002, announced that she wanted to study and live in New York City, when so many other cities in the world had first-rate universities to choose from? Despite her fear of flying, Juanita visited Aura in Providence and accompanied her to New York. Instead of assuaging Juanita's fears, that visit only made them more vivid. In Grand Central and Penn Station, squads of burly, camouflaged, heavily armed soldiers patrolled with German shepherds. Going into libraries and museums, guards inspected every bag and purse, even shining flashlights into them, and Juanita always carried a large handbag that required extra-long searches. When they went to the restaurant where Woody Allen performed on his clarinet, they were told he wasn't playing that night and that they needed a reservation anyway. Even Mexico City's subways were cleaner than New York's. Online, Juanita had sleuthed out information about the rapes and muggings of Columbia students in Morningside Heights and Harlem. But Mexico City had its own brand of terrorism, Aura reminded her mother. Had she read anywhere that New York City taxi drivers kidnapped passengers and took them at gunpoint to ATM machines, or worse?

Juanita's maternal grandparents were French, though she'd never been to France herself, and didn't speak the language. But even if Aura never realized her mother's dream of becoming a professor at the Sorbonne, she should at least become an academic in Mexico, at the UNAM, where she'd have instant job security, a decent and reliable salary, independence, and respect. Surely there was nothing wrong with a mother wanting such things for her daughter; by the time she was Aura's age, Juanita knew all too well about the treacheries that could befall a young woman without a career of her own. Someday, if a handsome, and preferably wealthy, young husband came along, so much the better, though in Mexico, as elsewhere—Aura's mother certainly believed, anyway—a husband was never somebody who could be counted on to stick around for long, or to stay sober or sane, to not end up throwing his own career, along with his family, into the garbage. In Juanita's opinion it made no sense for Aura to leave Mexico and the UNAM—where while completing her PhD she could already have a job as an adjunct professor—to study Latin American literature in New York.

Nevertheless, Juanita accompanied Aura to Columbia on the day of her interview in the Hispanic languages department's dilapidated Beaux Arts town house, where Federico García Lorca had once lodged, dazzling faculty and students at cocktail parties in the lounge. They decided that while Aura went for her interview, her mother would wait in the Hungarian Pastry Shop. It seemed that whenever anyone who'd ever had anything to do with Columbia University was asked a question such as, And where should we go to see what student life is like? the Hungarian Pastry Shop was the response. In Providence they'd looked up the Hungarian Pastry Shop on the Internet to copy the address, and found it described as a "a delightfully cozy café." It turned out to be a dank, crowded little place that looked and felt like it was in a basement, though with long glass counters invitingly filled with pastries. Maybe it was a test of your suitability for Columbia—if it seemed like only a dingy coffee shop to you, you didn't belong there. Juanita even remarked that if this café really represented *el colmo,* the summit, of student life at Columbia, then why go to New York—there were plenty of cafés just like it around the UNAM, not much better or much worse. Whatever, said Aura anxiously. She had to get to her interview. Her mother hadn't brought anything to read, so Aura left her with a volume of Borges's *Obras Completas,* festooned like a jubilee ship with brightly colored Post-it flags, and charged out the door.

The interview was with the department head, a blond milk-pale Peruvian, and it lasted about an hour. They spoke at length about the work Aura had been doing on Borges and the English writers. More than midway through the interview the department head told Aura that she was going to be accepted, and with a full department scholarship. When she returned to the Hungarian Pastry Shop, her mother was sitting at the table by the wall at which she'd left her, her coat still on. There was no coffee cup or pastry plate on the table. She didn't seem to have touched the Borges book. You didn't order even a cup of coffee, Ma? asked Aura.

Noooo, hija, said her mother, with a fed-up sigh. They have a very complicated system here. I suppose you need a genius IQ and perfect English to understand it. By the time I deciphered more or less how it works, I thought you'd be back from your interview any moment, y ya, I just didn't want anything anymore.

Ay, Mamá, please, don't exaggerate—

Exaggerate? You tell me, hija, if this seems like a normal process to make customers go through for only a cup of coffee. First you have to go to that counter to place your order—like the witness to a crime, Juanita pointed tentatively with her finger toward the counter, pausing as if to rehearse the whole terrible and confusing scene in her mind—and then they write down your order on one of those pieces of paper and you have to write your own name on it, too, and then you go back to your seat, and when it's ready, the waitress comes out carrying your order on a tray with the piece of paper and walks through the tables calling out your name until you signal to her that it's you she is searching for. For this, you have to be hoping that she is looking your way, so that you can catch her eye, and then raise your hand. But what happens if the waitress walks away from you, to the other end of the café? Are you supposed to shout your name at the waitress's back? And why should I be forced to call out my name in a crowded café? *Ees meee, Juaneeeta! The leetle Mexicana lady over here! Alo-o-o!* Juanita swung her hand up as if tossing something away over her shoulder—Ay, no.

Aura, laughing so deeply her eyes were squeezed shut, wheezed, Ay, Mamá!

No-no-no, hija. Why do I have to give them my name just to order a cup of coffee? Are they going to ask to see my passport and visa, too?

Nobody could make Aura laugh the way her mother could. Later, whenever we were in the Hungarian Pastry Shop, she'd recall her mother's tirade.

Her mother pointedly didn't ask Aura how her interview had gone. They decided to go for a drink at the West End Bar, another don't-miss-it venue of typical student life. They would have to cross the campus to Broadway. It was late afternoon, already growing dark. Aura led her mother through the university's wrought-iron gates and out into the middle of the quad, with its monumental library buildings at each end, a wintry Zócalo with students trekking across browned grass and hedge-lined pavement in every direction, coming and going from buildings projecting multiple geometries of light into the dusk.

Isn't it beautiful, Ma? said Aura, stopping and gesturing around her. This is where I'm going to school next year.

They resumed walking as if her mother hadn't even heard her. But by the time they reached the other side of the quad, her mother's cheeks were drenched with tears. Juanita hugged Aura and told her that she was proud of her, and that she knew how hard she'd worked for this. For that night, at least, a truce in their battle over New York City was declared. At the West End Bar, they drank and celebrated the shared saga of their twinned lives—the penniless abandoned mother with no job, professional skills, or prospects, who'd fled San José Tacuaya with her four-year-old daughter in a Volkswagen Bug that wasn't hers, to start a new life in Mexico City. Now that daughter was going to be a PhD student, on full scholarship, at one of the world's most renowned universities.

Aura saw her biological father only twice after she was four. She was twenty-one when the first meeting, in a restaurant in Guanajuato, took place. After some telephone negotiations, initiated by Aura and kept secret from her mother, she rode the bus from Mexico City to Guanajuato, and he drove across the state from San José Tacuaya, where he was still living, now with his new family. When her father walked into the restaurant that day, dressed in a navy blue suit and a beige shirt, Aura, sitting alone at a table waiting, recognized him right away. He looked older than she remembered, of course, his graying brown hair shorter than before. Recognizing her recognizing him from her table near the back of the restaurant, his coal-dark eyes opened wide as if in fright. But he walked toward her with his long arms held out and that gentle eager smile she'd never forgotten and was sometimes surprised by in photographs of herself, and she stood up for his embrace. He had the droopy ears that she'd inherited along with his long sloping nose (though in a nicer, softer, feminine version). The next thing she noticed was that one of her father's pant legs was covered with dried yellowish mud. It wasn't even raining. Why did he have mud all over just one pant leg? She'd heard from her tía Vicky that he wasn't doing well economically, but his suit seemed like an okay suit. She was too afraid of embarrassing him to ask about the mud, and he offered no explanation. In later years almost all of the aborted stories Aura tried to write about this meeting with her father included the muddy pant leg. You could tell that she wanted that mystery of the mud to stand metaphorically for the mysteries of her father and the past, but that she could never quite figure out how to make that work in a short story. The mud, she'd decided, must—or should—have a connection to the strawberry fields of San José Tacuaya—laboring in the muddy strawberry fields covering the plains outside the city was the most common livelihood of the poor there. In her short stories, Aura was always searching for a way to link the muddy pant leg to the strawberry fields and both to a father's first meeting with his daughter in seventeen years and to some as yet unrevealed truth about that long separation. Her father no longer had anything to do with the strawberry fields, though back when she was his adored baby girl and he was a rising local politician in the PRI, he'd campaigned and presided over many ceremonies on the strawberry farms, celebrating harvest festivals and new labor pacts; many times he'd come home with spattered shoes reeking of manure, which had to be taken off and left outside.

An inexplicably muddy pant leg and a man's never adequately explained abandonment of his wife and four-year-old daughter— could they really have anything to do with each other? Could the muddy pant leg really become a metaphor for whatever had actually happened seventeen years before? Aura's inability to come up with that plausible narrative link was one reason she never completed any of those stories.

Maybe young writers like Aura, along with readers, but also some older writers—those who haven't learned to recognize a futile task even when it hits them in the face—sometimes overestimate the power of fiction to reveal hidden truths. If any two things are alike in some obvious way—the muddy pant leg and the abandon- ment of wife and child both characteristics of the same man— does that mean there must also be less obvious correspondences between them? Deeper, revelatory or at least metaphorical ones? Aura was sure there had to be and dug many long deep tunnels without finding what she was looking for, which doesn't mean she might not have, eventually.

Or else maybe sometimes you just need somebody to tell you what really happened.

Pasted into Aura's first-grade scrapbook, amid drawings and pages from vocabulary coloring books, was this letter to her father:

> Héctor
> *Te amo papá no se porque se separaron.*
> *Pero de todas formas te sigo*
> *queriendo como cuando estábamos*
> *juntos. ?Oye tú me sigues queriendo*
> *como antes¿ espero que sí porque*
> *Yo hasta te adoro adiós papá te*
> *amo con todo mi* ♥.[2]

Aura claimed to have no definite memories of her parents' separation. Throughout her childhood, in later years, and probably right up to the last days—something Aura said to me near the end makes me think this is true—Aura regularly interrogated her mother about the circumstances of the breakup. Juanita could never have foreseen that Aura's love for her father, or that her obsession with him, would persist as it did. Providing a substitute dad by quickly remarrying had done nothing to loosen her daughter's fixation on the lost original; probably it had the opposite effect. What was it about that four-year-old girl's love for her father that, throughout the rest of her childhood and adolescence and even at twenty-five, it remained as lodged inside her as the sword in the stone?

In Mexico, about two weeks before Aura died, she came home one afternoon after a long lunch with her mother and told me that she was beginning to suspect that the "great events" of her past hadn't

---

[2] I love you papá I don't know why you separated. But I still love you anyway like I did when we were together. Listen, do you still love me like before? I hope so because I even adore you good-bye papá I love you with all my ♥.

happened exactly as she'd always believed or been told. Coming up the steep stairs to the sleeping loft, she found me sprawled on the bed instead of working or reading the book lying next to me, and before she'd even spoken I'd looked up at her with a hopeful expression and asked—imitating the playful way she often liked to speak these words, like a child inviting you to come out and play—¿Quieres hacer el amor? But she definitely wasn't the least bit in the mood. Instead, she said what she said about the great events, her voice brusque and a little rebuking, and I responded, ¿Ah, sí? and waited for her to say more. But she only picked some of her books and papers off the small plastic table she used as a desk when she wanted to isolate herself up there, and carried them to her desk downstairs. So, what had her mother told her that she hadn't known before? It's easy to claim now that I knew Aura didn't want to talk about it just then but that I was sure she'd tell me later. Maybe it was my own laziness or disinterest that stopped me from pressing the question—I was bored of her mother's dramas. I wanted to fuck, not talk about Juanita *again*. I also knew how protective Aura was of her mother. If Aura had been told a new version of the past that reflected badly on her mother—I can imagine now a drunkenly muddled confession, quickly recanted or rationalized, whatever coherence the conversation briefly possessed fading like ghost laughter—she really wasn't likely to tell me the whole story, at least not right away. I don't know if she would have told me eventually or not. I just don't know. Aura and Juanita shared a secret world.

7

Amid mud and unborn strawberries, still spreading roots beneath the earth and fertilizer, the women were holding her white legs apart and urging her on with a chorus of, "Push, Señora Primera Dama, push!" And the Señora Primera Dama, who regarding this spare narrative of the facts, of which, I should confess, despite the surprise or mockery of those who don't believe in this kind of prenatal memory, I also have unerasable recollections that manifest in dreams that lamentably frequently turn into nightmares—but let's return to the strawberries and the story of my birth.

—from "Of Strawberries," an unfinished
short story by Aura Estrada

Before getting to know them profoundly (before having learned all about their origin and cultivation) she adored strawberries. She ate them at all hours. And when she wasn't eating them, she liked to think about them; with cream, without cream, natural or *flambée*. It's not improbable to speculate that it was her love for the *Rosaceae Fragaria* that led her into a rushed marriage to the future guardian and procurator of the Strawberry State. That union would also deliver her to an unforeseen hatred of that earthy fruit.

—from "A Story of Mud," an unfinished
short story by Aura Estrada

Where does he lose his daughter, where does he recover her??? The guilt that one evades, until you can't evade it, until you find it, or it finds you.

What is the great metaphor for guilt? The mud!!!!

—from Aura Estrada's notes for "The Visit,"
an unfinished short story

8

Before her breakup with Aura's father, Juanita had never before driven a car by herself. A few Sunday afternoons, on the quiet industrial zone streets of San José Tacuaya, her husband had given her lessons, sitting beside her in his Ford Falcon, his hand hovering over hers on the steering wheel. But she packed two suitcases, took a bus across the mountains to Guanajuato with four-year-old Aura, and borrowed Vicky's Volkswagen Bug without telling her where she was going. Launching herself into the roaring truck traffic of the highway, she drove with her daughter all the way to Mexico City, a five-hour drive at least. Growing up, no matter how many times Aura heard that story, she was never able to recall anything about the legendary trip, not one detail.

Aura did remember her dad: his nose, chubby cheeks, gleaming dark eyes. Her dad was always picking her up in his arms, swinging her in the air, carrying her around while she sat on his shoulders. He sang and played Cri-Cri songs for her on his guitar, taught her words in English and French. A zillion times a day he told her that he loved her. Aura had an old photograph of herself sitting astride the soft hump of her father's belly while he lay sprawled on his back in the grass in their backyard, their snowy little terrier alongside, front paws raised, probably barking. Often when she studied that picture a giddy sensation quietly came over her, like the faint physical memory of tickling fingers, of tumbling forward, laughing, into his embrace, the bristle of his chin like singeing sparks against her cheek. That was the last time she ever lived in a house with a yard, except for that year in Austin, where the yard belonged to the boys who lived downstairs on the ground floor. That was one of the things Aura would always yearn for: a house of her own with a yard.

Héctor stopped loving me, Juanita would answer, usually with a tired sigh, whenever Aura asked what had provoked the separation. I begged him to take us back, nena, but he wouldn't. After that, I knew we had to get away from there and find a way to start over. We had no other choice, hija.

Aura did know the story—a story, at least—of how her parents had met. Juanita had met Héctor when she was a student at the university in Guanajuato and living in a rented house with two of the Hernández sisters, Lupe and Cali, and also Vicky Padilla—Aura's future tías. Juanita's mother, Mama Violeta, had sent her away from Taxco to Guanajuato when she was fourteen, to an all-girl Catholic boarding school. The Hernández sisters were day students there, and their mother, Mama Loly, virtually adopted Juanita, inviting her to move in with the family. She became friends with Vicky back then, too. Guanajuato, built on steep mountainsides, with its colonial architecture and churches and famous university and winding narrow streets and oblique plazas and bars, was then, like now, an international student town as well as a tourist destination. The midseventies were as boozy, druggy, and profligate a time in Guanajuato as anywhere else in the world. I can't say for sure what the Hernández sisters and Vicky, or even Juanita, were like back then, but each of those women, in her individual way, was regarded as a wild beauty in her youth and was destined in adulthood, in varying degrees, for heartbreak, calamity, and alcoholism. It was back then that Juanita met Héctor, at a party in their house. A few years earlier, he'd dated Lupe Hernández. What drew Héctor's attention to Juanita—so Aura always told me—was the leather miniskirt she was wearing that night, the way it showed off her shapely pale legs and thighs. Juanita had a loud laugh and liked to make bold and cutting remarks; black eyeliner, thickly drawn as if with moist Magic Marker, intensified her gaze's stormy drama. She intimidated boys her own age. But Héctor, a lawyer and local politician, was ten years older. He was dressed all in white that evening and carried a white guitar. He wasn't exactly handsome, Juanita always said, but his wheat-hued face was full of

character, he was soft-spoken and funny, and he had a sad, sweet
smile. A true orphan, adopted by a childless couple in San José
Tacuaya—an accountant-bookkeeper and his wife—he'd gone to
law school at the University of Guanajuato and shined there. A
brilliant mind, everybody said so, and a brilliant future—a rising
star in the PRI, even more so than Juanita's brother Leopoldo,
who was already an operator in the official party too. Héctor could
perform any Beatles song on his guitar, and when he sang "In the
Summertime," in English, he sounded just like Mungo Jerry's singer
with a Mexican accent. Juanita and Héctor were married about two
years after that meeting, and less than a year later Aura was born
in a hospital in León, Guanajuato. They lived in San José Tacuaya.
The PRI had selected Héctor to be the party's candidate for the
office of municipal president of that small city; it was like being
mayor. Back then the official party's candidates didn't lose elections.
Campaigning alongside his beautiful, fresh-faced young wife, with
her long, wavy, chestnut hair, who wore jeans and embroidered
peasant shirts, his own hair worn like Bobby Kennedy's, falling over
his big ears and into his eyes, Héctor represented the new image
of the PRI, a chastened revolutionary party that had learned how
to renew itself in the decade since the bloody cataclysm of the '68
student massacres, in touch with youth and the times after all. As
the Primera Dama Municipal, Aura's mother was forced to be in
the local public eye as much or even more than her husband, by his
side at ceremonies and banquets, presiding over women's lunches,
afternoon teas, benefits, and all manner of festivals and events on
the strawberry farms. Once Héctor had decided that he no longer
wanted her for a wife, Juanita knew that the public spectacle of her
and her daughter's abandonment would make life unbearable in
San José Tacuaya. It was unthinkable that she could raise Aura in
such an environment. Anyway, she hated that boring, crass little
city. One thing she would never in her life regret was the decision
to come to the Distrito Federal to start their lives over.

Was there another woman involved, Ma? Aura would sometimes ask her mother.

Who knows, hija. Nothing would surprise me. But Héctor was never much of a womanizer.

But what about me? Aura would ask. Why did he want to leave me? Why doesn't he answer my letters?

Sometimes even adults who've made the most wonderful child can fall out of love, Juanita would try to explain, and she'd tell Aura all over again how much her father had loved her. But Héctor changed, she would say. It seemed obvious now that something was wrong with him—psychologically, she meant. He always doubted every good thing life gave him, hija. So charming and brilliant, but on the inside, never able to overcome whatever it was that had predestined him to always ruin his own chances for happiness.

Things hadn't gone at all well for her father, Aura knew, since his glory days as municipal president. Instead of rising higher, he'd plummeted—swiftly or gradually, she didn't know. Tía Vicky sometimes had news about him: he was teaching law at a community college, but he also had a side business delivering bottled soft drinks to market stalls and collecting the empty bottles to bring back to the distributors. It was hard to believe that her father had fallen so far. And then, years later, as if the official party had never understood how much they needed the former young hotshot presidente municipal of San José Tacuaya to help lead them into the future, the PRI, rotted and loathed, had finally fallen, too.

Aura's earliest memories of their new life in Mexico City were of her mother sitting in the dark in the living room of their tiny apartment for hours, playing sad songs on her record player, her face soaked with tears. Aura could never hear any of José José's bathetic ballads without remembering that time. She wrote letters to her father. Her mother helped, until she could write them by herself. In some of these letters, she even asked why he wouldn't let her and her mother come home. Her mother mailed the letters, but her father never wrote back.

Before long Juanita had found secretarial work at the university, in the psychology department. Aura and her mother lived in a small one-bedroom apartment in the south of the city in a complex of tall

towers that provided inexpensive housing for university employees,
though many tenants didn't seem to have any link to the university,
and had probably moved in illegally after relatives and friends had
left, paying the required bribes. The apartment smelled of moldy
cement and gas. In high winds pieces of the buildings fell off, clat-
tering down the sides, cracking and shattering windowpanes. At
night, Aura could hear cats yowling and hungry kittens crying for
help inside the twelve-story stairwells but she was forbidden to go
to their rescue because, said her mother, drug addicts lived in the
stairwells, too. Aura used to imagine the drug addicts sleeping in
the stairwells upside down like bats, living off the blood of cats and
lost children.

    I know that to this day most people who work at the univer-
sity and live in those apartment towers really don't think they're
so bad. But Aura's impressions of what she sometimes called "the
Terrible Tower" hadn't only been shaped by childhood memories of
a desperate time—one night something happened there that Aura
had only fragmentary memories of, something she couldn't even
be 100 percent sure had really occurred. But it was as if those few
glinting memory shards had sheared her neurons in some way that
had left her vulnerable to certain stimuli, the way light flickering
through trees or flashing behind a barred fence, or even a vividly
striped shirt passing on a sidewalk on a sunny day can provoke
seizures in certain people.

    Aura, whenever we came back to Mexico during school breaks
or the summers, used to like to take me on long walks that were
guided tours of the daily routes of her childhood and adolescence
in the neighborhoods surrounding the Ciudad Universitaria and
across the campus itself, a semiautonomous city-state bigger than
the Vatican. Once, walking to a sushi restaurant on Avenida Universidad, while stopped at a corner waiting for the light to change,
she pointed out three towers clustered on the horizon, back from
the row of shopping centers and lower commercial buildings and
offices lining the avenue, and she said that there, in that unidad
habitacional, in the tower on the far left, was where she and her

mother had lived during their first few years in the city. The buildings had originally been constructed to house athletes for the '68
Olympics. Smudged by a haze of smog and smoldering sunlight,
they looked like bluish-gray construction-paper cutouts pasted to
the gray-yellow sky. While Aura described her memories, I stared at
the tower, trying to imagine stairwells filled with howling cats and
vampire drug addicts. When the light changed we crossed and went
on along the avenue holding hands. Because her mother was afraid
of having to bring trash out to the Dumpsters in the parking lot at
night, said Aura, she'd always ask their neighbor to come with her.
Their neighbor was a fat, quiet man who was a lab worker in the
university's school of veterinary medicine. Whenever he opened his
apartment door while Aura was standing outside, she could see a
mangy blue macaw on its perch at the back of his living room, and
the terrariums where he kept snakes and spiders. The neighbor also
had a little yellow mongrel dog that was as quiet as his owner, never
barking, though he always wagged his tail and wiggled all over whenever they met in the corridor. But that poor little dog, said Aura, had
a terrible elevator phobia. At least twice a day, the neighbor took
his dog out for a walk, and so at least twice a day they had to wait
in the corridor for the elevator, which always took a long time to
come and was grindingly noisy when it did, and while they waited,
the fat man would try to calm his dog, patting him and speaking
reassuring-sounding words, always to no avail, because as soon as
the elevator rumbled to a stop and the doors opened, that terrified
little dog would lose control of his bladder and pee on the floor. As
if addressing an exasperating but coddled child, the fat man would
softly scold his dog in a resigned nasal voice that Aura could still
imitate, *You have to wait until we get outside, perrito necio,* and then
he'd go back into his apartment to fetch his mop. No matter how
often the neighbors complained about the lingering smell of dog
urine in front of the elevators, no matter what a pain it must have
been to have to mop up every time he took his dog out for a walk,
their fat neighbor never once lost his temper, or even mentioned
the possibility of getting rid of the dog.

Is that an example of unconditional love or what? I remember saying as we walked along the sidewalk.

After a moment Aura said, Yeah, but I think it would have been even more loving if he'd taken his dog to live somewhere else, on the first floor.

Maybe he wouldn't move, I said, because he was even more in love with your mother.

Quién sabe, could be, said Aura. Poor Áyax.

Ajax, like the soap? I asked.

Áy-yax, she said, as in *The Illiad*, and she grabbed my chin and said, Ay, mi amor ¿por qué eres tan tonto? and kissed me. That was another of our routines, though my dumb remarks, contrary to what her teasing seemed to presuppose, weren't always intentional. Aura explained that in Mexico the soap is called Ajax, too, but in Spanish the Greek hero is Áyax. Anyway, her mother would only go down to the Dumpster at night if Áyax went with her. Maybe Áyax really was in love with my mother, said Aura, and would save up his trash, just so that he'd always have some ready whenever she knocked on his door, I wonder . . . That was when I realized that Áyax was the neighbor's name, not the dog's, and I was about to make some silly remark, but something stopped me. It was the way Aura said, *I wonder*, a note of sadness in her voice, like somebody pressing down once, gently, on one minor piano key.

What a funny story, I ventured, encouraging her to go on. But it was obvious that, just like that, her mood had changed. What was the dog's name? I asked. I don't remember, she said. She leaned close, resting her head against my shoulder while we walked, and she hardly said another word until we were sitting in the restaurant. By Mexico City standards, the sushi was pretty good in that restaurant. It was a family-run place, and the family was Japanese instead of the usual Mexicans dressed in kimonos and sword-master headbands. It was decorated in a traditional-seeming manner, with dark, intricately carved wood and red paper lanterns imprinted with Japanese ideograms.

Maybe it was by the Dumpsters where it happened, said Aura, not in a stairwell like I've always thought.

What maybe happened by the Dumpsters? I asked cautiously.

Something really terrible, she said. To my mother. I don't know, maybe. You can't imagine what my mother endured in those days, Frank. That's one reason, you know, I can never really stay angry with her. I don't think she'll ever tell me the whole truth about what happened. Not even when she's on her deathbed—Aura gave an exaggerated shudder, and embraced herself as if she was cold. She pulled up the sleeve of her cotton sweater and held out her arm. Look, she said. She had goose bumps. I took her hand in mine and her palm was sweaty.

¿Qué te pasa, mi amor?

She just stared sadly down at the table for about five minutes— maybe it was less, but it seemed like a really long time—while I sat nearly paralyzed across from her.

Well, I was only four or five, she finally said, so I don't really remember—now Aura held her gaze off to the side as she spoke, and her voice became deliberate and a little bit childish. We'd come home late in a taxi, I know that. My mother must have taken me with her to Vicky's house, or something like that. A vocho verde, a Volkswagen, like all the taxis back then, with the front passenger seat taken out. I was probably asleep—she must have woken me—and she said, Aura, stay right here, I'll be right back, I just have to go and get some money. Her voice was normal but she looked terrified, like she was making a huge effort to control herself; her face was quivering like it might burst open. Do I really remember this, or is it something I just made up a long time ago like a story, to fill in a blank or my confusion? I don't know.

You mean you're not sure if you really remember her saying that? I asked. Well, isn't that to be expected? It was so long ago. But is there anything you *are* sure you remember?

I remember the driver, said Aura, at least I think this must be a real memory. First, I remember the back of his head. He had a really huge head, but with short black hair, kind of flat on top. He must have had ears—she let out a slight, mirthless giggle—but I don't remember any ears, just his head. His head was like a dead planet. A dead planet radiating antimatter, you know what I mean? Second, his neck, because it was like a pig's neck. Third, his eye. He turned his head when my mother got out of the taxi, and that's when I saw his eye. Haven't you ever noticed—now Aura was looking at me almost pleadingly—how quiet I get whenever we're sitting in the back of a taxi and the driver has a huge head like that?

You mean just here in Mexico, or New York, too? I really hadn't ever noticed anything like that.

Mainly just here, she said. In New York the taxis are different, with those, you know, partitions, between you and the driver.

Maybe I've noticed something a few times, without realizing that the driver's head was the reason, I said.

When I saw his eye, it scared me.

Scared you how?

Aura turned her head to the side and narrowed her eye to a slit.

That is pretty scary—I smiled, but she had that expression on her face that says, I know that seemed really cute to you, but what I need is for you to believe and understand what I'm trying to tell you. I asked, So what do you think happened that night?

They left me alone in the taxi, she said. They both got out, the taxi driver and my mother. He probably locked the doors, I don't remember. Can you imagine what that was like?

No, I can't, I said. Though I could picture four-year-old Aura sitting splay-legged in the taxi's backseat like a forgotten doll, chubby doll cheeks and eyes full of incomprehension and fear.

Maybe they walked across the plaza in front of the building, said Aura, and went inside, but I don't know. I don't remember if there was anybody around, or how long it was before my mother came back. But when she did come back, she pulled me out of the taxi and carried me; I remember hiding my face in her shoulder. I was probably crying. But I think that's all I remember.

Aura said that she'd pored over those fragments of memory countless times over the years, including in therapy, trying to piece them together, but she'd also asked her mother about the incident. Ayyy no, hija, not now!—that's how Juanita usually responded to her questioning—Are you going to try to tell me you really remember that? It was nothing. ¡No pasó naaada! Once, when Aura persisted, asking, Did you at least call the police, Ma? her mother responded with a blast of fake laughter: Of course! Isn't that what anybody would do? Call the police? So they could buy the cabrón a tequila and toast him? Toast him for what, Ma? Aura asked her, and her mother just stared at her, then said, For robbing me, hija, what else?

Aura fiddled at her napkin. After a moment, her voice quiet and shaky, she said, Frank, sometimes I feel so afraid I lose it completely. It just takes over me. You've seen that, you know what I mean.

I got up from my side of the table and sat next to her, put my arms around her. I had seen that, and would again. A late-night conversation about the 3/11 train bombings in Madrid, which had happened about five months before, had ignited the fit she must have been referring to, up to then the only one I'd witnessed. Though Aura hadn't been in Madrid or anywhere near on the day of the bombings, her seizure of trembling and weeping over that act of mass murder hadn't struck me as excessively histrionic, in fact it had seemed kind of magical, like the clairvoyant empathy of a holy child, and I remember thinking that everybody at least now and then should react like that to the world's murderous horrors. The next time it happened, though, we were home on a cold winter night in Brooklyn, watching a DVD of the movie about the capture of the Sendero Luminoso terrorist leader Abimael Guzman. Early in the movie Guzman was still spreading death from his sunless hiding place, and there was a close-up of Guzman's waxy face, his sinister sneer and a serpent's glint in his cold eyes, and that's what ignited Aura's terror. She backed away from the television and cowered in a corner of the bed, her arms over her head, and soon she was violently shaking and weeping. It didn't matter that it was just an actor we were watching, it was as if Guzman's murderousness and his indifference to the suffering he caused and even the satisfaction he took from it—in other words, actual evil—had somehow leaked into our bedroom through some fissure in the television screen. Aura's terror so overwhelmed her that night that it scared me to think of how much worse it might have been if I hadn't been there to hold and reassure her. Those fits, though they happened only a few times in the four years we were together, were like a combat veteran's unhinging flashbacks.

Since Aura died, it's as if I inherited, but just somewhat, that manner of feeling sometimes attuned to something dreadful out there. Usually I don't shake and cry out like she used to but I definitely kind of lose it. One afternoon back in Mexico City, I went to an exhibition commemorating the fortieth anniversary of the Tlatelolco student massacre, and afterward I walked over to the plaza where it had happened, a few blocks away. A shabby housing complex, an architectural relative to the Terrible Tower though only several stories high, overlooks one side of the sunken concrete plaza; on its opposite side the plaza is bordered by an archaeological site— the ruins of Tlatelolco where, after a battle, Spanish conquistadors had supposedly left some forty thousand slaughtered native warriors decomposing in the surrounding canals and amid the cannonaded rubble. On the afternoon of the '68 massacre, soldiers had stealthily crossed the ruin site to take up positions at its edge, and from there had fired down on the people in the plaza, student protesters mostly but also neighborhood children and other bystanders. That afternoon when I stood looking down from where those soldiers had been, the plaza was mostly empty, just some litter and children playing and it was very quiet, as if everybody who lived in the building had fallen silent in unison, turning off their radios and televisions as if to better hear whatever was coming. The plaza's pavement was a charcoal gray, the sky was a paler gray, the tepid sweaty air felt like it was breathing, and the hanging rain clouds were like the ghosts of soldiers taking up their killing positions again. There was a hopscotch game crookedly drawn in chalk on the plaza and even that looked sinister, as if it were camouflaging a secret hatch. I thought of Aura and of how she might easily have found the thing that terrified her here. You sensed death hiding in the shadows, in the light, breathing in the air, blowing stray bits of litter across the plaza. Death as something stronger than life, ready to burst out of the air with a banshee shriek or to fall silently upon the children playing in the plaza, or on the whole world.

Maybe what I felt that day was a quieter version of the terror Aura was talking about in the Japanese restaurant. That conversation gave me a new inkling of the depth of Aura's bond with her mother, like something stored in a bank vault twelve stories under the earth that only they knew the combination to. Didn't I have a responsibility to share some of what Aura felt for her mother, that mixture of pity and awe and grateful reverence? I did share it, at least partly. It was all new for me, this degree of intimacy and trust and its requirements: an expansion of attention and a concurrent narrowing of focus to be able to take in everything, past and present, inside the radius of Aura's life that I could; to try to understand at least as much as she would allow; to be able to anticipate and protect, to be always ready. Love was new to me, believe it or not. How did I get well into my forties without ever having learned about or discovered this? And later, a little more than a year after Aura's death, I was already feeling panic that I was losing or had already lost this ability to care about someone else in this way.

9

Juanita had Aura's ashes. I had Aura's diaries. She was keeping the ashes from me, and I kept the diaries from her. I rarely risked taking them out of the house, and spent whole days at my desk, poring over them, copying out sentences and paragraphs. The diaries from her childhood were sometimes disorienting to read because the love they aroused wasn't the one I was familiar with, it felt more like the love of a parent. That was a delusion, maybe. Never having been a parent, how can I know what a parent knows or feels?

I copied down phrases like this one, recorded by Aura in her diary:

¡We're called los bichitos!

That was probably the first diary she ever kept, its baby-blue plastic cover decorated with Little Bo Peep and baby sheep. Bichitos was her tío Leopoldo's nickname for the small herd of children in pajamas—his own three children, Aura, and the new girl—romping in his walled-in yard. I pictured Leopoldo watching with a napkin-wrapped tumbler of scotch and soda in his hand, mustache and goatee framing his thin, acerbic-looking mouth, his expression both paternally stern and bemused. Why did this seem to make six-year-old Aura so happy? Because it was funny to refer, with such a straight face, to one's own children and niece as *little bugs*. She also liked feeling included with her cousins. Aura and her mother had been living in the Terrible Tower for about a year, and Tío Leopoldo lived nearby in Coyoacán, with his wife and their children and servant in a renovated colonial house of yellow stucco and black volcanic stones. Aura saw a lot of her cousins back then. Later, after Leopoldo and his wife divorced and the children went to live with their mother and her wealthy new husband, she hardly ever saw them. (They didn't come to our wedding; only one came to the funeral.)

That evening there was a new girl in the yard, Katia, tall and pretty. She stood off to the side as if she didn't know how to play tag, until Aura's cousin Rafa pulled her by the hands into the game and after that nobody could catch her; she bounded around the yard like a startled deer. Katia's father was Rodrigo, a tall, sinewy man with an erect posture, black hair down to his shoulders, and sharp almond eyes. His coppery skin was darker than his daughter's; Juanita's was lighter than her daughter's. Juanita and Rodrigo came into the yard to say good night, then left together to go somewhere else, and a little later los bichitos were put to bed. In the morning, as they had their breakfast and watched TV, Aura waited tensely for her mother to return, and Katia waited for her father. Finally, around noon, they came back:

> Mamá and Rodrigo were wearing the same clothes they had on last night!

Aura noted in her diary. Soon after, Rodrigo and Katia moved into the too small apartment in the Terrible Tower with Juanita and Aura. From now on Aura was to call Rodrigo *Papá*, Katia was to call Juanita *Mamá*, and Aura and Katia were to be sisters. But who was Katia's mother, and where was she? Her name was Yolanda and she was living in Orlando, Florida, near Disney World. With no warning at all, Yolanda had fled from her husband and daughter; supposedly no other man was involved. Why had she done that? Because Yolanda had her own dream to pursue. Her dream was to start a new life, in Orlando, USA. During her childhood Katia would visit her mother in Orlando only three or four times, during school vacations. As time went by, Katia had less and less contact with her mother, until finally she had no contact, not even telephone calls on her birthday. Yolanda had found work as a hostess in an Orlando restaurant, and it was there that she'd begun her self-education in the "high-end food service business." Eventually she became, of all things, a sommelier. Of course, she became a U.S. citizen, too. They knew this because a magazine called *Good Life Orlando* published an article about Yolanda that she mailed to Rodrigo's relatives in McAllen, Texas. Her personal life remained a mystery to those she'd left behind. The article made no mention of a husband, past or present.

Rodrigo and Yolanda were both from Culiacán, in the rugged, hot, dry north. He'd come to Mexico City to study at the university, where he majored in sociology and starred for the baseball team, pitching and playing the outfield. Though Rodrigo was a serious jock, university life and the times turned him into a hippy and into a supporter of leftist political movements, a marcher and protester and vehement political arguer. He vowed to find a career where he could make a difference in the life of the poor. But soon after graduating he found himself with a wife and baby to support and went to work for an uncle's construction company. Within a few years he no longer had a wife to support, but he still had a daughter.

His willowy little girl, who had her mother's silky brunette hair, large, glossy brown eyes, and pale rosy-cheeked skin, would always be, wherever she went to school, the prettiest girl in her class, the best behaved and the politest, the most popular among the popular, with the best study habits and nearly perfect report cards. Aura, two years younger than her new stepsister, was a good student, too, though not as disciplined or as consistent in her grades, and while her behavior was often amusingly mischievous, it was also occasionally odd and troublesome. For instance, the year when Juanita was summoned to the Colegio Kensington several times by the principal, Miss Becky, because Aura was caught stealing, daily, from her classmates' schoolbags and knapsacks: a Spider-Man mechanical pencil, a Hello Kitty wallet, a Wonder Woman ruler, and so on, and it seemed that no classroom punishment or warning could put a stop to her larceny. Juanita and Rodrigo had promised Aura that if she was well behaved in school that year, as a reward she would be allowed to go with Katia to spend part of the summer at Yolanda's house in Orlando, near Disney World. Aura was on the cusp of being expelled from school when Juanita finally understood that there was nothing her daughter wanted less than to go to Orlando with her stepsister and the sommelier. When she rescinded the promise, Aura's crime spree ended.

Soon Rodrigo found the job that he would hold for the next two and a half decades, at least, at a consulting firm that advised local governments throughout Mexico on developing public housing projects. It was as close as he would ever come to his dream job, and he traveled the country, meeting with officials, building boards, community leaders, and the like, listening to their ideas, offering his recommendations. The firm matched those governments with private contractors, receiving a commission from the latter when the contracts for the projects were signed. Rodrigo didn't have much to do with the contractors; he just delivered his reports and recommendations to his boss, the firm's sole owner. The boss, Rodrigo's former urban studies professor, grew wealthy from his dealings with the contractors. The job kept Rodrigo on the road, traveling all over Mexico, often as many as five days a week, which he seemed to like; it paid very little.

Working as a secretary for the head of the psychology department, part-time as a research assistant, and taking an evening shift in the library, Juanita earned more than twice what Rodrigo did. She alone paid the down payment on the new apartment in the Copilco residential complex, definitely a step up from the Terrible Tower. Rodrigo and Juanita shared a bedroom and the girls shared the slightly smaller one across the hall. There were two bathrooms, a separate kitchen, and a central area that was both living room and dining room. A gated entrance with a guardhouse just off the avenue led into the walled-in parking lot. Here the children could play outside, ride their bikes, and roller-skate in the parking lot; you didn't have to fear stairwells or walking to and from your parked car in the dark. Aura had a friend in the complex whose parents even allowed her to take the trash out to the Dumpsters at night—

something my mother never lets me do,

she wrote in her diary. Those were the years of Mexico City's pollution crisis, when children were often kept home from school because
the air outside was too poisonous to breathe, and asphyxiated birds
plummeted from the sky. A dead bird once landed directly in front
of Aura's bicycle as she was pedaling in circles in the parking lot.

    Aura and Katia had, or at least each seemed to set about
determinedly developing, opposite personalities. If one little girl's
side of their bedroom was always the model of neatness, the other
girl's—guess whose?—was a mess. Katia had a mild, at times perky
and outwardly confident disposition, and she never cried or lost
control, but she was also an emotionally distant girl, easily able to
tune out everybody and everything around her. Aura was a cham-
pion crybaby, antic chatterer, back talker, and tantrum thrower.
Katia from a young age was fastidious about clothes and even on
the family's tight budget knew how to help her stepmother outfit
her in a way that always made her one of the best-dressed girls at
school. Aura preferred jeans, corduroys with elastic waists, baggy
sweatshirts, and overalls; she liked bright-colored sneakers, rubber
rain boots and flip-flops, eccentric hats and big sunglasses. The older
stepsister never broke her toys. The younger one reliably broke her
own toys, and her stepsister's. Katia liked Barbie dolls. Aura liked
dolls, too, but also Transformers, Power Rangers, Teenage Mutant
Ninja Turtles, Robotix, Atari, et cetera. Both girls liked books, but
Aura liked them more—

I read a book in English, *Little Women,* and I understood it very well,

she wrote in her diary when she was nine; a few entries later, she
rebuked herself for often preferring comics—*Mafalda, Betty and
Veronica, La Familia Burrón,* to "real books." Katia excelled in team
sports. Aura liked riding her bicycle and roller skating. The two

girls were sent to ballet school together. At first it was thought that Katia was a natural ballerina but she soon lost interest, bored by the drudgery of classes and rehearsals; she preferred spending her spare time with her friends. Aura, though she didn't really have a ballerina's physique like Katia, was surprisingly devoted to ballet and kept at it for years, becoming a lead soloist in school recitals and an assistant instructor of beginning students, an honor she'd long aspired to. There was even talk of sending her to Cuba to study at Alicia Alonso's famous ballet school. In her diary Aura confided that she wished she didn't have to share her bedroom with Katia so that she could turn it into a ballet studio, with a floor-to-ceiling mirror and dance barre.

With Rodrigo rarely at home during the week, it was Juanita who got Aura and Katia off to school in the mornings, took them to doctor, dentist, and eventually to shrink appointments, to ballet and confirmation classes, birthday parties, Girl Scouts, French and math tutors, the Freemasons' summer day camp, and all the rest. Living walking distance from the university was a convenience. Also, many of Juanita's closest friends from Guanajuato, the tías, were around to help out a bit now, having moved to the DF one after another, fleeing broken marriages and relationships, with children of their own in tow. Juanita hired a housekeeper, Ursula, who came in the mornings from the city's outskirts and left at four in the afternoon for her long commute home to prepare dinner for her own husband and children.

My mother was basically a single mom who raised Katia as her own daughter, Aura used to say. If anything, she treated Katia better than she did me. Katia was Little Miss Perfect and I was the one who had all the problems. It was always important to Rodrigo that Katia be the well-adjusted one, the less ruined and happier one. He'd defend her no matter what. And in those days, mostly because she was afraid of being dumped again, my mother would go along with whatever Rodrigo wanted.

Aura talked about all the time she spent alone as a child. Her mother often didn't get home from work until nine or ten at night.

After school, Katia liked to be with her friends, and was usually invited to play at their homes outside the Copilco complex; she never included her little sister in these outings, and rarely brought her friends to Copilco—one of the few times that Katia did was also the last. Going into the kitchen to see what there was to serve as a snack to her friends, Katia found a tray of green ice cubes in the freezer, flavored, she supposed, with lime Jell-O or Kool-Aid. Aura had made the ice cubes, but the green color came from Lysol. Aura loved the smell of household liquid cleaners, and she'd discovered that when mixed with a bit of water and frozen in an ice tray, they had an especially refreshing tang. You held the tray close to your face, touched the tip of your nose to the ice—which in itself was a nice sensation, as she demonstrated twenty years later for her husband in their Brooklyn kitchen, though with just normal ice in the tray—and breathed in deeply: *mmmmm*, such a tart tingling blast to your nasal passages! Aura already had allergy-related sinus problems, worsened by the city's pollution. Later, at thirteen, in her rebel-girl stage, smoking cigarettes so heavily that her school nickname was La Pipa, she would undergo sinus surgery. Katia served a green ice cube wrapped in a napkin to each of her friends. She gave one to Aura, too, who held hers to her nose, inhaled, and looked around happily to see if everyone else was enjoying their frozen Lysol, but what she saw was Katia and her friends, pink tongues out, licking. Later, Aura was unable to explain why she hadn't warned the other girls; it hadn't even occurred to her that they would be so stupid as to lick the Lysol cubes.

¡*Diabla idiota!* shrieked Katia, You poisoned my friends! There were panicked girls wailing, Call an ambulance! Aura gaped. They were just joking, no? A few of the girls, gagging and sobbing, phoned their parents. You're going to jail for the rest of your life! screamed Katia. Aura shut herself into the bathroom, squalling in bewildered terror and shame. For all the hysteria, nobody had gotten sick, or even vomited; after one or two licks, all the girls had flung their cubes onto the carpet. Later, it must have been hard for Juanita not to be overwhelmed with pity for Aura, but still, she had to be punished. No riding your bicycle for two weeks! Some of the girls were forbidden by their parents to ever visit Katia in her home again—a cruel overreaction that caused Katia deep embarrassment at school.

I could have come home to find six dead girls lying on the floor! Aura heard her mother bemoaning into the phone to Mama Violeta, her grandmother. Juanita worried that the reason Aura had trouble telling fantasy from reality was because she spent too much time alone in the apartment. But she had to work late to make money to pay for both girls' schooling. What could she do?

So that Aura could have some company in the afternoons, Rodrigo and her mother bought her a Scottie puppy in a market. Aura was overjoyed. But the puppy's health quickly deteriorated, and after just one week it died. Her mother tried to explain that it wasn't Aura's fault, that the pet sellers in the market had knowingly sold them a mortally ill dog.

In the unfinished short stories and fragments that I later found in Aura's computer, little girl narrators are always being tormented by older stepsisters:

> "It's your fault our housekeeper quit."
> "It's not true," I replied forcefully, almost shouting.
> "It's your fault that *my* father didn't drive us to school today," she went on.
> I swallowed my saliva and repeated my words without conviction.

About two years passed, during which Rodrigo and Juanita were married. In her diary, Aura wrote:

I have everything, even a diary, and the love of my parents. I'm 10, and my sister is always busy. You know, I like to write stories, and I sent one to the newspaper, *La Jornada*.

My ma gave a lecture at the university, it was padrísima, I felt so happy!

I just got dressed and I'm fed up, Mamá is impossible, I don't know what's going on with her but the truth is I'm not really liking her that much, let's say just the opposite, it's just that we can't get along anything I say she gets angry, even when I haven't finished the first word of my sentence. But maybe I'm just in a bad mood and so I'm going to go outside and skate.

Something has happened, it feels weird, nothing is the same as before. Papá is always away, and when I see him on weekends, something isn't right.

I think I need a new kind of friend. I'd like a friendship full of love, where we'd always be telling each other how much we love each other, talking in signs, forming a great team, but so far I haven't found that kind of friend.

Today has been the same as others. I didn't get bored but I didn't have fun either. But in the afternoon we're going to Perisur to buy Katia a bathing suit.

I went to eat and as I can't stand eating with Katia I went to the kitchen with Ursula. She was finished but I promised to eat fast and quietly, then I sat with Ursula and had tea with a sweet bun and I said things to her in English and explained what the words meant.

Cárdenas got various votes including those of my mother and father and I support them. We went and stood outside the

Congress building to support our party. The people from the PAN made noise but we just made V for victory signs with our hands and whenever somebody from the PRI came out to talk we all turned our backs. My mother knew one of them from the PRI and when he came over she started insulting him. I carried a sign that said

NO

AL FRAUDE

Today I've been happy and I learned that just because a mother can't be with her daughter all the time, that doesn't make her a bad mother, it's not the amount of time that matters.

I'm wearing a bra!

Dear Diary:

Surely you are asking yourself why I am writing to you. Again, problems with your mother, or feeling lonely? No, today it's not that, I just felt like writing. I'll tell you everything that has happened—

We went to Disco Patín at night. There was a big rink and a little one, all lit up. We were skating in the big one—some poor mongolotito was following us, but they made him leave. I met an instructor.
I don't know why Frida got mad at me.

I feel like a flea, nobody pays attention to me, I feel like I'm going to cry. To feel like a flea is humiliating and too painful for me. I just have to hear that little laugh from my "PERFECT" sister who only receives praise, congratulations and love, and my heart feels tossed into the trash. But I suppose that's just the way life is, some people are superior to others.

Played Atari like crazy, rearranged my Barbie house, watched television, read, set the table.

Entering secondaria [middle school] has been incredible. The worst has been my relations with my mother. I can't stand her anymore because if she has no interest in my things, why do I have to be interested in hers?

Advice on how not to be like my maldita perra mother
1. Don't discourage your children.
2. Don't yell at them.
3. Make it so that they spend every day marvelously and never even find out what boredom is.

I'm a total pendeja of a girl. I never pay attention to anything and I'm fed up with myself, I HATE MYSELF. I want somebody I can tell all this to, somebody to hug, a lot and very tightly. But I look around, and I find no one.

Dear Diary:
Mamá isn't here, I'm alone in the house so I can do what I want, my mother has forbidden me from going outside but I don't care I'll go out anyway, with that man with the motorcycle, the truth is he drives really fast.

I go with him, he lets me off at the wrong place and I'm hungry so I go into the store and slip some chocolate bars into my pocket but the employee sees me and I run out into the street but he catches me by the shoulder and takes the chocolate bars back, the next time I steal I better take more precaution.

Then I went to that horrible market and I ran into Luís who gave me whiskey, at first it was really strong but then I got used to it. Around 10:40 a.m. I decided to go home just in time to deceive my mother.

We had eggs for breakfast but I wasn't hungry, the whiskey was more than enough. Then I had to accompany my mother to work and while she thinks that I'm sitting here at one of the many desks, I go down to the 1st floor, to the coke machine, I find it and carefully, without anyone seeing me, I bang the machine and pull out a soft drink. Mmmm, yummy. Then I go upstairs, and my mother doesn't know anything that I've done today.

Maybe Aura suspected that her mother was snooping in her diary, or else that last entry was just a fantasy. By then, though, Aura had started tagging along with the older kids in the Copilco complex, and some of the stories she told me weren't so different from that one, so who knows?

Juanita and I never had the chance to sit down together to talk about how to divide Aura's belongings; we never came close to having that conversation. I would have given her almost whatever she wanted, the childhood diaries for sure. I did get a phone call from Juanita's cousin, who told me that Juanita wanted Aura's computer, but I said no, and not only because I'd bought it for Aura, but because so much of what was on it belonged to both of us, or was a part of our relationship—photos, music, the wedding site, texts we'd worked on together, and all Aura's fiction was saved there. What I did instead was take the computer to a technician and pay him to copy the contents of Aura's hard drive onto disks, minus, on the advice of a lawyer, her e-mail accounts. But about a month after Aura's death, I received an e-mail from Juanita's lawyer—a lawyer from the university, one of Leopoldo's colleagues—giving me two days to vacate the Escandón apartment where Aura and I had been living. Actually, it wasn't even an e-mail to me, it was sent to a friend of mine who'd come down for our wedding and also for the funeral, a lawyer in New York, but Juanita and her lawyer seemed to be assuming that he must be my lawyer, which he wasn't, though he did help me to find one in Mexico. They probably had no legal right to evict me, the widowed husband, so abruptly, even though it was technically Juanita's apartment, but I had no desire or will to fight. It wasn't that I was afraid of what they could do to me. I fled from having to confront the full force of their hatred and blame. I took everything in the apartment with me. That must have surprised Juanita. She probably expected me to leave most of Aura's stuff behind, including that old steamer trunk in which she kept her childhood diaries and her old school papers and such. I took the disks with the contents of Aura's computer back to Brooklyn with me, too.

One thing I did leave behind in the apartment was a copy of Leopoldo's book of political aphorisms, inscribed to Aura. I put the book down on the floor, open, spine up, and stomped it, imprinting it with my footprint, and kicked it into a pile of trash. I left behind our cheaper furniture, too, including the pine dining table from the Tlalpan carpentry market, with Aura's old school papers and old family photographs neatly stacked on top; also an envelope in which I'd put the silver charm bracelet that had belonged to Juanita when she was a child, "Juanita" engraved on its little plaque, with a note explaining that Aura had worn the bracelet into the ocean that last day.

I have an uncle who's going to hate you, Aura had told me shortly after we started going out. And you're going to hate him.

But I didn't hate Leopoldo. He was one of Aura's few relatives, she loved him, and he seemed to love her, so I did my best to get along with the guy. Anyway, he was funny. He liked to speak in aphorisms. Watching an elderly couple making a crabby, gesticulating scene with a waitress in a restaurant we were in, he remarked, in the same light dry tone he must have used when he charmed six-year-old Aura by referring to her and her cousins as bichitos:

Los viejitos sólo deben salir para ser amables, Old people should only go out in public to be sweet.

But he was also a haughty, vain, and pretentious man who knew exactly how he came off and, at least in some instances, seemed to enjoy making people wonder if he was really as appalling as he seemed, or if it was all just a twisted performance. As she had with Juanita, Mama Violeta had sent Leopoldo away at a young age, but to a military school in Tabasco where, as an intelligent, sensitive and lonely boy, he'd suffered horrors. The seething wound of those years was the source of his ramrod stiff bearing, his antiquated formality, and his general misanthropy and hostility.

I never really understood that he hated me until, at Aura's funeral, I caught him staring at me. I was weeping, friends were pressed around me, it seemed I couldn't greet anybody or receive an embrace without breaking down. I turned my head and caught Leopoldo aiming a stare of cold hatred directly at me. I remember thinking, What's that about? but I quickly dismissed it, it seemed perfectly right for everybody to be acting crazy. Soon I understood that stare better. There was more to it than hate. There was scrutiny in it, the cold reflection of a developing suspicion and logic. He stared at me like he thought he was investigator Porfiry Petrovich and I was Raskolnikov.

10

That first winter of Aura's death I was fixated on not losing my gloves, my hat, or my scarf. Since first being entrusted with the responsibility of looking after gloves, hat, and scarf in kindergarten, I'd probably never gotten through a whole winter without losing all of them. Aura was just the same, probably even worse. There were about a dozen single unpaired gloves, hers and mine, scattered around inside our big closet like unmated birds in a forlorn aviary. At least once every winter Aura would fall in love with a new winter hat, winter hats still being a novelty to her, and she'd wear it everywhere, even when it wasn't cold out, and when I'd swoon over how cute she looked and want to cover her winter-glowing cheeks in kisses, I'd think, It's just a matter of time before she loses this hat, and I was never wrong. One morning there I'd be, trying to reconstruct our path through the city the night before, phoning every bar and restaurant we'd been in, often speaking in Spanish to morning restaurant cleanup crews or kitchen workers and describing the hat Aura might have left behind. Everywhere I went that first winter without Aura, I was always patting the pockets of my down jacket to make sure the gloves were there, the pocket zippers closed, no matter how drunk I was, I'd suddenly remember to do that. If I noticed that a pocket's zipper was open with a glove stuffed inside, if I saw any part of a glove or finger protruding, I'd gasp or even curse myself and zip it closed with such emphatic self-recrimination that, on the street or the subway or at the next table, I often drew alarmed and curious stares. Mi amor, I'm not going to lose these gloves, I promise, I'd mutter away, as if they were her gloves and she was depending on me to bring them home to her. And I didn't, all that winter, for the first time ever that I remember, lose either my gloves or my hat. But I did lose my scarf, during a long night of drinking in January, in Berlin, where I spent three weeks during that first winter without Aura, when I'd wanted to flee Brooklyn during the holidays, and then I refused to buy a new one, despite that city's winter cold that feels like it blows in off Russian steppe battlefields strewn with frozen corpses. When I got back to Brooklyn about a week later I started wearing one of Aura's scarves instead, a black pashmina with a white pattern, embroidered with silvery threads. People would say, What a nice scarf, or, What a pretty scarf, and I'd say, It's Aura's, and sometimes people, especially women, would respond, Yes, I thought it must be, or they'd give me a little pat on the shoulder. That was the scarf I was tying on again as I got ready for my second winter without Aura.

This time I didn't even get as far as mid-December before I reached into the pocket of my jacket one evening as I was coming out of a subway exit and realized that I'd lost a glove. I went into our closet and found an old left-hand glove from some other separated pair, and when I soon lost that glove, too, I didn't care. But I was still determined not to lose my hat, a gray cloth aviator cap with synthetic-fur-lined flaps. Aura was with me when I bought it for ten dollars in Chinatown during our last winter.

Aura lived in the Copilco apartment from about the age of six until she went away to the University of Texas. After she came back from Brown she lived in her mother's new high-rise condo apartment for a few months, before moving on her own back to Copilco, where her mother hadn't sold that apartment yet. Copilco was where Aura and I spent our first night together. So many of the turning-point moments in Aura's life happened there. When she was eleven her grandmother Mama Violeta came from Taxco for what was supposed to be a month's visit, maybe longer; there was even a chance that Mama Violeta was going to move in and live with them. But within days a fight erupted, overheard by Aura in her bedroom, her grandmother horribly insulting her mother, and her mother's indignant shouts ordering Mama Violeta to leave. And Mama Violeta did leave, except she didn't just storm out and stalk around the parking lot until she calmed down and came back and tearfully apologized to her daughter for the terrible things she'd said and vice versa, as Aura had expected; instead she packed up her suitcase and left, and never again spoke to her daughter, or even to her granddaughter. Back then Juanita rarely drank alcohol, and she went jogging with Rodrigo on weekends and took aerobics classes; her body was firm, her skin smooth and fresh, and she always dressed nicely. Oh, she was so lovely, you can't imagine, Aura used to tell me with an adoring little girl's pride. Aura never discovered, or never told me, what had caused the fight, but she believed that if one moment marked the beginning of her mother's long, at first almost invisible, decline, it was that rupture with Mama Violeta.

Six years later, Juanita expelled Katia from the Copilco apartment, too. By then Katia was no longer considered so perfect. Excited by the possibilities of her own beauty, boy crazy and headstrong, she'd been battling Juanita throughout her adolescence. And then, despite her excellent grades, she'd failed the highly competitive UNAM admission exam. But when Katia, who wanted to study business administration and dreamed of a career in fashion, was admitted to a private university, Juanita somehow came up with the tuition money and gave it to her. Some weeks went by. In the afternoons and evenings, Katia came home with shopping bags from Palacio de Hierro and other upscale stores, once sporting a pair of new Italian leather boots that in Aura's memory became so iconic that years later, whenever she shopped for boots in New York or stopped to look in shop windows, it was always as if she saw Katia's boots among the ones on display, barely worn, a little dusty and tragic, and she'd remember her stepsister who'd suddenly vanished from her life after having practically dominated it, like a tyrant really, for so long. For years Juanita, so as not to upset Rodrigo, had nearly turned a blind eye to Katia's daily bullying of her younger stepsister. But when Juanita found out that although Katia had been pretending to go off to classes in the mornings she'd never matriculated and was spending the tuition money on clothes, on those boots, and on her boyfriend, she banished Katia from the household. Rodrigo did not defend his daughter, maybe didn't dare to try. Katia was nineteen, no longer a child, and she'd committed a crime of seemingly demonic ingratitude; well, now she would have to learn to be responsible for herself. And Katia wasted no time in taking control of her life, as if being expelled from Copilco and her family was just what she'd been wishing for. She found a place to live, some modeling work, and then steadier employment as a secretary in an economics institute, and went back to school part-time, paying her own tuition. Rodrigo went on seeing his daughter more or less in secret. Juanita never forgave Katia. But Katia never forgave Juanita, either, and never apologized or gave any sign of wishing for a rapprochement. Ten years would go by before Aura and Katia saw each other again.

Though Aura hadn't seen or spoken to her grandmother since she was eleven, she kept a framed photograph of Mama Violeta in our bedroom in Brooklyn. The photograph showed a fair-skinned, if wrinkly, European-looking woman with long bony limbs, flaccid cheeks, slack-mouthed (Juanita's mouth when she was sad, exactly), and a familiar turbulence in her hurt-looking, intelligent eyes. A frilly cushion that Mama Violeta had embroidered with Baudelairian purple, pearl gray, and crimson black-stemmed flowers and "AURA" stitched across the flowerpot in yellow was on our bed, atop the quilt of many colors.

Aura's famous first therapy session, when she was eleven:

Do you feel that your mother listens to you, Aura?

Does *your* mother listen to *you*, Doctora?

Juanita, worried about the effects of so much traumatic leaving and cleaving on the girls—Aura's father, Katia's mother, Mama Violeta—had made separate appointments for each with Dr. Nora Banini, a psychoanalyst on the faculty of the psychology department. The elfin girl with the animated face and raspy voice, hair falling over her eyes, sitting forward on the soft leather couch, elbows propped on her lap, chin resting upon interlaced fingers, stared directly back at Nora Banini, seated opposite, who serenely persisted.

You seem angry, Aura, but you've just met me, so I don't think you can really be angry with me. Is it your mother you're angry with?

But I *do* want to get to know you, Doctora. Are you angry with *your* mother?

Please, Aura, call me Nora. Maybe you're feeling angry with your mother for bringing you here today? Why do you think she wanted us to have this chance to talk?

Let's talk about *your* mother. Is she nice to you? Why don't you want to talk about your mother, Doctora?

Aura would keep on seeing Nora Banini until she was twenty-seven, though by then only when back on visits from New York. Katia, paying for her own sessions, would keep on seeing Nora Banini, too, until she was into her thirties, married and a mother.

In the summer of 1990—Berlin Wall down, Soviet Union on the cusp of collapse—Aura was sent to a summer camp in Cuba. By then Juanita, as much to antagonize Rodrigo as for any other reason, had transformed into a jeering antileftist. So why send Aura there? Aura had once dreamed of studying ballet with the great Alicia Alonso, but those dreams were past. At thirteen, radicalized by Mexico's stolen presidential election and the U.S. invasion of Panama, Aura was noisily declaring herself a Communist and a Cuban-type revolutionary and Juanita foresaw, or so Aura would always claim, that all it would take to demolish her daughter's utopian illusions would be a few weeks in Cuba itself. The camp was by a beach and brought together young adolescents from all over the world, many from the Scandinavian countries. They were housed in what seemed to be an old hospital, with long green-painted corridors lined with airless green rooms, six cots in every room. That first night Aura couldn't get to sleep; she was kept awake by the room's suffocating heat, the pitch darkness, and the sonar weeping of another Mexican girl in a neighboring room whose wallet, stuffed with dollars given to her by her parents, had already been stolen. Within her first few days there, Aura lost her sandals on the beach, and then her sneakers were either lost or stolen, too. She ended up going barefoot. Every meal was rice and beans, and after each meal the campers had to scrape their leftovers into buckets that were brought around so that this could be added to the rice and beans served at the next meal, making an increasingly gluey and muddy-looking gruel. Aura stopped eating. When her mother went to pick her up at Benito Juárez Airport, Aura had lost so much weight she was holding her pants up with her hands, she was barefoot, her sun-caramelized skin was spotty with scratched-raw insect bites, and her clothes hadn't been washed since she'd left Mexico. When Juanita asked her how she'd spent the three weeks at camp, she answered cheerfully:

Making out with Danish boys, Mami!

For Aura, "Communism" would forever after provoke a retch-inducing recall of communal buckets of rancid rice and beans. But her new scrawniness gave her a gamine prettiness that even she couldn't deny. The anxious delight stirred by what she discovered in the mirror when she got home quickly developed into a borderline anorexia that would endure well into her twenties. Within weeks she met the boy who would become her first boyfriend, at an all-night outdoor rave in the Bosque de Tlalpan. Juanita, naturally, had forbidden Aura to attend raves, an impediment solved via the ruse of fake sleepovers at girlfriends' houses. That ruse exposed soon enough, Aura was grounded for two months, a period she always recounted fondly because of her discovery one Sunday afternoon, in Tío Leopoldo's study, of a blue-bound volume of the selected works of Oscar Wilde, a name she recognized from Gandhi bookstore calendars and also from a T-shirt worn by *un dark* known as O.D., who painted his fingernails and eyes black and was a friend of the boy she'd met at the rave: the sad-eyed, jowly visage and folded-wings hairdo imprinted on O.D.'s T-shirt had reminded her of Mama Violeta. Aura brought the volume back to Copilco to accompany her through the remaining weeks of her imprisonment. In pink felt-tip pen, on the cover of her notebook, she wrote, "I never travel without my diary. One should always have something sensational to read in the train," surrounded by a little flock of pink hearts. Fifteen years later, when we moved into the Escandón apartment, she unpacked that same hefty blue volume from a box of books, held it up, and told me the story; now it's in Brooklyn.

Dos Santos was the name of the boy she'd met at the rave, and he was eighteen, five years older than Aura. Dos Santos was actually his surname but Aura only used his first name whenever she phoned him at home and one of his parents answered. In the old steamer trunk where Aura also stored her diaries, I found Dos Santos's poems, hundreds of them, reams of photocopied pages stuffed into plastic grocery bags. Around when they met, Dos Santos had also finished writing a six-hundred-or-so-page novel that he gave to his father to read. His father eagerly did so and, when he'd finished, told his son that it was worthless garbage, lacking any sign of talent or promise. For all his diffident airs, Dos Santos was a trusting and even naive boy who revered his dad, an eminent economist at the ITAM. Utterly crushed, he swore he'd never write again, even though he claimed there was nothing else worth living for.

Aura had never before felt so needed by anyone other than her mother. If there's one thing young writers should never do, Aura told Dos Santos, it's share their writing with their parents: sound advice that she'd rarely follow herself. She read Dos Santos's tome and it thrilled her. Honestly, she wasn't just saying that to make him feel better. Pages of wild prose that invented their own grammar, filled with silly and inscrutable jokes, and such a weird imagination he should be grateful his father hadn't locked him up in an asylum! (The novel wasn't among the writings of Dos Santos that I found in the steamer trunk.) Aura's enthusiasm and praise, probably accompanied by kisses of the sort refined with Danish boys on the beach in Cuba, restored Dos Santos's conviction in his own literary powers and rebel spirit, and that conviction, after all, had made Dos Santos who he was, a teenaged personage, El Poeta or whatever, not just some eighteen-year-old loser who hung around with a thirteen-year-old girl. Aura and Dos Santos became each other's most indispensable companions. He was the secret sign-language friend she'd been longing for.

Where's your sense of humor, mother?
Love

It was not abnormal: love. For a person to fall in love, to construct a love that was young and innocent, it is terrible. Nothing abnormal either about believing that everyone was against me—according to Freud, paranoia is a natural reaction of young love. Except that in my case the paranoia was not without basis. It sat firmly on my mother's shoulders, her whole body its pedestal as a frown descended over her face and she lifted her hands to the sky and groaned when the black object of her hatred came to visit: my First Boyfriend, sitting there— in HER CHAIR!— sporting dark glasses on a dark autumn Friday, under the obvious influence of marijuana. Lighten up, Ma; where's your sense of humor? But my mother, my single mother, in particular with respect to her thirteen-year-old, pubescent, menstruating daughter, has no sense of humor. Not a drop. My single mother in particular is weighted down with suspicions, rigid with severe admonitions founded on statistics, opinion polls, worst-case scenarios. All of which had nothing, or very little, but more likely nothing at all to do with the fact that her daughter was in love for the first time. Instead of tenderness and concern, the punishments and prohibitions rained down like leaves dropping prematurely from the trees. That autumn never went away: it toppled the future before it in a domino reaction. *Fast forward*, when what I wanted was *rewind*.

—Aura Estrada

An authoritative mother's unyielding disdain for her adolescent daughter's boyfriend will usually win out, and Dos Santos and Aura were a couple few half-awake mothers would encourage. Dos Santos did eventually recede from Aura's life, as if being slowly pulled away in an undertow that not even he noticed until he was disappearing into the lost years of his midtwenties. But Aura never stopped believing in Dos Santos—as years later she believed in me. Whenever we were just back in Mexico City and went into a bookstore, I always knew what she was hoping to find on the table of new books: Dos Santos's just-published first novel or poetry collection. And I'd think, but I'd never say, He's well into his thirties now, if it's going to happen, isn't it about time?

The last time I saw Lola, Aura's best friend at the UNAM, who was also raised by a single mother in Mexico City, she said:

I used to wish I had a mother like that, who I knew would look out for me and fight for me no matter what. Do you know what I mean? A mother who fights for you like a mother should, but also the way a father should.

More or less, I understood. I suppose I could have used a parent like that, too, when I was a teenager, my father having been, actually, the opposite of someone who would fight for you.

That conversation with Lola took place last New Year's Eve in a bar on Ludlow Street. She was still working toward her PhD at Yale and, just as she used to when Aura was alive, she came regularly to New York by bus on her way to see Bernie Chen, a PhD student at Cornell, now her fiancé. Five years earlier, when I had first met

Lola, right after Aura and I started going out, she'd taken me aside to offer a drink-fueled candid warning:

If Juanita is okay with Aura being with you, then she'll be with you. But if she's against it—Lola slowly shook her head no—then she won't be. You know that, right?

So you're saying that if Aura's mother doesn't want her to be with me you think she can break us up.

Juanita's power over Aura is like something in a myth, said Lola. It's like she can throw thunderbolts from Mexico.

I'm meeting Juanita in a few weeks, I said. In Las Vegas, if you can believe it.

Lola tried to cheer me up. When Juanita sees how happy Aura is with you, she said, everything will be fine. In the end, that's what matters to her most.

With banished Katia no longer an expense, there had been more money to spend on Aura's education. To become a doctoral student in comparative literature, Aura would need to be fluent in three languages, and so she was sent to Europe during the next three summers: twice to Paris to study French, once to Cambridge for courses in English literature. The only trips out of Mexico that Juanita and Rodrigo had ever taken were just across their country's borders, by automobile, mostly to Texas, but one time into Belize. It was impossible to show enough gratitude for her mother's sacrifices, but Aura tried. *A twenty-four-hour daughter to a single mother*—that's how Aura described herself in her diary. Aura persisted in referring to her mother as single, partly because, with Rodrigo away so much, for all practical purposes she was. Even if she couldn't yet put into words what it was that filled her with foreboding, Aura often felt consumed by worry about her mother. Every weekday she rushed home from the university and took over the kitchen from the housekeeper, Ursula, to prepare lunch for her mother, giving Juanita a chance to leave campus and be alone with her daughter for a couple of hours instead of spending the time at the usual restaurants and *fondas* with faculty and coworkers—meals at which her mother, Aura knew, was sometimes unable to resist that second or third tequila, or even more, when the others were drinking, too. Like her mother, Aura didn't really know how to cook—Ursula left their suppers prepared before she went home in the afternoons—but she began to teach herself from an English cookbook of international recipes that she found in the Gandhi bookstore's sidewalk bargain bins. Nearly every weekday she took her shopping list to the supermarket. Aura liked to cook fish because it didn't take long and was supposed to be healthy, but the English fish names in her cookbook didn't correspond to those she found in the seafood section at Superama. Most fish was too expensive, too, but there was an affordable one called *punta de venta* and these packaged fillets were always available. We're having punta de venta, Ma, she'd announce, phoning her mother at the university to tell her to hurry home, and whenever Juanita replied, Again? Aura would reassure her that she was cooking it a different way from the last time, whether that had been baked, fried, *à la veracruzana*, or even *à la meunier*.

One day Juanita said, Aura, you know, you really don't always have to buy punta de venta, I'll give you the money to buy something fresh, we can afford that. ¿Cómo? asked Aura, confused. Her mother asked if by chance Aura thought that punta de venta was a species of fish? Of course she knew, said Aura, that it was a fish. Wait, you mean, it's *not*? Then what is it? Her mother explained that punta de venta was what the supermarket labeled any kind of fish that was discounted because it had reached its sell-by date. Ohhh! They were laughing themselves silly when Juanita said, You know, mi amor, you don't really need to cook for me every day. A brief silence fell. Aura asked, You mean you don't want me to cook for you anymore, Ma? Hija, said Juanita, this driving between work and home and back just to eat every day is going to kill me, el tráfico está de la chingada. Aura gave a short laugh, which her mother echoed with a forced guffaw, provoking another round of laughter, not as rollicking as the first. Hija, corazón, Juanita gently pleaded, isn't this a bit much for you, too, all this shopping and cooking; can you really spare the time? Wouldn't you rather eat with your friends?

We're all just a fantasy, Juanita remarked one day, during another conversation that Aura recorded in her diary.

None of Aura's tías were actual family. Not blood family. They were fake or pretend family. Prosthetic family, as Aura called them.

And what am I supposed to do with that? asked Aura. How is it supposed to help me, to know that I'm a fantasy?

We both are, not just you, her mother answered. And you should enjoy it, and be grateful, instead of always arguing with it the way you do.

Did Juanita consider her husband, or both her husbands— maybe even all husbands everywhere and always—to be prosthetic relatives, too? Detachable, just part of a fantasy family? Were only mother-daughter relations real?

Reading in Aura's diary about the months after we first met, when she returned to Mexico from Brown and went to Guanajuato for Christmas, it felt strange not to find myself included among the so-familiar cast—the tías, Mama Loly, Vicky Padilla, the god-parents who were also Aura's professors, Fabiola—all of whom I'd be spending the holiday with one year later as Aura's new, older, boyfriend from New York. Juanita's boss, usually referred to as el Dramaturgo, also came to Guanajuato that Christmas. In his twenties he'd written a sort of Angry Young Macho play that was still regularly staged in Mexican schools. Aura had acted in a production at the Colegio Guernica, playing the macho's spir-ited but relentlessly mistreated young wife. "I hate digging bullets out of my own body, carajo!"—that had been one of her lines, and at home it had become a joking refrain wielded in moments of actual or ironic distress by all the females of the household, even Ursula. Now in his fifties, el Dramaturgo was rector of the humanities, one of the university's most powerful posts. Soon after the student strike that sent Aura away to Austin had ended, el Dramaturgo had hired Juanita as his administrative secretary of the humanities, a significant post in its own right. Now Juanita had her own office one floor beneath his, with two secretaries and a respectable salary. It had been a smart if unconventional choice to hire Juanita—no one understood better the mazes and murk of the massive university bureaucracy; there was hardly a university functionary, file clerk, security guard, or campus bus driver with whom Juanita wasn't on a first name basis. She could have switched careers, become an important official for the university workers' union—people had let her know how valuable she could be in that role—but Juanita's heart and loyalties were with the academic side of the school, with the teaching and research faculties that had given her a way to survive when she was newly arrived in the capital with her baby girl. The university was like a Renaissance city-state that had taken Juanita in as a foundling in order to nurture her into one of its great ladies, a connoisseur of the wielding of power within its walls.

At least, Aura wrote in her diary, she was too old now to be ordered to call el Dramaturgo "Tío." Her first morning in Guanajuato she went out into the streets, charged by her mother with the errand of buying a gift in the market that she would give to el Dramaturgo—she chose a carved wooden penholder—and flowers for the party in his honor that afternoon in Tía Vicky's mother's house, where they were staying. One of Mexico's last surviving Golden Age movie stars, Carlota Padilla now mostly played grandmothers and wise old family servants on telenovelas. Though she lived in Mexico City, she owned a restored hacienda house on the outskirts of Guanajuato that resembled one of those colonial-era convents that are converted into five-star hotels; it had an old walled orchard out back and a swimming pool. Aura felt happy, wandering the streets on her party errands, admiring the colonial architecture and the steep mountains encircling the city. (She often liked to quote drunken Dr. Vigil's line from Under the Volcano: "Guanajuato is sited in a beautiful circus of steepy hills.")

I bought the flowers (Mrs. D, of VW) and went back to the house and found el Dramaturgo already there, tequileando with my mother, kicking off the alcoholic activities which, for me, have ended in horror. Conversations. Flattery—sincere and false. The meal. Meat. I abstain. Tequila. Iced tea for me. I clear my own plate, get up from the table; I dance alone in a corner, watch television. More tequila—my mother and her jefe. My mother's husband adopts unexpected positions during a vehement political argument. Another dramaturgo arrives, this one has come all the way from Guadalajara just to visit el Dramaturgo. More tequila. My mother starts to touch on upsetting subjects. To such a degree that later, as he's leaving, dramaturgo #2 whispers to me, Follow your own destiny. Do I have one? My nerves are on edge. I want to start my doctorate, go to a prestigious university, write, study, work, have a life. My godfather is good. He flatters me every which way. I'm not sure I believe him. If even half of what he says about me were true, I'd love it. He's drunk. Like my mother.

Which upsetting subjects might those have been, mi amor? Maybe another mocking disquisition on how absurd it was to go away to study Latin American literature at a gringo university? Hadn't Juanita raised and prepared Aura to do just that, to go away to study abroad? Now she didn't want to let her go. Juanita dreaded being without Aura, dreaded being left alone in her marriage to a man who no longer loved her, and who wasn't going to help her because the only way he could help her was by loving her. That dread was passed on to her daughter, the heaviest of the suitcases she'd bring with her to New York. Aura couldn't love her stepfather if he wasn't at least trying to make her mother happy. It wasn't only his fault, she knew, but it was only her mother's happiness that she cared about.

Why did you leave me to grow up without a dad? Aura had asked her father, face burning, in the restaurant there in Guanajuato that first time in seventeen years that she'd seen him. Why didn't you ever even answer my letters? So far, so good, she told herself. I haven't cried. But then she did. She lay her head down on folded arms and sobbed and her father moved from his seat to one beside her and put his hand on her back and undoubtedly wondered why he was doing this to himself, and why was she doing this to herself, and why live at all anyway when life turns out to be such a fucking mess, sitting there with his sobbing daughter who he hadn't seen in seventeen years, mud all over his pants.

Well, of course she was going to cry. But he said what he had to say, his slender hands folded on the tabletop, the explanation that he'd probably rehearsed on the drive across the state from San José Tacuaya:

I thought you should have only one father, hija. After your mother and I separated and she married Rodrigo, I wanted you to regard him as your father, and to love him. I thought that would be best for you. It's not good for a child to have two fathers. Of course I've always loved you, and always missed you.

Thank you, Pa, she'd said. I've always loved and missed you, too. But thank you for what? The more she thought about her father's answer, later, the more it saddened and even angered her. Her real father, she'd perceived that day, was an intelligent, sensitive, flawed person who lived in the world much as she did, always wanting to apologize for his existence. Everything about him—his gentle eyes, his hushed voice, his politeness, the mysterious mud on his pants—had filled her with compassion. She could tell they would have been strengthened by each other's love, by their smart father-daughter complicity. Something essential, that both needed, had been ripped from them. This was the man who should have been her father.

The day after Christmas, having gone to Mama Loly's to say her good-byes to Fabiola and the Hernández clan, Aura returned on foot to the Padilla house and she was just raising the key to the lock when the old timber of the big zaguán door shook in its frame as if from an earthquake aftershock, followed by a burst of metallic fidgeting within the lock, which set the door handle quivering. She waited a moment, put the key in, turned it, pushed the heavy door open, and found Héctor, her father, on the other side, in the stone-paved vestibule, looking flustered, his mussed graying hair dangling over his forehead. His hands fluttered toward the door in futile pursuit when she let it close behind her. They looked at each other, exchanged cheek kisses, a slightly awkward embrace, holiday greetings, then Aura said, What a surprise, Pa, what are you doing here? He was dressed the same as the last time she'd seen him—same suit, she was pretty sure—only without a tie, but he looked older, as if he'd aged a decade in four years. He looked drained and haggard. I couldn't figure out how to make the door open, he said, and he smiled crookedly. I heard from Vicky that you were here, he went on, and I decided to drive over to say hello, hija, but I'm sorry, now I have to go, as you see, I was just leaving. Está bien, Pa, she said, Feliz año, pues—confusion made her voice listless. Igualmente, hija, he said—I hope the New Year brings you all the happiness you deserve—and he bent to kiss her on the cheek again, and then he said, Perdón, Aura, this door, there's some trick to opening it that eludes me. She opened it, pressing the lock lever while unlatching it on the side, and she said, It is a bit tricky, Pa, and she pushed on the door with both hands and held it open with her arm extended, smiling and making a little bow from the waist that he didn't seem to notice as he thanked her and fled out the door as if freed from a cage.

At the end of the walk he gave her a nervous wave good-bye and turned into the street and that was the last time Aura ever saw her father. In a shadowy corner of the spacious living room she found her mother and Vicky sitting at a table like a pair of shady fortune-tellers, lowered eyes, curling cigarette smoke, and a bottle of tequila between them. They'd just been laughing, she could tell, and had stopped when she came in. They were laughing at my father, she thought. She wasn't going to give them a chance to perform their mocking account of his visit, would ask them nothing, would go directly to her room to pack and leave for the bus station in an hour. But Vicky asked, Did you see Héctor? so she had to answer, and said, Yes, tía, he was just on his way out. He only came because he wanted to see you, said her mother, not looking up. Vicky phoned to let him know you were here. I know, said Aura, he told me. Thank you, tía . . . well, I have to pack. What happened, said her mother, is that he remembered he had to go and collect empty bottles at the market, that's why he was in such a rush. Both women sniggered. Aura said, *Yayaya*, and went on toward the bedroom. She was going to the beach with P., who'd been her boyfriend on and off since the summer. They would travel from the DF by all-night first-class sleeper bus to Puerto Escondido, Oaxaca, and then catch the local bus along the coast to that undeveloped stretch of three adjoining beaches separated by bluffs and rocky promontories: Ventanilla, San Agustinillo, and Mazunte. She'd longed to see these beaches since she was fourteen, when groups of her school friends had first begun going there on trips that her mother never allowed her to join. There wasn't a single resort or conventional tourist hotel there, but there were lots of places that rented hammocks and a bit of shelter; other travelers just strung their own hammocks in groves of trees, or pitched tents on the beach and paid nothing. Aura's relationship with P. would last only a few more months, but her new love for that stretch of coast would persist.

Over the next four years and seven months, she would visit those beaches at least eight more times, five with me, as if yielding to the pull of an irresistible destiny: geography and fate one and the same. P. took her to Ventanilla, the wildest of the three beaches, which lacked even the most rustic backpacker hostels. The largest dwelling there was a kind of two-story hut with a twin-peaked, thatched roof over a wooden floor that had a slatted half-wall running around it, the living quarters, itself held up by long palm trunk poles. A thatched overhang extended from the front of the structure over the brown sand. For a small price the fisherman who lived there with his family rented hammocks or allowed travelers to hang their own from the poles under the overhang, or to pitch a tent in the sand, as P. and Aura did—what they were paying for was access to the outhouse and, during the day, to hammocks in the shade. The kitchen, a short distance from the house, was in an open-sided palapa where the fisherman's wife and her sisters cooked their family meals and ran a simple restaurant serving breakfast and, throughout the long afternoons, the fish, shrimp, and lobster brought back by her husband and his brothers in the launches that they pushed off the sand and into the waves in the dark predawn.

With its vast spaces of ocean, sky, and beach, and the peaceful and simple life led by the fisherman and his family—a way of life that it seemed one could join or borrow just by renting a hammock—Ventanilla changed Aura, a girl from the megalopolis, raised in a small apartment where there was no escape from the other taxing personalities living there, where often, as she reflected in her diary, she had no better option than to just sit there *buzzing with anger* opposite her antagonist of the moment, and where she'd had to *master the arts of argument and the cutting remark to survive*. She hadn't known that there was space inside herself for a place like Ventanilla. She discovered a new way to be there, she thought, a self that had always been hidden from her, truer, she felt convinced, than the anxious, self-protective, and defiantly lippy girl of Mexico City.

Ventanilla was a paradise, she wrote in her diary, that was also a labyrinth because there was so much that she'd never seen or experienced before. Even the flavors of the papayas were unlike any she'd ever tasted. The disciplined industry of the pelicans, drawing long straight lines of flight while skimming the water for fish with their enormous bills. White herons perched pensively on the rocks. The ocean wind blowing in her face all day, robust, scratchy with sand, but also caressing. The discovery that it was possible to spend almost a whole day in a hammock, reading, writing, staring out at the ocean, daydreaming, or closing her eyes and listening to the shouts and laughter of the fisherman's children, their windblown fragments of speech like lines of experimental poetry.

The days were so long that by late afternoon she couldn't be
sure if what had happened in the morning had actually happened
yesterday; evening always came as a welcome surprise, cooling the
burning sand, filling the sky and air with diluted fruit drink colors,
until finally it became too dark to read. So little was demanded or
expected of the night that it was almost like being a child again.
Falling asleep listening to the mechanical crunch of the waves, the
comfort of knowing she was safely out of reach. The fisherman's
children spent hours playing fútbol with a plastic ball so deflated it
was more like a hat, and the chatty little girls who went to a one-
room schoolhouse in Mazunte never ran out of stories to tell. The
girls carried their pet baby parrots and kittens around with them
like favorite cloth dolls. She learned all the children's names and
couldn't stop taking their pictures, on that first visit and subsequent
ones. But the long line of jungle and palms at the back of the beach
spooked her, there must be snakes in there, and she imagined eyes
watching from within the green shadows. In the dense mists of
early morning the figures walking on the sand looked like ghosts
from Comala.

At one end of the beach rose a steep bluff with a large solitary
cross on top. Millennia of erosion had opened a triangular window
in the formation of enormous boulders jutting into the ocean at the
foot of the bluff, the beach's eponymous window, in which sunsets
were framed like detached pieces of sky; she spent much time trying to imagine when and how wind and ocean had penetrated the
rock, the instant when light and spray had first broken through,
what could that have been like? The beach at Ventanilla was *mar
abierto*, open wide to the ocean, bringing treacherous currents and
ferocious waves. Everyone warned about the dangers of swimming,
though the surfers seemed fearless.

The ocean surrounds you as soon as you go near it, she wrote
in her diary, and pushes and pulls you and seduces you with the
whispering of its foamy withdrawal over the bubbling sand. The
heavy waves suspended in the air for miraculous instants in front

of your gaze. They fall fall fall with fury, and fling and drag you with more force than you'd calculated.

Most days, when I open my eyes in the morning, the first thing I see, projected out of my brain and eyeball sockets like lasers of horror, is Aura when they told me she was dead and I rushed back to her bed and saw her. Or the wide swathe of ocean foam receding, uncovering her floating facedown, and I always shout, NO! At any moment it comes back. Panic shooting up through me like silent antiaircraft fire, or down through me, because it's also like the sensation of falling in your sleep except you're awake. Hot flashes on my brow, sweat down my spine, chills. Fuck. Shout out, sometimes softly, sometimes loudly enough that heads turn. Standing on a subway platform or in the street or in a dark bar, hands clenched at my sides, staring down, head bobbing, going No No No no NO NO no no NO! NO!—waking from it with a start, looking around.

I'm terrified of losing you in me. Back in Brooklyn I still sometimes find myself trying to skip down our sidewalk as you used to, my angel. Aura used to challenge me to try it, and I would, and there she'd be, face scrunched, laughing at my spazzy effort. That agile hopscotch-like skipping she used to do on the sidewalk, a winged-heel blur, heel-kicked-back heel-kicked-back while also moving forward in an exhilarated burst down the sidewalk as if propelling herself back to her childhood in Copilco, the other girls huddled in the parking lot like lambs in the twilight, watching. I wish that everybody walking on Degraw Street could pause to remember Aura hop-skipping down the sidewalk like she used to, instead of noticing me trying to recall her in my half-century-old limbs, doing my clumsy stomping-stumble on the sidewalk, startling and baffling neighbors and other pedestrians with my futile widower's dance.

11

February 2003 (DF)

My infancy wasted in my mother's bottomless handbag, a lip
pencil and a makeup case, prohibited evidence maybe: a blue
vein pulsing in her forehead. Lowered eyes seeking forgiveness.
Anguish and, later, insatiable rage.

There's too much noise in my head, memory doing its
thing, memories I'd rather forget return, return. This place is
going to finish me off. My mother's shadow. *Aura*, that damned
book, a story and its coincidences. Fiction became reality. Or
I'm a fiction. A nightmare of my mother's. I can't be me. Maybe
thus the recurring idea of death. The only way for me to affirm
myself, find myself, to be an individual, to commit a completely
voluntary act. At least to find a language that she doesn't understand, my own. But at the same time anxiety, nausea, guilt.
Shitty psychoanalysis that doesn't resolve anything in practice.
To know is not to act. This place where I'm living: pure tears.

Romantic disillusion.
My childhood destroyed: a ruin.
An aged youth: I let hope die.
With her, everything is anguish, skepticism

March, 2003, Copilco—Been having these dreams. Men chas-
ing me, having to save a bunch of guys, my mom drowning in
the sea, my real dad coming back and abandoning us again, a
swimming pool eaten by the sea.

May 25, 2003—I miss being in love, involved. In the morning I left P.'s house feeling angry, feeling so nothing, so unloved. The sensation of being a red cube in the middle of the desert.

June 3—power comes to me only when I feel safe. For two weeks I function, then for two weeks I'm a comatose vegetable who can't even read. I wasn't made for academia. Since I was 18, I've felt pursued by the idea that I should have dedicated myself to something else entirely. Some profession that doesn't demand of me this commitment to solitude. I don't know how to commit myself, not to a profession or to a person. There is something in me dedicated to destroying the confidence that I so slowly construct. Then I pass two weeks feeling creative and sure of myself and I begin to feel good in company with my solitude and my books (Chesterton, Yeats) but these two blessed weeks end and then again, spiritual ruin, dead motivation, all day in bed or staring nowhere in particular and anxiously waiting for the phone to ring, and for the masculine presence of the bars at night and that absurd companionship that only leaves me feeling more alone. Who am I kidding, it's all got to do with menstrual periods and hormones.

I have so many friends and I feel so isolated here in this house, the house of my childhood, where I spent good moments but mostly just nerve-wracking ones.

Dead all in the same week:
Bolaño
Compay Segundo
Celia Cruz
Lupe Valenzuela (ex-wife of el Dramaturgo)
Bolaño born the same year as Dylan Thomas's death (and Stalin's, too)

Ventanilla, July 3—I'm in front of the ocean again. They are surprised that this time I didn't come with P. I hope they will like me just for myself. It was weird when I decided to come here, I didn't even think of P., of us, here. I just thought of the pleasure of seeing the beautiful brown faces of the children again. The fisherman's wife is 24, and she already has five children. Sometimes I try to imagine what it will be like to study for a doctorate, I try to figure out if that's really what I want and I am overwhelmed with confusion. At least I have Kafka with me right now, his exquisite posthumous stories, *The Great Wall of China*. . . but I'd better get back to reading Derrida for professional reasons . . . I hope writing won't abandon me.

Thought is an agent of change, it has repercussions in life.

September 2003—I'm in New York. The departure has happened. The beginning is difficult. As for new ideas—cobwebs obscure my thoughts, threads of death woven with fear of failure and of never belonging anywhere. I'm afraid of myself. I don't understand this compulsion of mine to seek out the street and the night when it does me so much harm. "You're a public danger"—my mother is right.

February 2004 (Paris)

Où sont les axolotls?

12

That's a robot?

Aura was showing me, in her notebook, a drawing of a pair of lace-up shoes surrounded by tiny handwritten notations, sketched patterns of angular and undulating lines.

They're shoes that come when you call them, she said.

You mean you call out, Shoes, come here, and they come walking to you wherever you are?

Yeah, she said. Well, you can't be *too* far away. And they can't go up and down stairs.

You can wear them?

You have to be able to wear them. Robots, she explained, have to be useful, or else they're not really robots.

We were in Copilco, sitting on a couch in the living room. The notebook, a plain spiral one with a red cardboard cover, was open on her lap. The robot shoes were her invention, though still no more than an idea. Aura had a bit of a thing for robots. She explained that each shoe would have sensors programmed to respond to its owner's voice and that the shoes would walk toward that voice when called, in a room or apartment, or inside a house within a certain range. For situations when you didn't want to call out, for example if you needed to slip out of a dark apartment without waking anybody but didn't want to leave without your shoes, there would also be a remote. The robotics would be built into the shoes; the engineering of the walk was complicated, but imagine it, she told me, as a *synchronized iambic pentameter that makes the walk.*

That's a pretty awesome invention, I said. She dipped her head like a proud circus pony, said thank-you, and turned some more pages of her notebook, stopping at one with a sketch of a dress she'd designed. It was an odd-looking dress, drawn in colored pencil with blue and yellow and red hoops seeming to twirl around the skirt. You'd really wear that? I asked, and she said that she would. Designing dresses was one of her favorite ways of doodling and I found sketches of dresses in all her Columbia notebooks. This was our "first date." Nine months after the night when I'd met Aura in New York—I hadn't seen her since, or even had any news of her—in late August in Mexico, she'd turned up in El Mitote, a dingy bohemian and cokehead hangout on the edge of the Condesa. I was drinking at the bar with my friends Montiel and Lida, and there she was, standing before me. Hello again, my death. I felt as if I were staring at her through a thick haze—the cigarette smoke in the air, my own shy amazement and inebriation.

How come you never answered the e-mail I sent you? she asked. I answered that I'd never received any e-mail from her. She'd sent me an e-mail, she insisted, in which she'd thanked me for having mailed her my book, and also telling me that she was coming to New York again. I didn't think she was the kind of person who wouldn't thank someone for having sent her his book, did I? Well, I don't know what happened to that e-mail, I said; it must have gotten lost.

That night in El Mitote, you wouldn't have guessed just by looking at Aura that she was a grad student. Her hair wasn't quite so chic anymore; it was messier, and falling into her eyes. She'd come with a small group of friends who were on the other side of the bar. She was leaving for New York City in just three days, she told me, to begin her PhD studies at Columbia. That news lit a silent burst of sparks in me. I'd be flying back to New York myself in another two weeks. Then there's no time for us to get together before you go, I said, but she said, Why not? There's time. And we agreed to meet the following night at the San Angel Inn, a restaurant and bar in an old hacienda mansion where you sit on sturdy leather couches by the patio drinking margaritas and martinis served in individual miniature silver pitchers set in small ice buckets. I'm sure I wasn't the first guy to have tried to impress her by inviting her there, but at least she wouldn't think I hung out only in dumps like El Mitote.

On the beige vinyl couch in Copilco, she turned some more pages in the notebook and came to one filled with writing from a turquoise roller-pen. This was a short story she'd recently finished. Do you want to hear it? she asked. It's really short, only four pages. I said of course, and she read it to me. The story was about a young man in an airport who can't remember if he's there because he's coming or going. It was written in a lonely minimalist airport tone, with a sweet deadpan humor. I wasn't listening with the best concentration, though, because so much else was going through my mind. At dinner, I'd already been casting my hopes forward, plotting how quickly I could see Aura again in New York. Then she'd taken me completely by surprise, inviting me back to her apartment. Did she only want to read me a story? Sitting close to her, I watched her lovely lips form the words she was reading and wondered if I was really going to kiss her in the next few minutes, or hours, or ever.

Aura's parents had moved out of Copilco to their new place a year before. Left behind in the living room there was only the couch we were sitting on, and the round dining table, metallic gray and white, where Aura had sat through thousands of family meals. Most of her books and things were packed into cardboard boxes now. The steamer trunk was there. There were word magnets on the refrigerator door, and a "Keep Austin Weird" bumper sticker; inside the refrigerator there was a quart bottle of Indio beer, half empty and recapped, and Jumex orange juice in a glossy cylindrical container that I would drink from the next morning after brushing my teeth with Aura's toothpaste on my finger. Empty beer bottles stacked in the corner, pizza cartons wedged behind a trash can. Aura had been living alone here for the last six months or so. Friends who still lived at home with their parents would come and stay the weekend, crashing on the couch and the floor. She'd been teaching introductory-level classes in English poetry and Latin American fiction at the UNAM while finishing her master's thesis on Borges and the English writers, preparing for and taking her exams, months of pressure and nerves but also crazy nights. No other city where the night is longer, more excessive and absurd, than in the *Dee Effeh*. Every time in recent years that she'd started to make a real disaster of her life, she was convinced, it was because she'd given in again to the Mexico City night, where she might easily go off course *forever*.

For months the date of her departure for Columbia had seemed impossibly far off. But just the other day she'd put a load of clothes into the washing machine and thought, The next time I wear these socks, I'll be in New York. Oh, but she was going to miss Mexico, too. She was still chirping away with grateful excitement over the party her mother had thrown for her two weeks before in Tía Cali's penthouse apartment, with its roof patio, to celebrate her passing her exams and receiving her master's degree: a live band, dancing, the new scarlet party dress she'd worn—four years later, that would still be her favorite dress to wear to weddings and fancy parties. She was carrying snapshots of the party in her purse and had showed them to me earlier that night at the San Angel Inn.

When Aura finished reading her story about the young man in the airport, I told her that I really liked it, and she thanked me and asked what it was that I liked about it. While I spoke she held herself perfectly still, as if she could hear my pulse and was measuring it like a polygraph. Then she said that I hadn't meant what I'd said, that I'd only said what I'd said because I liked her. I laughed and said, It's definitely true that I like you, but I liked the story, too, honestly, and I practically narrated back to her the part where her protagonist picks a discarded printed flyer up off the floor and reads that in celebration of a Mexican airline's new route to Hawaii free drinks are being offered at Departure Gate 37, and he goes there for his drink, enters a raffle to win a trip to Hawaii, and doesn't win. She laughed, falling over sideways with her eyes squeezed shut, as if someone else had written it and she was hearing it for the first time and found it hilarious. That was the first of many conversations we would have in the coming years about her writing that would proceed more or less exactly like that, beginning with her claims that my praise was calculated to win her affection or some sex or just domestic peace. That night, on the couch, we began to kiss, and ended up in her bed, kissing and touching. I was so surprised by her warm sweet-smelling and supple youth and by this unexpected development in my life that I was in danger of getting carried away like a romping puppy in a field of tulips, and silently I urged myself not to lose control, to make love to her like a grown man, not an excitable teenager. But then she asked if I minded if she kept her jeans on. So we weren't going to fuck. I said, That's okay with me, really; no big hurry. I spoke gently, though maybe there was a trace of letdown or defensiveness in my voice. Plaintively, but also defiantly, as if not at all reconciled to an undesirable though inevitable-seeming task, she asked, Do I have to blow you or something? I laughed and said, Of course you don't have to blow me, and wondered, What is it we do to our girls? I said that of course I wanted to make love to her, but only when she felt ready. Muy bien, she said. With my nose pressed into her hair, I said, Hmm, you smell so good, not just your hair, your whole head smells good, your head smells like cake. She giggled and said, It's not true. It is true, I insisted, your head smells like cake, like tres leches, yum, my favorite. I put my nose in her hair again and inhaled and kissed her and even pretended to take a big bite out of her head and told her again, Your head smells like cake! A little later we fell asleep in each other's arms, Aura with her jeans on. On her ceiling were hundreds of little glow-in-the-dark stars—she and Lola had taped them up there, carefully following the constellation map the stars came with.

In the morning, when I was in the bathroom, she leaned out of the bed and took my wallet out of my pants on the floor. When I came back into the bedroom she was holding my driver's license in her hand. She looked up and exclaimed, Forty-seven!

Yup, I said, embarrassed.

I thought you were at least ten years younger, she said. I guessed you were thirty-six.

I guess I'm supposed to say thanks, I said. Nope, forty-seven.

She'd never asked my age. Still, I was surprised she didn't know. I thought Borgini, at least, would have said something about it. Aura was going to a wedding later that day, a Saturday. She said she'd be back early; she had so much to do to get ready to fly to New York the next morning. She'd be staying at her mother's. I phoned her there that evening and Juanita answered. That was the first time we ever spoke, but she already knew my name. Frank, she called me. Hola Frahhhhnk, that Mexican pronunciation that coming from Aura sounded like a happy goose honk. Juanita spoke to me in such a friendly way on the phone that day that I thought Aura must have told her mother about me and that she must have said something nice. Aura wasn't back from the wedding yet, but she'd taken her mother's cell phone with her, I guess she'd lost or misplaced her own. Juanita gave me the number and when I phoned I got Juanita's voice-mail message. Aura phoned back later that evening. She spoke through a background din of music and voices. She said she'd had a good time with me, and apologized for having forced me to listen to her airport story, and I told her that I'd loved hearing it, and also about the shoes that come when you call them. I told her that I'd call her as soon as I got to New York, in another ten days. When I put down the phone, I thought, In another ten days her life will have totally changed.

For the previous six years, I'd rented an inexpensive apartment in Mexico City that I'd usually sublet whenever I went back to Brooklyn. Back in the eighties, when I'd worked as a freelance journalist in Central America, my paychecks had sometimes been wired from New York to banks in Mexico City and then I'd have to go up there to get them and convert them to cash. The first time was in 1984, when Aura was seven, when the megacity struck me, compared to Managua, Tegucigalpa, or Guatemala City, as radiant and inexhaustible, crammed with opportunity and surprise. I hadn't even been in the DF twenty-four hours when I met a punky slip of a girl in tight pogo pants and neon pink sneakers in the Rufino

Tamayo museum, a nineteen-year-old art student at Bellas Artes who had a delicate, Mayan princess face and who made out with me on the museum steps. But I never saw her again; the next day she was off to the Yucatán, where her family was from, for Christmas. They kept my passport as collateral at the desk of the cheap hotel downtown where I was staying, until the banks reopened after the long holiday vacation and I could pick up my money and pay them, and where one afternoon in the hotel coffee shop two whores—older than me, probably well into their thirties—asked if I wanted company and then came up to my tiny room, two beautifully ripened women, it turned out, in underpants like in the *Life* magazine ads of my childhood, one with a thin streak of black pubic hair like a wisp of flame licking up her soft broad tummy to her navel, the other lighter-haired and muscular, with small breasts. That's still the only time I've ever done it with two women at once, on the single bed with its flimsy spring-coil mattress, they zestfully applauded every orgasm, theirs and mine, and when it was over I paid with my portable shortwave radio because I didn't have any cash, and the black-haired woman said we could do it again the next day if I got my hands on something else I wanted to trade for sex, and I had the intuition, nothing more than that, that they were a pair of housewives and bisexual lovers who did this mainly for fun. The next time I returned to Mexico City was more than a year later, about six months after the earthquake. The hotel was gone but part of its old brick back wall was still standing, and from the opposite sidewalk you could see how the floors had collapsed into a multilayered concrete sandwich with rubble spilling out the sides. The city was full of ruins like that, more prevalent in some zones than others; the south, where Aura lived, was not built over the soft dirt of the ancient lake bed as in the center and was the area least affected. (Just now I wanted to call out, "Aura, what is it again that you remember about when the earthquake hit?" She told me about it once or twice, but now I can't remember exactly what, it's lost.) I'd followed the earthquake in the news and knew many journalists who'd been sent up from Central America to cover it, and some had come back totally shaken. Having no overt political narrative to impose on the worst of what they'd seen there, at least not one having to do with geopolitics and war, seemed to make it even more devastating. I had a friend, Saqui, who'd covered more war than anyone my age I knew: Afghanistan, Africa, and the Middle East, as well as Central America. Saqui told me about walking out of his hotel on Avenida Reforma the night he got to Mexico City, two nights after the quake, the air thick with smog, pulverized cement, and acrid smoke, and how, when he was crossing the avenue, he saw, in one of the lanes closed off to traffic, a dead child laid out on the pavement, a little girl in sweatshirt, jeans, and sneakers who looked like she'd been rolled in flour. There were two Mexican men standing over her, and my friend told me that they looked at him in a way that so sorrowfully but menacingly warned him not to come any closer that he swerved away as if they were pointing guns, not daring even to glance back until he'd crossed onto the opposite sidewalk, where he turned and saw the two men still standing over the little corpse as if they were waiting for a bus, and he thought that it was the saddest, most terrible thing he'd ever seen. And the weeping mothers standing outside schools that had collapsed when the quake hit, in the middle of the school day. Sixteen collapsed schools, thousands of dead children—schools that were supposed to have been earthquake-proof but weren't, the direct result of the PRI's corrupt dealings with building contractors—*there* was a political narrative, whatever comfort that gave. And the volunteers from all over the world who joined hundreds of thousands of Mexicans in the search for survivors in the rubble and the exhausted cheers that went up whenever someone was found still alive. Yet what most astounded Saqui was the way the city so relentlessly and quickly drove itself back to life, the avenues filling with traffic while the human moles of the rescue parties were still digging and the groups of mothers were still waiting and crying and the stench of death in the air was growing stronger every day.

At least once a year I went back to Mexico City. I developed a fast allegiance to the city and was enthralled by its medieval mysteries because something about post-earthquake DF was like a medieval city celebrating the end of a death plague with carnivals and mystery plays. In 1993, my girlfriend and I even lived there for a year, in Coyoacán, when we must have walked by fifteen-year-old Aura hanging out with other scruffy teenagers and hippies in the plaza—she went nearly every weekend—or browsed alongside her in the Parnaso and Gandhi bookstores, or passed her rattling down the cobblestones of Calle Francisco Sosa on her bike. In 1995, when that same woman broke up with me, she stayed on in our apartment in Brooklyn and I moved down there, to the DF, feeling liberated from a failed relationship and exhilarated to be starting over, fueled by the romantic fantasy that I was going to find and marry that girl I'd kissed on the Museo Tamayo steps a decade before. I was definitely that kind of romantic fool, and though I was pretty sure I remembered her name, Selena Yanez, it's not true that fortune always favors the fool, and I never found her, nor anyone who even knew her.

Over the next few years, I ended up spending much more time in Mexico City than I did in New York, until I got a part-time post at Wadley College. The plan was to live in Brooklyn only when I was teaching, and in Mexico the rest of the year. My apartment was on Avenida Amsterdam in the Condesa, a rambling, five-room, barely furnished place in a nearly century-old building neglected in every way by its landlord. (He's in prison now; a few years ago he was arrested for being the money launderer to a kidnapping ring.) There was a permanent gas leak in the kitchen; perilous, ancient light fixtures; spongy wooden floors painted a peeling viscous bathhouse-brown; and the French windows had termite-churned frames, with a few missing panes that let the rain and sometimes stray birds in. The only furniture I kept there were my cheap Dormimundo bed, two tables, a few chairs, and an old set of drawers that had come with the place. Trees stood outside the front windows, and during the long, rainy summer afternoons, I thought it was the most peaceful place to write I'd ever found. When I'd first moved there the Condesa was still a quiet residential neighborhood of middle-class homes, art deco apartment buildings, random old mansions, tree-lined streets, parks, circular plazas with fountains, and a few surviving old Jewish bakeries and musty Eastern European cafés, remnants from when Jewish immigrants and refugees had populated the neighborhood before prospering and moving their families to Polanco and the suburbs. But the Condesa was also on the cusp of what was going to be a speedy transformation into the city's and maybe all of Latin America's trendiest hipster neighborhood, triggered, went the usual explanation, by the return of those same Jews' artistic, bohemian, entrepreneurial, and coke-snorting Mexican-born descendants.

Those first few months in Mexico, while I searched for Selena Yanez, I had an exuberant string of affairs and seductions, just what I thought I needed because I'd been in relationships, one after the other, since college, serially and sometimes overlapping. D., who I moved to New York with from college; Gus (we were married and divorced before I was twenty-six and now she was probably my closest friend); J.; then M.; and finally S. Then, practically before I knew it, I fell into yet another on-and-mostly-off-again nightmare, the most obsessive frenzied self-destructive relationship of my life. She was a heartbreakingly self-thwarting woman, a gifted artist probably destined never to realize her potential, thirteen years younger than me, acrimoniously self-exiled from her upper-class family, the only one of four sisters not to live at home until she married. It was still a fairly new phenomenon in Mexico City for young women of a certain upbringing to strike out on their own, living in tiny apartments like their counterparts in New York or Paris. She hardly knew what to make of herself. Damaged and full of conflict, she was also maniacally controlling: the first time I slept over at her apartment she threw me out in the morning for hanging a towel on the wrong rack in her bathroom. A *niña perversa,* as she liked to call herself, sultry and gorgeous, her enormous dark eyes an opaque glower, and yet so gentle and shy beneath all that. I don't think I'd ever met anyone who so craved love, which she couldn't help but spurn; it seems that everyone knows this type, though it seems I didn't.

Shouldn't I have known what was coming after that first fuck in my apartment, when she declared that we were only going to have sex for one week and then never again? For a week she dutifully turned up at my door every afternoon; she'd ring my buzzer and I'd see her through the peephole nervously twirling a finger in her hair, and after that week was up she was gone. I nearly went insane, waiting for her outside her apartment, howling into the phone, leaving little love poems on strips of paper folded like Chinese cookie fortunes into the nameplate by her door buzzer. After about a month, she gave in, and we started up again. I seriously debased and fucked myself up with Z., that's the truth of it. I didn't have a friend who didn't try to convince me to flee the torments of that relationship. That I wasted so many years on it is sad proof that I was missing something that every mature, functioning man should possess, except I didn't even know what that something was. When it was finally over I had to confront, for what felt like the first time, the fact that even if I let someone really get to know me, and did my very best to love them, that it wouldn't necessarily be enough to make them love me back. Gradually, I fell into a long funk. I dated, was rejected a lot (though almost never by anyone I cared that much about), and on a few occasions did the rejecting myself. By any measure that wasn't deluded, I wasn't young anymore. One year led to another and then to another, until it became five years of loneliness, with no affair that lasted more than a few weeks or days, and all of those a year or more apart. I worked on my novel like a dreamy tinkerer, without any urgency or drive to finish; did very little journalism; went to the gym; frequented places like El Mitote or El Closet, a strip club; ended up in after-hours dives like El Bullpen and El Jacalito and others whose names and addresses I don't remember. Now I look back on that whole time as a long dress rehearsal for the real thing, the grief and melancholy and loneliness and dissolving of self that lay far ahead and that maybe now will never end. My father was slowly dying during those years. He took a long time to die, in and out of the hospital for about five years, battling for life with desperation and panic, starkly terrified of death, and suffering a lot, and I was always being summoned back to Boston from wherever I was—from Mexico, once from Barcelona, once from Havana where I was doing research—to his bedside for what was supposed to be the end at last, except he always pulled through.

A few nights after that first night with Aura in Copilco, before I went up to New York, the Argentinean woman to whom I was going to sublet the apartment came by to give me a check and pick up the keys. She was a graphic artist, maybe in her midthirties, just separated from her Mexican husband; she had sad brown eyes, a dimpled chin, thin straight dirty blonde hair, and she was wearing tight faded jeans and a flannel shirt that revealed the top of her shadowy cleavage. After we dealt with the apartment, we went out for a few drinks, then she drove me home. It was late, the street was empty and dark, and somehow we ended up having sex right there, her straddling me in the passenger seat of her car after she'd wriggled out of her jeans. Looking over her shoulder I noticed, amazed, how quickly the windshield fogged, the glare of the streetlamp behind the trees above making the moisture glow like pinkish ice. When was the last time I'd fucked in a car?—in college, I think. It was the first sex I'd had in many months. Why this totally unexpected episode now? Was I coming back to life? I never saw her again.

Back in New York, I didn't rush to see Aura. I wouldn't call it a strategy, but I sensed that to have any chance with her, I shouldn't in the least crowd her. She'd quickly become immersed in her new Columbia life, I was sure: her studies, new friends, brilliant young men from all over the world—dashing robot scientists! Why shouldn't she forget about me? I readied myself for disappointment, vowed not to hold it against her. I hadn't been back in New York a week before my mother phoned to tell me that my father was back in the hospital. I went to Wadley, gave my first classes of the semester, and then headed up to Boston in the late summer heat to see him. By then, I'd sent Aura an e-mail saying hello, and from her new Columbia account she'd responded with her telephone number. The first time I phoned, so nervous and excited my belly felt like a basket of writhing eels, her roommate, the Korean botanist, answered. She had a young cheerful voice that came through the phone line like a fresh breeze of spring. Aura was in the shower, she told me. She was *in the shower*. That phrase evoked so much—it was about six or seven on a weekday evening, normally not an hour for showering unless she was going out, most likely on a date, or whatever it is, I thought, that grad students call "dates." Even now it hurts to imagine her engaged in that sweet ritual for anyone other than me: coming out of the bathroom with her hair turbaned in a towel, another wrapped around her torso, choosing her dress, blow-drying her hair, putting on the dress, studying herself in the mirror, applying makeup, taking off the dress and putting on another—one that's less pretty and sexy but that's cut in a way that covers the yin-yang-faced sun-moon tattoo on her chest above her left breast that she's had since she was fifteen—reapplying her lip gloss with a Zen calligrapher's perfect touch, padding around the apartment in still bare or stockinged feet, in that state of restrained excitement just before going out into the night. I left my name, asked her to tell Aura I'd phone again, and a few days later I did. We talked awhile about her courses and professors—the department head, the pale Peruvian who'd told her she was accepted, had taken a job in Michigan, and decamped, just like that!—but she sounded happy, told me she'd thrown a party for the students in her department, that she'd been able to find all the Mexican ingredients in Spanish Harlem that she needed for the food she'd served, even the bottled Mexican syrups and a big block of ice and ice-shaving instruments to make raspados. She loved giving parties. I asked her if she was free for dinner one of these nights. She asked if we could meet for lunch instead. I said that I never met for lunch, because it inter-rupted my working hours. Why did I say that? Because I thought that her saying she wanted to meet for lunch was her way of letting me know that she wanted to be just friends. It didn't take much, in those days, to discourage me. Before she hung up, she repeated that she was always free in the daytime. I wonder if eventually I would have given in and gone up to Columbia to meet her for lunch, or for afternoon coffee in the Hungarian Pastry Shop, and how that might have affected our fates. But our standoff was interrupted by my father's rapid decline. He was moved from the hospital in Boston to a bleak Medicare hospice in Dedham, just off Route 128. It was understood that the move to the hospice meant that the end was finally at hand, yet my father had escaped death so many times that I was sure he would again, though by now nobody really wanted him to, my mother especially.

My parents had a miserable marriage. I never saw them kiss, not once. He was eighteen years older than she. During my last year of high school they finally separated, something my sisters had been urging my mother to do for years. But the separation never became a divorce. After he retired, at age seventy, my father bought a little condo in Florida, where he'd stay in the winter, driving himself back up to Massachusetts in the spring. He had a condo in Walpole, too, but after a few years he sold it and went back to living with my mother in our house in Namoset whenever he came north, on the pretext that my mother couldn't handle the house on her own—paying the bills, the landscapers, and so on. At eighty-seven, when my father started getting sick and couldn't do the long drives anymore, he sold the Florida condo, too. Living with my father year-round again, dealing with his illnesses and cantankerous nature, so wore my mother out that within a few years she seemed almost as old and doddering as he. In his youth my father had been an athlete, a high school football and semipro baseball player, but during his last years, while a slow-moving cancer in his intestines was devouring him, he had the wasted skinniness of the decrepit Fidel Castro. In 1999, he choked on vomit in his sleep and spent eight days in a coma, from which he miraculously emerged with a crazy glint in his eyes, skinny limbs electric with dancing-skeleton energy. The coma left him with memory loss and disorientation, though four years later he still did the *Times* crossword puzzle every day and was opinionated about everything. Sometimes he'd say something strange and spookily suggestive, as if his coma had opened a leak from which dream logic seeped unchecked, like when we were on the phone right after 9/11 and he said, Frankie, why aren't you out guarding the airports? I had no idea what he meant. Frankie, he persisted, all the young men are out guarding the airports, why aren't you with them?

About two weeks into September, I went directly from Wadley to see him at the hospice. The room he was in was a cement box and he was hooked up to the familiar IV tree of nutrient and piss bags and monitors. My father spent his last days in that horrible place mostly just lying on his side, staring at the wall. The nurses were rough and bad tempered; my mother told me that she hadn't met one yet who was nice. When I asked him to tell me what his mother had been like he started to sob. I'd never seen him break down like that, boohooing away. His mother had died years before I was born and I'd never had much curiosity about her. My father was from a Russian immigrant family that had fled the pogroms; he was one of the youngest of eight or nine children, and he came of age in the Depression. He'd worked his whole adult life, until he was seventy, as a chemical engineer for a dental products company in Somerville, leaving for work every morning at six-thirty a.m. His mother, he told me that day in the hospice, was "a foul-mouthed fucking bitch," always fighting with his father and her children, making everybody's life miserable. It was close to the opposite of how I'd heard her described years before in what must have been the abridged for-children version. But the way my father wept, as if in helpless rage, as he spoke about his mother surprised me even more. I think he knew that if I was asking about his mother, it could only be because his death was imminent. He probably figured that it must be my novelist's opportunism: better get this info now before it's lost forever. He'd had what some might think was a pretty shitty life, but he'd sure loved its few pleasures: his flower and vegetable gardens, betting on horses and football, his spy novels and American history books. At eighty-six, he'd still drive out to Fenway and buy a standing-room ticket to watch Roger Clemens pitch. In most ways he'd done better than I: he'd owned a house in the suburbs, helped put his kids through college, had married a beautiful Central American woman—a bilingual secretary at the plant where he worked when they met, a future schoolteacher, who never really loved him, just as he probably never really loved her. But not being loved by his wife wasn't making it any easier for my father to let go of life. I told him I'd be back in another week. He was going to hang in there, I was sure of it, I figured probably even for another year. Pretty soon, Daddy, I said, we'll be watching the Red Sox in the World Series. We used to joke about how there was no way he was going to leave this life until the Red Sox finally won the World Series. It wasn't going to be that year, 2003, though it still looked like it might be. I'd already bought my train ticket to Boston for the weekend, when, sitting in my closet-sized office at Wadley College, I got a call on my cell phone from the hospice telling me that he had died. Nobody had been with him, he'd died alone, facing that wall, or so I pictured it.

You could say I never really had a chance to grieve for or mourn my father, but I don't think I would have mourned him that much anyway. One night I woke from a bad dream and he was sitting on the edge of my bed, only where his face should have been there was just a shadow-filled oval, like the portal to a black hole. It was a little more than two weeks after the funeral that Aura phoned and said she needed urgently to speak to me; she needed my advice about a problem she was having. She wanted to see me that very day; could I? I told her to meet me at two in the Barnes & Noble in Union Square. I was standing by one of the new-books tables in the front of the store when she came up to me. She was wearing faded jeans and a striped jersey under a hooded zippered sweatshirt; with her bangs partly hiding her eyes, her smile looked magnified. Slung over her shoulder was a cloth book bag emblazoned with the Columbia emblem; she was even skinnier than when I'd last seen her in Mexico six weeks before. My only friends have turned against me! she blurted. Those were the first words out of her mouth. I've made such a mess! She laughed as if embarrassed at herself, the damsel in distress. I suggested we go outside and talk in the park. It was a sunny fall day, just like the day of my father's funeral, limpid azure sky, a few white clouds, trees patched with color, the air clean and brisk, a beautiful day that turned Union Square, I told Aura, into the Luxembourg Gardens minus the statues of the queens. The queens have escaped, I went on, but look how they shed their long, brown stone dresses so that they could run away, do you see? See all those crumpled brown paper bags blown against the curbs and mixed in with the leaves, and balled into those trash cans over there, and that one standing up straight on that park bench next to that man eating a sandwich? Those are the queens' dresses. Aura slowly looked around at all the paper bags, as if what I said might be true, and grinned. And where did the queens go? she asked. That's what everyone's trying to find out, I said. Well, maybe I can run away there, too, she said. We sat down on one of the benches and she told me about the problem she was having with her friends. During her first days at Columbia, two girls, inseparable best friends, neither of them first-year students, had adopted Aura as the proverbial third wheel. One, Moira, was from the Dominican Republic and New York, the other, Lizette, was from Venezuela. At an academic conference sponsored by the department, Moira, a very pretty mulatta but also a total neurótica and a *pinche obsesiva de controlar todo*, got a crush on a guy from Princeton who'd come to give a presentation on the subject of his dissertation, "The Representation of Childhood in Three Latin American Female Writers." Here we digressed into a brief conversation about the three female writers: one, Clarice Lispector—Clarice L'Inspector, Aura called her—was a favorite of us both; she liked Rosario Castellanos, too, who I'd never read; Aura said the third, who I'd never heard of, was practically the only contemporary writer the professors in her department approved of, and that was because her novels *are so well suited to theoretical readings*. The Princeton guy had initially seemed interested in Moira, he'd even made plans with her to get together the next weekend, but ever since he'd gone back to New Jersey he'd been phoning Aura. Worse, he e-mailed Moira to tell her he'd fallen in love with Aura, going so far as to describe himself as a victim of the *flechazo*, love's arrow, and Moira had immediately forwarded that e-mail to Aura and the other friend, Lizette, and probably to other people in the department as well. After a series of distraught confrontations, Moira and Lizette had written Aura an e-mail formally ending their friendship, as if she'd signed some sort of friendship contract and now they were abrogating it. Aura had gone to both of their apartments, but her knocks had gone unanswered, though she was positive she'd heard muffled voices through the door at Lizette's. So, here she was six weeks into her first semester, without friends, being unjustly portrayed as a man stealer.

After an interlude of apparently sage mulling, I asked, Did he pick that as his dissertation topic because he's more interested in women's issues than in any other subject, or because he wants other women to think he is?

Aura laughed. Oh, but there must be easier ways to pick up women, even in academia, she said. He's obsessed with his mother, and I'm obsessed with my mother, so that's what we talked about. But just because a guy is obsessed with his mom doesn't make me want to go out with him. Probably the opposite.

Well, I'm not obsessed with my mom, I said, so you don't have to worry about that.

Aura's bag was heavy with books and her laptop. Was she going to the library? I asked. No, but she did have some reading to do. There wouldn't be a day the rest of her life when she wouldn't "have some reading to do." She was thinking of going to a café. If she wanted, I told her, we could go back to my place to read for a while, and then I'd take her to dinner. We rode the subway back to Brooklyn and spent the rest of the afternoon and into the evening sitting in my apartment, she on the ugly blue- and-white striped couch that was destined to be the first piece of furniture she was going to jettison, and soon I was being lulled by the soft rapid clicking of her keyboard.

We had dinner in a restaurant on Fifth Avenue in Park Slope, a Mediterranean place; it was still warm enough to sit outside in the garden. I tried to kiss her on the sidewalk after. She turned her head away with a winsome smile. What, she wasn't going to kiss me? I laughed, as if I didn't care whether she kissed me or not, ever.

We walked back to my apartment and made love until just about dawn and again in the late morning after we woke up. But when she was leaving I actually said,

Will I see you again?

She looked at me, a little disconcerted, and said, Of course you will. She came back that night.

13

My mother and her friends belong to the Shaky Grasp Generation, Aura told me once. Of reality, she added. The post-'68 generation stranded in a Mexico City that had turned out not to be San Francisco, New York, or Paris after all, just the same old Mexico City, only more traumatized and disorienting than ever before.

Among the Shaky Grasp Generation's Mexico City intelligentsia, an enthusiasm for psychoanalysis took hold. The promise of a higher, more just, and poetic organization of life—according to Aura—was now to be sought and perfected in the individual's intimate core and within the circle of the nuclear family and closest friends, before, surely someday, it could be brought to the masses. Certain Mexican shrinks were almost obsessively discussed and gossiped about among her mother's and uncle's colleagues and friends. Some seduced and had love affairs with their patients. And it became a fashion, represented as an enlightened duty, among the Shaky Graspers to send their domestic servants—women and adolescent girls who were almost without exception uneducated and illiterate—into therapy. In Mexico, of course, even an administrative secretary can afford to hire at least a part-time housekeeper, because domestic workers are paid so little. Aura's uncle was among the first to send his live-in "muchacha" to the family psychotherapist. If he and his wife and their children were in therapy, Leopoldo had explained, it could only benefit the household gestalt for the family servant to undergo therapy, too.

Those were the circumstances that inspired the novel that Aura worked on during the last year of her life, and that she'd tentatively titled *Memoirs of a Grad Student*. The grad student in the novel is named Alicia, a young woman from Mexico City who is studying for a PhD in literature in New York. Alicia doesn't want to be an academic, but doesn't dare defy her mother to pursue her secret dream. Real-life Aura didn't always keep her yearning to write a secret from her mother, but she knew her mother disapproved. Her mother believed that Aura needed to focus all of her mercurial energies on her academic career if she was going to succeed.

Aura completed two chapters of her novel, and left many fragments. The novel's first chapter is about Alicia as a little girl in Mexico. There we meet her mother, Julieta; the family's domestic servant, Irma; and Julieta's former boyfriend, Marcelo Díaz Michaux, a psychoanalyst who has just returned to Mexico City after years of study and practice in France. Later in the novel Marcelo Díaz Michaux was going to convince Julieta that her housekeeper, Irma, needed to become his patient, and then he was going to send her to an experimental utopian asylum in France. Like real-life Ursula, Irma is a cheerful, talkative, and dwarfish woman who is described as having a ten-year-old's body even though she's about forty. I remember Aura laughing about what those first therapy sessions between Irma and Marcelo were going to be like. A household servant as witness to family secrets, a lonely little girl's closest after-school friend and confidante, those would also have figured into Aura's scheme.

The novel's radical French asylum also had its counterpart: a renowned institution a few hours outside of Paris called La Ferte. Aura had already corresponded with the asylum's eighty-seven-year-old director, arranging a visit so that she could research it for her novel. We were planning to go to La Ferte the next year, in the spring of 2008.

These were the last bits of her novel that Aura wrote, which I later found saved as a separate document in her computer:

Marcelo Díaz Michaux:
      Even Julieta as the dead mother played a number on me. And now there's no beating her . . . although we'll see about that. I'm young—sixty is the new thirty—she's dead, so who's winning now? Of course, she has left me homeless,

along with Alicia, my wife, and our child, having decided, at the last moment, to leave the house to our long-time maid, Irma Hernández, who now resides in France, somewhere outside Paris, where I'm flying to right now.

The Characters

Marcelo Díaz Michaux

Born in 1946 in Mexico City to a diplomat father and a devoted housewife. Raised in Mexico City by his mother (mostly). He attended (in Mexico) the French Lyceum where he met Julieta. At twenty-six, Marcelo went to study psychiatry at the Sorbonne. Two years later, when he received Julieta's wedding invitation, his downfall began. Fifteen years later he returned to Mexico to set up his office to practice a kind of Lacanian psychotherapy. On the side he started working on an essay about clouds as an ideological construction.

Alicia—Julieta's daughter

She was born in 1977: frond, rings, marooned, barreling up, lewd, skein, squall, crevice, drumstick, divot, crocuses, encroach, flinch, slither, daft, cadge, baksheesh, a spider spinning.
    In 2008, Alicia is thirty-one.

Alicia is the same age Aura would have reached had she lived another nine months, until April 24, her birthday, in the spring of 2008. If all had gone according to our plan, we would have visited La Ferte in the spring of 2008, and Aura would have been pregnant.
    Was I a model for Marcelo Díaz Michaux? On the surface, we didn't seem to have much in common. She'd made him a decade older than me, which may have been an expression of anxiety, or an anxious joke, about our age difference. Of course Julieta couldn't have been too happy about that nutjob, her old boyfriend, marrying her daughter. But as an eminent Parisian shrink, Marcelo

would have had a lot more money to spend than I did. Thus, in the summer of 2007, Marcelo and Alicia would have vacationed in Tulum, or somewhere in the Yucatán, like the Riviera Maya, on the placid Caribbean, not at a Pacific hippie beach with tumultuous surf in Oaxaca. Having gone to Tulum, and not to Oaxaca, Alicia is alive in the spring of 2008, when she turns thirty-one. Why didn't Aura and I go back to Tulum that summer, where we spent five days during the first week of 2004, instead of to the beach in Oaxaca? Because I couldn't afford to rent a cottage for two weeks in Tulum, though I could in Oaxaca.

frond
rings
marooned
barreling up
lewd
skein
squall
crevice
drumstick
divot
crocuses
encroach
flinch
slither
daft
cadge
baksheesh
a spider spinning

I memorized that list, and often meditated on it, sometimes focusing on just one word until I found Aura in it, and laughed as if she were there with me and we were sharing a giggle over what she'd meant by "drumstick." Or I chanted the list of words and waited for whatever came: images, memories, other words, visions.

* * *

Crevice: cenote. On the dirt road just past our hotel in Tulum, before you entered the Maya Biosphere Reserve, there was a small cenote by the side of the road, a seemingly bottomless crevice filled with the crystalline water of a subterranean river. We pulled our rental car over—we were in bathing suits—and got out to swim alongside the local kids who climbed up into the scraggly trees on the banks to dive into the water. I did that, too, provoking shy grins and laughter, launching hairy-belly-hanging-over-bathing-suit and winter-pale barrel-torso into the air, making a big splash as I went under, driving my arms and kicking as hard as I could to see how deep I could go into the chilly purplish depths until, overcome by fear of accidentally swimming into a cave and not being able to escape, I turned and kicked frantically upward. The Yucatán peninsula, we learned from my travel book, is one immense slab of brittle limestone flattened millions of years ago by a giant meteor, the impact filling it with deep fissures and cracks through which all rainwater seeps, feeding the underground rivers running beneath the peninsula's arid surface. Whenever there's a collapse of rock above a watery void, or the shifting of tectonic plates opens a crevice in the limestone strata, a cenote is formed.

Portal to the underworld is how Aura and I heard a guide at a Mayan ruin site explain a cenote to his package-tour gaggle, that one's smooth pea-green surface hiding the sinkhole's murky depths and the skeletons of human sacrifice victims tossed in after their hearts were cut out. *Hell-Ha* was the name Aura gave to the Mayan theme park Xel-Ha, a mobbed tourist trap that we went to because it promised cenotes and lagoons to snorkel in, though underwater there were many more pairs of human legs dangling and kicking from inner tubes floating by overhead than there were fish to see below, and lots of drifting, semitranslucent bits of crud.

* * *

There was also that little lagoon or lake or pond that we found one afternoon in the Maya Biosphere Reserve. We'd driven far into it on a rough dirt road that was filled with muddy ruts and swampy craters, unbroken scrub jungle on both sides, when off to the right we saw a small parking area and an observation tower, painted bright yellow, rising above the low trees like a lost lifeguard's chair. We parked, got out, and followed a path until we reached the tower, then climbed the zigzagging stairs to the platform on top. It was a surprise to see the blue Caribbean no more than two hundred yards away, at the far edge of jungle canopy across the road; also, it was later than we'd realized, the sun falling in the sky, orange and pulsing.

When we climbed down, instead of heading right back to Tulum, we followed the trail farther in, to that hidden lagoon, where we sat on a low wooden dock, no one else around. Soon we were watching the iridescent pastels of the sunset spreading over the water and blazing in the sky above the strip of jungle between us and the ocean, the whole place throbbing with bird calls, as if every glowing tree and plant hid a boisterous bird or two, and we both felt stunned into separate peaceful meditations on the crazy sublimity of what we were witnessing, each of us filling with a sense of mystical wonder and loneliness that merged into one mystical wonder and loneliness together. It was as if we'd just been married in a secret ceremony conducted by the birds. Sometimes I think that if cenotes really are portholes to the underworld and I can go through one and be reunited with Aura, it's on the shores of that jungle lagoon that I'll come out and find her waiting.

Well, Hell-Ha, mi amor. No happy memory that isn't infected. A virus strain that has jumped from death to life, moving voraciously backward through all memories, obligating me to wish none of it, my own past, had ever happened. But I'm like a sentry who keeps nodding off at the quarantine gate, letting the inmates stream past. Still, it's lonely to be left with only my versions. Aura can't say: But it wasn't really like that, mi amor, it was more like this. Someday it was going to be her, holding my boney hand, leading me through our memories of falling in love. That sweet elation of waking up and finding her beside me in bed. The apartment filling up with music I'd never heard before, tuneful, clever, girl music—Belle & Sebastian—on the happiest mornings of my life so far. (Four years later I still hadn't gotten over it, the daily surprise of happiness.) She brought her own CDs those first nights she stayed over. "Dear Catastrophe Waitress," "Wrapped up in Books," "Judy and the Dream of Horses," and

> If you find yourself caught in love
> Say a prayer to the man above
> Thank him for every day you pass
> You should thank him for saving your sorry ass.

Was this really happening? In my life? I can't listen to those songs anymore without fogging up. Soda Stereo, Charlie García, Smiths, Pixies, OOIOO; her beloved Beatles and Dylan. And what did I turn Aura on to? Iggy Pop and the Stooges, I guess. Te quiero aún más hoy que ayer, I love you even more today than I did yesterday—every morning those were the first words I'd say to her, like the superstition of rabbitrabbitrabbit being the first words you speak out loud on New Year's morning. It would be months before the morning came when I'd forget to say it. Aura pretended, for about two minutes, to be indignant, What, you're falling out of love with me already? The next morning I remembered but in less than a year repeating those words did finally begin to feel too automatic. Still, it wasn't something to toss away as if all used up, there would still be mornings when I especially wanted her to hear it, or just wanted to say it again. One morning, back during that first or second week, she led me from bed to stereo, put in her Bjork CD, and advanced it to "It's Oh So Quiet," the song about falling in love, where Bjork's lullaby *shhh-shhh*s turn to euphoric shrieks of WOWWW WOWWW...THIS IS IT!!!—I could inspire *that*?! Bjork-like was the slant and shape of Aura's eyes, the fall of her hair, her air of a mischievous sprite. Another night, sitting on my lap, she read out a poem from the Carol Ann Duffy book she'd brought with her: *At childhood's end, the houses petered out . . . till you came at last to the edge of the woods.* It was in a clearing in those woods that the poem's speaker, Little Red-Cap, first *clapped eyes on the wolf.* With *wolfly drawwwl*, the old wolf, wine-stained snout, was reciting his poems, book held in *hairy pawww*—Aura lowered her voice into those internal rhymes, the crimped black points of her tights over her toes rising on the beats like cat's ears lifting toward sound. *What big eyes . . . what teeth*, hahaha, *and bought me a drink, my first.* Why does Little Red-Cap want to go with the old wolf? Aura pressed her warm forehead against mine: *Here's why. Poetry.* She repeated it: *POETRY.* Little Red-Cap wants to be a poet, too.

What little girl doesn't dearrrly love a wolf?

—ebulliently chanted and drawn out like the chorus of a favorite rock anthem. Except the poem didn't end happily, not for the wolf anyway. After ten years of listening to him perform the same old songs without finding a voice of her own, Little Red-Cap cuts the wolf open *scrotum to throat* with an ax, finds her *grandmother's bones* inside. Oh no, I said, Please, my love, don't ever do that to me, I won't stifle your voice, I'm not *that* kind of old wolf!

Our first Sunday in New York together, we went to Katz's Deli so that Aura could have her first pastrami sandwich. The plan was to go from there to the Metropolitan Museum, then maybe walk in the park, drinks in some romantic hotel bar, go to a movie, and someplace for a late dinner. The sandwiches at Katz's being so enormous, I suggested we split one, and order two matzo ball soups, because she'd never had that either, but she so liked the sample tidbits of pastrami the counterman gave her and was so excited by the look of the sandwiches, the piled juicy meat spilling out the sides, that she wanted one just for herself. She devoured it. Then, on the sidewalk outside Katz's, she said that her stomach hurt. She had a bewildered look in her eyes, her face was drawn, and when I pressed my lips and nose to her cheek it was clammy and smelled slightly of mustard and meat fat. Ohhh, she moaned, bent over, arms clasped over her abdomen, I have to go home. You mean, to my place? I asked. She nodded. I waved down a taxi and we went back to my apartment in Brooklyn, where she spent the rest of the afternoon in bed, while I made her drink Alka-Seltzer, dashed out to the supermarket for chamomile tea, read, watched some football with the sound off while she napped, tickled the inside of her forearm like I already knew she always wanted me to, feather-lightly raking my fingertips up and down over her skin. By night she felt better, and for dinner I ordered her chicken-and-rice soup from the Chinese take-out place around the corner, Sing Chow Mei Fun for me, and we watched a DVD. I'd pretty much forgotten that it was possible to spend a Sunday the way Aura and I spent that one.

Now, whenever I pass near Katz's Deli, I stop to stare in a mute muddle at that sidewalk, at the long blackish snake of the curb, the empty air above. Sometimes I go and stand where it happened and whisper, You mean, to my place? Descending into memory like Orpheus to bring Aura out alive for a moment, that's the desperate purpose of all these futile little rites and reenactments.

To celebrate Juanita's fiftieth birthday, two of the tías, Lupe and Cali, and a few friends, including Aura's childhood dentist, had invited her and Rodrigo for a long weekend in Las Vegas. Aura had classes on Friday and Monday, so we flew there on Saturday morning just to have dinner with her mother that night; we were flying back the next day. A black, flat-topped mountain, or maybe it's a butte, overlooks Las Vegas, rising out of the Mojave Desert against the horizon like a giant black van in an empty parking lot, hot and shiny in the blazing sunlight. Aura and I decided that it radiated evil, spraying it in continuous arcs, like long-range cat pee, over the gleaming city. Our taxi driver was at least partly responsible for this lasting first impression, driving us from the airport as if he was under orders to deliver us in the fastest possible time to the sinister mountain, where his Lord Master, the judge and ruler of our fate, was waiting in his cave. Speeding down a long straight avenue behind the glassy Las Vegas strip, tires squealing as he jolted forward from every red light, he drove like he was in a rage, as if he already knew our fate and was powerless to prevent it. Aura was gripping her seat, gasping; we traded expressions of alarm. The driver's first name, according to his taxi ID card, was Boguljub, and his taxi was an SUV with an electronic message board facing the backseat that only amplified the claustrophobic frenzy, flashing announcements for shows, casinos, and discount steakhouses. We passed a billboard for Siegfried and Roy, Masters of the Impossible, though one of them, I forget which, had been mauled and nearly killed by one of their tigers about a month before—a white tiger that dragged Siegfried or Roy around the stage, jaws clamped around his neck and shaking him, I recalled from a news report, "like a rag doll." (How and why did *he* survive?) Boguljub turned left, pedal to the floor as he shot up the long side street to our hotel, the Venetian. We weren't going to the mountain after all. Beelzebub, of course, is how Aura and I forever after referred to him, though with his sandy hair and blue eyes he less resembled the anvil-headed taxi driver of Aura's childhood terror than the evil mountain did.

For all my alarm over Lola's warning that Juanita could break Aura and me up just by commanding it, I don't even remember the moment we met. Hola Ma, this is Francisco, and Juanita's eyes locking on me for the first time—no memory of that. I had to go and look at the snapshots we took with our disposable camera. Juanita, Rodrigo, and Aura sitting at a table with unwrapped presents and cocktail glasses on top, Juanita holding up a pink T-shirt with "New York City" glitteringly imprinted across it and smiling as if it really was the most remarkable gift. Aura was always a last-minute and impatient gift shopper—in the coming years, I would often be the one to pick out her parents' presents. The photos show a glassy atrium area, Juanita's face flushed and overjoyed, Rodrigo in a baseball cap pulled low over his eyes, Aura looking Audrey Hepburn–collegiate, in cream sweater, gray wool skirt, with her hair in a loose bob, happy to be with her mom. Not much fuss was made over me. Perhaps this was partly shyness, theirs and mine, but also, I was just one more boyfriend; Aura's boyfriends came and went, so why shouldn't I? Maybe they didn't know yet how old I was, that in less than three years I'd be celebrating my own fiftieth birthday. Aura doted on her mother, *baa*ing "Mami" and making Juanita grin giddily. I didn't yet perceive, beneath his quiet, collected demeanor, Rodrigo's often-brooding separation. At one point I caught Juanita studying me across the table. She looked away when she realized I'd noticed. The next time I caught her looking at me, later that night, I think she'd made up her mind. Aura and I, like other charged-up lovers, could shut others out, lean in close and laugh at everything either of us said no matter what. The first time I caught Juanita spying on us during a moment like that was about six weeks later, in Mexico, at the ostentatious New Year's Eve gala in the Salon del Lago that Leopoldo invited us to, her expression more thoughtful, sadder, than when she'd fixed her sight only on me. She looked like a maternal Prospero, all powers waned, helplessly spying on a closely huddled, inexplicably enamored Miranda and Caliban.

But in Las Vegas, I was paying attention only to Aura, and don't recall caring much about her mother's reaction to me. Most of our other Las Vegas photos were taken in our gaudy Venetian hotel room, me posed like a gargoyle atop an armchair that resembled a papal throne, Aura vogueing, playing posh in her luxurious hotel bathrobe amid the pretentious furnishings. Another of her after sex, sitting up against piled pillows, the bathrobe's parted lapels revealing her small tattoo and the soft upper slopes of her breasts, her eyes a little sleepy but looking directly, confidingly, into the camera—an axolotl gaze.

Later that night, at a blackjack table in the Bellagio casino, Aura, with her first bet ever, won fifty dollars. Fortune's child! We'd joined up with her parents and the Hernández sisters and their friends—so far, I'd barely glimpsed them, they were always off gambling or shopping—to go to the birthday dinner. The Bellagio seemed as endless and grand as the Louvre, hall after hall of gambling tables, bars, restaurants, shops, and tourists snapping pictures. One moment Aura and I were walking with the others, absorbed in our own conversation, and the next we looked around and were alone in the crowd, Juanita, Rodrigo, the tías, their friends, all vanished, nowhere in sight. We didn't know the name of the restaurant we were headed to, or under whose name the reservation had been made.

For nearly two hours Aura and I wandered from restaurant to restaurant—there were at least a dozen—poring over reservation lists and begging snooty maître d's for permission to walk through their dining floors one more time. We repeated the circuit twice, thrice, within the vast Bellagio. The third time we stopped at Le Cirque we were turned away with a stony, *Your parents are not here*, before we could open our mouths. We'd flown all the way out to Las Vegas for this, to have dinner with Juanita on Saturday night. Finally, we took a break from our search to stop at one of the casino bars for a round of drinks. What if I never see my mother ever again? asked Aura. Where are we anyway, Francisco? I spoke reassuring words. But this being Las Vegas I knew that nothing was impossible and tabloid headlines—*Mexican Family and Friends Vanish without Trace inside Bellagio*—were already flashing through my mind as if on the electronic message board inside Beelzebub's taxi. We went back to wandering the casino in a drifty stupor, holding hands like children afraid of being separated. Another half hour or so went by. ¿Cómo se dice una cobija de indios? Aura asked out of the blue, but before I could answer she said, Indian blanket? ¿Se dice así? and gave a little shout—there was Rodrigo, blocking our path, lifting a strong hand to each of our nearly touching shoulders as if to prevent us from escaping. He'd left the restaurant to look for us. After waiting a long time for us to turn up, they'd all finally eaten. Maybe we could still catch them for dessert. He led us to a cafeteria-style buffet restaurant that we hadn't even noticed. Another happy reunion

scene between Aura and her mom, and with the tías. Afterward we
went for a walk outside on the neon boulevard with its illuminated
fountains, a fake Eiffel Tower. Late the next morning Aura and I
flew back to New York. On the plane, while she studied, I watched a
movie about a racehorse. During the climactic racing scenes, horses
stampeding down the homestretch, I bobbed up and down in my
seat like I was the jockey, though I didn't realize I was doing it until
I felt a nudge, turned, and saw Aura imitating me, bouncing in her
seat, staring at the screen, exaggerating my absorbed expression,
and she laughed and began to kiss me, while I grinned madly, the
surprise victor, riding my prancing heart down the dung-splattered
track into the winner's circle!

Nearly a year after Aura was gone, her cousin Fabiola told me that
Juanita had tried to persuade Aura to leave me. Aura told Fabis, but
she never told me. She has to understand, Aura would say to Fabis,
I'm in love. Fabis also said that when she'd visited Aura at Brown,
Juanita had phoned around eight nearly every morning to discuss
Aura's plans for the day, the progress of her thesis, and so on. Fabis
said, I was surprised at how sweet Aura always was with her mother
when she called, no matter how late we'd been out the night before,
and I remember wishing that my mother cared about me like that,
though now I'm grateful that she didn't, that she respected my freedom. After Fabis accompanied Aura up to New York to help settle
her at Columbia, Juanita phoned to thank her. She told Fabis that
she'd saved her from the ten sessions with a psychiatrist she would
have needed had Aura flown to New York by herself. What did she
mean by that? asked Fabis. Ten sessions with a psychiatrist? I still
don't get it, she said. Fabis's account struck me as holding possible
clues to a scene that had long disturbed me, though I'll never know
what actually ignited it. I'd come into our apartment with a friend
one day and found Aura sitting cross-legged on the kitchen floor,
bent forward and clutching the telephone, crying and repeating in
an extremely anguished tone,

No, Mamá...

NO, Mamá...

Nooo...

No Mamá, NO...

We closed the door quietly behind us and went to buy a bottle of wine on Atlantic Avenue, several blocks away. When we came back Aura was off the phone and didn't even seem rattled, though she was still subdued. I asked about it later and all she said was, Oh, nothing. You know, my mother... But I can only think of one or two other times that I saw Aura so distraught. Her mother must be especially in despair, I remember thinking, maybe even threatening suicide, not really meaning it but totally freaking out her daughter.

No one hates Romeo more than Juliet's mother—that's the line I was ready to wield were Aura ever to bring up her mother's hostility to me. But Aura never did, so I never got to use it. Now I knew, thanks to Fabis. But it couldn't have been that easy for Aura to shrug off her mother's maternal counsel. It couldn't have been only a simple matter of, But I love him, Mami, and that's that. There was an earlier episode that I'd nearly forgotten. We were in Mexico for the monthlong Christmas break, not three months after we'd started going out, though already we were living together in Brooklyn. We were staying in my Condesa apartment. (My Argentine subletter had gone back to her husband after less than two months.) After the way I'd talked it up—making it sound practically like a whole floor with a view in a sunny Florentine palazzo—Aura was disillusioned. She saw no charm in the rotted French windows with their missing and cracked panes, the kitchen window that opened on a well-like patio that bred mosquitoes in the rainy season, the constant seep of gas from the kitchen, the crudely carpentered furniture bought on street corners, and worst of all the windowless bedroom, its walls and ceiling speckled with dried mosquito splatter from the many grisly insomniac hours I'd spent over the years, standing on my bed or stalking around the room clutching a rolled-up magazine or swatter. This was probably the first time I'd so disappointed Aura. What did it mean? What if I was like that bedroom? A negligent, aging romantic goofball, his enthusiastic promise exposed as a gloomy, suffocating, cell of killing walls with an uncomfortable, cheap bed. Yes, yes, of course he's like that, hija, that's all you'll ever be able to expect from *him*, you don't think I know about men like that, niñotes from my own generation who refuse to grow up?

I have no proof that Aura and her mom ever had such a conversation. But for three days and nights in a row, Aura was cold and even cruel to me in a way she'd never come close to being before, or ever would again. She made love to me only once, so listlessly my dick fell and crept under the bed. In the mornings, she was off even before breakfast, with errands at the UNAM across the city and plans to see her mother, friends, past professors, even her old therapist, Nora Banini. She seemed not to want to introduce me to her friends. During the long days, she didn't even phone. Was she with an old boyfriend? Borgini, for fucksake? (Juanita, I know now, had eagerly encouraged Aura's relationship with Borgini.) But I knew Aura wasn't like that. Was she? I was beside myself, every bone saturated with dread. She was treating me the way a woman treats a man when she knows she's finished with him and is getting herself ready—going over her arguments, rehearsing with her mother and friends—to break up.

What's the matter? I wailed when she came home. What did I do? You're right, this apartment is a shithole, I'll get rid of it. Oh, God, you don't love me anymore! Just like that?!?

Her eyes were cast down. She was across the bed from me, straightening the covers, the old feather-spurting comforter. The silence in that room crept toward death. The legs of the carcasses on the walls began to quiver, and also the wings, mosquitoes resurrected to zombie life by my breaking heart, which they would soon be sucking every last drop from.

Finally Aura said, quietly, It's not that, Frank. Don't worry, it's nothing, it will pass.

And it did, the next morning. Like a fever, it lifted, and there she was, as if she'd been mischievously hiding underneath it, back to how she was before, pestering me to go everywhere with her. That morning she wanted me to accompany her to the Ghost Building. We never even spoke about why she'd been so cold to me. I was happy to leave those three days behind as if they carried a deathly contamination.

The Ghost Building was the most notorious eyesore on Insurgentes, a huge semi-abandoned condominium building, fifteen stories high— much taller than any building nearby—with broad, angled facades, capped by a concrete construction that resembled a fire-gutted airport control tower. It looked like it had barely survived the bombing of Dresden. An editor had offered Aura the chance to write a piece for the Talk of the Town–like section of a new magazine that a lot of younger writers were eager to write for, but she'd never done that kind of writing before. She'd just spent her first semester at Columbia taking classes that practically required her to learn a new language— critical theory—including one with professor Gayatri Chakravorty Spivak, probably Columbia's biggest lit-crit superstar since Edward Said. Aura was intimidated and baffled by Spivak but also adored her. Yet here she was, thrilled by the chance to write for a magazine that told Distrito Federal trendies where to eat, shop, and party.

She'd decided that she wanted to write about the Ghost Building. All I knew about it was that those all-night lowlife bars, El Bullpen and El Jacalito, used to be in the ground floor around the back but had been closed down. What goes on in there? I asked. Crack dens? Probably, she said, but I don't know; that's why we have to go. There'd been a murder in the building over the summer, she told me, a lawyer who had his office there. Oh great, I said, that makes it sound safer, lawyers have offices in there and they get murdered. We stood on the sidewalk, gazing up at the scorched-looking walls. Dun-colored sections of tile and concrete were cracked, cratered, and broken off. The windows had a sooty glare, some with shabby curtains or lowered blinds. Higher up, nearly floor-length sections were burned-out black voids. We didn't trust the elevators, so we went through a small door off the lobby into a stairwell that smelled of rancid damp and piss. Fast light footsteps, a scrofulous kid coming down the stairs, dirty sleeveless T-shirt, tattoos—the crude blue-ink prison kind, a stingray of hair down his back, a rolled-up paper bag clutched in one hand, eyes down; he darted past without a hello. We climbed to the second floor and found ourselves creeping down a murky corridor, no lights, doors closed, silence, a musty rodent smell. Scattered doors held printed signs or plaques, one reading *Oficina Jurídica*—a criminal law office. We turned the corner into another corridor that was so long it seemed to vanish into gloom. We retreated to the stairwell and climbed to the next floor, and then to the next, each more abandoned-looking and claustrophobic than the one before. I wanted to get out of there. Anything might happen to us, and especially to Aura, in that barely inhabited ruin, and I'd be responsible. But in the next stairwell, when I began to lead Aura down, she pulled on my arm and whispered, Higher, let's go higher—like she was under a spell. We're not going higher, I said. We're getting out of here. Later, she and Fabiola had a laugh over that. Me, the former "war correspondent," afraid of the Ghost Building!

> Señora Gama, administrator of Insurgentes Condominiums and the responsible party for the closing of two businesses on the ground floor of the battered building—the well-known dives El Bullpen and El Jacalito—walks with assured strides along the cracked and dark hallway of the tenth floor, wearing an electric-blue jacket and miniskirt. With a forced smile she makes way for her possible future tenants—two young women looking for a space to open a sewing business—to descend the staircase to the eighth floor. This is the highest floor to which the only one of four elevators to survive the 1985 earthquake arrives. It is adorned with colorful and unintelligible graffiti, and takes them down to the fourth floor.[3]

[4] La Sra. Gama, administradora del Condominio Insurgentes y responsable directa de la clausura de dos de los lugares que amurallan la entrada al maltrecho inmueble—los conocidos antros El Bullpen y El Jacalito—camina segura en su traje de saco y minifalda azul eléctrico por el agrietado y oscuro pasillo del piso diez. Con una sonrisa forzada, invita a sus posibles futuras inquilinas,

So opened the piece, "The Ghost Building," that appeared in the magazine *D.F.* a few weeks later. The two young women who wanted to rent a space for their sewing business were Aura and Fabis. Without telling me until later, Aura had cajoled her cousin into going back there with her.

> Curious to find out what lies beyond the tenth floor, the girls climb the frightful stairs. The view of the city is spectacular. When they get to the top, they find a sign that reads, *Private property. Entry prohibited for all personnel.* They peer down the deserted hallway. They see a wide pillar, burned and covered with graffiti. Where once there were windows, there are now only charred frames, filled with cloudless sky. There's a radio playing somewhere. They follow the music and at the end of the hallway, beyond a door left ajar, they see a red carpet inside an apartment, and two men reading on a sofa. They hear footsteps approaching. Frightened, they look at each other and without a word run to the staircase.

When Aura handed her piece in, the editor was delighted with it and gave her a new assignment. We started staying in Aura's old apartment in Copilco, in the bedroom in which she'd spent most of her life. There was hardly any furniture left and the telephone had been disconnected. Though it was no secret that we were there, we felt as if we were hiding out like teenaged runaways.

But Aura was soon to have her own apartment. Young architects were converting an old warehouse at the edge of Escandón into a condo-complex of loft apartments. Fabiola's mom, Odette, knew one of the architect's parents and bought two ground-floor one-bedroom apartments at a discount price before construction

---

dos mujeres jóvenes buscando un espacio para empezar su negocio de costura, a tomar las escaleras hasta el piso ocho (el último que alcanza el único elevador sobreviviente de los cuatro que existían hasta el temblor del '85 y cuyas paredes están adornadas por coloridos e inteligibles graffitis). Bajan en el piso cuatro.

began, one for Fabis, another as an investment, and Juanita bought an apartment for Aura on the same floor, investing all her savings in the down payment. It was an extraordinary gift, intended to provide Aura with security and independence at the start of her professional career. The apartments would be ready to move into by summer.

The weekend before Christmas we went with Aura's parents to Taxco, where Juanita had grown up, to spend the weekend in a recently restored grand hotel, Los Ángeles de Las Minas, as guests of the hotel's owner, a good friend of Leopoldo. I hadn't met Aura's uncle yet—the one who, as Aura had warned, was supposedly going to hate me, and who supposedly I was going to hate back. He turned out to be the man standing in front of the hotel wearing a yellow construction hard hat, with architectural blueprints rolled under his arm, the top three buttons of his crisp white shirt unbuttoned to expose a hairless swimmer's chest, a soft yellow sweater loosely knotted by the sleeves around his neck—Juanita's sole brother, six years older, the law professor, former diplomat, and author. With his sharp black goatee, he had a Mephistophelian presence that seemed cultivated, supercilious, vain, and powerfully intelligent in a way that didn't exactly warm your interest but put you on guard instead.

We exchanged polite if brusque introductions and greetings. There was no reason for Leopoldo to be wearing a hard hat because construction on his new cottage hadn't begun yet; he was only going with the contractor to look at the lot. Maybe the rolled-up blueprint paper didn't even hold architectural drawings. He was like a small boy dressing up, with grave ceremony, as Bob the Builder. I told Aura later that her uncle's dressing up like that made me like him.

On the way up to our hotel room we paused at the display case of a silver-work shop in the lobby. Later that afternoon, when I came down to the bar to pick up a bottle of wine on the pretext of not wanting to wait for room service, I slipped into the shop and bought a necklace that Aura had seemed to like. That's how I was, buying her presents, an overjoyed spendthrift piling up credit card debt with squirrelly endeavor. Overcoming that mysterious three-day crisis had strengthened our love—our mystical wedding with the birds in Tulum was just two weeks away. I took a picture of Aura, in sleeveless black shirt, standing on the balcony outside our room in the late afternoon, a hazy blue mountain backdrop, her cheeks and nose flushed, a bashful smile and tilt to her head, a soft vulnerable shine to her eyes, all of this making her look even younger, startlingly and preposterously younger, like an enamored, just-ravished quinceañera, I recognize with some disbelief every time I look at that photograph. As evening fell, the mountainside grew so feverishly alive with sparkling and moving lights it was like a shaken-up snow globe, and a faint electric noisiness filled the air, as if coming from insect-sized motors and music boxes floating across the valley. We sat on the balcony, drinking wine. I pulled the necklace from my pocket.

When I look at that photograph of Aura now, I feel more aware of our age difference, more uneasy about it, than I ever did when we were together. Juanita rarely said anything, in my presence that is, to make me feel embarrassed or apologetic about my age. I think that wasn't so much out of consideration for me as for her daughter, playing along, pretending to see us as Aura wanted others to; or maybe it was for herself, too. Juanita almost always spoke to me as if I were closer in age to her daughter than I was to her, but it's not as if it would have been better for any of us if we'd spoken like two parents. What shames me now was the way, when we were with Aura's mother, that I sometimes let immaturity masquerade as youthfulness, so that when I was spoken to as if I were practically still an adolescent, or a man-boy, a *niñote*, I'd allow myself to feel camouflaged and even flattered. Sixty is the new thirty. But that's not how I was with Aura. Now, I have to guard against the danger of confusing how Aura's mother regarded me or spoke to me with *any* aspect of how Aura did—one of death's corrosive betrayals.

* * *

Aura said, This is where I spent the happiest days of my childhood.
We were standing on a steep street in Taxco, looking at Aura's
grandmother's house, the one now occupied by Mama Violeta's
longtime maid and her family, though Mama Violeta was still very
much alive. Painted a rich indigo with bright yellow shutters and
decorated with tiles, the two-story house stood on a corner, embedded in the hillside. From that elevated part of the sidewalk it seemed
that with a running leap you'd be able to land on the rooftop if it
weren't surrounded by dense strands of barbed wire and broken
bottle glass. The house was packed with small shaded patios and
secluded rooms, and had windows on two sides opening on views
of the mountaintops where the silver mines were, including the
one where Aura's great-grandfather, a French mining engineer, had
worked. During her summer vacations from school Aura had sometimes spent as much as a month at a time here. Now Mama Violeta
no longer even spoke to any of her children from her first marriage.
Leopoldo had sounded out his half siblings and learned that Mama
Violeta really did intend to leave the house to her former maid
when she died. Mama Violeta's four children from her second marriage all lived far away, one somewhere in Texas, the rest scattered
around Mexico, like the daughter she was now living with, on an
avocado plantation in Nayarit. Their father, Mama Violeta's second
husband, couldn't have been more unlike her first, the dissipated
actor. An accountant at one of the silver mines, he never drank
alcohol, coached boys' fútbol teams, and was a regular churchgoer
who participated in Holy Week processions. He died when Aura
was still in elementary school.

   Mama Violeta was also a gifted dressmaker and seamstress,
and in her youth had dreamed of moving to Paris to pursue a career
in haute couture; maybe, if her first husband hadn't died so young,
she would have. In a family where looks were often made too much
of, Leopoldo's elder daughter, Sandrita, and Katia were regarded as
the indisputable beauties and rivals, yet Mama Violeta often treated

Aura as if she was her favorite. Mama Violeta once spent many weeks sewing and embellishing a dazzling party dress that she'd designed herself. Who was it for? Mama Violeta wouldn't say. All her grand-daughters coveted it and dreamed it would be theirs. Mama Violeta told eleven-year-old Aura that she was making it especially for her, but that she had to promise to keep it a secret. Aura didn't even tell her mother. When the dress was ready, Mama Violeta gave it to her cousin Sandrita, who was a year older than Aura. She said she was giving it to Sandrita because she was the most beautiful, and from its cut it seemed clear that she'd been making it for the tall, long-legged, rail-thin Sandrita all along; that's why when Aura started sobbing and told her mother about Mama Violeta's broken promise, nobody believed her.

Madness runs in families, of course, said Aura on the sidewalk that day in Taxco. Supposedly, more among women then men. For three generations it gets passed down mother to daughter, and then stops. Maybe that's just folk wisdom, she said, but that doesn't mean there's no truth to it. Well, my grandmother is obviously crazy, and my mother is crazy, so what I need to find out is, was my great-grandmother crazy, too?

Mi amor, you're not crazy, I said, I promise. But what about that great-grandmother? Her great-grandmother, said Aura, had gone back to France for a visit to her own mother, who was soon to die, and had never returned to Mexico; she fell ill while she was over there and died. Ill with what? I asked. Aura didn't know. Mama Violeta had been on the cusp of adolescence when that happened. Her father, who never remarried, went on raising her alone, then died a few years later.

That would be a great place to write in, said Aura, pointing at a corner room on the second floor. If only we could convince Mama Violeta to sell the house to us, she said. Aura and I agreed to start saving money to buy the house. This was Aura's long-held dream. She wanted to restore the house for her mother, too, who now refused to even come and look at it. But Aura hadn't seen or spoken to Mama Violeta since she was twelve, since that day her mother and grandmother had had their terrible fight in Copilco. Maybe next summer, said Aura, we'd drive up to Nayarit and surprise her grandmother with a visit.

That last day in Taxco we bought the carved, whitewashed wooden angel with the lewd but friendly scarlet lips that hung over our bed in Brooklyn, perpetually watching us, slowly turning away, watching.

¡Ay mi amor, qué feo eres! That funny silent laugh of hers, mouth open, eyes squeezed shut, wagging her head.

¿Soy feo?

Síííí mi amor, pobrecito.

I looked like a frog, too, she liked to tease. ¿Cómo está tu papada? she'd say, as if the loose skin under my chin, not quite a froggy wattle, possessed an independent life. She'd tug on it with both hands, laugh, and huskily say, Tu papada, mi amor.

Pobrecito, no tienes cuello. Poor you, you don't have a neck.

Poor you, you're old. She'd say that sometimes, too, whenever I couldn't stay awake if we were in bed watching a DVD or television. It's true that even if I liked the movie or television show we were watching, I usually dozed off. That only happened in bed, hardly ever in theaters. I always fell asleep reading in bed, too. Was that a symptom of age?

I've never returned the last DVDs that Aura ordered from Netflix. I found the envelopes, but two of the discs were missing. I didn't know what she'd done with them, didn't really know where to look. I went on paying the monthly fee; I'll probably have to for the rest of my life, an eternal contract, even if I never order another DVD, which I probably won't. Aura still owed astronomical amounts at every DVD rental store in our neighborhood and around Columbia. I'd stopped watching DVDs at home anyway. I didn't like being alone in the room with the DVD player. Its mechanical click-clicking and whirrs, furtive little lights, its autonomous lifeless companionship depressed me, made me feel like the last person left alive on earth.

One cold winter night, I fell asleep beside Aura while she was reading in bed. An hour or so later, she shook me awake.

I gasped, What?

She gestured at the light switch on the wall—it operated the lamp that the angel hung from—and said, Turn off the light, mi amor.

I gaped at her.

Impishly pleased with herself, she cracked up.

I got out of bed and turned off the light.

Gracias, mi amor.

. . .

It's cold! I didn't want to get out of bed!

The way she pronounces Frank when we're alone, and the way it wakes up my heart. I can hear and feel it inside me, that soft near-honk caressed by plush lips, a down-stuffed vowel that floats on her breath past *n* and lightly smacks *k*. But in her writing, in her e-mails, she always called me Paco.

She would occasionally say, Why couldn't you be ten years younger? Then everything would be so perfect!

It was an imperfection, my age, no doubt about it. But did my so-called youthfulness—not just that I looked younger than my age but my immaturity—make us more compatible? Probably it did, at times, but it also worried her. How had I gotten to be my age without having saved more money, or having planned better for the future? She didn't think of me as a failure, but I worried that she would, that someday she'd even be justified in thinking so. I worried about her leaving me over that—I was determined to work hard, to earn money—more than I did about our age difference. Maybe this was delusional, but we both claimed that I'd surely inherited my father's hardy constitution, and that I would also live vigorously into my nineties, that I was going to be one of those barrel-chested, squarely built, ornery and horny old men, the Picasso or Mailer type, though happily loyal to just one woman! In the past, when I was younger and had girlfriends who were somewhat older than Aura, people had sometimes asked if I was the father, that most common humiliation of the older male lover. But that never happened to me when I was with Aura. How could that be? I guess when we were together in public, we just didn't give the impression of a father out with his daughter.

My father used to munch on whole onions as if they were apples, I'd told her once. I thought of it as evidence of his hearty Russian peasant appetite and ways. No one who ate onions like that could have a weak constitution. A few days later, alone in the kitchen, I impulsively took a bite out of a red onion, to feel what that was like. In the bedroom, all the way at the other end of the apartment, Aura heard the crunch and shouted, Did you just bite into an onion?! Don't you even *try* to kiss me now!

How did she know it wasn't an apple?

In department stores, she'd pester me about male cosmetics, antiaging facial creams, and the like, even Botox. Please, mi amor, for me, don't you want to look young for your young wife? I used to wonder if she was serious: if I actually came home one day with my face looking like a frozen piecrust after Botox, wouldn't she be horrified? She'd send me e-mails with links to information about calf hormone antiaging creams or whatever, and where to order them online. She knew I'd never use such creams. Creams you have to slather all over your face before bed, and again in the morning, imagine. But Aura was a fanatic about facial creams. During our last trip to Paris, which was a short one—just two full days, because I was there only to promote a book—I spent four hours following Aura through the Sephora superstore on the Champs-Élysées. Aura, it can't be that we're spending one of our two afternoons in Paris in a makeup store, I complained. She said, But they have things here they don't have in New York! Then they confiscated most of her Sephora treasures at airport security in Charles de Gaulle because she'd packed all those tubes and bottles in her carry-on.

We were on the subway, that first fall, on a morning when I'd walked Aura to the Carroll Gardens F train stop and she'd talked me into coming up to Columbia with her. The train was being held in the station. She was kissing me, on my lips, all over my face; that morning she couldn't stop kissing me, and I was laughing and kissing her and I glanced aside and saw a well-known book critic who lived nearby standing there in his dark raincoat, halfway down the subway car, staring at us, his mouth a dour slit between downward creases and a nose like an old marshmallow. Whenever I saw the critic around the neighborhood he'd rarely say hello, maybe a quick nod and often not even that, but I'm certain he knew who I was, and because we'd occasionally coincided at parties some twenty years earlier, he knew he was about my age, though even back then, barely out of college, he'd looked middle-aged. So there he was, gray-haired and balding, pallor nearly gray, his raincoat a greasy gray-green, watching us with the lusterless longing and thirst of a mummy. I remember that I even felt a slight shudder of suspicion and fear, as if his gaze might carry a curse. The train started to move and he sat down and opened his newspaper.

Aura never comes back to sit in her Journey Chair on the fire escape, it's a one-way journey she went away on. I tried to feel braced by the tough antimysticism of that. Some mornings I'd come into the kitchen and look out the window and see the chair covered in snow. The boughs of the trees in the backyards weighted with snow, snow striping the floor of the fire escape, about five inches' accumulation on the seat. It reminded me of that haiku Borges wrote: This hand is the hand that touched your hair. Snow that sits where you used to sit.

14

December 2003
Everything changed. Another path opened, and I don't know where it's headed.
Era of: Us against the World.
World against Us.

I still don't know how to write in a diary.
Diary: another year is drawing near. It never ceases to surprise me that each one, since I got out of high school, has had a special event. Some definitive act that has sent me in a new direction. Hopefully my life will obey that law for many more years. Right now I don't know how far into the future this road will reach . . . isste caminho . . . nao sel . . . en si sei que en estou contenta. With doubts and bad moods like always, but in general, very, very pleased with life and its surprises and gifts. Indeed I have to say/write how grateful I am. Before Paco the world had darkened. I'd erased myself. Loneliness struck me down. I'd lost hope. The pain of deep solitude, a Heart that didn't belong to anybody.

Paris 2004—(one year later!)
Party upstairs. My life upside down. Unrecognizable. I am fat, no longer skinny. 27 years old. Pissed. Attempting to write je ne sais quoi. Life so beautiful. I feel the guilt of beauty. I feel the guilt of being. What am I doing!?

December 24, 2006
We're alone. Only Paco and me on Christmas. This is the

second time, the first was Paris and it was magical. We're on a plane, we've spent most of the day traveling, Paco asleep on my shoulder. Love is a religion. You can only believe it when you've experienced it.

15

Aura was stuck in a broken elevator in Butler Library—she phoned me on her cell when I was at Wadley. There were other people in the elevator with her, someone urgently ringing the emergency bell, spritzing panic through the phone. I told Aura to stay calm, that surely it would be fixed within minutes, and to call me back as soon as it was. When after fifteen minutes or so I hadn't heard from her, I phoned and there was no answer. Class was about to start. (We were discussing *The Street of Crocodiles,* the book she'd have with her at the beach that final day.) I didn't turn my phone off. About midway through, I told the students I had to make a call and stepped out—I got her voice mail and left a message asking her to let me know that she was okay. I pictured horrifying scenarios: air running out, Aura gasping, claustrophobic hysteria. Class was a disaster. When it was over and she still didn't answer, I phoned the Columbia switchboard, was transferred and put on hold until finally someone at campus security told me there'd been no report of a stuck elevator at Butler Library that day. It was as if the elevator had vanished, with Aura and the others inside, and no one had noticed.

Within seconds of her call to me, it turned out, the elevator glitch had fixed itself, the door had slid open, and Aura had proceeded directly into the reading room, where she was required to turn off her cell phone, and there she'd stayed studying for several hours, until finally she checked her e-mails, saw my frantic messages, and remembered . . .

Or that time we had to go to a cocktail party in Manhattan. Aura was at home and I was a few subway stops closer to Manhattan, down in Dumbo, where I was subletting a friend's inexpensive writing studio for a few months. The plan was that she would take the F train to the York Street stop, find me waiting on the platform, and then we'd ride the next train into Manhattan. One train came, its doors opened, a few people got out; another pulled in several minutes later. The station, winter trapped inside, was a grimy cement and iron deep freezer. The pay phones were broken. My cell phone didn't work down there. Robotic rats on the tracks, eating electricity and iron filings. How could this be happening? We'd timed it, I'd phoned her and said, All right, I'm ready to go to the station, and she'd said, Give me five more minutes, and so I'd waited five more minutes. She's still trying on clothes, I thought, pulling dresses on and taking them off because they're too sexy or too ostentatiously fashionable or because they show off her breasts too much or reveal her tattoo. She liked the way her most prized dresses, including some of the ones I'd bought for her, looked in the mirror, she just wouldn't wear them out of the apartment. Four trains had passed. My fingers and feet stung from the cold, my nose was running. I climbed the long stairs out of the station to phone her from the street. I had to walk nearly a block before my phone regained its signal. Wind gusted off the East River, whirling litter like frozen bats. She didn't answer her cell or our telephone at home. I went back into the station and, as I descended the stairs, I heard coming from far below, like the crash of rough surf, the sound of a train entering or leaving the station. On the platform, looking into the tunnel, I saw the dwindling green lights and orange dot of a Manhattan-bound F train. What if she was on it? I waited another half hour, then climbed out to the street again. I phoned the apartment where the party was, but she wasn't there, either. That déjà vu sensation of loneliness, bafflement, and sadness, of, Is this really happening? Then—I didn't know what else to do—I redescended into the station. If I described all of this to a psychoanalyst as a nightmare I'd had, wouldn't it seem to be about separation and death?

What had happened, it turned out, was that Aura had gotten on the train at Carroll Gardens and ridden it only one stop, to

Bergen Street, and had waited for me there; she'd confused Bergen with York Street, two stops farther on, or had spaced out when I'd told her the plan. Finally, she'd trudged back toward home, feeling as bewildered and sad as I was, and she stopped into Sweet Melissa for a hot chocolate.

Arriving back from abroad to New York airports, we always had to join separate lines at U.S. Immigration, even after we were married, with Aura in the much slower line for foreign visitors. I'd always clear passport control well before she did, then wait by the wall in front of where foreigners came out. Sometimes guards would tell me that I couldn't stand there, and I'd retreat to the luggage carousel, but often they left me alone, my unease stirring as the minutes passed and still Aura hadn't appeared. Finally, I'd see her step up to one of the booths and I'd feel a new surge of nerves, because what if there was something wrong with her papers again, or the agent was in a bad mood, or just liked to harass Mexicans, and turned her away on the slightest pretext; we'd all heard stories like that. Someone at the U.S. embassy in Mexico had told Aura over the telephone that even having a Fulbright scholarship was no guarantee anymore of a student visa. What if at any moment, here at the mouth of the gate, she was going to be pulled back and returned to Mexico without even being allowed to speak to me. I rarely got to spy on Aura from afar like that, watching as she obediently pressed her fingers down on the fingerprint scanner and answered questions, meeting the customs officer's eye, smiling or even laughing in response to some remark from him, or else remaining serious and composed—this always brought back memories of being a small boy watching my mother talking to a policeman who'd just given her a parking ticket, or to a bank teller, or to a butcher in Haymarket Square, my awareness of their awareness of my mother's delicate prettiness and foreignness, my own sense of an unbreachable apartness—until finally I saw the shrug of the officer's shoulder as he stamped her passport, and within seconds Aura was walking into my embrace.

*   *   *

Moments of temporary separation and absence and even loss that were like little rehearsals for what was coming. Not premonition, but actual visitations, death coming through its portal, taking Aura away, putting her back, receding back into its hole.

Death, a subway train going the wrong way that you can't get off of because it makes no stops. No stopping for hot chocolate in Death.

That week after our first Christmas and New Year's together in Mexico, we took a room for five nights at a boutique hotel on the beach at Tulum. The first three mornings we wound up having to drive from Tulum to the passport office in Cancún and back again in the afternoon, almost a hundred miles each way. Aura had realized, before we left for the beach, that since arriving in Mexico a few weeks before she'd lost her passport. Tía Lupe express-mailed Aura's birth certificate from Guanajuato to the FedEx office in Cancún. Mexican bureaucracy is notorious: long lines stretching all the way back to the Aztec empire; multiple appointments to schedule at this teller window or that counter; many official forms to buy at those tiny stationery stores always owned by nice old ladies, to fill in, have notarized, then buy and fill in again because at one window some bureaucrat found one stupid infinitesimal thing filled out incorrectly, then renotarize, and so on. Aura was a veteran of Mexican bureaucracies, the UNAM's being among the worst. It was captivating to witness the unruffled manner with which she endured it all, her serene, polite, and even pleasant interactions with the clerks and secretaries, winning over even the most bristlingly petty or hostile ones. All this opened a window into her temperament, I thought. I loved waiting in those passport office lines with Aura, even though it was how we were spending our Tulum vacation instead of at the beach. That mostly two-lane highway that we spent so much of that brief vacation driving on, beaches and cenotes and ruins hidden from view, was like any ordinary highway, despite the billboards announcing resorts and water parks with Mayan names and motifs. Our rental car had a CD player, and at a gasoline station, because I told her I didn't really know his music, Aura bought a CD of José José's greatest hits. That was the only music we listened to on the long drives between Tulum and Cancún, the same sad ballads her mother had listened to in the Terrible Tower, weeping over her abandonment.

On the Tulum-bound drive we kept seeing small hand-painted signs directing us to "Subway," which must be the name of a Mayan town, I deduced, pronouncing it *Soobway*. I even said, Maybe it says Subwaj and we're not getting a good look at the signs. But no, it was a *y*, not a *j*. For some mysterious reason, someone was trying to lure travelers to *Soobway*. But it turned out to be Quintana Roo's first Subway sandwich franchise, in a small shopping plaza off the highway by a golf club outside Tulum. Aura hardly ever again passed by a Subway anywhere in the world without remarking, There's your pueblo Maya, mi amor—*Soobway*. To reach the beach where our hotel was, we'd turn off the highway onto a long stretch of dirt road, the car hitting the softer surface at nearly highway speed, bouncing and seeming to lift off and float through a brown cloud of churned-up dirt as if riding one prolonged note of José José's sonorous voice, and that sense of dislocation again, of being propelled through a portal, from an in-between world, back into the beach town of Tulum. In the end, a bureaucrat at a window finally told Aura she could get her passport only in the state of her permanent residence. Why wasn't she told that on the first day? There is no answer to that question.

Aura beside me in bed: What would happen to you, mi amor, if I ever left you?

I would die, mi amor, you know that.

You would, I know, you *would* die, wouldn't you?

I really would.

And she laughed, with a kind of childish delight, and said, Or if something happened to me, if it was me—

No, Aura! No, stop!

—if it was me who died—

Then I would die, too. I would. Aura, don't even say that!

You *would* die, wouldn't you? Ay, mi amor—sadly shaking her head.

You are so lucky, Francisco, she would say. You are the luckiest man on earth, to have a young, intelligent, talented wife who loves you the way I do. Do you know how lucky you are?

I know, mi amor. I'm the luckiest guy alive.

You are, Francisco, you really are.

I am, I know.

And if you're going to be a father at your age, you're going to have to keep yourself in top shape. Babies weigh a lot, you know, and you have to carry them everywhere.

That's why I go to the gym so much. I'm getting ready.

And you have to pay attention all the time to what's going on around us when we walk in the street. If neither of us is good at paying attention, then I'm not having a baby with you.

I know, mi amor, I'll pay attention for both of us, I promise.

Every day a ghostly ruin. Every day the ruin of the day that was supposed to have been. Every second on the clock clicking forward, anything I do or see or think, all of it made of ashes and charred shards, the ruins of the future. The life we were going to live, the child we were going to have, the years we were going to spend together, it was as if that life had already occurred millennia ago, in a lost secret city deep in the jungle, now crumbled into ruins, overgrown, its inhabitants extinguished, never discovered, their story never told by any human being outside it—a lost city with a lost name that only I remember—*Soobway.*

On the Ninety-sixth Street subway platform where, after a late lunch at the Columbia Ollie's, we were waiting for the express back to Brooklyn, Aura was saying Ohhh, you know, it's a text that's about the way texts generate discourses among texts, so no reason even to mention authors or authorial intention. Well, okay, I know that's true, but . . . But in her class that afternoon, taken up by a discussion of Borges's short story "Pierre Menard, autor del Quijote," no one had laughed even once. But Frank, *Frank,* she exclaimed, didn't anybody realize that Borges was being *funny* when he wrote that story? The story's narrator, she recounted, is a mediocre critic who is indignant because his late friend Pierre Menard was left out of some catalog of important writers assembled by another critic. Okay, but does anyone else agree that Menard was so great? The baroness and the countess, they agree, said Aura, both of them friends of Menard and the critic. But they're just the baroness and the countess! she exclaimed. And the French countess, she lives in Weechita or someplace like that now, married to a rich gringo, don't you think *that's* a clue? A clue that Borges was also being silly *and* making fun of self-important bad writers. She mimicked a scolding professorial basso: No, *Ow-rra,* wrong. Silly? *¿Qué? Bad* writers? That's not how we read texts *here, Ow-rra.*

The red-and-pink tassels of yarn dangling like bunches of dwarf bananas, three on each side, from the Andean earflaps of Aura's ridiculous pointy wool hat and the spiky red tassel that crowned it jiggled in unison with her bobbing cheeks and the peal of her laughter. Aura was having fun, too, her eyes gleaming; she'd go on like this, chattery, ebullient, all the way back to Brooklyn. Aura was discovering in those days that she wasn't like the other grad students, ideologically prohibited from considering the person and mischief of the author. She wasn't always so giddy to revel in or acknowledge these differences, she was often tormented with worry—I'm going to be expelled! They're going to take away my scholarship! They're going to send me to the Gulag!

Do you think Jim has a wooden leg? she asked, switching the subject to one that had lately preoccupied her. Valentina's husband, Jim, the super-rich investment banker, also quite a bit older than his wife—hadn't I noticed? Wasn't that a wooden or prosthetic leg limp that Jim had? From the knee down, she said, his shone bone, his shun sheen, what do you call it? What if she asked Valentina if Jim had a wooden leg and it turned out that he didn't, would she be offended? Valentina was already so insecure about how prematurely aged Jim looked that she wouldn't let him come anywhere near Columbia. Well, even if his shin is made of cheese, I said, it won't be just some ordinary Camembert, that guy makes a ton of money. Ay, mi amor, she said sweetly, ¡qué tonto eres! One night a few months later, coming out of a movie, we let ourselves lag behind Valentina and Jim on the sidewalk so that I could study his walk. Maybe he does, I thought. That summer they invited us to their country house and we went swimming—arthritic stiffness was all it was.

Waiting for the train to Brooklyn, listening, looking down into her face, so full of puppyish excitement and her own particular innocence: What was that innocence? What was Aura innocent of that I wasn't? Much past experience of failure and disappointment. Was love making me innocent again, wiping that history away? Aura was innocent of the power of her own gifts and that, her innocent promise and humility, sometimes made her seem so fragile to me. At such moments, there on the subway platform, practically dizzy with love for her, I would sense how vulnerable she was—so caught up in her own excitement, not paying attention, so physically slight—to a shove from behind by some fiendish lunatic off his medication, into the path of an oncoming train. This recurring fear of a crazed subway pusher was sometimes so strong that I would almost feel the urge to push her off the platform myself, as if the fiendish lunatic was me and I needed to get the inevitable over with, or as if I just couldn't endure so much love and happiness one more second, and simultaneously, in a silent burst of panic, I'd pull her to safety, away from the edge of the platform. My hands around her waist or on her shoulders, I would gently pull her back into the mass of waiting passengers and put my own body between her and the tracks, and give her a relieved kiss on the cheek. I never understood it, this awful urge to push her off the subway platform while simultaneously pulling her to safety, rescuing her from phantom fiends but also from myself.

16

The first time I put on my down jacket in November, heading into my second winter without Aura, I found an empty pink condom wrapper in the zippered pocket on the outside, over the breast, and for an instant I couldn't remember how it got there. I stared at the words printed on it, *Extra feucht, Zartrosa,* as if they were code I'd once understood but had forgotten. It was from last winter, those few weeks in Berlin. One night I'd gone to a bar with a young woman, just a girl really, a Mexican art student visiting Pancho Morales, a writer I knew from the DF who was in Berlin on a German DAAD grant. She was studying in London but knew Berlin inside out, and we were going on to another bar when she realized that she'd lost her hat, a sort of iconic art object of a hat that she'd made herself—another Mexican girl into her hats—and she wanted to go back to Pancho's apartment to see if it was there, and it was, hanging on a coat peg in the hallway. There was a Christmas tree in the hallway, too, completely stripped of bark and foliage, its pale branches decorated with what looked like snowflakes and icicles that turned out to be delicately tied strips of medical gauze and shards of broken mirror hung from white threads. What a beautiful Christmas tree, I said to her, because it really was, and it turned out that she'd made it for Pancho and his wife. Your art must be amazing, I said, and she said that I could see some of it on her computer if I wanted. We went into the room where she was staying, took off our shoes, sat down on the futon on the floor, and she opened up her laptop and started showing me her art, and before long I was kissing her neck and, as she leaned forward, her shirt rode up, exposing the skin of her waist and the small of her back, and I kissed that, too, and then she asked, Do you want to eat me out?—just like that, with disconcerting frankness; all this like an echo of my first night with Aura, when she'd read me her airport story and shown me the drawing of the robot shoes. Aura and I didn't fuck that first night, but the girl in Berlin and I did, after I'd eaten her out like she'd asked, with a desperate hunger, for a long time. We used a rubber that she had in her bag and it had a pink wrapper.

She was only twenty-five, the same age as Aura when we'd met, but now it was five years later, when Aura would have been, was still, thirty. We slept, then stayed in bed until late afternoon; it was one of those Berlin days without daylight, that pass on silent wings like a soot-colored owl, and the apartment was silent. Pancho was out on one of his famous binges from which he wouldn't return for three days, and we saw or heard no sign of his wife. We fucked some more, went to a movie at the Sony Center, ate sausages and drank *gluhwein* at a Christmas market, and then at three in the morning I put her and her many suitcases into a taxi to the airport, and I went back to the apartment I was staying in, that belonged to my Guatemalan friend and his German wife. When I woke up later that morning it was as if those one and a half nights of sex and sweet female company hadn't happened, though of course they had, it just made no difference that they had. I felt the same as I did every morning, the same darkness and sadness, the same memories, images (Aura dead . . .). Sex and intimacy with a beautiful young woman made no difference, I could fuck all I wanted, or not fuck, and it wouldn't change anything—later, when I found the pink condom wrapper in my jeans I decided to save it as a reminder of that lesson, and put it back in the pocket of my down jacket. Over the next few weeks while I was in Berlin, and when I got back to Brooklyn, we exchanged a few e-mails, and then I never heard from her again, though now and then I looked at her Facebook page. She was snowboarding in the Alps. She'd decided to go on the wagon and stop using drugs. She was making sculptures from smashed mirrors.

*   *   *

Valentina, with Jim, was visiting me in my apartment when I asked
her for help in setting up my screen saver to rotate different pictures
of Aura—without Aura around, I needed outside help for even the
simplest computing puzzles—and she noticed that I had at least five
hundred photographs of Aura saved in my computer.

Why do you have so many photos of Aura? she asked.

Because I loved her, I said, and could never stop taking pictures of her.

Valentina turned to Jim and asked, Why don't you have pictures of me in your computer like Frank does of Aura?

Jim's gentlemanly lack of expression said, So pictures in a computer are a sign of love, but the Gramercy Park town house we live
in isn't?

Some nights I would meet Valentina and some of Aura's other New
York friends, like Wendy, or Juliana, a Chilean who was also at
Columbia, in a bar near my apartment or in another neighborhood,
sometimes even in Manhattan. They missed Aura, too, and sought
connection to her through our conversations and through me, just
as I looked for Aura in them, always encouraging, hectoring, begging them to describe every detail they could recall of even the most
ordinary moments they'd spent with her. There were complications
and dangers in allowing ourselves to get as close as we did during
those months, that first winter and spring of Aura's death, just before
I went to Berlin and, especially, after I came back.

Valentina was a norteña, with long slender legs, the upright
posture of a lifelong rider of horses, and the brash informality and
swagger of a spoiled rancher's daughter. Except her parents were
music teachers who owned a little musical instruments store in a
Monterrey shopping plaza, and Valentina had spent way more time
in mosh pits than anywhere near a corral. Before Jim, she'd serially
dated self-destructive junkie rock musicians and the like. Now she

dressed like a rich emo girl, with fantastic hairdos that always made her look like she'd just come directly from Tokyo's hippest hair salon. She shared with Aura some of that childlike volubility, and they ignited bouts of goofy hilarity in each other. *Raua* was what Valentina called Aura; *Navilenta,* Aura called Valentina; they liked to talk, to e-mail each other, in a nearly made-up language. They loved each other, but their friendship had sharp edges, and Aura was wary of Valentina's sometimes stunningly insensitive tongue. Aura used to be intimidated by Valentina, until, as the years passed, she realized that she shouldn't be. Valentina was smart and fun to talk to, but like a lot of New Yorkers from the art-hipster-money world—her husband was one of those high-finance guys who haunt Chelsea and Williamsburg art galleries and rock and experimental music clubs, dressed like an aged punk rocker though one who drank only very expensive wine—Old Man Sex Pistol, I liked to called him—a lot of that talk was intellectual fashion, which doesn't mean that it was empty, or not often clever, but it usually adhered, however loosely, to a recognizable script. Valentina wasn't happy in her marriage. It had been in a long crisis that she was always trying to *work out.* She desperately wanted a baby but Jim, with two grown sons from his first marriage, didn't. It wasn't easy for a middle-class Mexicana, into her late thirties now and still struggling to finish her PhD thesis, to even contemplate walking away from a twelve-million-dollar town house on Gramercy Park and all the perks—private masseuse, at-home pilates and yoga instructors. I found myself feeling drawn to Valentina, seeking her out, craving her attention, even. I'd stand as close to her as I could, looking down into her face, trying to ignite in her some of the silly playful banter that she used to share with Aura, and whenever I succeeded I was surprised by the intensity of the longing it aroused, a sugar rush that, when it faded or burned out, plummeted me into a vacant stupor.

But Valentina could also be so callous in what she said that I'd wondered if she suffered from some form of autism. Why can't you just go back to being the way you were before you met Aura? she said to me during one of those nights when we had met up in a wine bar. Her tactlessness seemed to suggest other laxities, and I found myself fantasizing and wondering more and more about whether or not I might be able to fuck her. Valentina aroused me in a confusing way. It was as if I preferred to be misunderstood or ignored than to be sympathized with. I'd discovered that I almost never liked it when people tried to be sensitive to me.

It also annoyed me that Valentina thought she knew certain things about Aura and me that were probably not so great—I didn't know what those things were, but I had some reason for believing that they weren't necessarily true. I wanted to know, and didn't want to know, what she thought she knew.

One evening Aura had come home from hanging out with Valentina and, standing penitently before me—penitently but also playing it up, comically theatrical in her distress—she'd pressed her forehead to my chest, remorsefully shaken her head back and forth, and blurted: I said some bad things about our marriage to Valentina that aren't true but I only said them because she's so unhappy with Jim and I wanted to make her feel better. I won't do it again, I promise! Frank, am I horrible?

I thought that must be what lay behind some of Valentina's occasionally mocking attitude. She liked to remind me that she knew sides of Aura that I didn't, but also that no one has the right to claim an authoritative knowledge of anybody else anyway—this was a huge theme of Valentina's—that there was even something fascistic in such presumption. When Aura's friends and I ended up in conversations about this, ephemeral alliances would form: Wendy glaring coolly at Valentina while she extemporized, and then indulging me in the most old-fashioned of widower-coddling ways, with lamp-eyed affection and *douceur*, stroking my hand while I quietly/exaggeratedly fumed, blinked my eyes, and said, Of course I knew Aura, you can't tell me I didn't know Aura. (*la douceur*—the revolutionary nineteenth-century technique of treating the mad with "gentleness," picked up in my research into *l'histoire de la psychanalyse* for Aura's novel.)

When I told Valentina what Aura had said about making things up about us just to make her feel better during one of their bad marriage conversations, Valentina left the bar, indignant and humiliated. It was cruel of me to have told her that. Juliana was with us that night and I expected Juliana to hurry after her, but she didn't, she stayed behind in the bar. She downed her glass of wine in a few gulps and ordered another. A silent nervous melancholy descended on us. We'd never been alone together before. I was drinking bourbon. Oh, Francisco, Valentina misses Aura so much, Juliana blurted with a soft moan. I know nobody misses her as much as you do, she said, but this isn't a competition, Francisco, we all miss Aura, but Valentina really really misses her. I wasn't Valentina's best friend, Aura was, and sometimes I feel that she wants me to be like Aura was, and I just can't. Juliana had brown fox eyes with long, curling lashes, and dark-reddish hair that fell around her thin pretty face, neck, and shoulders in a viny way that I found incredibly attractive. On the cab ride back across the Brooklyn Bridge, I remembered how Aura used to like to gaze out the window at the bridge and the view, often exclaiming over it. I remembered one night in particular, when she'd twisted herself around in a taxi to look out the window, her leg hooked behind her on the seat, her dress riding up a bit to unveil the supple underside of her dancer's thigh, her naked heel coming out of her shoe, the lights of the bridge and the skyline illuminating her like lightning, and how all that had made me almost crazy with joyous lust. The next instant, I was kissing Juliana in the backseat of the taxi. We went back to her place in Park Slope and fucked deep into the night, and again in the morning, as if this was going to mean something. The wedding rings on the silver chain around my neck jingled and bounced in her face; I watched her flinching beneath them. She didn't smell like Aura, her skin, her lips, her saliva; neither had the Berlin girl's, but with her it had not been a turnoff. I already knew before we got out of bed that morning that we were never going to do this again. *Why did this happen?*

Juliana asked just before I left, and I replied, lamely, Because we felt lonely and we both miss Aura.

Later that same day I waited for Valentina in the small West Village park across the street from where I knew she went twice weekly for harp lessons, from three-thirty to five in the afternoon. As soon as she came out, wearing dark glasses, her mid-thigh, orange coat with fur-lined hood, and black leggings and ankle boots, I called out to her. She crossed the street and didn't seem much surprised. I apologized for what I'd said in the bar. I held her beautifully manicured long fingers that were learning to play the harp and kissed them, one by one, then her lips. We began to say things, as if each of us had been storing it all up, waiting for just this moment. It was crazy. We decided that we'd run off to Mexico to live together, but not yet, in a few months, when a year had passed since Aura's death, when it wouldn't look so bad. Yes, when it won't look so bad. We parted, madly kissing, uttering little exclamations between breaths, is this really happening? She headed west, like a spy after a rendezvous. There was an A train stop just blocks away, and I headed back to Brooklyn, and I kept imagining her lying in her million-dollar bed, her shapely thighs apart, slowly masturbating herself with those painted, pliant harpist's fingers while I watched. The next day I wrote her an e-mail telling her that, aside from my apology, I hadn't meant a word of what I'd said. Later we had an argument about whose idea it had been to run off to Mexico, and who had actually first said the words, "after a year is up, when it won't look so bad." Why had any of this happened?

We were all trying to find Aura in each other, I guess, though I don't think we recognized it. We were lonely, still in shock, frightened. It was deeply frightening for each of those young women to have lost a beloved friend in such a sudden and horrifying way. Everybody was unhinged. Of course they reached out for the embrace of someone who understood, who was also frightened. Maybe I was trying to find my still-recent former self, the husband, using women and their bodies to try to connect, as through a medium, with the lover who was accustomed to giving and receiving love every day.

Now, fifteen months after Aura's death, none of us were even speaking to each other. But Valentina was finally pregnant with Old Man Sex Pistol's child, their marriage was saved. The second year of death was going to be lonelier than the first.

One afternoon soon after I returned from Mexico that second summer, in the supermarket around the corner from our apartment, the chubby, bespectacled Ecuadorian checkout girl said, Oh, you're so tanned señor, have you been to the beach?

I answered, No.

And how's your wife, señor?

Oh, she's good, I said. Tú sabes, back in school, studying, really busy.

But she was scrutinizing my face the way a concerned physician might as you lie about your symptoms, and then she said, But I haven't seen her in so long.

You haven't seen her in more than fifteen months, I thought. Did I just imagine that she was looking at me as if she could tell I was lying? There was another supermarket on Smith Street, across the street from Café le Roy, about a ten-minute walk. I'll start going there, I decided.

Mexican workers in New York restaurants were especially drawn to Aura, often pausing in whatever they were doing to have a conversation with her. Aura looked like a classic Mexican girl-next-door, sunshine in her friendly black eyes, hair worn in two black pigtails over her shoulders—though she only sometimes wore her hair like that, and looked so utterly lovely whenever she did. She was like Mexico's sweetheart in a contemporary equivalent of a Mexican World War II movie, visiting the soldier boys overseas. Often, even in the fanciest restaurants, not just busboys but even the kitchen workers in their splattered whites would come out and stand around our table, just to talk to her. She'd ask them where they were from in Mexico, and they'd tell her little stories about themselves, and ask her questions, too. There was something so genuine about those

encounters that I never saw a restaurant manager get annoyed at
the workers, or hurry them back to work. Sometimes they'd ask for
her phone number, too, but she wouldn't give it to them, of course.
Once, very early on, in an idiotic excess of enthusiasm, I gave one
of those guys our number, and he phoned every few days for weeks.
It was almost always me who picked up the phone when he called.
He had a rustic accent, always asked to speak "con la paisana," and
I would say she wasn't home and, finally, that she'd gone back to
Mexico.

Café le Roy, our regular weekend brunch spot, was the only
place on Smith Street that had Mexican waiters, not just busboys
and kitchen workers. There was an exceedingly pretty waitress who
looked like a young Nefertiti, with eyes like long dark gems, and a
satiny hollow between delicate collarbones that it was hard to keep
my gaze from. She was from Puebla, like most of her coworkers, and
was studying for her teaching degree at one of the city's community
colleges. When this waitress, whose name was Ana Eva, confided
to Aura that she was in peril of failing her literature course and
that if she did she would be expelled, Aura met with her in the
neighborhood on two separate weekends to help her. Ana Eva had
to write a final paper about any twentieth-century poetry movement
that she chose, and Aura decided that she should write about the
Mexican poets known as Los Contemporáneos. She helped her with
her research and corrected her first draft and, in the end, Ana Eva
pulled an A-minus. I hadn't been back to Café le Roy since Aura's
death. I wondered if Ana Eva even worked there anymore.

Then one afternoon, when I was in the New York Public Library
doing some reading (Freud's essay "Mourning and Melancholia"—
mourning's "function is to detach the survivor's memories and hopes
from the dead." You're supposed to accept that and work at it. Freud
believed the process should take between one and two years. But I
didn't want to detach or accept, I did not want to, why did I have
to want to be "cured"?), I felt a soft touch on my shoulder and I
turned my head and it was her, the waitress from Café le Roy, saying, Hola, Francisco... I didn't even remember her name at that

moment and my flustered smile gave that away; she said, Soy Ana Eva, la mesera del le Roy... Her Egyptian eyes, chiseled cheeks, perfectly arched lips, dark-reddish lip gloss. I'd never seen her when she wasn't in her prim waitress uniform of white collared blouse and black slacks. Now she was wearing a loose gray sweater that might have been a boy's, a blue cotton skirt, hem well beneath her knees, red Converse high-tops with black ankle socks peeking out, her long, thin, smooth, brown shins. A college student. The top of her black-haired head at the level of my chin, a couple of inches shorter than Aura. I groped for something to say.

You're still in school?

I've wanted to talk with you, Francisco, to tell you how sorry and sad I am for you and Aura, she said. But I didn't know how to reach you.

We went outside, into Bryant Park. I bought some coffees at the corner kiosk, and we sat at one of the green metal tables. It was early November, not too cold. She wore a denim jacket and a black velvety scarf. It was an overcast day, the grass still green, the leaves mottled brown and pale green; I thought of Paris, and the runaway French queens. Ana Eva said that she'd found out about Aura when she'd seen a little notice in the weekly Latino section of the *Daily News* about a memorial ceremony and reading organized by Aura's classmates. She was in a regular city college now, at Baruch, in her last year there, and working at a restaurant near the college, but she still lived in Brooklyn, in Kensington. Her beauty and gentleness lifted me into a heightened alertness that I hadn't experienced in a long time, as if I'd woken up from a lower state of wakefulness that was perhaps a form of sleep. I remembered some of the thoughts I'd had when Ana Eva would lean over refilling my coffee, and Aura's occasional chiding after she'd moved off: Oh, you like her? Aura sometimes used to like to make herself jealous. There was never any real justification for it, but she'd make herself feel jealous anyway. She used to tease me that I would have been happy to fall in love with any mexicanita who'd come along, and that I'd just been incredibly lucky that the mexicanita who'd come along had turned out to be her. I'd laugh, but now, as I found myself gazing a little too intensely at Ana Eva's young face, I heard Aura saying, Cualquiera mexicanita, ¿verdad? and I must even have laughed a little, because Ana Eva, smiling quizzically, asked, ¿Qué pasó? And I said, Oh, nothing, perdón, I was just remembering how much we liked going to Café le Roy for brunch. It's a good thing you did, said Ana Eva, because if you hadn't, I might not be in college now. When Aura helped me with my paper, she saved me. Nobody else in my life has ever done such a generous thing for me, Francisco. I didn't know what I could do for her in return, or give to her that would show how grateful I was and how much I admired her. I always thought that someday I would find a way to thank her . . . Ana Eva hoisted her narrow shoulders, for a moment looked like she was about to cry, then she sighed and her shoulders dropped. I thought about how young Ana Eva was, and began preparing an excuse to be on my way. Ana Eva said, Sometimes I feel Aura inside me. Her spirit visits me, I'm sure of it. Just a few days ago I heard her voice inside of me, asking me to take care of you, Francisco. But I didn't know where to find you, or what to do. At the restaurant they told me you don't come there anymore. Then today I run into you in the library, as if Aura wanted me to find you.

I'd given a lot of thought, of course, over the preceding year and several months, to the question of where Aura's spirit could be. I'd wonder, What would she want me to be doing now, supposing that she's been able to think about me, or even watch me (but not watch me, I hope). I believed either that Aura's spirit had faded into nonbeing, into pure energy, after the forty-ninth day of her death, as the Buddhists believe, or else that her spirit had never left Mexico. She's probably taking care of her mother, I'd thought. So when Ana Eva told me about Aura's spirit visiting her, I believed that *she* believed it, which is probably the essence of the matter anyway, since who could prove her wrong? Maybe she'd really had such a conversation with Aura in a dream. I guess that's where it started with Ana Eva Pérez, with my deciding to believe her, or to behave as if I did.

Look after me how? I asked.

She looked down. I don't know, she said, with a slight embarrassed laugh.

Cook for me, maybe? Do you know how to make turkey meat loaf? Aura used to make that for me three different ways. Also, on some Sunday mornings she'd make chilaquiles con salsa verde for breakfast, yum, my favorite, except it always took her so long it would practically be dinnertime before they were ready. She'd be in the kitchen for hours, unless she bought the salsa verde in the supermarket.

I can make chilaquiles, said Ana Eva, smiling. Do you cook?

I used to, I said, when I was married. Maybe you should let me cook for you first. Then, if you like the way I cook, you can make chilaquiles for me.

That was somewhat nonsensical, but it's what I said, and she agreed. We traded telephone numbers. When I phoned her a few days later I felt a nervous fluttering in my stomach—butterflies!—and even panic when she didn't answer and I had to decide whether or not to leave a message, and then I did, cringing over my affected casualness. I hadn't felt like this since phoning Aura back when she lived with the Korean botanist. Was it a sign that I was ready to try for a relationship? I'd begun to think about when, if ever, I'd be ready for another one; or if I'd even be able to find a woman who would love me and who I could also love. The first time I'd had to think about it was at the funeral, when, in front of the other people grouped around us, Aura's mother had suddenly said to me,

You'll still have another chance, but I'll never have another daughter.

I hadn't known how to respond to that. Juanita had lost her daughter, her only child, and would never have another. Should I simply affirm that? Was there also an accusation in her words that I should respond to? Looking straight at her, I said, Yes, I know. Inside, I vowed, No, I won't. Your loss isn't greater than mine. But was it greater than mine? Was there a way to measure? What if it *was* greater? What did it mean about my grief, or about me? Should I

vow never to fall in love again and make a pact with Juanita to show
her how much I loved her daughter? Was that what she wanted?
No, she didn't want that.

I'd never loved anyone in my life as much as I'd loved Aura,
not even close, not any parent or sibling or any previous lover, and
not my first wife; maybe I'd never really loved anyone before Aura.
I believed that I loved Aura as a husband is meant to love his wife,
in the most sacred conjugal manner, and much more.

But Juanita was right.

The grief and bereavement literature, all the scientific studies
of widows and widowers that I'd sought out in libraries and online,
were confusing on this matter. Often, in these studies, widows and
especially widowers remarried quickly, because this is what they
knew how to do, they knew how to love and to assume the responsibilities of a marriage; to compound grief with a collapse into a
barren existence of daily meaninglessness was too much, and they
fought back by finding a new partner as fast as they could. One psychiatrist even wrote that remarrying quickly following the loss of a
beloved spouse should be considered a living tribute to that spouse
and the quality of the marriage. But the studies also showed that
most of those quick remarriages didn't work out, leading to quick
divorces. Bereaved spouses who'd had happy marriages were much
more vulnerable to what the grief specialists called pathological
mourning—"extreme emotional loneliness and severe depressive
symptoms"—than people who'd been in unhappy marriages, and
that this was especially so if they were widowers of around my age.
Widows and widowers from happy marriages had more health problems than the survivors of unhappy ones. If your spouse was what
they called an "attachment figure"—someone who you considered
the source of your happiness, and of your own identity as a respon-
sibly functioning and reasonably happy man in the world—then
you were especially fucked. The studies found that strong support
groups of family (which I didn't have) and friends (which at times
I did have) made no difference. If on top of everything else, the
death of the beloved was sudden, unexpected, or violent—Aura's

death was all three—then you were particularly "predisposed to a pathological reaction," including post-traumatic stress disorder, like a combat vet. Traumatic grief, I read, made you more prone to cancer, heart disease, increased consumption of alcohol (*isí, señor!*), sleep disturbances, unhealthy eating, and "suicidal ideation." All in all, widowers of beloved wives lost ten years off their life expectancies; happily married guys widowed in their fifties were on average dead by the time they were sixty-three, unless they'd managed to remarry successfully. And what if the dead wife was heartbreakingly young, beautiful, brilliant, loving, good, on the brink of realizing her promise and most ardent dreams (writing, motherhood), and her family blamed the surviving husband for her death—blame that he was more than disposed to accept, though not at all in the terms or by the means that they expressed it? I found no studies with widower cohorts like that.

All of this said to me that for my own sake I should try to try. I missed being a man with responsibilities to another person, engaged with life. I'd been good at marriage, not counting the piling up of credit card debt—me, along with millions of other decent American husbands—and being unable to move to a bigger, more expensive apartment. On the night of the presidential election, the returns coming in, victory declared, and during the nearly nationwide euphoria that followed, I lay on my bed under the angel and sobbed. Our child would have grown up in this better, changing, more dynamic country; well, at least it sure seemed so that night. What stake did I have in it now? More affordable access to a government-funded old-age home someday? Better homeless shelters, should it come to that?

Yes, self-pity. Why the fuck not.

But I could fight it. I could still be a husband and a dad. Ana Eva was twenty-six. Wasn't that too young for me? Hadn't Aura and I managed to push age difference to its workable limit? We might even have become an Alpha couple. Aura, with her Ivy League PhD and blooming bilingual literary career, was going to be extremely hirable, in New York, Mexico, or anywhere. I'd had a decent job, not bad paying, my salary padded by contracts for books which, whatever else you might say about them, reflected an energetic engagement with the world. Now I would have to start over. Ana Eva was an admirable, intelligent, hardworking young woman. She wanted to be an elementary or middle-school teacher. She had an interest in literature. If we got married, she'd be able to get her green card. She insisted she didn't mind our age difference. She claimed there was no meaningful difference between her age and Aura's. Because of her school and work schedule, it wasn't easy for us to find time to be together, but soon Ana Eva was spending all her free time with me. I took her to restaurants in Brooklyn, mostly in our neighbor-hood, usually pizza and pasta places. She knew about wine from being a waitress, and liked to pick what to order. When we went to the sushi place on Court Street that Aura and I used to go to and that I hadn't been back to since, the Israeli owner greeted us as if he was surprised and delighted to see us again, and I realized he was mistaking Ana Eva for Aura. Sometimes she came to my apartment to study, or we met in Wi-Fi cafés to do "homework" together. I bought her presents, though I didn't go crazy—I didn't buy her a new laptop to replace her slow and outmoded one. We kissed on our first date, made love on our second. I cooked for her at my apartment, using pots and pans and utensils that had been untouched since Aura had last touched them, feeling like I was rousing them from their stoic mourning, forcing them to submit to a betrayal. Shut up, pots and pans, this is part of *moving on*, like we're all supposed to. I phoned my closest friends in New York and Mexico to tell them that I'd fallen in love, and waited like a hungry dog for words of congratulations and approval; if I discerned even a trace of skepticism in their voices, I became belligerent. I told Ana Eva that I loved her, and she said that she loved me. She lived with two other immigrant City College students in Kensington, both of them young men, one from Turkestan, the other from Slovenia. She'd answered an ad for a roommate on a bulletin board at school. The two boys shared one room, with separate beds, and she had the other. I didn't like to go there, not to that neighborhood, where there wasn't much to do at night, and definitely not to that drably male and peculiar apartment. So we went to my place. We made love on our bed, under the angel, by the wedding dress hung over the mirror, the bureaus and closets still stuffed with Aura's clothes, jewelry, cosmetics, bags, and shoes. Didn't this bother Ana Eva? She said that it didn't, that she thought it was beautiful, that she felt connected to Aura, that she was sure Aura was happy we'd found each other. I promised I would take the dress down and decide what to do with all Aura's stuff after the second anniversary; Ana Eva said that would be fine. I tried to remember to toss the wedding rings on my chain over my shoulder when we made love. She liked to inspect my tattoos, and to ask questions about them. All but one were the result of an impulsive off-my-rocker three-day spree back in late August, done by a young female tattoo artist named Consuelo who worked at a parlor in the Zona Rosa, who always wore a loose-fitting black leather vest over her bare cinnamon-brown skin and blueberry-hued tattoos; the smell of her skin lotions and musky armpits like a pleasurable drug as she leaned over me, working, her long black hair tickling my skin in mesmerizing contrast to the burning-pulsing tattooing needle. She listened to me like a shrink would have, processing my vaguest suggestions into tattoo ideas, the quiet, concise, almost Chinese-sounding patter of her voice drawing those suggestions out of me. I'd already had one tattoo, a now faded one on my upper arm of a Posada skeleton riding a comet that I got in Mexico, in the eighties, when I'd wanted to mark my "rebirth" after the end of a relationship that I barely remembered now. The new tattoos included one on my forearm that read *Natalia 17/1/09*—Natalia was what Aura wanted to name our baby if she was a girl, Bruno if a boy, and I'd decided that she was going to be a girl, that she was going to be Natalia, and that the seventeenth of January, 2009, was going to be her date of birth (now, in bed with Ana Eva, it was only months away); over my heart, the image of a heart cracked in pieces, 25/7/2007 written over it and *Hecho en Mexico* beneath; on my rib cage, a pretty line drawing of Aura in her wedding dress with a guadalupana corona of stars, and our wedding date, *20/8/05*; on a shoulder blade, the sad clown with a dark teardrop falling from his eye and the words, *laugh now, cry later*; and tattooed in tight cursive script, like a necklace beneath my collarbone, these words from "Exequy on his Wife," by Henry King, Bishop of Chichester:

ev'ry Howre a step towards Thee

But you don't really want to die, said Ana Eva.

Sometimes I really did, I think, Ana Eva, until I met you.

I brought my copy of "Exequy on his Wife" to bed and we went over the poem. It gave me a way to talk to Ana Eva about what had happened: Aura's death, my guilt, her mother's blame, how love survives loss and the challenge of how to carry that love forward, and, of course, the language of the poem itself, the expressing of seemingly obvious and eternal grief emotions that probably can't be expressed any better or more truly than they are in that poem, though it was written more than three hundred years ago. This is why we need beauty, to illuminate even what has most broken us, I said, sounding a bit like my old teacher self. Not to help us transcend or transform it into something else, but first and foremost to help us see it. Ana Eva solemnly nodded, the respectful student, and said quietly, Yes, to help us see it.

So take that you fucking Sméagol, you and your Latino straw man marvelous quirkiness of love, go sodomize yourself with your fucking sock puppet, you idiot pendejo!

Ana Eva gaped at me. What had set this off? Why this outburst of ranting only seconds after she'd just been so sympathetic about the poem?

She was frightened. She'd drawn back into a corner of the bed. What's the matter? Was it her? Why was I screaming at her about some Sméagol?

Oh Ana Eva, no, no, it has nothing to do with you. I'm sorry. Something Sméagol, a book critic, wrote. He gave us the evil eye on the subway. He fucking killed Aura, not me.

Oh Paquito, cariño—she lithely crawled toward me over the bed. You didn't kill Aura, nobody did. It was an accident. Ana Eva cradled my head in her hands, while I sank into appalled remorse. I never used to rave like that in front of Aura. With her, I'd held myself, always, to a higher, more self-controlled standard of behavior. Once, very early on in our love, I'd gotten into a fight with an Arab taxi driver who hadn't wanted to take us to Brooklyn, and though he did drive us back to Brooklyn, inside the taxi our argument, a heated trading of insults, had escalated and finally blown up and we'd ended up standing in the pouring rain outside the taxi in the Cadman Plaza exit ready to fistfight, screaming curses at each other, and then the driver ordered Aura and her friend Lola out of the taxi, too, and though I shouted at them to stay inside they obeyed the driver and got out into the rain and Lola ran off into the sparse woods off the exit to hide. The taxi drove off. Aura and I went into the woods to look for Lola, shouting her name, and finally found her crouching like a drenched kitten behind a tree. Lola had run off to hide, she told us, because she'd never witnessed such violent hatred as between that cabdriver and me; she said it had terrified her. Soaking wet, we waited for another cab. Later, Aura said, There's nothing more classless than people who fight with taxi drivers and waiters and workers in stores. My stepfather used to do that and I'm not going to put up with a boyfriend who does. If you ever fight with a taxi driver again, Francisco, I'll leave you, I mean it! I never did again, not once. From then on I was a docile, polite taxi passenger, protesting only when it was occasionally called for, in a respectful and moderate manner. Love does change your behavior, it does force you to aim for a higher standard. You can change. But look at me, raving about Sméagol, raving the way my father used to.

Ana Eva asked me once what Natalia's full name would have been, and I told her, Well, Natalia Goldman. But there'd also been the possibility, I told her, that we were going to use Aura's last name, Estrada, or even my mother's maiden name, Molina. Aura and I had talked about that. The kid was only going to be a quarter Jewish. Why saddle her with the planet's most Jewish-sounding surname?

Why should Natalia go through life always having to put up with wiseass remarks about Goldman Sachs!

I think you should be proud to honor your father by using his name, said Ana Eva.

You do, do you, I said. Well, I don't particularly second that emotion. I had a memory of my father a few years before he died, standing on the plush baby blue carpet at the top of the stairs in our suburban Massachusetts house, and ranting: My dumb fucking father, that stupid Russian peasant, comes into the country and lets them stick him with a fucking Yid name like Goldman. He was a goddamned baker; he could have said, Give me the name Baker. He made pickles, too. You know what? Call me Pickle, why the hell not? Or I'll hang on to the name I already have, thank you very fucking much. But Goldman, no, thank you. Then the genius goes and changes his own *first* name from Moishe to Morton!

I had been stunned. For more than eight decades my father had stewed with resentment over an ugly surname that wasn't his, that had been arbitrarily imposed on him, and he only let this be known after that coma had loosened screws in his brain. That was when I found out that in Russia my grandfather's last name, our family's true last name, had been Malamudovich. I did like that surname much more than Goldman. Why couldn't we have kept it? I agreed with my dad, what was the matter with that dumbfuck Russian peasant? Malamudovich Molina—I liked that even more. If I could do it all over again, I'd call myself Francisco Malamudovich Molina, my true name.

But I can't even say it, said Ana Eva.

Paco M&M, then.

I still like Goldman better, she said. It's like a superhero name. The man who is made of gold.

Yeah? Well, what about Pickleman? The man who is made of pickle.

When I took Ana Eva to Katz's Deli because she'd never had a pastrami sandwich, she agreed to split one. It's like Proust's cookie, I mumbled, taking my first bite. She asked, Who's Proust? What? A pastrami cookie? She didn't even finish her half of the sandwich. I'd begun to measure what Ana Eva said against what Aura had said, or would have. Ana Eva plaintively asked one day, Do I ever say anything funny? I don't, do I? Oh, I wish I knew how to be funny.

The qualities I'd liked best in Ana Eva at first, such as her tranquil disposition, began to irritate me. She had that frankness about sex that I'd noticed in other young women. But her appetite for daily fucking was much greater than Aura's. Aura always had a zillion things on her mind and a zillion things to do. You could make out with Aura in the middle of the day and it would be delicious but it wasn't required to lead directly to fucking. Ana Eva had a methodical approach to existence in which everything else waited patiently in line behind sex, and the lines formed daily. When you made out with her, she quickly grew shivery and hot, and if you put your hand on her breast, or inside her thigh, she'd squirm away like a virginal schoolgirl, and say something like, ¿Qué ha-ces? in the most breathy, girly way, and press her mouth to yours even harder, or else she'd push you away a little and suddenly lift her shirt or her dress off over her head and reach back to snap off her bra, freeing her small pretty breasts with their hard dark nipples big as bumble-bees—that moment always made me catch my breath. She had long, skinny fawnlike legs, and smooth, thin arms, and it seemed as if I was spending half my waking time entangled in those limbs, in their sinuous liveliness, the long shivers and twitches that traveled up and down them. Sometimes she'd come into the apartment, drop right down onto her knees, and unzip me. I began to feel that she had too much sexual hunger and energy for me, that I couldn't keep up, and I began to attribute that to the difference in our ages rather than to a difference in our natures, though it was probably both. One night I told her that I was too tired for sex and just wanted to go to sleep, and she got angry. She didn't just sigh impatiently or hold herself stiffly apart from me in the bed. Her eyes flashed like a knife fighter's, she wanted explanations. It was the first time I'd seen her so demanding. I'm just tired, I repeated. I can't necessarily fuck every night, I said, and maybe I don't even want to. Why did I want her to sleep over, then? What was the point, she asked, if we weren't going to make love?

From that night on I began having resentful sorts of thoughts and feelings about Ana Eva. I grew short with her, and she must have realized that I was often bored. I felt the depression that had more or less constantly accompanied me since Aura died descending again, but now it felt heavier, murkier, with a whole charged atmosphere that went right through my skin and corroded my nerve endings. One evening Ana Eva and I were in the kitchen talking, and I realized someone had left a bottle of poison out on the counter, a bottle that looked like it was mezcal but that held poison, and couldn't have been more clearly marked anyway, with the word *VENENO* and black skulls on it, and I said, This shouldn't be left out on the counter, and I picked up the bottle and put it away in a cabinet. Ana Eva asked, Why are you putting the grapefruit juice away in the cabinet? I heard what she said, realized it was a carton of grapefruit juice as soon as she spoke and that I was indeed putting it away in a cabinet instead of in the refrigerator, but when I looked at her it was as if she were far away and in some other room behind a wall of smoked glass and I said, with a sense of futilely pushing words out into some too gelatinous atmosphere, Because it's poison, Ana Eva. I think that was when they began, those diffuse daytime hallucinations, my eyes open and able to register who and what was around me, my ears hearing what anyone was saying, but somehow I was also dreaming at the same time, dream images spilling into the day like crude oil from a sunken tanker. One night we went to a movie, a story about teenaged runaway lovers. At the end the girl dies, and it's the boy's fault; the girl is in the back of the ambulance, her white dress covered in blood, her soft round cheeks, life slowly fading from her eyes, and I began to shake all over, I was muttering and then almost shouting, No, no! Don't! NO! I stood up and staggered down the aisle, biting the heel of my hand and crying, Ana Eva trailing me, holding on to me though I kept walking, pulling her along, and didn't stop, didn't say a word until finally I found myself sitting alone at the downstairs bar in Rexo with five drained mezcal shots lined up in front of me, staring out the window at Avenida Nuevo Leon, devoid of traffic, green-tinged by the street lamps, four streets feeding into it at different angles, one of Mexico City's deadliest traffic intersections taking the night off, *the haunted intersection*. A few years before, my friend Yunior, visiting from New York, had stood looking across the street at the corner Rexo is on and the grimy curb in front of it and said, Someone died there once, and I'd known instantly that he was right. The adrenaline and panic triggered by the movie's ending had finally drained out of me, replaced by an alcohol-soothed emptiness and a loneliness that felt like forever. I stared through the bar window out at the glowing pavement of the mostly deserted avenue and thought, This is never going to end. But the bar was on Houston Street, not in Mexico, and they were tequila shots and Ana Eva was sitting silently on a bar stool, half asleep, beside me.

A few nights later she woke up in bed as if from a nightmare, clutching her head in her thin brown arms, which looked like tri-angular paper clips. Her breathing was like soft shrieks, and then she was saying, I'm sorry, I can't anymore, I can't sleep next to her wedding dress anymore, and feel her all around me, I can't, I can't, lo intenté pero ya no puedo, *Ayyy, Aura, perdóname!*

When we broke up a week later I told Ana Eva it had nothing to do with her, that she was wonderful but that I just wasn't ready to have a regular lover. But don't you think Aura would want you to be happy? she pleaded. I was mystified that she took it so badly; I thought by now she must be yearning to flee. When she kneeled before the Aura altar and the wedding dress to say good-bye, I recalled Flor, our former cleaning lady. There Ana Eva went on about our "poor dead little love" sounding like a lost child, and she begged Aura to forgive her, said that she'd tried her best to look after me like Aura had asked but that I hadn't let her. Her shoulders shook and shook. Our relationship had lasted almost a month from start to finish.

*   *   *

Later, when I looked it up, I found out that Malamudovich means "son of a scholar," or "learned one." And what did my father learn from his father? And what did I learn from my father?

Aura and I both grew up around parental unhappiness, rage, and, to different degrees, violence. I didn't dwell on it much, but it was something else that gave us a common understanding. We knew what we'd come from and what we were determined to avoid in the life we were making. One evening, when I was twelve, I'd come home from playing football with my friends later than I'd probably been told to. We were supposed to be going to Aunt Sophie's for dinner that night—maybe it was one of the Jewish holidays—and now we were going to be late. My father beat me up inside the front door, at the foot of the stairs; that was the usual treatment when I did something wrong, but this time he kneed me in the back with so much force that I crumpled to the floor and when I tried to get up I couldn't, I was paralyzed from the waist down. In the hospital emergency room, as I lay on the examination table, my legs slowly, tinglingly coming back to life, the doctor, his expression stern, asked how it had happened. It was my father who answered. He said, Frankie got hurt playing football, doctor. I should have spoken up and sent him to jail, or at least gotten him into trouble, but I kept quiet. How I hated him. For years I swore that all I wanted was not to be like him. Nothing could so discourage me, or fill me with more self-contempt, than to feel that rage that fed his tantrums and bullying in me, too. I told myself, insisted, that my temperament was more like my mother's, we were the easygoing ones, putting up with and repressing a lot, essentially sweet-natured people though almost always too passive to speak up for ourselves. We rarely—in my mother's case never—answered back or vocally expressed our anger.

But wasn't anger one of the recognized stages of grief? Where was mine? I'd been lots of things since Aura died, but not angry. What would be an appropriate expression of that anger? Did it even have to be appropriate? When I ranted crazily about Sméagol, was that progress? After I broke up with Ana Eva, I felt a black rage riding shotgun on my shoulder. I stalked around like everybody better watch out. I wanted to hand out celebratory cigars: It's finally here, the anger stage. And I waited for something to happen.

One evening in the gym I came into the locker room after my workout and a guy in a suit, no tie, was standing in front of my locker, talking on his iPhone. His brown-orange hair was still damp from his shower. His polished leather briefcase was on the bench, neatly folded *Financial Times* and *Wall Street Journal* protruding from the side flap. A finance guy, there were a lot of them in my gym and I often overheard them in the locker room complaining and commiserating about their troubles. I took off my sweat-soaked T-shirt. The locker room etiquette was for him to step aside or at least to move his briefcase so that I could sit at my locker. I caught his eye, gestured with the towel in my hand at my locker. He stared at me blankly and kept talking. I waited, staring back at him. He turned slightly away. He seemed pretty involved in his conversation. Finally I said, Could you please move your stuff. And just like that, I saw the motherfucker roll his eyes and sneer as he turned his back on me, still talking into his phone. My hand shot forward and grabbed him by the shoulder and jerked him around—NOOO it didn't; I wish it had, but it didn't. I was shaking with a murderer's pent-up violence, I swear, but he was slipping his phone into his pocket and snatching up his briefcase. He swept past me without even a glance. A few other guys had noticed, and I felt them staring at me and silently laughing, staring at my tattoos—*laughing at me,* while my anger dissolved into humiliation like it was an acid bath. I went and took my shower, and stood under the water a long time.

Meanwhile, I kept on paying Aura's monthly fees at that gym. Couldn't get it together to send in the paperwork: notarized death certificate, et cetera. And that was all—my anger stage fizzled out like a wet firecracker.

Soon Aura's savings would be used up and all my credit cards maxed out. Then what? What should my love and my loss turn into? I found

myself observing homeless people with too much curiosity and interest, the way I'd once observed famous and even published writers
when I was in my late teens and early twenties—though not quite
in the same way. I remembered being a college freshman, sitting in
an upstate New York motel room with Ken Kesey, reaching out in
awed disbelief to take the shocking pink joint he was passing me in
his huge fingers. Earlier that night I'd been told that Ken Kesey had
signaled me out in the audience from the stage during his reading,
turning to the creative-writing student, a senior poet who'd been
awarded the honor of introducing him, to ask her, Who's that curly-
head cherub? I bet all the girls like to mother him. That's what Ken
Kesey had said about me. Curly-head cherub, who all the girls like
to mother. Impressed, the poet had invited me along with some
other writing students to escort Ken Kesey back to his motel. He
must have wondered why I didn't say anything, why I just sat on
the edge of the bed, sharing his pot, staring, laughing whenever the
others laughed, looking away whenever he looked at me; or maybe
he didn't wonder. Where is my homeless mentor, who will single
me out on the sidewalk or a crowded subway car to say, Who's that
curly-head loser? If he doesn't get his shit together, he's on his way
down here fast. Dude think he's the only one who's ever lost a wife?

According to the grief books, those written by psychoanalysts anyway, the mourner's dreams should divulge the inevitable if slow
process of his or her detachment from the Lost Object. In one case
study that I read, when a middle-aged widower, after a long and
difficult mourning, had a dream about a little smudge of excrement
on a piece of white cloth, his psychoanalyst interpreted it as a sign
that he'd made important progress. As much as the widower loved
his wife, he was putting death and loss in its appropriate place. He
was ready to reengage with life, to love again. One night I dreamed
that Aura had left me. I was alone in a very messy but large apartment that wasn't ours. Then Aura came in through the door. She
was sad, heartbroken, because she'd fallen in love with a hippie

puppeteer from Spain and run off with him to Vermont but now the Spaniard had rejected her. Please come back to me, I pleaded. You know we love each other. Her eyes didn't even register my presence. She lay on a divan, looking disheveled, wan, and kind of wobbly headed but most of all distant and preoccupied. Finally she got up to leave. She didn't even say good-bye. So listlessly, she walked across that debris-strewn floor to the door. She was halfway out the door. I was never going to see her again. But I ran to her and caught her by the arm and pulled her back inside. Next thing I knew, Aura and I were madly kissing and saying mi amor, mi amor, and in the dream I knew I'd cheated destiny and won her back, and oh, we were both so happy.

Then it was the second New Year's Eve. Deep in the lost jungle city of *Soobway*, Aura's belly was growing huge, the kicking coming night and day, Natalia's birth only seventeen days away. In the lost city, I'd accepted that tenured high-paying teaching job at a mediocre northeastern university that I'd been offered that last spring—one hundred and sixty-five grand a year. A heavy workload, there wouldn't be much time for writing, but that was okay while Natalia was a baby and Aura was finishing her first novel. Save money. In a few years, maybe we'd move to Mexico.

I'd spent the first New Year's Eve without Aura in Berlin, with Moya and his German wife, Kirsten, in a Vietnamese restaurant with a bright orange plastic-seeming interior that we'd stopped into because soon it would be midnight. We'd been walking awhile—earlier, in their apartment, we'd drank a bottle of prosecco called Bella Aura that I'd discovered in a supermarket—and hadn't found anywhere else to pass New Year's Eve. We ordered food and a bottle of champagne. The restaurant owners and their relatives were out on the sidewalk with some of their employees, who were stringing firecrackers onto a stepladder. In the streets of Berlin New Year's Eve is celebrated like

a holiday about war, or else as a sort of exorcism of war, with firecrackers, exploding rockets, small bombs going off all over the city,
groups of youth crouched with fingers in their ears behind mortar
tubes on every dark street corner, the smell of explosives saturating
the cold air. As the countdown drew near, I told Moya and Kirsten,
This won't mean anything to me, the only date that marks the passing of the years for me now is July 25. But when Moya and Kirsten
got up to stand by the door with their champagne glasses to watch
the fireworks and celebrate the stroke of midnight with the other
customers and restaurant staff, I followed. Aura and I had spent four
New Year's together; only four. When midnight came it hit me hard
anyway and after I'd embraced Moya and Kirsten, I moved away
down the sidewalk into the shadows to be by myself. We'd spent
New Year's Eve in Paris a few years before, when we'd rented an
apartment in the fifteenth *arrondissement* for a month. Gonzalo and
Pia, friends from Mexico who'd moved to Paris, invited us to dinner
at their apartment in Montmartre. They had small children and so
did Gonzalo's brother and his wife, who were visiting. It was one of
those dinners where half the adults are always away from the table
tending to children, but the children are also the entertainment. I
played Super Mario and had a sword fight with little Jero. It was a
low-key but pleasant, married couples' New Year's Eve. Aura and I
left before one in the morning and decided to walk down through
Pigalle, with its seedy bars and clubs. We stopped into one with
steamed-up windows and a small cover charge where a live African
band was playing. The place was packed with Africans and Europe-
ans, and nearly everybody was dancing. The band was great, with
pedal steel and electric guitars, talking drums, and a saxophone,
and the lead guitarist-singer was a dynamo. We danced there until
dawn, when the band finally stopped playing and the crowd began
to thin. Out on the sidewalk, sweaty and exhilarated, squinting
against the stony glinting light of a Paris winter morning, we decided
to walk instead of taking the metro. We walked all the way to the
Luxembourg Gardens to see the statues of the queens and Babar's
castle, and then into the streets around the Sorbonne, and we went

and looked at the old apartment building across the street from a small medieval church where Aura had shared an apartment with two Japanese girls in the summer of 2001, when she was studying French. We found a place open for breakfast, had perfect omelets and *pommes frites* and champagne, and afterward took the Metro back to La Motte-Picquet–Grenelle. So had begun 2005.

Now it was going to be 2009. I was meeting Lola and her fiancé Bernie Chen at a bar on Ludlow Street at two in the morning. They'd come into the city from New Haven to watch the ball drop in Times Square. I don't know why they wanted to do that. I'd been drinking alone at home, watching college football. Maybe it was because I was already a little drunk that shortly after midnight I decided to head out to a neighborhood bar for a drink or two before I had to catch the subway into Manhattan. In honor of the holiday, and of seeing Lola and Bernie, I put on my suit. The suit had been made for me by an elderly Mexico City tailor a week or two after Aura's death, a tailor recommended by a friend's girlfriend who worked in the government, who said he made suits for her bosses. I wanted a raven-black mourning suit, of coarse, heavy cloth, which I imagined myself wearing every day for at least a year. The elderly tailor who came to our Escandón apartment—this was several weeks before I was forced to leave it—to measure me was an elegant grandfatherly man with kind, lively eyes in his drooping age-mottled face, who in his suit lapel wore a small round sponge with pins stuck into it. He told me that he didn't believe Aura would want to see me going around all the time in a black mourning suit. Gesturing at the photographs of Aura all over the apartment now, the tailor said, I can see from her eyes and her smile that your wife was full of life, Francisco, and I know she wouldn't want you to drag yourself down like that, showing such a heavy sadness to the world. Can I recommend a charcoal-gray wool? It's dignified, but it has some lightness to it. And he opened his book of fabric samples.

When I reached the bar on Ludlow Street, Lola and Bernie were already there. I was cold because all I was wearing was my suit over a sweatshirt, and my hat, the same Chinatown hat with earflaps that had made it all the way through the first winter. The bar was full of people standing, but Lola and Bernie had a table, which seemed lucky, a good way to start the year. Lola was only drinking bottled water and Bruce had a vodka tonic. Lola and I hugged tightly and when we parted she blinked her eyes a little and said, There's so much that I need to talk to Aura about, sometimes I think I can just phone her and then I can't believe it, that I can't. Me, too, I said. But I had a hard time following the conversation. Maybe they were mostly talking to each other, but no, they were looking at me; in fact, Lola was telling me a story about Aura and her mother. Spread over part of the tabletop was a garland of seaweed intertwined with oatmeal and splatters of raspberry jam. It looked like a flattened octopus. First I tried to lift it off between two fingers but I couldn't and then I took a napkin to try to wipe it off, but when the napkin touched the tabletop, there was nothing there. I wasn't sure if they'd noticed. Lola was telling me about the day they'd had to hand in their applications for Mexican government, foreign-graduate-school scholarships. Juanita drove Aura and Lola to the building where, inside, students were waiting in long lines to hand in their applications, but because they were with Aura's mom, they didn't have to wait; Juanita led them right to the front. Lola remembered the resentful stares of the other students and how mortified Aura was. Afterward, in the car, Aura wept like a child: she didn't want to take the scholarship exam, she was exhausted from studying and working on her master's thesis, she needed a break from what felt like years of unbroken pressure and studying. So Aura had ended up not taking the exam that time, which was why Lola had left for graduate school a year before Aura.

They had news. Not only were they getting married that summer, in Bernie's home state of Hawaii, but Lola was pregnant. The baby would be born before the wedding. Lola was beanpole skinny, but when she stood up and pulled her sweater taut, you could see the bump, like a small round pumpkin. They already knew that the baby was going to be a girl. That's why they'd especially wanted to see me. They wanted to name their daughter Aura, but only if I was okay with it. Was I okay with their naming their baby girl Aura? Oh, Lola, Bernie, of course I'm okay with that, much more than okay with that, this is the most wonderful news! I really did feel moved, it wasn't just a pretext for ordering another bottle of champagne, even if I ended up pretty much drinking the whole bottle myself. Incredible how many of Aura's friends were having babies, just around when we were having Natalia! Lola, Valentina, and the wife of Aura's friend Arturo from Austin who also lived here in New York now, and two other couples we knew in Mexico, all pregnant!

Lola and Bernie were taking a taxi to Penn Station to catch a train to New Haven. I decided that instead of a taxi I'd take the F train home, and so I got into the taxi with them, and got out at West Fourth Street. Bye! I love you! Congratulations. Happy New Year! Next year we'll celebrate with baby Aura! I remember heading toward a side street, thinking there might be a bar still open a block away. I heard a bang, like a small bomb going off by my left ear, a car door slammed with more force than I'd ever heard a door slammed before, echoing up and down the street and making everyone in the stalled traffic jump in their seats, including us in the car that Juanita was driving, Aura in front, me in the back, and we saw the strapping young man who'd just slammed that door stalking rapidly down the sidewalk away from the car, which was in a driveway, the shadowy figure of a young woman behind the wheel, and the young man was weeping—the woman in the car must have just shattered his heart—and through her lowered window Juanita loudly jeered at him, *Ay, no llores (no YOHHH-res)*, Aww, don't cry.

I woke up to a man cutting my suit jacket off of me with what
looked like gardening shears. They were pulling up my sweatshirt,
clapping monitors to my chest. The metallic sheen of an ambulance
roof. I was in an ambulance, following you, mi amor . . . My hat!
Did I leave it in the bar? Shit! Where's my hat? I asked, but no one
answered. Then I was being wheeled on a gurney through a cascade
of fabulous light, like sugar falling through a hole in the night sky,
into the dark cavelike opening at the back of a hospital and into a
grungy reception area. A policeman. People stood over me talking,
asking questions, and then I must have faded out again. Then I
was in an elevator, alone with a tall black man dressed all in white.
What's going on? I was being taken down for another CAT scan.
Another CAT scan? The second one, yes. Am I going to be okay?
And the man in white answered, You might die, sir. Just like that,
in a deep stern voice. You might die, sir. Oh, I thought. Okay, mi
amor, you see? I *am* following you, está bien. The elevator opened
and he wheeled me out. Resignación, señor, resignación. Hell-Ha,
mi amor. So this is what the spider has been spinning. It's okay.
This is all absolutely a-okay. Here we go, down into the true velvet
underground, it's really not so cold in Alaska. You have no idea
how much I've missed you. Oh, every second, a step toward Thee.

17

We'd rented a huge house in San Miguel de Allende so that Juanita and Rodrigo and some of our friends could stay with us the week of the wedding. But Tuesday night I left on a bus for Mexico City, because I had to be there at eleven the next morning to pick up my foreigner's permit to marry a Mexican in Mexico. I sat at the front, to watch the landscape. The bus was a ways out of San Miguel when I pulled the manila envelope out of my backpack to look over the paperwork, my duplicate copies of the submitted application forms, birth and health certificates, and so on. That's when I realized that I'd left my passport in San Miguel, at the house. Without the passport, they wouldn't give me the permit. And I would need the permit back in San Miguel on Thursday for our license to marry in the state, and to procure a justice of the peace to perform the wedding. By Thursday night guests would already be arriving, some from as far as Europe. The wedding was on Saturday. The rehearsal dinner and prewedding cocktail party was on Friday. But if I didn't have my passport with me tomorrow morning in Mexico City, there wasn't going to be a wedding. Aura was at the house in San Miguel and I phoned her, and she quickly found the passport. One of the wedding planners was with her, and she hatched a plan. I went and knocked at the door of the bus driver's booth. The door opened and I spoke to him over his shoulder as he drove. I explained the situation, and that my wedding was at stake. By now we were at least twenty minutes out of San Miguel. He said all right, he'd drive in the right-hand lane as slowly as he reasonably could to give the wedding planner's driver a chance to catch us. If he hadn't caught us when we reached the busy multilane toll highway at Querétaro, it would be too late.

The wedding planner's assistant was driving a black SUV. I sat in my seat, eyes riveted to the right-side passing mirror, in which was framed the narrow highway behind us and some of the arid landscape. Traffic was light and I could see the headlights of trucks and cars pursuing us at varying speeds, slowly overtaking us. In the mirror, the darkening light began to dissolve the highway's pavement, the sky filled with towers of blue-black clouds, and the horizon resembled evening over a wintry ocean just after sunset. I looked at the clock on my phone. Nearly forty-five minutes had passed. What was I going to do if the wedding was canceled on account of my carelessness? Why did Aura and I always have so much trouble with official papers and documents, lost and forgotten passports, the U.S. student visa she hadn't realized was expired until she was at the airport counter in Paris? Would our lives have turned out differently if we were the types of people who never lost anything, who always had their papers in order? Mishap is the mother of comedy. Those days of waiting in line at the Cancún passport office, laughing and chattering away while we were supposed to be at the beach in Tulum, without a moment of exasperation or recrimination between us, had revealed as much to us about the character of our young love as sex, probably even more. Mishap is the father of displacement: unexpected journeys and detours, lost and shamed wanderings in the desert, but also providential visions, like when that black dot with headlights appeared in the mirror on the crest of the dark horizon. I tried to judge the speed of its approach. It was coming fast, like an airborne object.

Mishap: mother-father of death: yours, then nearly mine. The first two CAT scans had revealed a spot of blood on my brain. If the spot grew, it would mean I was hemorrhaging, and then I might die, sir. Two dark spots on the horizon, one growing, and the other, well, until the next CAT scan they wouldn't know.

There were already signs for Querétaro and the toll highway. My cell phone rang. It was the wedding planner's assistant. Is that you? He blinked his headlights on and off. Yes! I knocked on the bus driver's booth, told him, thanked him profusely. The bus decelerated to a stop in the break-down lane. Space shuttle dockings in outer space. The doors opened, I bounded down the steps into the open air, breathing in sagebrush and manure and diesel fuel beneath the first stars in the gravity-less purplish sky. The black SUV pulling in behind us in a festive spray of pebbles, the passenger door opening and Aura stepping out with my passport in her hand; I was lost and now I'm found, that funny, slightly stiff-legged run of hers, like a ballerina running off the stage; an embrace by the highway, Ay, Francisco ¿qué te pasa? Don't you want to marry me? Francisco, you better stay out of the cantinas and away from those cocainómano friends of yours. I will, I promise! The rescued bridegroom climbed back onto the bus waving his passport and the passengers broke into applause. ¡Viva México, cabrones!

I opened my eyes and found Gus—Augusta—my first wife, sitting in a chair beside me in the emergency ward. We'd gotten married when she was twenty and I was twenty-four, back when she was putting herself through Columbia by dealing coke to students at Cannon's Pub. I went off to Central America to work as a journalist during our second year of marriage, and that was basically the end of that. Now she was my closest friend, more like family than anyone in my actual family. I'd given her phone number when they brought me into the hospital, though I had no memory of that, and they'd phoned her at five in the morning. She'd been asleep for not even three hours, and was still a little drunk. Her husband had driven her in from Brooklyn, and then he'd driven home to go back to bed. She had bags under her bleary blue eyes, her chestnut hair was a tousled mess. The emergency ward was packed: New Year's Eve was St. Vincent's second busiest night of the year, after Halloween. On one side of me was a beefy guy with an Eastern European accent who'd fallen through a store window, the big panes of shattering glass slicing deeply into his back, arms, and thighs. His girlfriend was crying into her hands and he kept shouting at her to stop. On my other side was a long pale transvestite with smeared, sky-blue eye shadow and a Southern accent who'd tried to commit suicide with an overdose of pills. He was better now and wouldn't shut up, launching into his life story almost as soon as he noticed I was awake, how he'd run away from home when he was thirteen and come to New York. He was a drag performer, and when he told Gus she looked butch, she told him to fuck off. My head was caked with mostly dry blood but I was still bleeding from my left ear. Gus kept yelling at nurses to clean me off whenever they rushed by, but they said there were more urgent cases. I asked Gus what had happened to me, and she said nobody was sure. Maybe someone had attacked me with a metal pipe or a hammer, or maybe I'd been hit by a car and fallen on my head. Anyway, I'd been found unconscious in the street, lying by the curb. My ear was a mangled, pulpy mess, though the most serious wound was in the back of my skull. Also, I had three broken ribs. The police, Gus said, had asked her if I had any enemies.

Enemies? I took that in. Mishap: mother-father of death, but also of shameless melodrama. Did you tell them about Aura's uncle and mother? I asked, sort of joking. It wasn't conceivable that Leopoldo could have hired someone to trail me from a bar on Ludlow Street to the West Village. The next time I woke up I was somewhere else; I'd been wheeled into a corridor. Gus was still with me. I told her to go home but she said she wouldn't until I was in a room and they'd cleaned me up and dressed my ear. They were taking me down for another CAT scan soon. I was going to have to stay in the hospital, even though I no longer had insurance.

What's wrong with my ear? Is it going to be deformed?

It looks really bad. I'm sorry.

I touched it, felt its throbbing stickiness.

Not Leopoldo. Who else might actually try to harm me? I thought of the last journalism book I'd done, about a murder: Mono de Oro, Tito, and their homo assassin chafas, la pareja diabólica, no worse enemies than those, but trail me from a Lower East Side bar on New Year's Eve to run me over or whack me in the head?

Gus, did I tell you that I lost my hat? Can you believe it?

Later that morning they moved me from the corridor to a room. Gus went home to sleep, promising to come back in the afternoon, though I told her she didn't have to. I was sharing the room with another patient, hidden from view by the drawn curtain. The little sink was wedged between the bed and in the closet was my shredded tailored suit in a plastic bag on the floor. The aluminum rails around the bed, the monitors. Why was I hooked up to an IV, what were they giving me? The silent television mounted high in the wall. Plastic wristband. Oh, the memories—hello, Dad. A glimpse of New York City brick and a wintry sky outside the window. This was the hospital where the AIDS pandemic had first hit in New York, where it raged for years; how many young and not so young men had died in this same room, on this same bed? A memory of seeing black balloons rising over West Village rooftops, and knowing why. Memories of my first years in New York, when I used to work in restaurants, usually as a busboy, faces and voices of waiters but only a few names not forgotten now, Sandy, Gino, their lewd dirty talk and teasing, sometimes hilarious, sometimes disturbing; Danny, who used to sneak up behind me at the busboy station to sing into my ear, Whatever Lola wants, Lola gets . . . All those dead waiters, how many of them had died in this very hospital?

They'd stitched the back of my head with a staple gun and it seemed my ear was going to heal into an ugly clump. A small team of robed doctors came in to see me. The spot on my brain hadn't grown, one of the doctors told me. I was very fortunate not to have hemorrhaged. I had a severe concussion. They wanted to keep me under observation for a couple of nights. That weirdly pleasurable ache in my side was my broken ribs. When I woke up again late in the afternoon Gus was back. Guess what, she said. You were hit by a car, a hit and run. A teenaged girl from the Bronx. The teenaged girl confessed to her father because she thought she'd killed you and he made her phone the police.

I mulled this new information. Then I said, I remember now. A car, yeah. It drove onto the beach, around this big sand dune. I stared at Gus with that now familiar sense of being mystified by my own words even as I spoke them. The car came right at me, I said, over the sand, really fast. Gus stared at me, lips parted. I shut my eyes. Where was Aura in this scene? I wasn't making any sense. That tall dune, the parking lot behind it, that was a Cape Cod beach I used to go to as a teenager.

Well, I don't think so, said Gus, because you were hit by a car right off Sixth Avenue. No sand dunes around there that I've ever seen.

I didn't remember anything about it. Someone had found me lying there and phoned 911. In my hospital room later that same day, or maybe it was the next day, Gus told me a story about coming over to the house I'd rented in San Miguel on the afternoon after the wedding. Aura, hungover, had retreated into the cool shadows of our bedroom, and was lying facedown on the bed. I was outside, in the garden, with friends. We were driving back to Mexico City that afternoon, and then the next day Aura and I were flying to the Pacific coast for our honeymoon. Gus was in the living room with Juanita and some others. Aura's wedding dress was draped over a sofa. Juanita picked up the dress and held it in her arms; with one hand she lifted the ripped, mud-splattered, danced-on ruffled skirt hem to look at it more closely, and she smiled to herself. It was *such* a lovely smile, said Gus.

When I was released from the hospital the woman in the administration office told me that my hospital bills would be paid by the insurance of the girl who'd hit me. She gave me forms to fill out. She said that I ought to be able to get some money for myself out of this, too, and told me what to do. It won't be much, prob- ably, she added, but something. Seems you were pretty inebriated yourself, she said. I would have to come back in about a week for an MRI, and then to get my stitches out. If I felt nausea or had a severe headache or had double vision or trouble walking, I was to go straight to an emergency room. Gus and her husband drove me home. I felt woozy for days, weak in the knees, my insides a trembling gelatin. I felt fucking *old*. In the hospital they'd given me stuff to treat my ear: disinfectant, creams, cotton, gauze, tape. A weird clear liquid, as if from a runny nose, constantly dripped from the ear. I went home and lay on the bed, near Aura's wedding dress, and kept the heavy beige curtains drawn. The stillness and silence in that room, those long days, the crepuscular light. I read some in the books on death and grief that I'd been amassing for over a year. I thought about the peaceful sensation that had filled me when the orderly in the elevator said, You might die, sir; that sense of following Aura down a dark velvety tunnel. Well, I didn't die, didn't follow. In the evenings I turned on the television. I got up from the bed a couple of times a day and went into the bathroom to wash my ear and replace the gauze bandage covering it. In the morning I went outside to buy coffee and the newspaper, walking slowly, like a decrepit old man. But after a few days I no longer felt so trembly when I walked. I did a little bit of work. Ordered takeout. When I took a shower, I used Aura's tea-tree mint treatment shampoo.

18

As she listened to the professor, her legs im[*handwriting unintelligible*] opened, her body thrust downward, like a sinking ship.

In a warm mid-September day, as she listened to her professor read in a perfect Cuban-Spanish accent the words of Nobel winner poet Pablo Neruda, her mind easily wandered the abysses of the white page she had in her lap. Having arrived late, she had been confined, not unhappily, to one of the corners of the non-air-conditioned room—until the feeling of an intent look forced her to lift her head. Her involuntary head movement coincided with the end of Neruda's poem. What she found upon lifting her head should have warned her of what was to come, but at the moment, not knowing what the older girls knew (she thought she must be mistaken) it could not be that the professor's green eyes made bigger by magnified seeing glasses were locked on her bossom. It simply could not be. Not in front of the whole class, not while reading Neruda (oh, but specially because of reading Neruda). Not only did the professor's eyes remain fixed there or so it appeared to Guadalupe's (wild) imagination—but he even dared to ask her a question: ¿Qué piensas del poema Guadalupe? Before she could answer the professor was already unpassionately engaged in a diatribe against Neruda and his "corny poetry." "Neruda," he said, "no lo vamos a leer, clase, porque no me gusta." Guadalupe thought this sudden censorship rather odd for a graduate level course and the same question that had been haunting her since she set foot in JFK's famous airport popped into her head like a popcorn in a microwave (the head being the popcorn, the classroom the microwave): what am I doing here? Why did I come here? Who am I here? Okay, so it was not just one question haunting her, but three, or, rather, that first question unfolded like a paper Chinese fan—other questions, all part of the same bucolic, enigmatic scene in red, white, or black. Then she thought of her mother. "Yes, my mother," she answered to an imaginary judge in an imaginary trial of the Academic Law of Justice System. She also pictured the judge—a sort of blurry Derrida-Lyotard-Foucault triad—heartily, heavily, unheartily, laughing . . . Followed by the judges, the person who tapes trials (the trial-taper?), the audience (all wearing glasses, painstakingly taking notes of what not to answer, of how not to be) laughing at her. "Laughing at me."[4]

---

[4] An uncorrected fragment, handwritten on yellow legal paper, with many cross-outs, scribbles, and corrections, found among Aura's papers. It's from her first semester at Columbia, when her English was still rusty.

19

The professor who didn't like Neruda did like words of his own coinage, such as "foota nota." In class, he'd say, As it says in the *foota nota*... Aura told me that she'd cringed and looked over at Valentina, who'd rolled her eyes: the first spark of friendship had passed between them. In Spanish lit and Cultural and Latino studies departments all over the country, clever academics were dissing Neruda, or whomever, and dazzling their students with Spanglish witticisms like foota nota. Behind his back, his students called this professor Mi Verguita. (*Ver-gee-tah*) My Little Penis. Mi Verguita discovered references to phalluses in every text, and was always guiding his class into discussions of phallic subjects and contexts that often included the amusing or strained references to his own "privileged signifier" that had earned him his nickname. But Mi Verguita had also published some fiction, and displayed in his office a flyer for a reading he'd once given in a Barnes & Noble; thus, at least some of the other professors in the department despised him, and were conspiring against him.

Mi Verguita lived with his wife and children in Boston and traveled to New York every week to give his classes. Aura took a class with Mi Verguita—the one in which he trashed Neruda and unveiled foota nota—during her first semester at Columbia. At first the class was held in a seminar room but then they met in the evenings in Mi Verguita's university-supplied apartment. He always brought a gallon jug of red Chilean wine to those classes, and often rum as well. After class, Mi Verguita would put on music—from the Spanish Caribbean, mostly—and encourage his students to dance. Soon he was especially focusing his attentions on a shy, pretty, usually conservatively dressed student who'd come to study at Columbia directly from Bogotá, Colombia—a young woman, it so happened, who was married to a civil engineer who'd put his own career on hold to accompany his wife to New York so that she could earn an Ivy League PhD, and who now worked downtown in a computer repair shop. She was dazzled by Mi Verguita; who knows what he whispered in her ear when they danced after class, but it always made her lift her chin and look into his eyes, smiling and biting her plump lower lip like a rabbit with a secret. One afternoon Aura sent me an e-mail from Columbia with the news that Mi Verguita had been suspended. Supposedly the student's husband, after his wife hadn't come home after class, had gone to the acting department head to accuse the professor of having seduced his wife after plying her with drink. Within days Aura and her classmates found themselves at the heart of an Academic Law of Justice System sexual harassment investigation.

Mi Verguita was the last, or maybe next to last, full-time Latin-American literature professor in the department. Professors who still taught novels and poetry in their classes were being forced out. Specialists in critical theory and cultural studies were taking over. Aura had unwittingly enrolled in a department where a purge was under way. The department was finally, belatedly, modernizing, bringing itself in line with other cutting-edge programs around the country. Where was it written that every department that taught Spanish owed a special allegiance to fiction and poetry? What percentages of the world's native Spanish-speakers had ever read a novel or were even literate enough to read one?

At the end of her second year at Columbia, on May 29, 2005, Aura wrote in her notebook:

I do not wish to be an academic.

I wish to be me. I am not me when I am an academic. I am not an academic nor will I ever be. La imaginación/las imágenes se avalanzan en una corriente de descarga poderosa una vez fuera del tanque que es/se ha vuelto/la Universidad. Casa Pánica. Las restricciones que no se entiende a si mismo. No confía en si mismo. Hay mejores maneras de la desconfianza que la auto referencia pedestre y estéril. Mi vida está en otra parte.[5]

Why NYC?

I want to stay. [Here Aura drew eight floating hearts]

Clarice L'Inspector.

A short story collection. Variaciones sobre la verguenza. [Variations on shame, or embarrassment; *verguenza* can be translated either way. Aura listed five short stories she'd either already written or planned to write.]

I wish to kill my TV.

I wish I did not have one.

I do not need a TV.

I don't know how to begin the summer. Maybe I'll never write great literature. It's enough to write. And write.

An X-ray of my early childhood.

NO ESCRIBIR CON ESPERANZA NI DESESPER-ANZA, SÓLO CON ESMERO. [Write with neither hope nor hopelessness, only with great dedication.]

---

[5] The imagination/the images that pour out on a powerful current once outside the tank/that the University/ has become. Casa Pánica. Restrictions that they themselves don't understand. That they don't believe in themselves. There are more interesting forms of doubt than the pedestrian and sterile self-referential. My life is elsewhere.

Among Aura's papers I found her marked-up photocopy of Foucault's canonical essay "What Is an Author?" Out of curiosity, I read it. I haven't read much critical theory. As I understood it, according to Foucault, this is how we should now regard "the author": as just a name that is useful for classifying texts, for marking some books off from other books. It was easy to imagine Aura finding that a pretty funny Borgesian idea. Did her professor and classmates parse this essay as solemnly as they had Pierre Menard? I don't know. The essay seemed to me like a dazzling web woven by an insane genius spider. I read to the part where Foucault cites Saint Jerome's contention that even an author's name has no credibility as an individual trademark, because different individuals could have the same name, or someone could write under someone else's name, and so on. Foucault then asks, "How then can we attribute several discourses to one and the same author?" The weary student glances ahead at the next several pages of dense text. Foucault's answer is going to take a while. The afternoon light is fading. Aura has been at this a couple of hours. She asks herself, Wouldn't I rather be reading *The Portrait of a Lady*? Isn't that basically her problem, maybe her biggest problem in life *right now*? Wonder what's for dinner . . . wild salmon?

In her class on critical theory, taught by the new acting department head, a California Chicano whose name was Charly García, same as the Argentine rock star, each student was required to give an in-class presentation on a contemporary theorist. Aura chose Gayatri Spivak, the reigning luminary of Columbia's comparative literature department, whose class Aura had taken during her first year. In her presentation Aura explained the development of Spivak's ideas from her famous translation and preface of Derrida's *De La Grammatologie*, through her seminal text, "Can the Subaltern Speak?"—in which the self-referential gesture, said Aura, is taken to its ultimate consequences—up to her most recent work at the time, *Death of a Discipline*.

Then Aura got to her main point, the reason she'd chosen

Spivak for her presentation. She put the following question before the class:

What is the role of literature in this theoretical scheme?

And she answered:

In fact, a predominant one. Spivak doesn't abandon the study and criticism of literary texts, said Aura, and she went on to explain a few of Spivak's ideas about the importance of literature. One of those is that literature, books, permit a kind of teaching that is *unique* and *unverifiable*. The unverifiable aspect of literature is key here, said Aura, because, for Spivak, it's what distinguishes literary discourse from all other humanistic discourses. Then she dutifully went on to describe some of the criticisms of Spivak. How could Spivak be the leading exponent of Subaltern theory and still defend literature, which can't even attempt to represent the voiceless marginal Other, the Subaltern, without committing an act of colonization? Spivak, Aura said, is not afraid of contradictions.

Charly García complimented Aura on the presentation, but said he disagreed with Spivak's attitude toward the literary text. I just don't understand it, he said, emphatically bouncing his fists off his lap. I just don't understand how Spivak can still defend the literary text.

Aura's thesis was going to be on some of the young writers and artists who'd emerged in Mexico in the nineties and just after, with the fall of the PRI. I remember seeing her at her computer, into her fifth or sixth draft. She looked up and wailed, I used to write so beautifully, and now I'm forgetting how! Look what they're making me do! By beautifully Aura partly meant in the style of criticism and essays published in the kinds of journals she liked to read, the *London Review of Books*, say. Now she had to write a jargonized political and economic analysis of the fall of the PRI.

Students who weren't up to the exacting standards of the new regime were being expelled. One of the first to go was Moira, Aura's friend-nemesis from her first weeks at Columbia. Aura convinced herself that she was next. At home, it was almost all she talked about. She had insomnia almost nightly. Why did Aura make this so hard for herself, choosing for her thesis adviser the brilliant Uruguayan Marxist literary theoretician and taskmaster Pilar Segura? Because the Uruguayan was the department's new star hire, the professor that hotshot students clamored to work with, and Aura was competitive. In the fall of 2005—we'd been married that summer—during one of their thesis meetings, the Uruguayan said, Oh, Aura, really, you are still so innocent. We have to get rid of this naive love you have for the literary text.

The love of literature isn't innocent or naive, thought my wife. Anyway, is the love of Marxist theory less naive?

Aura decided to apply to a City College MFA in Creative Writing program. She hardly ever showed her writing to anyone but me, and sometimes to Lola, but somehow her thesis adviser's condescension gave her the courage to expose herself to the judgment of whoever it was at the MFA program who decided which writing students to accept. We got to work translating three of her short stories for the application. It had to be top secret: her Columbia scholarship required a full-time commitment; studying at any other institution simultaneously was forbidden. I know plenty of people around the world who disdain younger American writers who enroll in MFA programs for taking such a safe, conventional, even bureaucratic path to a writing career that usually, in the best cases, is actually a creative writing *teaching* career. Aura's choice was maybe the bravest of her life. Even by just applying, she was putting her PhD at risk. She was terrified of rejection, even of criticism, of exposing her dream of a writing career to the test of her talent and determination. She wasn't going to tell her mother—not yet—she didn't need any more stress, wasn't she already enough of a nervous wreck? So that she could relax while putting her application together, I took her to Mohonk for the weekend, a place she loved. Mohonk Mountain House is a huge rambling Victorian castle in the Hudson Valley that felt like the perfect setting for a Gothic horror movie or an Agatha Christie murder mystery. Aura made me take pictures of her lying sprawled like a murder victim in the long, door-lined corridor. Then she photographed me playing dead in the corridor. They had a spa; she had massages. There was a big outdoor Jacuzzi where you sat in the churning water, steam billowing off you in the chilly November air. Hiking trails. The clientele was mainly middle-class families, plus quite a few elderly, and scattered younger couples. If you wanted, you could just sit around playing board games all afternoon, drinking hot cider or hot chocolate, eating freshly baked cookies and pumpkin pie. Big plush armchairs and couches in front of stone fireplaces with fires perfect for roasting a stag. We sat together in front of the fire, computers on our laps, translating her most recent story, "*Un secreto a voces*."

Three months later, in March, she received an e-mail from a writer—an actual Famous Irish Writer—who taught in the MFA program. He told her that he liked her stories but that he needed to speak to her. Could she come into the college for a "chat"? An appointment was made for later in the week. Over the ensuing days, this impending chat dominated our conversations. Were they going to accept her or not? Why would the FIW waste his time by asking her to come in for a meeting if he didn't want to accept her into the program? Maybe, I said, he just needs to know about your visa status. But Aura anguished, she was sure something was wrong, maybe they also had a rule against studying in two places at once. When she went to the college the FIW was waiting for her in his office, and so was the older, even more Famous Australian Writer who directed the program. The two were friends, and they'd obviously discussed Aura. They asked her some questions about herself, and she answered. No problem with her studying at Columbia at the same time, they told her. They had a different, well, not a problem, a concern. The stories she'd submitted were impressive, but they were translations, and it seemed she hadn't even done the translations herself—at the end of each story, she'd typed, *Translated by Aura with some help from her friends*. But the program was conducted entirely in English. They were now satisfied that she could converse in English, but could she write in English? To be in the program, she would have to. They gave her twenty-four hours to write an autobiographical statement in English of no fewer than six hundred words explaining why she wanted to enroll in the creative writing program. She went home and did it. A few days later the FIW phoned again, this time to tell her that she was accepted. For another week she heard nothing else. Shouldn't there be an official letter? Maybe the FIW had spoken before consulting with the FAW, who didn't agree. Oh, Aura, I said, you're accepted, just send them an e-mail and ask. She did. A few days later, the FAW answered, "Dear Aura, Everything is okay. You are in. You have been accepted into the MFA program. You will receive a letter on letterhead, but this is the REAL LETTER. We are proud and happy to have you." That evening we met downtown for oysters at a small French restaurant with a zinc bar. We split a bottle of champagne, and then went to see a movie with Valentina and Jim in the Village. Afterward Aura pulled me to a near stop on the sidewalk so that Jim and Valentina would walk ahead of us. She wanted me to take a good look at Jim's walk. Was that a prosthetic left leg limp? Maybe it was. I wasn't sure.

One of the short stories Aura had included in her application was about a little girl who is caught stealing every day from her school-mates' knapsacks and lunch boxes. Her parents, summoned for a meeting by the school's principal, are baffled by their daughter's behavior. *They looked at her as if a totally unknown person was standing before them.* Previously, the mother had promised the little girl that if she was on her best behavior, she could go with her stepsister to her stepsister's mother's house in Orlando, Florida, for the summer vacation, and the reader perceives that that is why the little girl is stealing, because she doesn't want to go to Orlando. As punishment, the mother forbids her daughter from riding her bicycle in the parking lot of the residential complex where they live. The little girl disobeys, going for a ride not just in the parking lot but, for the first time in her life, she pedals out into the dangerous traffic of the avenue. Encouraged by her admission to the MFA program, Aura sent the story, "*Un viaje fallido,*" to a South American online literary magazine and they accepted it. Her first published short story! She told her mother the good news. But when Juanita read the story, it upset her. For one thing, she didn't like that the mother in the story doesn't figure out why her daughter is stealing. In real life, she'd figured it out, hadn't she? That was why Aura hadn't gone to Orlando with Katia. Why was Aura publicly airing turbulent episodes from the past, and distorting what had really happened? Aura tried to explain that it was fiction, and that if the story had gone on longer surely the fictional mother would have figured it out, too. But the story's meaning was in the bike ride, the little girl's brief, reckless dash toward adventure and freedom—and to a McDonald's down the avenue, where on weekends there was always a clown and children playing on the big plastic slide, but that on that weekday afternoon was deserted and dirty.

Several months later, when Aura had another short story published, this one also set in a Copilco-like residential complex, about a single mother and her daughter, her mother reacted similarly. Were these stories Aura's first attempts to write an *X-ray of my early childhood*? Dangerous and troubling secrets were embedded there. Don't many young female writers eventually write about their mothers?

The story should conclude with the central character happily embarking on a journey to unknown lands. The enthusiasm pales for the reader in light of his awareness of the disaster. But the disaster will have a resplendent obverse side.

Those words, from Aura's notes for the novel she wanted to write, seem cryptically prophetic. But if they are prophetic they pose an obscene riddle because how can there be a resplendent obverse side to Aura's death? I think she was referring to graduate school. In the novel, meant to be told backward, the unknown lands that the fictional Alicia happily embarks to include New York City and the hallowed university where she is to study for her PhD. That was going to be the disaster: her academic experience. Not anything or anyone else. Am I right about this?

20

Four nights after Aura's funeral, her mother telephoned me. She got right to the point. She'd obviously prepared the words she was about to speak, maybe even had rehearsed them. Juanita said:

Aura was a graduate of the university. I have always worked at the university and so has my brother. The university is our family and the university looks out for us the way a family does, and what the university lawyers tell me is that it is very suspicious that you didn't give a legal statement.

As I listened, I could see myself reflected in the two-stories-high glass panes separating our Escandón apartment from its little patio: cordless phone held to my ear, standing next to the pale wooden stairs leading up to the sleeping loft. Dwarfed by the apartment's vertical spaciousness, the high yellow wall, I looked like a miniscule figure with blurred features in the lower left corner of an immense painting. The sliding door was open and I could hear the whispery rustle of the bamboos at the back of the patio. I'd planted the bamboos myself, six in all, never imagining that they would grow like fairy-tale plants, now nearly two stories high. Less than a week before she'd died Aura had stood not far from where I was standing and looked up at me as I came down the stairs. I love this apartment, she'd announced. The apartment was ours: her mother had bought it for her. It had been empty and new when we'd moved in. Over four years, she'd been slowly and carefully furnishing it just as, within our means, she wished. A carpenter was building us bookshelves that we'd arranged to have delivered after we came back from the beach. Now I was back from that beach without Aura, and on the telephone with her mother. What was she accusing me of? What did she mean when she said that according to the university lawyers it was very suspicious that I hadn't given a statement?

It was Juanita who'd decided that Aura should be cremated. That meant that we—Fabiola and I, along with Juanita—thirty or so hours after Aura's fatal accident in the Pacific waves, had had to go directly from the Mexico City hospital where she'd died to a nearby *delegación*, a mixture of a neighborhood police station and district attorney's office, to give witness statements about Aura's death that were meant to verify that we weren't trying to hide anything by requesting authorization to cremate her. There would have to be an autopsy, too. They split us up, Fabiola was taken into one room, or else it was a cubicle, Juanita to another, and I to another—or was Juanita with me?—my memories of this are confused, but I do remember the grim bustle of the delegación: handcuffed prisoners in street clothing sitting on a bench against a wall, police and criminal-lawyer types coming and going, the walls, the furniture, the grungy hues of yellow and brown. I hadn't slept since our last night at the beach. It was afternoon or early evening or maybe it was already night. I sat in a chair at a steel desk across from a clerk, an overweight fortyish woman with a sluggish expression who was sitting at an old desktop computer—black screen, neon green lettering—who told me to tell her what had happened. So I told her, and she typed, never showing any emotion, her fingers powerful and fast on the keyboard. It was the first time I'd told the full story of Aura's accident and death, and probably I told it with more detail than she needed, but she steadily typed every word as soon as I spoke it, that at least was my impression. I was still in my bathing suit, sandals, and a T-shirt. Before, when we were waiting in the delegación, I'd been shivering with cold, but now I wasn't. When I was finished giving my statement, she asked for my identification. I had none. I'd left my passport back at the beach house we'd rented in Mazunte. All I had in my wallet was a credit card. Since I didn't have any ID, the woman behind the desk said that my statement couldn't be accepted. All that typing for nothing.

But Juanita, I said into the telephone, I did give a statement. You were there. At the delegación. It wasn't accepted because I didn't have any identification. I left my passport back at the house in Mazunte.

Drawing out every word—I knew this voice, Juanita's most sarcastic, sneering voice—she said, *Ayyy,* what a pretty story. What a pretty story. (Qué bo-*neee*-ta his-*tohhh*-ria.) You didn't have your *paaassport.* You left it behind at the *beeeeach.* You can tell your pretty story to the lawyers and judge.

Juanita, I said. What are you accusing me of?

My advice, she said, is that you consider fleeing the country for your own good.

I'm not fleeing the country, I said. I have no reason to flee the country.

The university lawyers want to have you arrested and imprisoned right now, she said, her voice quickening. But I've stopped them. I am acting as your protector in this. I don't want to see or talk to you, not while you're under investigation. My brother is acting as my attorney. From now on, anything you have to say to me, you should say to him.

That was the last conversation I ever had with Aura's mother. When I got off the phone I immediately phoned Leopoldo to ask him what was going on. Why had Juanita spoken to me that way? That brief conversation with Leopoldo, the last I ever had with him too, ended with him telling me to put whatever I had to say in writing; then he hung up on me. Later that same night, or maybe it was the next night, Juanita phoned Fabiola and told her that she should keep away from me, to not talk to me or be seen with me while I was under investigation so that she wouldn't be pulled into the investigation, too. Fabis left her apartment and crossed over to ours and knocked on the door. I found her almost in a state of shock, like a traffic accident survivor; she was shaking and trying not to cry and could barely tell me what had just happened. She phoned her mother. Odette was indignant. That night she took Fabis and me out for dinner, to a crowded restaurant, so that anybody could see that we weren't hiding anything.

21

The sensation that my brain was leaking, spurting dream images into the day. Fatigue like a hand inside an old soft leather glove, softly gripping my brain, the discernible pressure of its twitching fingers. Waking at around three or four in the morning, and instead of just desperately staring into the dark, slipping back into one snatch of dream or nightmare after another; waking from each with a jolt in the same instant that I registered relief that I might be sleeping. Finally I'd give up, let go of the pillow clutched over my head, get out of bed feeling shaky and drained, mentally rummaging and kicking through the debris of images and scenes that had been so jerkily streaming through me.

Aura was the blue color of a Popsicle, or one of her old frozen household liquid cleaners, but she didn't feel cold, curled alongside me, legs drawn beneath her, slowly bending over to kiss me, and that's when I was jerked awake. Then I was in a department store's grimy bargain basement, where in a plywood bin I found Aura's dresses for sale, tightly folded into brick-sized rectangles, each with a crisp cardboard band around it; I picked one up, recognizing which dress it was, same with a few more, and then I was awake again, staring up into the dark. I dreamed that I'd been on a date with her, in Parque Chapultepec, and now I wanted to phone her and ask her out again, but I couldn't remember her name. Who was that nice, brilliant young woman? I asked. But I did remember her face and, especially, the pretty freckles on her nose. From that one I woke up with a grin. As if my forgetting her name had only been one of her supernatural jokes.

*   *   *

The wedding-cake molding at the tops of the walls, the angel and the wedding dress and the altar; the shimmery heart made of hammered Mexican tin that hung on the wall; her desk, her books, her computer, her crowded pencil holder, chocolate Valentine's Day heart, Orphan Annie eyes of the woolen stuffed cats from Chiapas; mismatched bedside lamps from neighborhood antique stores, one with a red shade and a rooster painted on its ceramic base; her RoboSapian atop the dark-wood bureau; her clothes in the dressers and her makeup and perfume containers and bottles; the long drawn curtains through which light barely filtered; the steamy gurgling and hissing and the tiny ecstatically trumpeting elephants inside the radiator pipes, keeping the room snug, along with her humming space heater, during those dark winter weeks after the accident that I mostly spent sprawled on the bed on our multicolor quilt. Her books, her things, her music, her enduring if faint smells or else the warmed smells of all her things. Waking to the squeaking tires of a car driving through predawn snow, the airport-runway rip and thump of a snowplow passing by.

On Degraw Street one night I watched her coaxing a stray or lost cat out from under a parked car, bent over in her down winter coat, clucking and cooing to it, dancing her mitten in front of its crouching stare; this went on for at least ten minutes, until the cat crept out and she picked it up in her arms; it was a black and white tabby, already at home in her embrace, paws dangling over her forearm, Listen to that purr! The cat aimed a hostile stare at me as I approached. She said, Francisco, we're taking this cat home, and I said, No, Aura, we're not allowed to have pets, you know that, and I said, Anyway, it's probably a stray, who knows what diseases it has, and I said, No, Ow-rra, we can't.

*   *   *

I'm sorry that we didn't move to a new apartment, sorry we never got a dog or a cat, sorry we didn't rent the downstairs apartment when it came open so that we could have stayed here in New York that summer tending the garden instead of going to Mexico—I wrote e-mails to Aura about all of that. I'm sorry about your mother, I wrote. I'm sorry I don't know what to do about your mother. I'm sorry I haven't been able to help your mother. What could I possibly do to help your mother—throw myself off the Brooklyn Bridge? When I returned to Mexico nearly a year after your death, people told me that everyone at the university believes that I'm to blame for your death. That at the university whenever anyone mentions you or me or us, someone inevitably remarks, Ohhh, but nobody knows what really happened there. Something happened, they say, but who knows what, it's all very mysterious. He didn't even give a legal statement, you know; he fled the country without even giving a statement, very suspicious. Even your godfather, the literature professor and poet, goes along with this because he's afraid of your mother's and Leopoldo's power at the university. He even refused an invitation to take part in a memorial reading your friends orga-nized more than a year after your death because I was going to be there; he said, I have to be loyal to Juanita. Your godfather, to show loyalty to your mother, said that he wouldn't even read a poem or say a few words about you at your memorial reading, because I was going to be there, and he had to be loyal to your mother. Why shouldn't they go crazy? Why shouldn't they be deranged with hate and accusation? To try to understand and even sympathize is the least I can do; probably also the most I can do.

The last novel Aura read, which she'd begun in Mexico City and finished the day before we left for the beach, was Onetti's *La Vida*

Breve, and now I had it with me in Brooklyn but I couldn't bring myself to read it yet. I did read her copy of Thomas Bernhard's *The Loser,* and also her *Under the Volcano,* underlined and with notations in her hand throughout. I was glad to be reading some fiction again after so many months of grief and mourning books and also books that I thought might help me imagine the radical French psychoanalysts and asylums of Aura's novel. One day, opening my paperback copy of *Pnin,* I discovered and followed the fairy trail of Aura's green ink markings and wasn't even out of the first chapter before I felt her laughter welling up inside and tumbling out through her parted lips when poor Pnin realizes he's taken the wrong train to Cremona; next laugh stop, the squirrel that gets Pnin to press the button on the drinking fountain. Aura had drawn little green brackets around such phrases as "a rustling wind" and "in the silvery sun" and had neatly printed the word "weather" in the margins. Why would anyone write "weather" next to every description of weather in a novel? I knew why. In her creative writing workshop, the FAW had given the assignment of keeping a weather diary. Observe the weather, describe the weather, it's not so easy. Pay attention to the literary uses of weather. Every day that semester—while she was also preparing to defend her doctoral thesis proposal—Aura had dutifully described the weather in her notebook. Later, Wendy told me that only two students in the workshop actually wrote in their weather diaries every day: she and Aura.

Sometimes that was like a holy gift, the memory-sensation of Aura laughing inside me. I could never will that laughter, but sometimes, like while reading *Pnin,* it just arrived, as if crossing over from the spirit world. I could, however, slightly push the corners of my lips back into my cheeks, just enough to make my cheeks bulge a little, and hold them there, like two warm, peeled soft-boiled eggs, and that always conjured Aura's smile in repose, her soft, everyday expression, as if three-dimensionally superimposing not just her face over mine, but some of her disposition, so much more gentle and pleasant than mine. I was still always flicking with my thumb at the base of my ring finger, expecting to touch the ring; the ring had fit loosely and I was always clamping my thumb over it whenever I had to throw something away in a trash receptacle; flutters of panic whenever I was surprised by that finger's nakedness, calmed a split second later as my brain issued its incredulous reminder—*Still?* I have to tell you this *again?*—that the ring was on the chain around my neck with Aura's.

During those weeks after my accident, I also tried to reread *Lord Jim*: I had the idea that it was time for me to do what Lord Jim does, disappear with my shame and wrecked life, hide myself away in some remote and demanding place where maybe I could start over. But now I felt baffled by that book, by the fear of death that drives the characters, the grotesque antics that didn't even deserve to be called cowardice; unfunny clowns, those men struggling to ready the lifeboat under cover of night to flee the Malay pilgrim ship they are mistakenly convinced is sinking, falling all over themselves, one so panicked that he even collapses and dies from a heart attack, and Jim's fateful leap into the lifeboat—it reminded me of that time in the hospital when my father, a week or so after he'd come out of his coma, ripped out his feeding and oxygen tubes, the IVs out of his arms, and flung himself over the bed railings and landed on his side on the floor where he lay running in place while a nurse and I grabbed and held him down, his hospital gown hoisted around his hips, his thin, old-man's dick flapping, the shock of his wild animal energy in my hands as he kept trying to *run away from death*. Instead of being impressed by his life force, if that's what it was, it disgusted me, made me ashamed, or maybe I *was* impressed—because it was impressive, no doubt about that—and then ashamed later, after the nurses had bound him into the bed, his wrists to the rails with leather straps, like some dangerous psycho. My father's hysteria, that's what the death-panicked sailors in *Lord Jim* reminded me of. And I remembered a conversation I had with my mother as we sat in his hospital room just after—little did we know my father would live another four years—when I asked her, Why is Daddy so afraid to die? and my mother said quietly, Who knows, that's just the way your father is. You know, he's always been a hypochondriac.

Was a terror of death, I wondered, a form of hypochondria? A few minutes later, after I'd slipped back into my usual hospital routine of staring off into space, my mother said, I'm not afraid to die, with her delicate titter and an expression of prim, almost embarrassed conviction. I said, Me either, not like that. I don't think we meant we wouldn't feel any fear as we faced death, but that how to face death was something that at least my mother had thought about and decided on. Don't eat with your mouth open like your father; Don't slurp your soup like your father; Don't beat up on your kids like your father; Don't *not* fuck your wife like your father; Don't face death with panic and cowardice like your father. I was fearful of many things, did that make me like my father? Wasn't a fear of dogs related to a fear of death?—a primordial fear of being ripped apart and devoured by beasts, your own blood bubbling from their nostrils, their snouts soaked in it. When I was about three, in our front yard, I yanked a dog's tail from behind, a short-haired gray mongrel with a tail like a cobra, and the dog whirled, snarling, and pounced, slashing my forearm with its teeth as I lay underneath it shrieking until a neighbor came running with his rake. I still have the tiny scars and, ever since, menacing dogs—though I actually liked dogs and had several as pets—dogs that barked, growled, or charged at me, had sent fear, adrenaline, panic coursing through me, though I'd learned to disguise it; even by early adolescence I could almost always proceed with outward calm, heart pounding, instead of running away or climbing a tree. About a week after Aura's death, Odette and Fabiola invited me to their country house in Malinalco so that I could rest and get some sleep. Every day I went on long walks into the countryside, on muddy roads through cornfields and pastures, startling peasant farmers, some of them on horseback, who'd probably never seen a man like me, middle-aged, comparatively light-skinned, clearly not a local, walking along those roads with tears streaking his cheeks and sometimes even bawling like a child—I bet, hearing me from a short way off, the farmers thought it was laughter and looked to see what was so funny. It was during those walks that I discovered that when dogs chased me now, or stood alone or in packs in the middle of the road baring their teeth and growling, or frenziedly barked from behind gates and fences as I passed, I no longer felt fear, that whatever used to set off those riotous alarms in me was now stone.

During her last night, the long night before her death, Aura must have realized she was going to die, or that at least probably or very possibly she was going to die. That abyss that she faced all by herself that night, without me, was what I feared now, more than I'd ever feared anything, my darling. I couldn't even begin to edge close, to contemplate it, without feeling my body react as it used to when threatened by dogs, cringing, shrinking back though still urging myself forward, sometimes halfheartedly, eyes half shut, throat suddenly dry and tight, too much—. What did she feel, what did she know, what was it like, what did she think? The lonely terror that must have flooded her with an intimacy unlike any I or anyone else ever reached or touched inside of her, and that I cannot bear even to try to imagine, or just can't. Not even when that orderly said, You might die, sir, not even close, because, at that moment anyway, I didn't really care anymore, or maybe I didn't really believe it, and I know Aura cared, and that she must have believed it. That night when she must have felt more frightened and lonelier than I am able to imagine was also when she might have judged me. Her judgment of me might have been one of her last conscious thoughts.

Fue una tontería, that's what Aura said to her mother, at two in the morning, in Mexico City, as they wheeled her from the ambulance into the hospital emergency entrance. *Una tontería*: dumbness, a stupid act, an idiocy even, Aura told her mother. Those were the last words I ever heard Aura speak, in that tone of willed cheer she often used with her mother—the plucky camper. How did I spend my summer vacation? Making out with Danish boys, Mami. Fue una tontería, Mami. My tontería? But she didn't say that, not at all. She did not sound as if she was blaming anyone. She sounded like a hero. I do remember her mother crossing her arms, face pale, staring at me with hatred and blame, and why shouldn't she have? Bringing her daughter home to her like that, paralyzed from the neck down, from her accident in the waves. But that is a cloudy memory, maybe more an imagined re-creation. Maybe I didn't even register Juanita and what she allegedly said to me as I followed behind Aura as they wheeled her into the hospital after our twelve-hour journey from the beach. Maybe I didn't really care about her mother at that moment, maybe I just don't remember, maybe I've *repressed* it, because Fabis told me that what she distinctly remembers is me reacting to Juanita's words with a stunned glance of, Why did you say that? but that without breaking stride I followed Aura into the hospital. Fabis told me that what Juanita said to me, as they wheeled her daughter past her into the hospital where twelve hours later she would die, was, *Esto es tu culpa.* This is your fault.

There was a week or so, in 2005, months before our wedding, when Aura lay awake every night, worrying that she was condemning herself to a miserable early widowhood by marrying me. I'd wake and find her staring into the dark beside me, her warm insomnia breath like pulling open the door of an oven, her body steamy. Wasn't it logical to assume that I would die at least twenty years before she did? Shouldn't she think ahead, spare herself that ordeal? We talked about it more than once. I told her, Don't worry, mi amor, I won't stick around longer than seventy-five, I promise. Then you'll still be in your early fifties, you'll still be beautiful, and probably famous, and some younger guy will want to marry you for sure. You promise? she'd say, cheered up or at least pretending to be, and I'd promise. You'd better keep your word, Francisco, she'd say, because I don't want to be a lonely old widow, or end up like your mother; she knew how taking care of my father had worn out my mother. But even if I don't die by seventy-five, I'd say, you can just warehouse me somewhere and go and live your life, really, I don't care. As long as we have children, I won't care that much. Just give me a kid, one kid, that's all I want. And she'd say, Okay, but I want five kids. Or maybe three. Well then we'd better move to Mexico, I'd say, so they can go to the UNAM. I wanted to move back to Mexico anyway; it was Aura who, for now, wanted to stay in New York. One afternoon during that final spring, after she'd turned thirty, Aura turned to me from her desk while I lay on the bed reading, and she said, We have everything we need to be happy. We don't have to be rich. We can get jobs in universities if we need them. We have our books, our reading, our writing, and we have each other. Frank, we don't need more to be happy, we are so lucky. Do you know how lucky we are?

Another day late that last spring Aura also announced that she'd decided that she wasn't going to be one of those women who in her thirties is consumed with being as thin as she'd been in her twenties; she was going to allow herself to be *rellenita*, a little filled out, did I have a problem with that?

Esto es tu culpa. This is your fault. Did Aura think that, at all, even
once, during that last long night? That it was my fault? It was not
my fault. Of course it was my fault. If I truly believed it was my
fault, would I be able to go on living? Apparently, yes, I would be
able to go on living, if I was only as afraid of death as I'd once been
of dogs. Except I'm not afraid.

During those first weeks of death, Aura, I was pretty sure, made her presence known and even visible to me. But afterward I'd convinced myself, with my rational New York–New England skepticism, that I didn't believe in the spirit world. I didn't believe Aura could ever come back and sit in her Journey Chair, or that I'd ever come home and find her standing in the middle of the bedroom in her wedding dress, confused about where she'd been and how long she's been away. Those first incidents, I argued myself into believing, were really projections of shock and longing. Everywhere I went those first few days after Aura's death, for instance, I heard Beatles songs that she'd loved: "Octopus's Garden" blaring from a car window just as we were going into Yosh and Gaby's building, where friends arriving from New York and elsewhere were gathering that night; "Lovely Rita" in stalled traffic outside the Gayosso funeral home; "Lucy in the Sky" in the supermarket where we went to pick up liquor to bring back to the apartment after; there were several instances like that in the coming days that startled everybody, and that Aura's Mexican friends commented on with knowing glances. Was Aura signaling to her friends with Beatles songs? The Beatles never went out of fashion in Mexico: wherever you go there, you hear the Beatles. So it was not even a surprising coincidence, right?

Three nights after her death, I was sitting in nearly the front row at an outdoor concert in the Zócalo that a friend took me to— people led me around from place to place during those days—where the singer was going to dedicate a song to Aura, and I looked up and saw, hovering over the stage and the centuries-old buildings overlooking the Zócalo, Aura's face luminous in the night sky as if floating inside her own sphere of moonlight, her most sweetly excited, loving smile, and I smiled back, tears blurring her. I felt her love that night and was grateful for that, but I also had the idea that she was enjoying the novelty of death and its magic, that it was as if she still hadn't understood what it meant. Two nights in a row she woke me in bed in the middle of the night, weightlessly on top of me, the naked lusciousness of her breasts filling me with that same shy rapture as always because I thought that not even young Marilyn Monroe's breasts could have been so buoyant and splendid as Aura's, they always startled me, probably because she was so modest and even secretive about her breasts. And, oh, that sexy honey in her gaze when she said, the way she always used to, ¿Quieres hacer el amor? How I jerked off in our bed during those first few weeks without her, with a grim, self-hating, tear-it-out-by-the-fucking-root fury, or like an insatiably horny ape or psychotic dementia inmate; it was hideous. A friend's mother made an appointment for me with a psychoanalyst, a thanatologist—an elegant Jewish-Mexican woman who was also a serious Buddhist, who gave me a prescription for sleeping pills. She was the one who told me about the Buddhist practice of visualizing recently lost loved ones inside a white glow to help them leave and find peace, and one day as I was trying to do this, I saw Aura struggling to make her way back to me, lifting her hands to me in a pleading gesture, looking bereft and terrified about "disappearing into the light." A few days later, during spinning class at the gym, I saw Aura again, standing in the corner, extremely distinct though the transparent shade of a ghost, looking lost and as if she really understood now what death was going to mean, gesturing to me as she had inside the white glow, begging for help, for me not to let her disappear, but this time with a wild panicked confusion.

I suppose anyone would think it was reprehensible that I was back at my Condesa gym two weeks after Aura's death, at a spinning class no less, mainly surrounded by women trying to keep their weight down and gay telenovela supporting-actor types. What a ridiculous fucking *fresa*, anyone would think. But not much else was left of my old daily routines, or was possible, without Aura. Spinning class, an hour of hard pumping on a stationary bicycle to pounding music, was at least a way to tire myself so that maybe I'd be able to sleep a bit, and also to sweat out my hangovers. In the middle of class one evening, pedaling away, I thought, What is this awful new feeling? Inside me, lodged between spine and sternum,

I felt a hard hollow rectangle filled with tepid blank air. An empty rectangle with sides of slate or lead, that's how I visualized it, holding dead air, like the unstirred air inside an elevator shaft in a long-abandoned building. I thought I understood what it was, and told myself, The people who feel this way all the time are the ones who commit suicide. I wanted to just get off the bike and run away, or drop to the floor in fetal position, or raise my arm and call for help. But I kept pedaling hard, moving to the music and the instructor's commands, and the rectangle full of dead air slowly faded. I didn't feel *good* after, but it went away, that sensation of absolute emptiness and dread eroding me from within with geometric precision, like a mathematical proof of the meaninglessness of life, or of my life.

It comes back pretty often, but so far it has always gone away. During those first weeks and months after Aura's death everything I did felt futile and absurd anyway. I sought out friends to drink with every night; they understood, and being Mexicans, they were willing to drink with me, not the same friends every night, of course, they took turns, I was the only one drinking as if trying to turn my blood to tequila. Stunned silent hungover days. Went to the gym, then to the cantinas. Once, well after midnight, when there was nobody around to drink with and I just wanted to drink a while more and no place else was open, I went into El Closet, the Condesa's venerable strip club or table dance place—*un teibol*, as they call them—that often stayed open until dawn or even later. I hadn't been back to that place since before Aura. I climbed the stairs, past the floor with the kitchen where you often spied the teiboleras in their glittering G-strings scarfing down meals, and then up to the next landing where, standing in the entrance to the dark foyer leading into the rooms for fucking, I was surprised to see Blanca, the homely, stumpy lady who attended to those rooms—bringing condoms and towels, cleaning up after—standing there in that same old disheveled white janitorial outfit and droopy dark cardigan. Blanca scowled at me and exclaimed *¡Pero Fraaank! ¡Esto es PECADO! ¡Tu estás CASADO!* This is a SIN! You're MARRIED! It wasn't just that she remembered my name after all this time, it was the realization that news of my having found love and a wife had somehow reached her and that she cared, that's what blew me away, left me momentarily speechless. Blanca, who I'd once spotted trudging home through the tree-bowered streets of the Condesa at around nine in the morning, stooped back, stubby legs, having finally finished her chores at El Closet, probably headed to a Metro stop that would carry her to some distant slum barrio—this troll of a woman with her horrible job had been happy to find out about me and Aura, she'd been happy for me. *There's a man who needs to be married, who would make a good husband.* Could that really be what Blanca had thought, observing me in El Closet back then? Now, seeing me come up those stairs for the first time in five years, she was indignant that I'd betrayed her illusions. ¡Tu estás CASADO! But Blanca, I finally responded, it's not what you think, honestly, I'm just here to have a drink, and I turned into the club.

I sat at a table in a corner, far from the stage. At the tables and banquettes against the walls, as always, las teiboleras sat in groups, their own little cliques, talking among themselves, trying to get through their long, tedious shifts, occasionally looking out across the room for customers who seemed as if they might be worth soliciting a drink or even a lap dance from, if not something more; some getting up to patrol the floor like sultry sleepwalkers, or heading to the dressing rooms because soon it would be their turn to perform on stage. Some sat with customers at their tables, or were lap dancing for them in the shadows in the far corners of the room. Waiters in white shirts and black pants continually circled, pressuring customers to buy drinks for the dancers; a middle-aged woman who sold cigarettes, candies, little stuffed animals, and cheap perfume from her vendor's tray; the women in dowdy schoolgirl uniforms who walked the floor selling lap-dance tickets, or led teiboleras by the hand to customers who'd requested them. And sometimes a teibolera headed to Blanca's back rooms with a customer. On the stage, at the edge of my vision, almost as if through the wrong end of a telescope, teiboleras, one at a time, were doing their thing: dancing, taking off their tops, tossing them to customers, some but not all taking off their bottoms, writhing on the floor, performing their pole gymnastics. Cheap perfume, a smoky female muskiness, the warm heavy air like an intimate emanation from all the naked voluptuousness in that room. In my loneliest post-Z, pre-Aura years, I'd sometimes fantasized that I might marry a teibolera. Now and then you met one who was putting herself through college. Once, in another teibol place, I met a teibolera who was studying literature at the UNAM, who talked about Dostoyevsky and Rimbaud, and asked me to send her a copy of *Finnegans Wake* when I was back in New York because she couldn't find one in Mexico, and I actually did, though I never heard back from her and doubt that it was her real address, in Las Portales, or even her real name that she'd given me; I'd known that, but mailed her the book anyway. There in El Closet one night, long ago, I'd taken the lady with the vendor's tray aside, known to everyone just as Mami, and asked her who of all the girls working that night would make a good wife. Mami took my question seriously, her eyes slowly panning the room from one teibolera to another until she turned back to me with the gleefully wicked grin of a long retired puta and said, *Ninguna*. Not one.

It was a different cigarette vendor working that night, not Mami, and I didn't recognize any of the dancers from five years before, either; they'd all moved on in the years since I'd met Aura. I rebuffed all drink solicitations and made it clear that I didn't want company. But then a very young woman, in red lingerie, with chalk-pale, thin arms, long black hair, a gentle pretty face, makeup plastered over pock-scarred cheeks, sat down at my table and softly said, I've been watching you. Why are you so sad? I told her that something terrible had happened but I didn't want to talk about it, that I just wanted to drink alone. But she must have gotten me to talk a little, because I remember that she told me that she was nineteen, which could have been a lie, that she was a Protestant, and that she was only working there to be able to support her child, a little girl, which was the same reason, I knew, that almost every one of those women, certainly the Mexicans, worked there. Just before she got up to leave she said, I can tell you have a noble heart. Something good is going to happen to you.

I'd thanked her for those words and told myself, That was like being visited by an angel. I didn't disagree that, at least during my years with Aura, my heart had loved in a way that could be called noble. It seemed at least possible that a broken heart could still be noble, but I don't think a totally shattered one can be. If that angel teibolera could see me now, going on two years later, would she still say what she'd said that night? Was there anything left of my noble heart, as I hid out in our apartment in deep winter in the weeks after the accident? Might her prophecy ever come true? But the truth is that teiboleras and whores tend to be wrong about many things.

Aura didn't know about my past in the teibols. There were things she kept from me about herself, too, and that I didn't find out about until after—nothing nearly as sleazy as the teibols, though, just the modest, bad-girl transgressions of adolescence. Don't tell Frank what I used to be like, she begged Brasi, her old schoolmate from the Colegio Guernica, pulling him aside in the cantina where we'd gone to watch a telecast of a World Cup match from Germany with Fadanelli and his friends, including Brasi, who Aura hadn't seen in years. What did she mean? What didn't she want me to know about? Brasi told me later, when I was back in Mexico a year after her death, that during high school Aura had for a while had two boyfriends at once. One of these was the most conceited guy in their class: handsome, rich, a jock, phony, and shallow—yes, they have them in Mexico too. According to Brasi, the guy fell totally in love with Aura but she made a public clown out of him: lying to him, ridiculing him, putting the horns on him, sharing with everyone his conceited and moronic confidences, a kind of show trial of which only he was unaware. There was a kind of justice to it but, carajo, it was really cruel, said Brasi, though that didn't stop him from chuckling, these fourteen or so years later. The other boyfriend, though, he couldn't have been too happy about it. Was he Dos Santos? I asked. Brasi said he didn't know, that he didn't remember. It was hard to believe that Aura could have acted that way, there must have been more to it. But Brasi had known Aura since elementary school, and now he was a philosophy professor at the UNAM; I knew he wasn't just making it up. Aura, poor baby, had never even mentioned Brasi to me until we ran into him that night, as if she'd actually been in dread of what he could tell me about her at fifteen and had wanted to hide his existence. A few times since Aura's death, I'd met people who'd known her—though usually not that well—people I encountered in places like that cavernous cantina in Colonia Roma, La Covadonga, that had become so trendy and where people of around Aura's age came up to me out of the blue to introduce themselves, to offer their condolences, and sometimes to share their memories. Some had used words like *contestatária*, a back-talker, lippy, cutting, sarcastic, standoffish, or aloof. They spoke as if everyone knew those things about Aura, though I'd never heard anyone describe her like that when she was alive. Usually these recollections were offered in a tone of affectionate respect, as if they were saying, Oh, yes, Aura was so smart and funny, but you really had to watch out because, boy, did she have a fast, sharp tongue. I'd occasionally gotten a dose of that sharpness. Don't speak to me the way your mother speaks to Rodrigo, was how I'd usually respond, and sometimes that made her retreat, abashed, or else she'd fire back, Well don't be as stupid as Rodrigo, then.

But none of her closest friends ever described Aura in such a way—her closest high school companions, the ones who stayed friends with her for the rest of her life, spoke of her precocity, the brainy girl who was also their loving, loyal best girlfriend. In New York, at Columbia and in her MFA program, Aura was known as sweet natured and shy, someone who in class always had to be coaxed to speak up. She'd even suffered over this; in one of her Columbia notebooks, she described herself as a "zipped-up timid mouse." Why such a change? Maybe she'd identified that earlier personality—defensive, always on the preemptive attack with cutting words—as something that she'd inherited or learned from her mother, or that she associated with her mother. Aura didn't want to be like her mother, just as I didn't want to be like my father. In New York it was as if she'd taken that personality off like a suit of spiky armor and laid it on the ground.

Aura and I never spoke too explicitly about any of this, though maybe we should have, because who knows what the impact of an accelerated, more explicit self-knowledge would have been, maybe—the physics of our destinies being so kinetically compacted inside us, reactive to the slightest alterations and shifts—it would have led Aura to some other chain of decisions and choices, resulting, somehow, in her not even being at the beach in Mazunte that day in July, in her having gone to a summer writers' colony to work on her novel instead, or in our staying at home because she'd decided sooner that she'd wanted a baby and was too pregnant to go to the beach, or in her having left me; or even, if we'd ended up at that beach on that same day anyway, in her having gone into the water an hour later than she did, because maybe that final morning it would have kept her at her writing desk in our beach house one more hour; or, deep in thought—thinking to herself, Is that really what I did, did I really take off and lay down my mother's spiky armor?—it would have slowed her steps from her beach chair across the sand to the water just enough to make her miss that wave, or made her, distracted, her mind still absorbed, duck that wave instead of, given over to the moment— in that last fatal impulse of delight—decide to ride it just like I'd ridden the one before.

One thing that never changed in the four-plus years that we were together: once Aura passed her two- or three-drink limit, she'd start reciting poetry. Of course sometimes she went well beyond those two or three drinks, whether with me or out with her girlfriends, especially Lola. She was famous among her friends for always phoning the next day, voice thick with hangover and remorse, to apologize, and they'd tell her she had nothing to apologize for, that they'd all been drinking and had a great time. With me, on the other hand, whenever Aura drank too much, the night usually ended with her curled up in some corner of the floor, crying for her father. I didn't have a dad, she'd bleat, in that slurred voice of a little girl that seemed to possess her in those moments. My dad abandoned me! He left us alone! He didn't care about me! And she'd weep, while I did my best to soothe her. Sure, sometimes this exasperated me: was Aura really going to cry over her father like this for the rest of her life? But I'd also wonder with awed and mystified pity about that hole her father's abandonment had left inside of her.

My father, on the other hand, trying to keep his tight grasp on his family, had done none of us any favors. My sisters used to implore my mother to divorce him, especially in the wake of one of his rampages of abuse. He didn't beat up on my sisters like he did on me, he savaged them with words instead. They'd never had the strength or determination to get as far away from home as they could and should have, because they were so attached to my mother and always wanted to be near her; he denigrated them constantly. I don't know which of the two—the thrice-married, wealthy, real-estate sister or the poor, never-married, Holiday Inn desk-clerk sister—now curses my father's memory more bitterly or is more paranoid, defensive, and emotionally crippled. By the time you were thirteen, my mother has said to me, we never saw you anymore, you were always out in the streets with your friends, and then after high school you were gone for good. That is true, Mom, and it saved me. If Aura's parents had stayed together, if she'd grown up in a stable home as the adored daughter of a respected Bajío politician and lawyer, a princess of the Land of Strawberries, who and where would Aura be now?

The last two years we were together, Aura stopped crying over her father. Was that because in me she'd found a reliable replacement father? A pretty facile piece of psychology; I can even imagine Aura having a good laugh over that. She was convinced that of the two of us, she was the more mature. But that doesn't mean there might not be a bit of truth to it anyway. I was more than one thing to Aura. I played multiple parts, just as she did for me.

In the reception room at the Gayosso funeral home, outside the chapel where Aura lay in her white-enamel coffin, I saw a man in a rumpled gray suit come in. I'd never seen him before. More than his distraught expression, it was his bearing that caught my attention, the way he held out his arms as he walked. He looked like somebody charging back into a room he's just left, desperate for one more chance to plead his case. Or like he'd been walking around looking for somebody to hug for hours and now his arms ached with fatigue. He had a long, sloping nose and a shock of gray-brown hair falling over his forehead. He was searching, I deduced, for Juanita. This was Aura's father, Héctor; I knew it even before I heard one of the tías say so. From a short distance I watched his long embrace with Juanita. I went up to him. I'm Francisco, Aura's husband, I said. Oh, so you're Aura's husband, he echoed wanly. Though he'd seen Aura only twice in the last twenty-six years, he seemed deeply shaken by her death, I mean as much so as anyone, as if he also didn't know how he was going to get through the rest of his life now. I felt weirdly protective, but what could I protect him from? We really didn't have much to say to each other, not there, at that moment. But I sat next to him on a couch in a corner, hardly speaking, and felt relieved when Vicky came over to talk to him. I did learn that Héctor and his second wife had only one daughter; Aura had told me she had two half sisters whom she'd never met, though she'd never been really sure about that. Six weeks later, at the end of August, when I was finally getting ready to go home to our apartment in Brooklyn without Aura, I heard her say, silently but emphatically, inside my own thoughts: Francisco, before you leave Mexico, you have to go and see my father and find out what really happened between him and my mother. Also, find out why he had mud on his pants—I clearly heard Aura ask me to do this, as if I was her last chance to solve that mystery, which would allow her to finally finish writing her short story about the day when he'd come into that restaurant in Guanajuato for their first and only meeting in seventeen years.

At the funeral, Héctor had given me his telephone number and invited me to come and visit. I phoned and, a few days later, took a bus into that part of Mexico called El Bajío, where Aura was born and where we'd had our wedding, to San José Tacuaya. Aura and I had gone to San José Tacuaya together only once, the weekend before our wedding, to bring a basket of eggs to a convent of cloistered nuns so that in exchange they would pray for it not to rain on our wedding day. It was also local tradition to stick knives in the earth the night before a wedding, and we did that, too. It rained on our wedding anyway, though not heavily, and just for a short while. That day in San José Tacuaya, Aura hadn't wanted to try to find the house with a yard where she'd lived the first four years of her life, having no memory of what it looked like from the outside, or even any idea of what neighborhood it was in.

From Mexico City it was a five-hour bus trip to San José Tacu-aya. I left at dawn. Movies, one after the other, blared on the video monitors, making it hard to sleep. I ended up watching most of the second movie, which was about a blue-collar, Philly neighborhood guy who tries out for the Philadelphia Eagles and makes the team. It was dubbed into Mexican Spanish, with football players, white and black, snarling chinga tu madre and cabrón at each other and chanting ¡Viva los Aguilas! in the locker room. Then I remembered Aura and her quarterback drop back. Nearly all my life I've had an American boy's restless habit of imitating a quarterback's three-step drop back into the passing stance. I'd do it over and over, sometimes when watching the news on television, or while thinking about something or other, a form of pacing. One day Aura asked me to show her how to do it, as if it was an interesting dance step she wanted to learn. Nothing to it, I told her, it's just three steps backward. You hold the football here, by your chin, like this, I said, and take one step back, the first step, with the foot that's on the same side as your throw-ing arm—so I explained and did it, followed by the next two steps and the throw. But Aura took her first step back with the foot that was on the *opposite* side of her throwing arm. That turned her body so that she faced front and made her rock from side to side like an off-balance, backward-stumbling penguin while she tried to finish the drop back, invisible football clasped under her chin, her teeth biting her lower lip, eyes wide open. It was hilarious. She looked like Giulietta Masina clowning in *La Strada*. She must eventually have figured out the right way to do it, but she kept doing it the wrong way. Sometimes, if she thought I was feeling blue or not even, she'd announce, Mira mi amor, and she'd perform her spazzy quarterback drop back, just to make me laugh.

As the bus approached San José Tacuaya, the view became flat brown-and-green strawberry fields stretching to the horizon, and the highway was lined with small restaurants and wooden stands advertising fresh strawberries and cream. Closer to the city, the industrial outskirts began, gigantic auto plants and smaller factories. Aura's father now lived near the city's old colonial center, on a long street lined with drab storefronts; his address was easy to miss, being just a simple wooden door wedged between the facades of two businesses: a pharmacy and a dry cleaners. A minute or two after I rang, Héctor came out to meet me and led me back along a narrow corridor that led to a small, dank patio and an old, four-story house that originally must have been the home of a prosperous family but was now divided into separate apartments. Héctor and his family lived on the ground floor, in a cramped-seeming apartment with the kind of massive, old-fashioned furniture that reminded me of my grandparents' house in Guatemala City. We went directly into a study that was also the living room, where Héctor sat in an armchair and I on a low sofa alongside bookshelves crammed with an impressive collection of law books and other tomes, mostly scholarly, on politics and history. But the books were covered with dust, I noticed, and looked as if they dated from the seventies or earlier; it appeared as if a new book hadn't been added in twenty-five years. Héctor told me that he was semiretired, teaching law only part-time at a community college in the city. Naturally, I didn't mention his supposedly collecting bottles for resale at the market. His wife worked, too, he told me, and his daughter, Aura's younger half sister, was living in the DF, working as a waitress. That was a surprise. I wanted to ask where but sensed that I shouldn't.

That time during Christmas, in Guanajuato a few years ago, I asked, was that the last time you saw Aura? I knew it was. I felt, with some dismay, the scheming journalist in me awakening, strategizing, laying down a seemingly innocuous question in order to get him talking. He told me about the afternoon when Aura had found him struggling to let himself out of Vicky Padilla's mother's house, that final flustered and abrupt good-bye; afterward, when Aura had gone inside and found her mother and Vicky drinking tequila, something in their attitude had made her not want to discuss her father with them. His voice rising with indignation, Héctor told me that Juanita and Vicky had mocked him that afternoon, that that was why he'd left instead of staying to spend time with Aura. Juanita and Vicky had been complaining about money. But then Juanita had said, It's no surprise we're poor, but you, Héctor, you have no excuse; by now you should be a wealthy, powerful man but look at you, you're even poorer than we are! And then, he said, Juanita and Vicky had laughed at him. He recounted this in his quiet, tired-sounding voice, his hands loosely entwined between his knees, staring straight ahead instead of looking directly at me. In order to commiserate, I said, I know what Juanita and Vicky can be like when they're together. Then I brought up that other time he'd seen Aura, a few years before, when she was twenty-one and they'd met at the restaurant. It was during one of her breaks from the University of Texas. Wasn't that the first time you'd seen her in seventeen years? I asked. Were you surprised that your daughter had turned out to be such a beautiful and intelligent young woman?

After a moment, Héctor said, Yes, beautiful, of course, a wonderful girl, and he emphatically nodded and said that no, no, it hadn't surprised him, he'd always known how exceptional Aura was, even when she was an infant. It's obvious, he said, that Juanita did a magnificent job of raising Aura.

Oh, yes, I said. This was the moment I'd been waiting for. I said, But you know, Héctor, Aura never truly accepted Rodrigo as her father, because she never got over losing you. She never kept her love for you a secret. She never understood why you and Juanita separated. Aura was obsessed with that mystery, but also with why you so completely stayed away from her afterward. She knew plenty of children of divorce who still saw both their parents. Why couldn't she?

Héctor had been holding himself still and leaning forward as he listened, as if better to concentrate on my every word, but then he lost it; he sat back and covered his face with his hands and quaked from within with dry harsh sobs. When he'd recomposed himself, he explained his reason for that distance. It was the same reason that he'd given Aura: Juanita had remarried and he'd thought Aura should have only one father. But why, I asked, didn't you ever even answer any of the letters Aura sent you? Héctor said that he'd never received any such letters. Maybe my expression was openly skeptical, because he blurted, Juanita, you know, has always been a little crazy. Then, just like that, Héctor gave up the secret of their past, the one that had been withheld from Aura her entire life even though she'd witnessed it, the events she seemed to have intuited and perhaps half-remembered but had never found a way of exposing or even expressing.

He had *not* left Juanita, Héctor told me. Whatever marital troubles they'd had back then, he would never have done that, because of Aura, his little girl, whom he adored, he said. No, Juanita had left *him*. She'd run off to Mexico City with another man, a rival politician, and taken Aura with her. After that, said Héctor, I had to tear her from my heart. I tore Juanita from my heart. And so you tore Aura from your heart too? I thought. Later, Juanita had tried to come back to him, he said. She drove back to San José Tacuaya with Aura, and when he came outside to meet them, four-year-old Aura, from inside the car, announced, We can come home now, Papi! But Héctor wouldn't take Juanita back, he'd torn her from his heart.

I sat stunned. Was this what Aura had alluded to in her diary? *There's too much noise in my head, memory doing its thing, memories I'd rather forget return return.* Her childhood memories, silenced and denied, replaced by a fragmented narrative of lies, hurt, guilt, and senselessness. Memories she'd kept secret, as if, or because, she had no words for them.

Héctor was dry-eyed and calm now, as if spent. I sensed that if I were to ask him one more thing, it would be a brutal trespass. What he'd told me, all its implications, should be absorbed in silence, and very slowly. But I did have another question, and now was the time to ask it. That time you met in the restaurant, I said, when Aura was twenty-one. It wasn't raining out, it was a dry day, at least that's how she remembered it, but you came into the restaurant with mud all over one of your pant legs. I forced a smile. Aura always wondered why, I said. It was another big mystery to her.

He nodded, and said, On the drive over, I had a flat tire and got out to change it. Out there on the highway it had rained, and a truck went past, through a puddle, and sprayed me.

A moment later he got up and went into the kitchen to make us some coffee. I checked my BlackBerry. There was a message marked urgent from a friend in New York, Johnny Silverman, my corporate lawyer friend, a winningly extroverted guy who'd befriended Juanita at our wedding. Now Juanita had cast him as my lawyer, which he wasn't, and her lawyer, one of the university lawyers, had sent Johnny an e-mail telling him that I had two days to vacate our Escandón apartment. When Héctor came out, I told him that I'd better catch the next bus back to the DF But aren't you going to stay to eat? he asked, his tone somber and anxious. He was expecting me to stay for lunch; his wife, who'd be home from work soon, had prepared a special meal, a mole de olla. I apologized and said, I have no idea what to do about this situation, so I better get back and deal with it. I told him some of the story: the apartment Aura's mother had bought for her, how I'd offered to go on making the monthly payments while I tried to gather the money to buy the apartment outright. It seemed legally dubious, I said, that they could evict the widowed husband just like that. To move out in two days seemed impossible! Héctor said that under Mexican law, he was sure I had legal rights, that I wasn't merely a *third party,* as Juanita and her lawyer described me. Excusing myself, I typed a fast message to Johnny, asking him to request permission from Juanita and her lawyer to move four months later, in January, and meanwhile I'd go on paying the monthly bank payments. After that, I wrote, I would pack the apartment up and leave, and Juanita would owe me nothing; if Juanita wasn't amenable to that, could I at least have another week? Even if I could get the money together to buy the apartment, I realized now, there was probably no way Juanita would sell it to me. I left for the bus station, feeling guilty about not staying to eat. I'd promised Héctor that I'd come back to San José Tacuaya as soon as I could, though I never did. On the way back to the DF I phoned Gus in New York and told her everything.

Remember, it's only his version, she cautioned. That doesn't make it all true. Maybe leaving him was the best thing Aura's mother ever did. He sounds like a wimp. She probably knew he was going to fall apart and wreck his career anyway.

A politician gets his wife stolen by another politician in a small Mexican macho city, I said, where everyone knows everyone, you don't think that could have hurt his political career?

Oh, come on, she said. Take your wife and child back, for God's sake, and go and screw some other politician's wife if you need to. There are two sides to this. As always. You don't give up a daughter like Aura *for any reason,* she shouted into the phone.

After we'd hung up, I sat with my eyes closed, leaning my head against the mesh curtain over the bus window until I dozed off, falling into one of those half-awake dream states where I was on a lonely train ride like in the movie version of *Doctor Zhivago,* through the desolate Siberian wilderness full of howling wolves that had so frightened me when I'd seen the movie as a child. *Juanita is like a dark forest*—I thought that, or dreamt it; it seemed to spell itself out one letter at a time. She's the forest but she's also the mother of the forest, its queen, its great hunter, its spell-casting wizard. She's the wolves, the bears, the nourishing fish in the rivers. She's the woodpecker that haunts the forest, shattering skulls and eating memories like grubs. Now I'm trapped deep inside this forest, while with every day that passes I'll remember less of who I was before, until soon there'll be nothing left for the woodpecker to devour. Is Aura here, trapped inside this forest, too? I'll never find out, there are no answers in this forest.

I was still on the bus, about an hour outside of Mexico City, when I received an e-mail from Johnny, forwarding me the message he'd just gotten from Juanita:

Estimable lawyer Silverman, in response to your attentive request, I'd like to comment that I have no objection to Frank staying for another week, until the date that you've indicated, though nevertheless it is very important that he realize that after that date I will take charge totally and absolutely of my house.

I didn't even realize until nearly two years later, when I went back through old e-mails and found the ones that were written that day and in the ensuing ones, that I must also have asked Johnny to write this message, which he'd cc'd to me:

Querida Juanita:

Now that I've read with care your previous mail about Frank, I see that I must have omitted something that is very important. Frank has asked me to ask you if you can give him just a small portion of Aura's ashes to take back to Brooklyn. I apologize for asking this so bluntly, but I don't know how one is supposed to ask a question like this.

Later, I would hear that when, two days after the funeral, I phoned Juanita's apartment to tell her I was coming over, Juanita told the others gathered there that she had to hide Aura's ashes because I was coming to take them away. Madness of a mother's grief—it stabs my indignant heart with pity, for whatever that pity is worth.

The old tailor told me that Aura would not want to see me drag-
ging my sadness around in a heavy, black wool suit and recommended a charcoal gray. When Chucho, our favorite among
the security guards in the building at Escandón, a stocky fiftyish
man with kind, almost feminine eyes, saw me for the first time
after Aura's death, he came out from his booth to intercept me,
and said:

Resignación, señor. Resignación.

On what would have been the first Monday after our vacation at the beach the carpenter turned up, as we'd arranged, to
deliver our beautiful new bookshelves. It had been twelve days
since Aura's death. The carpenter lived in the far outskirts of the
city, and despite his working-class origins and life, he had rust-
colored hair and blue eyes in his craggy face. The morning when
he'd come to measure our walls, he'd noticed that both Aura and
I were hungover from a night out in the cantinas, and had given
us a gruffly paternal speech about his own youthful alcoholism
and how he'd given up drinking forever when he became a father.
Now I told him about Aura. After a long moment of silence, he
put the newspaper he was carrying—one of the city's many crime
and scandal tabloids—down on the table and opened it to a story
about a woman in Polanco who'd been struck by a car and killed.
There was a photograph of her lying on her stomach in the street,
in a blue dress, her hands open on the pavement, blood pooling
around her head.

The carpenter said, Look at this woman, hit by a car and killed,
a mother of two small children. These things can happen to anybody,
Francisco, and they happen every day.

Three wise men: the tailor, the carpenter, and the security
guard. In those first days and weeks after Aura's death, nobody
spoke sounder words to me.

Charcoal gray instead of black.
Resignación, señor, resignación.
These things happen every day.

I did, at least, heed the tailor.

On January 17, 2009, in Brooklyn, New York, our daughter Natalia wasn't born. How did I mark that day? I didn't even remember that it was the day until late in the afternoon. I dressed my ear, which seemed to be healing in a way that would leave it looking like the smashed torn ear of a boxer. Worked a bit. Went for a walk. I thought about stopping into a church to sit and think about Natalia and Aura for a while, but I didn't.

One frigid misty evening soon after, as I was walking back from a restaurant, I saw, in the tree at the end of our block, up amid the wet, bare branches shining in the streetlights' glare, Aura smiling down on me the way she had a few nights after her death when she'd seemed to be floating inside her own halo of moonlight over the Zócalo. Happiness and amazement dissolved my disbelief, and I stood on the sidewalk grinning back at her, warming with a loving glow of my own. I went to the tree, laid my hands on the trunk, and kissed it.

It seemed credible to me that Aura would choose a neighborhood tree to hide in, and especially that tree, the biggest on our block, a hale, silver maple, in summer lush with foliage though now its expansive boughs and intricate branches were bare. In the spring, Aura had walked up and down the streets photographing the trees with their bright new leaves and flowers; she'd bought a field guide to the trees of the Northeast so that she could identify them and learn their names. For the next several days, every time I came down the block, I found Aura in that tree, her smile and shining eyes floating among the branches, and sensed her happiness to see me, and I always stopped to kiss the trunk. But one afternoon I came walking down the block with something else on my mind and forgot to look up into the tree and I'd just passed by it when I felt a force yank my head back as if grabbing me by the hair. Disconcerted, chastened, I turned and went back to the tree, apologized, and kissed it. I wondered what the neighbors must think of this behavior. The tree happened to be directly in front of the brownstone where, in the basement apartment, a burly, aging biker-type with defensive-tackle biceps and a thick black-gray beard lived. I wondered what he would think when he noticed that I kept stopping in front of the gate to his apartment to kiss the tree. I wasn't worried that he'd harm me but I did imagine him coming outside to say something like, What the fuck are you doing? and I wondered what I would answer. So, after about a week of this, if there were people out on the sidewalk, or if I saw the biker's lights on and his curtains pulled aside, I only reached out a hand and tickled the trunk as I passed, while whispering, Hola, mi amor ¿cómo estás hoy? Te quiero. I felt an unaccustomed emotional lightness, something almost like happiness, during those days. Was I going a little crazy? It isn't really Aura in the tree, I told myself. Nevertheless, one cold night I woke around three in the morning and remembered that I hadn't stopped to greet the tree even once that day. I sprang out of bed, threw my down jacket on over my pajamas, put on my sneakers, and went outside. It had been a night of freezing rain. The sidewalk was slippery with ice and it reminded me of how Aura had never really mastered walking on icy sidewalks; she'd always slip and slide and I'd tease her that she was like Bambi on the frozen pond. Aura's tree had never looked more beautiful than it did that night, enameled and blazing as if a mix of liquid diamonds and starlight had been poured over it.

Francisco, she said, I didn't get married just to spend time by myself in a tree!

¡Claro que no, mi amor! I put my arms around the trunk and pressed my lips to the frozen rough bark.

My ear healed; it was as if Aura had come inside from her tree to give it a miraculous kiss in the middle of the night, or else it was the powers of the tea-tree mint treatment shampoo. If anything, the ear looked a little smoother and fresher than the uninjured one, as if it had grown a new layer of baby skin, the only scarring a few barely discernible minnow nibbles along the cartilaginous rim. And it made me think of Aura's big beautiful ears, and of how Natalia should have been born by then, with big beautiful baby ears of her own.

A few days later a check for $17,612 came in the mail from the insurance company of the teenager who'd hit me with her car.

On January 29, I woke before dawn to find Aura stretched out beside me in our bed, nearly invisible, a lighter darkness within the darkness of the room but with her distinct shape. Was I awake? Was this longing? Or was it the result of having read that same day a book written by a psychiatrist who'd studied the survivors of near-death experiences? What I'd experienced after being hit by that car fit with the recurring and overlapping details in the survivors' testimonies that had convinced that psychiatrist to posit the possible existence of some other spirit world beyond this one. Maybe the book was hokum, but it was suggestive.

Did you just come in from the tree? I asked Aura.

No, she said. Mi amor, that's your imagination. Pobrecito. She giggled. Why would I want to hide in a tree in the middle of winter?

So this is my imagination, too?

No, this really is me. Of course it is.

Aura, do you promise?

Sí, mi amor, it's me.

I don't get it. If you can visit me like you are now, then why don't you come all the time? I've been so lonely without you.

We're not allowed out that often, she said. If I were here all the time, then I would be a ghost, and I don't want to be a ghost. Ghosts suffer.

That makes sense, I said. And I thought, It really does make sense.

There was so much I wanted to ask her. Well, just imagine. But before I could get another word out, Aura said, Frank, I came now because I need you to do something for me. I want you to go to Paris to find my mother.

Your mother's in Paris?

But Aura was gone, dispelled back into the air, into the chilled early morning light.

I wrote an e-mail to Brasi and asked him to find out for me if Aura's mother was in Paris. He wrote back that same day to tell me that he was sure Juanita was in Mexico. He'd seen her that morning at the UNAM.

22

A novel I read in the weeks after I was hit by the car had been recently published: it was described as a 9/11 book, the horror of that day and its dark aftermath being the cause of a separation between the main character and his traumatized wife, who leaves him in New York and takes their child back to Europe. It was a lonely story, narrated by a depressed main character, but near the end of the book, when he gets his wife and child back, his circumstances seem to brighten. They take a trip to a tropical beach, where the narrator discovers bodysurfing and encourages his wife to bodysurf, too. He tells her that it's easy. What he describes as a slightly menacing wave comes along, and he says something like, Here we go, and he raises his arms and puts his head down, catches the wave, and surfaces however many yards away, exhilarated. But the wife hasn't moved. She could care less about bodysurfing. When he exhorts her to catch the next wave she answers that she'd rather just swim, and coolly floats away on her back.

Too uncanny, an impossible coincidence. Did the author know? When he made the wife reject her husband's invitation to bodysurf and she just swims away, did he know that he was saving her life?

Unbearable, if the answer to that question is actually *yes*.

23

At our wedding we put a disposable cardboard camera on every table, but afterward we left the cameras we'd collected in the apartment in Escandón, inside a plastic trash bag. It was only a few weeks after Aura died that I finally took them, about fifteen cardboard cameras in all, to a film lab in Mexico City to be developed. I was surprised by how many intimate shots of Aura and me there were among the two hundred or so snapshots that came back. The two of us kissing, whispering to each other at our table, standing together in the shadows at the edges of the party, dancing close. It was as if private detectives had been hidden among the guests, spying on us, gathering evidence. These pictures seemed more *close in*, somehow, than those taken by the professional wedding photographer. Yet not one of those disposable camera spies caught either of us with even an accidental expression on our faces that I wasn't happy with. My favorite of those snapshots, taken near the end of the party, is of Aura alone, from behind, carrying her bridal, platform disco shoes in her hand like an athlete leaving the field, one bare foot kicked back as she steps, hoisting the dress's hem, her blistered sole smudged with shoe dye, perspiration, and even blood from all the hours of dancing. It turned out that the quick eye and reflexes that caught Aura's naked foot just as it kicked back didn't belong to some lucky amateur but to our friend Pia, a photographer whose work is shown all over the world. The black-and-white photograph on our wedding invitation was Pia's, too—the invitations were Pia's and her husband Gonzalo's wedding gift to us—taken in a street near their Montmartre apartment. It shows Aura from the waist down in her winter coat and boots, one of my legs is on the left and our hands are joined in the middle; the heart of the image, though, is our stark shadows falling across the sun-brightened cobblestones, holding hands.

We didn't begin to look for a Catholic priest who could marry us until three months before the wedding. Aura's mother wanted this, and I thought my mother would be happy, too. Mostly, I wanted to appease Juanita. The wedding planning was getting out of control. There'd been plenty of tense conversations about money, and disagreements, especially between Aura and her mother, who had different ideas. That wedding is the concrete foundation of my credit card debt. Juanita and I were more or less splitting the costs. She was inviting at least a hundred guests—family, friends, and colleagues, from all over Mexico—and Aura and I were inviting about sixty friends. In the end, more than two hundred people came. Our wedding planners, a team of San Miguel de Allende gringa expats, had plenty of suggestions that were surely perfect for the sorts of weddings they usually put together and that they relentlessly pushed on us but that I was constantly having to push back against, while at the same time trying to avoid the impression, before the wedding planners but also before Juanita, that I was skimping because I couldn't afford it. No, we really didn't want the wedding-party cover band the planners always employed; we'd hire our own DJ in the DF. We didn't want illuminated thunder sticks, a Mexican hat dance, or a fireworks display. Yes, we did want the live donkey with flagons of tequila holstered to its saddle. We did want *papel picado* banners hung inside the tent over the tables, with "Aura & Frank" cut into them. It was Juanita's idea to also order some that read, "Viva Red Sox," in honor of my father's memory. We did want mariachis for after the ceremony and at the end of the party. We wanted the tequila to last until dawn. I told Aura that I wanted our wedding to be like the climactic village fiesta scene in that movie *The Wild Bunch*, minus the massacre. I teased her that my best men, Saqui and Gonzalo, and I were going to ride in for the wedding ceremony on horseback and dressed in charro gear, like Steve Martin, Chevy Chase, and Martin Short in *Three Amigos*.

But it turned out to be much harder than we'd expected to find a priest who could or would marry us. Mexican couples usually reserve their priests a year in advance, and are supposed to attend classes, and the priests expect to conduct the wedding Mass inside a church. None of that was in our plans. Couldn't we find some easy-going lefty priest? Aura knew of a Catholic school and monastery run by Dominicans in the south of the city that, because of its activist role in poor neighborhoods and Chiapas, had some kind of unofficial involvement with the university, and she made an appointment. The school's reception area was in an open corridor alongside a cement courtyard. The priest who came out to meet us looked like a high school football coach: a broad-shouldered man in windbreaker and jeans, with neatly combed gray hair, wearing silver-framed glasses. He was French, Padre Jacques. He sat against the edge of the reception desk, arms folded across his chest, while we sat before him like schoolchildren, in plastic chairs. We explained what we wanted: for him, if willing, to come to Atotonilco, the old Catholic shrine village outside of San Miguel, on the twentieth of August, to marry us. But instead of inside the church itself, our wedding would be on the grounds of a restored old hacienda we'd rented; if, under those circumstances, he couldn't do a whole Mass—we didn't actually want a nuptial Mass—we'd be grateful if he could say a blessing. We'd pay travel expenses, of course, and whatever else he charged.

Aura had had the normal Catholic childhood education—some Sunday school, catechism classes, First Communion—and as a baby I'd been baptized and confirmed. Mostly, we confessed, we were doing this to please our mothers. Padre Jacques seemed to understand, and didn't plumb us further. But he had plenty to say. His Spanish, however fluent, poured out sounding like French, his mouth making the forceful exertions of an excited French speaker, his chin jabbing at us. He only required six weeks of preparation classes. We still had time. Christ also reveals his oneness with us through the sacrament of marriage—so began the lesson part. *Misterio Sacramental hasta la muerte,* I definitely remember those words. Marriage, like all the sacraments, was best understood as a preparation for the final sacrament of death and for the eternal grace of salvation; that was his main point. It was about preparing our children for the eternal grace of salvation, and their children's children. On and on he went, repeating the words "Christ," "death," and "salvation," seemingly in every possible combination, getting more and more worked up and abstract. For some reason, this tirade made me feel like Woody Allen in *Annie Hall,* when he sits down to Thanksgiving dinner with the WASP family and they say grace and suddenly he turns into a Hassid. I was sharply biting the inside of my cheek to keep from laughing. Aura was straining to look attentive and serious, but I saw her eyes widen and her lips thin, and realized she was trying not to burst out laughing, too. Death, Christ, death, marriage, salvation, the Holy Ghost, the Trinity, on he went. Thank you, Padre, yes, we understand, our marriage is a preparation for eternal salvation. But Padre Jacques couldn't marry us anyway, not in late August. No, *c'est impossible.* Still, we needed to come to the preparation classes. Out on the sidewalk Aura and I leaned against the whitewashed wall, barking with laughter, jajaja. What a bizarro priest! Oh, mi amor, I was trying so hard not to laugh, me too, that was hilarious, the way he kept going on about death! Jojojo.

I don't think we're going to find a priest to marry us, I said. I'm ready to give up. Aura said, Yeah, I don't even want a priest anymore. She wasn't even sure she wanted a wedding, not a big one. She'd be happier, she kept insisting, if we just got married at city hall in New York.

Then how did we, Aura, too, in the end, all get so carried away? Maybe Juanita began to see it as the kind of wedding she'd always dreamed of putting on for her daughter, in scale at least, however else it fell short of her fantasy, beginning with the groom; a wedding she never could have afforded on her own. The wedding was also a new way to prove to Juanita how much I loved her daughter. Juanita who'd once grabbed my BlackBerry off a restaurant table, inspected it, and held it aloft while she announced that I couldn't be as in love with Aura as I claimed because I didn't have a single photograph of her in my phone. But that BlackBerry didn't have a camera, and I'd never e-mailed photographs from my computer to download them onto my phone because it hadn't even occurred to me to do that. I remember kind of marveling at Juanita, that she'd honed in on this one chink in a love that I was always so proud to show off, like the proverbial tiny slipup that undoes the perfect crime. The wedding planning was one more thing that strained Aura's nerves, but she got caught up in it anyway, spending hours organizing and updating the wedding planning Web site on her laptop. She burned CDs with music that she imagined would play before the ceremony and that always included winsome, girly, Spanish pop from her early adolescence, like Jeanette and Mecano, as if to evoke the mood of a girl's daydreams of marriage. Planning the seating, drawing diagram after diagram, analyzing why this person or couple should or shouldn't be seated at the same table with that one, was like turning gossip into a board game.

Aura and I understood our reasons for getting married; it wasn't just romantic impulse, like it had mostly been for me the first time, when I was in my midtwenties. We knew there were ways to commit, to "feel married," without undergoing the official rite. Had Aura and I been more radical-bohemian, planning to raise a family in Berlin or someplace like that, we could have forgone marriage. But we had practical motives, too, such as Aura's immigration status. Also: a wedding as public expression-recognition-celebration with family and friends. I *have* found my missing half. *We have found in each other.* Let's be joined in every way possible, including by marriage. Let's make children.

Our fat leather-bound wedding photo album that Natalia will so like to pore over, in childhood, in girlhood, in scornful adolescence: Look at Mom standing next to that little donkey in its straw sombrero, laughing, hair blowing across her face—okay, she does look beautiful—a bottle of tequila in her hand, a strap of her wedding dress fallen off her shoulder exposing that infamous tattoo she had until she got it lasered off just before I was born so that the whole world wouldn't see it every time she had to breast-feed me. Mom gaping in astonishment as Daddy cuts into the wedding cake with a machete! Tía Fabis and Tía Lida throwing rose petals over Mom, and she's smiling and jumping up into a cloud of falling petals, hands held out, so that she looks like she's levitating. But, yuck, Daddy dyed his hair. You can tell that he dyed his hair because it's so solid and black, not like in all the other pictures from back then. Mom made him do it. She said, Yeah, I made Papi dye his hair. See how your father would do anything for me? Poor ole Dad. Mom wanted him to look younger, especially in front of all Mama Juanita's friends, colleagues, and distant relatives. That was before Mom finally forced my grandmother into AA by telling her she was barred from baby-sitting me if she didn't go. Now Mama Juanita hasn't had a drink of liquor in fifteen years! That doesn't stop her from making fun of Daddy, who she treats like he's a giant brain-damaged ostrich, but she makes fun of everybody, she's hilarious, I love her; when I stay with her in her house in Taxco on school vacations I have the best time! After Mom wrote that famous book about the Mexican girl who goes to live with her shrink husband in a French lunatic asylum and invents the robot shoes, she and Daddy bought the house back from my great-grandmother Mama Violeta's former maid, but that's another story that I've heard a zillion times.

The wedding video and color photographs were a wedding gift from Juanita's cousin. But I can't stand to watch the wedding video. You'd think I'd want to watch it all the time, as it's the only video of Aura that I have. That video used to make me want to scream with embarrassment even when Aura was alive. Why so much more footage of me than of Aura? Why was the camera person so riveted by me? Because I looked like I'd just been miraculously cured of blindness, aiming my stretched Muppet grin all over the place. My exuberance is pure—it's not like I felt undeserving, or like I'd gotten away with something. But I'd stopped—long before Aura—expecting or imagining that a day like this one would ever come, and that's too obvious in the video. There was something unguarded, out of control, undignified in my comportment, going among the guests like a romping dog, showing everybody my enormous grin.

I had no family at the wedding. About nine days before, my mother had fallen and broken her hip, and my sisters were staying to take care of her. But I was relieved not to have to deal with them. The ceremony was on a small island in the middle of a pond on the hacienda, while the guests watched from the lawn. The civil judge who conducted it was a baby-faced twenty-six-year-old in his first year of practice. Pia took a photograph that captured Aura walking alone—before she reached her waiting stepfather who would accompany her the rest of the way—across the lawn toward the island, her white veil hiding her face, holding her bouquet; above her, fuming, dark clouds can be seen atop still sun-suffused ones, casting shadows and light on the Alamo trees. It's a lonely and disquieting photograph, the last in that roll of film, and sprocket tears pierce the image on the far right like scorching talons. It rained, a windy drizzle, and guests retreated to the porch of the hacienda house, but before the ceremony was over it stopped. I went through the vows grinning and nodding like a bobblehead doll. Aura looked attentive, serious, a bit overwhelmed. The Mexican civil ceremony is traditional Old Mexico, long but not so poetic. No phrase so memorable as "love, honor, cherish, and protect," though vow number four states that the man, as the principal source of courage and strength, owes the woman, along with nourishment and direction, his protection. The woman is lauded for her beauty, self-sacrifice, compassion, and intuitive insight; she should treat her husband always, says vow number five, with delicacy and respect. Afterward, Aura joked that they could edit those vows down to one line and save a lot of time—she dropped into her low voice: The truth of the Master is the Slave, and the truth of the Slave is the Master.

When it was over, mariachis started to play, and two boys led the little tequila-bearing burro across the wet lawn. The Mexicans surged into the big white, open tent and sat wherever they wanted, totally ignoring our painstakingly planned seating. When our hipster Mexican DJ led off his first set with Pérez Prado and some techno-cumbias, he provoked a stampede of middle-aged Mexicans, Juanita's people, to their parked cars; they came rushing back with Beatles and ABBA CDs in their hands that the DJ, though at first he protested—"Then you cannot say that DJ OXO played at your wedding"—obligingly mixed into his playlist the rest of the night. The dancing went on until nearly dawn. There's a Mexican tradition among wedding waiters to try to get the bride and groom totally smashed, probably once a great boon in a country where the bride was supposed to come to her marriage bed a virgin. Every time I turned, a waiter was waiting to refill my tequila glass. I felt like I was being hunted. I fell backward into the mud, laughing, as Aura and I climbed into one of the vans waiting to take guests back into San Miguel.

A wealthy friend of Juanita's in Guadalajara had donated a good portion of the tequila. A friend of mine who owns restaurants in the Condesa got me a wholesale price on the wine. And so on. That's how we pulled off our grand wedding. Its success did help establish a feeling of family unity, some trust, and a softening, I think, of Juanita's maternal angst. Even if Aura kept saying she would have been just as happy to get married at city hall.

How were we supposed to be, now that we were married? Should there be a change? There was some shyness or confusion about that, manifested as constraint, during the first day and a half of our honeymoon, at a remote eco resort with a baby-sea-turtle hatchery, on the Pacific Coast in Nayarit. What a beautiful sunny morning! Time to get down to the serious honeymoon business of reading serious literature in our hammocks! On the second day, we went horseback riding. My horse galloped away with me down the beach, ignoring my shouts and yanks on the reins. The comedy of our narrative was restored: Aura had fun evoking me bouncing helplessly in the saddle as the horse bolted, to the amused cackles of our cowboy guide. Our cabaña was on the ocean, lit at night only by candles and oil lamps; there was no electricity. Blue crabs scuttled everywhere and we took photos of them backed into corners, raising their samurai claws. There was a lagoon that we rowed across in a little boat to go to supper at night. In the dining room we drank margaritas and played Scrabble, allowing both English and Spanish words. Aura played Scrabble with a book to read in her lap at the same time. The other hotel guests also kept to themselves, and gave the impression of being rock stars and middling financial hoodlums on badly needed retreats, never removing their dark glasses and their baseball hats with the bills pulled low, staying out of the sun. The surf was too rough and treacherous for swimming; the hotel had signs on the beach that prohibited going in the ocean. There was a pool area sculpted to seem like a part of the beach. I went swimming in the ocean anyway, though it's more accurate to say I ran in just far enough to dive under a wave, then turned and charged out through the heavy rock-scrambled drag. A hotel attendant watched me come up the beach from the water with a disapproving expression. He pointed at the sign and called out, Está prohibido nadar, señor.

No matter what, Aura told her friend Mariana, she knew that she could count on me to protect her. She felt safe with me. I always looked out for her. I'd throw myself in harm's way before I'd ever let anything happen to her, Aura said to Mariana in Mexico City, a few days before we went to Mazunte in July of 2007, and that was one of the reasons she was happy in her marriage to me.

Even though, earlier that spring, I'd nearly gotten Aura killed. We'd gone up to New Bedford, where I wanted to do some research for a novel I was starting. Like many New Yorkers who don't keep cars in the city, I rarely get to drive. I'm more nervous at the wheel now than I used to be when I drove more regularly, though I'm not a hesitant driver. In Mexico City, where Aura had a little red Chevy hatchback that she kept at her mother's, she always drove, darting around in that clogged anarchic traffic like a whirligig beetle. But on our trip to New Bedford I drove, in our rented SUV. I missed a turn and, in a flustered burst, tried late to catch it, turning sharply across the lane to my right. The car in that lane screeched to a stop, the driver laid on its horn, and shouts of *You fucking asshole*, astounded and nasty stares, broke out all around me.

Aura was sitting in the passenger seat, where the car would have struck. Shaken, she blurted in English, You are a stupid, stupid man.

She'd never spoken to me with such contempt. Ashamed, I drove on, imitating a normal person who'd never even intended to turn. A few minutes passed before Aura softly apologized, almost mumbling: I didn't mean it. In that kind of situation people say things they don't mean. It's the adrenaline, she said.

A stupid, stupid man. I couldn't get it out of my mind; it nagged at me for days and whenever I remembered it made me feel sad again. It was a stupid, stupid thing to have done, to try to turn without even looking across that lane. Why such a panicked impulse over a missed turn?

24

I took Aura's pack of Camel Lights out of the kitchen hutch drawer, got some matches, put on my down jacket, and went outside. It was after ten at night and freezing; when I sat down on the stoop, the cement stung like dry ice through my jeans. A few parked cars were still crusted with last week's heavy snow, or, not yet dug out, trapped in their icebergs, but on the sidewalks and in the middle of the street, the snow was now reduced to scraps and a dirty frozen slush. I lit up. Locked to the inside of the black iron fence in front of the downstairs entrance and the trash cans was Aura's bicycle, half-buried in a mound of snow, missing its seat, rusting away. I hadn't been able to find the key to her lock. Every couple of weeks, it seemed, somebody used to steal her bicycle seat. Where were those seats now? How far away does the traffic in stolen bicycle seats reach? Was someone in Moldova riding around on Aura's bicycle seat? This was the first cigarette I'd smoked in thirteen years. I inhaled and coughed. I inhaled again, held the smoke down. Dizziness; a slowly whirling nausea rising up through me. My fingers and ears hurt from the cold. I looked toward the end of the block, at the black gnarled branches and wispy twigs of her tree against the moon hovering directly behind. A couple of bicycle delivery guys came pedaling down the street, sweatshirt hoods up from under their jackets, the crunch of their tires through mud-ice, the soft percolation of their Mexican Spanish, every few words a *güey*. I want my friend back, I thought; we talked in signs and formed a great team. Maybe I feel sick of people not understanding what this is like, but it's not like I wish for anyone else to live through this. I stamped out Aura's cigarette and lit another one.

Hold her tight, if you have her; hold her tight, I thought, that's
my advice to all the living. Breathe her in, put your nose in her
hair, breathe her in deeply. Say her name. It will always be her
name. Not even death can steal it. Same alive as dead, always.
Aura Estrada.

25

It's so cold in Alaska...

You were going to become a rock star. You didn't realize it yet, but you were going to drop out of Columbia—and probably end up dumping me, too—for the grungy glamour of life on the road and at least modest stardom. Raul, a kid you knew from Mexico City who was at Columbia, too, studying architecture, had formed a band that was playing at clubs downtown and around the Northeast. The band had decided that what they needed to get them "to the next level" was a female vocalist, and so they were holding auditions. Raul invited you to try out. For days you shut the French doors to our bedroom and sat on the floor playing that song on your laptop and singing along to it:

Stephanie says...

It's so cold in Alaska...

I knew they'd choose you. You didn't have a great voice, but you didn't need one. You would just need to be able to carry a tune and softly speak-sing the lyrics, well, like Nico. The band, I was sure, must above all be seeking a certain look, and you looked like a Mexican Bjork. I had to accept it. I'd vowed to avoid the carica-ture of the controlling older lover. The last thing you were looking for was a Tommy Mottola. Anyway, you didn't think it would be the end of us if you became a rock musician, it would only mean the occasional weekend away and rehearsal time. I knew all the things it could and probably would mean, but kept my mouth shut.

That was during our first winter together. I went with you to the Lower East Side the day of your audition, a gloomy February Saturday afternoon. While you went off to the recording studio

the band had rented, I waited in a coffee shop next to the Tenement Museum. I sat at the window, sipping coffee, telling myself to
feel happy for you, "Stephanie Says" playing over and over inside
me like the saddest good-bye song ever. I felt a kind of grief, not
the heavy eviscerating thing itself, but its predatory shadow, like a
shark's shadow, pass through me that day. Everything was about to
change. I had to accept it. Finally you came into the coffee shop,
with that tight goofy smile, sat on a stool next to me, took a sip of
my coffee—the startling vermilion lipstick smudge you left on the
cup's whitish rim—and then after you'd gulped down a big chunk
of my second order of carrot cake, your gap-toothed smile widened
into one of broad embarrassment and you merrily announced, ¿Te
cae, güey? Raul says I have the worst voice ever, that I don't have
the least idea of how to sing. But they were nice about it. Oh, and
the girl who went before me was so good, they have to choose her.
They made videos of all the singers who tried out. Frank, we have
to get that video back and destroy it.

I told you how brave you'd been to try and how proud I was of
you and that I loved the way you sang "Stephanie Says" and that I
would give anything to see that video.

You always felt destined for stardom of one kind or another. But
the fear that maybe that wasn't true wouldn't leave you alone. That
you were no more than the classes you'd taken, the schools you'd
attended, the books you'd read, the languages you spoke, your scholarships, your master's thesis on Borges and the English writers, and
so on, but nobody unique, with a talent only your own. You were
desperate for something that was yours alone. I was yours alone,
but that isn't what you meant.

26

"La Casa Grande" was what we called Columbia, and the MFA program was "La Casa Chica," the way in Mexico a man refers to the house where he lives with his wife and children by the former, the secret abode he keeps for his lover by the latter. Three days a week Aura taught undergrads at Columbia, while working on her thesis proposal, and helped organize an academic conference sponsored by her department. She had MFA classes two nights a week and a steady stream of reading and writing assignments. She accepted every invitation to write for Mexican magazines and the occasional English-language literary review. Was it possible to take on such a heavy workload without eventually being overwhelmed by it? Not really.

We just have to make it to the summer, we exhorted each other. This summer we'll spend two weeks in Mazunte—our favorite Pacific beach. Neither of us in our lives had ever spent more than a week at a beach. Our honeymoon had lasted six days.

At Columbia only a few of Aura's closest friends knew she was in a writing program. If found out, she'd probably be expelled; she might even be sued or deported. Deportation was our midnight fear. She was in the United States on a student visa through Columbia, and what if it was revoked? City College's policy toward undocumented students was don't ask, don't tell; Aura's being enrolled there would hold no sway with the ICE agents. Marriage to a citizen no longer automatically brought a green card and we'd been warned that getting one was now an extremely slow process, embedded with traps. We knew we'd better get an immigration lawyer but so far all we'd managed to do was tape to the refrigerator the telephone number of a lawyer recommended by Silverman.

In the MFA program, Aura's being at Columbia didn't have to be kept so secret, but she played it down as much as she could. Many writing students, Aura had quickly discovered, didn't read much. Or they read mostly from the same bowl of U.S. contemporary fiction soup, a few Brits, Irish, and the like floating in there, too. When the Famous Australian Writer assigned the opening chapter of *The Portrait of a Lady* in "craft class" as an example of "how to introduce multiple characters and their relationship to each other," some of the other students complained. What's this? Boring and old-fashioned. How is this supposed to help us manage multiple points of view in the contemporary manner? But Aura and her friend Wendy immersed themselves in those pages, meeting the night before class to go over it line by line. For Aura, being able to read this way again, letting every word convey meaning and emotion she was under no pressure to discount, was a revelation. I think being in an MFA program gave Aura a new perspective on Columbia: that in combination the two were adding up to what she'd originally hoped for from graduate school. Applying her doctoral readings, however inappropriately, to her fiction led to something like new muscles; deeper patterns and layers. Her writing in English was overcoming its second-language fuzziness; she took more confident risks.

> And you thought, Sure! God would like Baby D's harp and accordion the same as he likes the androgynous angels music; and perhaps you will find out when you go to heaven, after your gig with the Shanghai Bureau. And perhaps you will find your bear costume in a closet in Heaven . . .

That was from a class exercise assigned in the FAW's workshop, and when Aura read that piece aloud, a hush fell over the class, impressed, disconcerted; and I felt my heart break again, more than a year later, when I heard the FAW read it aloud at the memorial service—"a fragment . . . of a fragment . . . of a fragment of a life," he called it—that fragment of a life that was still everything to me.

But reading her thesis proposal is painful. There she seems either like a butterfly thrashing against flypaper or like a figure skater laboriously hitting her compulsory marks in the short program: "performativity in crisis," the "larval fascism of subjectivity," the market, globalization, and so on. But ideas like the Deleuzean one about literature being part of the same disease against which it fights, playfully infiltrate her fiction, like in the story "The Belgian Artist," where the artist is reading a book called *The History of Germs* and a young woman comes to his bookshelf-lined apartment and says, "I can't stand books. They make me nervous." She was working on her novel, and also beginning to publish pretty regularly: an essay on Bolaño and Borges that was noticed by young literary writers in New York; more short stories. Later that spring, in May, for *Gatopardo,* a sort of Latin American *Vanity Fair,* she wrote a profile of a Mexican tailor in Nashville who used to design outfits for Elvis; also for Dylan. That was the first time she was ever flown anywhere by a magazine to write an article. In the pictures I saw of Aura in Nashville, at the tailor's annual Cinco de Mayo party, she looked so self-possessed and mysterious, as if she belonged there, among those Southern strangers in their redneck-hip Western wear, a world I could never have felt at ease in.

Still, as her thirtieth birthday approached, none of this—a few publications, work, ambition—was enough to soothe her. Aura could recite the names of every writer more or less of her own generation who'd published a novel or book of stories or essays in English or Spanish before they were thirty and she began to drive herself and me crazy with this scorekeeping. Aura, my darling, this desperation was something you were going to have to overcome. Those other writers hadn't spent their twenties studying for PhDs they didn't even want, I kept telling her. They'd devoted at least part of those years to their writing. It was okay! She'd started a little late but she was doing great! Better than great! Couldn't she see how great she was doing? Hadn't she realized that everybody saw how gifted she was?

Well, not everybody. She'd been roughly criticized in a work-shop by some of the students and hadn't taken it well. (A story that has since been posthumously published in *Harper's*, no less.) If one student said only one negative thing, she fixated on that and tuned out all praise.

This summer, mi amor, two weeks at the beach in Mazunte. We'll rent a beach house. Just three more months to go!

She endured another of those stretches where every morning she woke before dawn and lay awake worrying. She got out of bed feeling dizzy and exhausted. Sometimes she put coffee grounds in the coffee maker but forgot to put in water before turning it on; or she put in water but no coffee. Maybe all this was a normal symptom of turning thirty? She phoned Lola, soon turning thirty, too, and asked what was the first thing on *her* mind when she woke in the mornings, and Lola said, To go and pee.

It didn't help matters that I was finishing my own book, which made me seem remote and self-absorbed. Aura would sit at her desk in the next room sometimes pounding out gibberish on her clatter-ing keyboard to drown out my relentless typing. My inattentiveness irritated and wounded her. Every day she upbraided me about forget-ting to make the bed, or for leaving gunk in the sink after I'd washed the dishes, or for not shutting a drawer in the bedroom bureau. My workload wasn't quite as brutal as Aura's but I was under pressure, too. I was teaching two classes and was behind on the book, which had to be turned in by May. It was a narrative nonfiction book about a case of political murder in Central America, hard-fought in the courts and with ties to organized crime. The case was rife with violence—witnesses, potential witnesses, and other people related to the case kept getting murdered or disappeared—and had a cast of sinister and even psychopathic characters, including a few who'd become somewhat entangled in my life, if at a seemingly safe distance. The reporting was pretty much finished; I made one last short trip that spring, and was keeping up by Internet. That book sometimes took over my inner life in a way that I hated, infusing it with a silent obsessed frenzy and violent emotions that made me feel isolated in a world I was determined to shield Aura from. I worried about revenge too, about killers who might know that harming Aura would be the surest way to ruin me. No such thing was likely to happen, but my fear that they could easily reach us in Mexico if they wanted to—some of them had ties to narcos, to the Cartel del Golfo and Los Zetas—demanded precautions. That was why I told Aura that, with the book coming out in the fall, this would be our last summer in Mexico for at least two years. In three years, I figured, the most dangerous of those enemies, if they were still alive, would have fresher targets.

We'd spend the next summer in France; somehow we'd manage that, I promised her. And this summer we'd spend in Mexico, with those two weeks in Mazunte, rent a beach house there; I promised that, too. But it turned out that Aura was conflicted about spending even that summer in Mexico. She kept saying that she wanted to experience at least one summer in New York. If I said summer in New York was awful, hot, noisy, smelly, she said she wanted to find that out for herself and that I had no right to spoil it for her just because I'd lived there so long. Her friends loved summer in New York! At times she became fixated, again, on wanting to move to a new apartment, one with a garden, where we could have a dog. She spent hours cruising Craigslist for rentals, for a place that would allow pets. What she really wanted was to devote her energies to herself for once, to her own writing. It should have been obvious to me what was making her not want to go to Mexico. Even if it would have been impossible that summer for Aura not to feel that she had to be near her mother—and I believe it would have been impossible; but *would* it have been impossible?—I could have insisted that we go for only a month. We shouldn't have gone at all. I should have helped her be as ruthless and selfish, for once, as perhaps she was yearning to be. I could have found a garden apartment to rent, in a cheaper neighborhood. Our downstairs tenants actually moved out in April and that apartment was briefly available. There was about a five-day window when we could have snagged it. The backyard had rosebushes, two apple trees and a fig tree, shrubs, vegetable and flower plots, and grape vines on the fence, most of it requiring constant upkeep so we couldn't go away for the summer and let the grass turn to hay and everything be choked by weeds, withering in the summer sun. Also, that apartment rented for a thousand dollars a month more than ours. And you still weren't allowed pets. No, *Ow-rra*. I wanted to go to Mexico. Universal jury, if you want to find me guilty of something, find me guilty on that count. We should have stayed in New York that summer, tending our garden. *¿Le gusta este jardín?*

For years, Aura had worried that Rodrigo was going to leave her mother. Juanita's drinking, which had worsened, was usually his stated reason for their marital problems, though there were others. With more urgency than before, Aura had been begging and nagging her mother to seek help. During their nearly daily phone calls and Internet chats, they often fought furiously about it. One night in Mexico over Christmas break, Juanita and Rodrigo had come to meet us in a Condesa cantina-restaurant. We sat at a large round table drinking with our friends. When it was time to go, Juanita, leaning forward in her chair, reached across and around the table to snatch up glasses to drain the dregs, eyes fastening on each drink as if lining up a pool shot. Jaime, the deep-voiced Spaniard, murmured one of his kind jaunty jokes, Ay, caray, she beat me to it— something like that. Aura tried to be stoic but seeing her shame and anger went into me like a dagger. Her cheeks turned almost gray and with her grim expression, the sobered-up sadness in her eyes, her tightly downturned lips, it was like getting a glimpse of what a middle-aged Aura would look like if her life turned out to be a bitter disappointment. She shot a glare at her stepfather, helplessly-guiltily standing there, and went to her mother's side. Rodrigo had left a self-help paperback on divorce on the backseat of Juanita's car at least a year before and it was always there, like a sleeping skunk no one dared wake. Aura was convinced that her mother's terror of being left by her husband was what lay behind her drinking, that and her long rupture with her own mother, a constantly bleeding wound. And there was Aura in New York, growing into a woman, married, pursuing her own ambitions, who had less time for her. Abandonment, loneliness, helplessness, fear, all circling, closing in, that's what Juanita's life had become. For all Rodrigo's threats and insinuations that he was going to leave, Aura didn't fully believe he'd go through with it, for one thing because he didn't earn enough money to live somewhere halfway decent on his own. He was away, on the road, almost every week and, lately, on weekends, too. He was an athletically fit, still youthful-seeming man; it was hard to believe he didn't have a lover. And when he was around he inflicted plenty of cruelty, in his passive-aggressive, stolid jock way. Yet, despite everything, you sensed that he was still devoted to Juanita, that it wasn't just the home she provided. There was an undeniable voltage in her character that he, ordinarily a low-wattage guy, couldn't unplug from. She kept him on tenterhooks.

But we'd also perceived that Rodrigo, now a grandfather, yearned to spend more time with his grandchildren—two boys and a girl, the boys about four and two, the girl a newborn. In the past, Rodrigo had spent holidays with Juanita and Aura, choosing his moments to discreetly phone or go off to be with his long-banished daughter, Katia, but now that he had grandchildren his priorities had changed. That increasing attachment to his family, against Juanita's ongoing refusal to even acknowledge Katia's existence, would be, Aura had fretted, what finally drove her stepfather away from her mother for good. If the family could be reunited, at least on holidays—Christmas, Father's Day—might that be enough to keep Rodrigo from leaving? It was me who'd come up with that theory and, after clearing it with Aura, I'd spoken to Rodrigo. That was how our secret meetings with him and Katia began. I was the special envoi in this round of high-stakes diplomacy. Aura hadn't seen her stepsister in twelve years. Our negotiations, Aura insisted, had to be kept secret from her mother. So far, we had met with Rodrigo and Katia twice, once the previous summer and again in the winter, in two different restaurants. Both times, Katia came with her husband, who had a midlevel managerial position in a multinational appliances plant outside the city. They dressed like a young suburban couple: Katia, for that first meeting, in a gray jumper dress worn over a white blouse, with unflashy gold earrings and necklace; her husband in a scarlet sweater and dark slacks. Katia still had the perky air of the high school popular girl. Her chestnut hair was long, lustrous, and neat. She had a friendly smile—at least I thought it was friendly—but behind the liveliness of her eyes there was something very guarded. I sensed darkness inside of her, from her childhood, from her wayward years, that she probably never discussed with anybody anymore, except Dr. Nora Banini. I think that was what made me feel that I liked her; I was interested in her, felt an intuitive complicity with her. I had a lot in my past that I kept hidden, too. We'd both done well to survive our own selves and to be where we were now. I told Aura that I couldn't understand a parent, even a stepparent, banishing even a nineteen-year-old from home with such finality, forever refusing to try for any rapprochement. Of course, Katia had never sought to forgive or be forgiven, either. This was before I understood about Katia's childhood cruelty to Aura; before Fabis told me about it later, and as it was exposed in Aura's diaries.

But I couldn't have missed noticing, in Katia's barely restrained cheeriness, how deeply satisfying our first meeting was to her. We'd come to her, to ask her to help save Juanita's marriage. Katia let us know that she wasn't, in principle, against the idea. She looked at Aura across the table and said that she'd missed her little sister. Aura smiled back at her, said she'd missed her, too, and sank down a little lower in her seat. Under the right circumstances, said Katia, she could see us all getting together for Christmas, but . . . but . . . To encourage Katia, I blurted out a passionate little speech about the importance of family, describing myself as a "family-first person." Rodrigo and Aura both gaped at me and Aura said, with a little laugh, You're a *what*? I felt my face turning red. They knew I wasn't a family-first person, that no member of my own family had even come to our wedding and that I could have cared less. Look, I'm trying to be a diplomat here, I could have argued, not Moses or Jesus. What I meant, I said to Aura, is that as far as *you* and *your* family and the family *we're* going to make together are concerned,

I'm a family-first person *now,* and I always will be. Katia lit up: Aura, you're having a baby? Nooo, said Aura, not yet. Someday, I interjected, and Aura nodded, and Rodrigo grinned at us with affection and delight and said, Órale.

It was Katia's husband who openly came out against what we were proposing. He seemed clean-cut, sturdy, a little somber, but when he had something to say he was blunt. Why should they risk it? he asked. He knew that Juanita was a difficult woman. Why should he expose his wife and his children, the tranquillity of *his* family, on Christmas no less, to this difficult situation and to this difficult woman. Really, it was years too late for this. Katia had no stake in trying to save her father's marriage, no reason at all not to wish to see it end. The slightly nauseated look on Aura's face—it was as if she'd just crammed down an entire pastrami sandwich again—showed that she felt she was betraying her mother just by being there. Aura could at least have allowed herself to silently exult a little: she was the one living in New York, enrolled in a PhD program, on her way to becoming a writer like she'd always dreamed. But I doubt Katia thought she was doing any worse, living a straight middle-class life, with a little starter home in the suburbs. She had beautiful kids, a young and devoted husband, a part-time job of her own as a data analyst for a market research company. At our next meeting, Katia's husband said that it would have to be Juanita who made the first gesture of apology and reconciliation. He probably believed this was a conciliatory offer. If making it had been solely his idea, it would have been.

Aura said, I'm only here for one reason, to help my mother. If Papi leaves her now, when she's so vulnerable, it will destroy her. If there's a way to repair our situation and that will help Papi want to stay, then I have to try to ask for your help. But if you know my mother at all—she looked directly at Katia—then you know she is never going to apologize first.

Katia and her husband agreed to continue our negotiations when we came back from New York that next summer. In the end it was all for naught. In the spring, about a month before Aura's thirtieth birthday, Rodrigo left. One late morning while Juanita was at work and he was supposed to be, Rodrigo came back into the apartment, hastily packed his things in boxes, carried them out to the car, and drove away. He snuck out like a rat, said Ursula, the housekeeper, on the phone to Aura. It wasn't even his own car that he escaped in; he took Aura's little red Chevy, which he'd lately been driving as if it were his own. Where is he going to live, scoffed Aura, under a bridge? That joke became her way of making light of the loss. I hope Rodrigo is sleeping comfortably tonight, under his bridge. We didn't know where he was living; probably with Katia, we reasoned. I was surprised at first that this second paternal desertion hadn't affected Aura as I'd feared it would, stirring up old trauma, but what Aura had always insisted on turned out to be true: only one Dad narrative ran through her life. To her, Rodrigo was first and foremost "the husband," and now he wasn't going to be. A few days after he moved out, we flew down to Mexico, the first of two such trips we made that final spring, leaving Friday afternoon after Aura's last class. On those weekends, instead of going home to our own apartment in Escandón at night, we stayed with Juanita. I slept alone in the foldout couch in the study and Aura slept with her mother in her bed.

Though supposedly nobody had stayed in our Escandón apartment since I'd been forced by Juanita and her lawyers to vacate it, Fabis, who lived across the corridor, told me in an e-mail that there'd been a few nights when she'd seen the light on in our bedroom. Coming home late from a night out with Juanca, her boyfriend, when she'd stood outside the door sentimentally scratching at the steel panel alongside it with her key—that was how she and Aura used to summon each other—and saying Aura's name, the lights, she said, had flickered on and off. Spirits in the electricity, signaling by turning lights on and off, wasn't that a cliché of ghost stories? That last summer, Aura and I had flown down on July 3. A year later, when I flew down to Mexico alone for the first anniversary, I again left on July 3, on that same evening flight from Newark, and went directly to Fabis's apartment.

Our apartment had a long horizontal window of frosted glass facing the corridor and, upstairs on the sleeping loft, a vertical window covered by a curtain. The lights were off when I got there but I stood outside our door, stroking it with my hand, whispering to Aura. No lights flickered on and off. Fabis said that she'd last seen the lights on only about a month before. It was hard to believe that Juanita might have come and slept there, in our bed, which I'd left behind. But sometime during the last few weeks someone had disconnected the telephone answering machine. I'd been phoning from Brooklyn for months, to listen to Aura's hoarse-chipper greeting, until one day it didn't pick up, and then it never did again. But Fabis had already found out, from one of the tías, what had happened. Rodrigo had taken the answering machine to use in the new apartment he was renting somewhere in the city. He was still driving Aura's little red Chevy, too. In the weeks after Aura's death, Rodrigo had stayed by Juanita's side; he'd been there for Juanita, as much as he could be, but that hadn't led to their getting back together. Before he found his own place, had he been sneaking into our apartment to sleep?

A wall of industrial concrete about eight feet high separated the rear of the parking garage from our apartment's little garden patio. I could see our bamboos rising high above it, covering the flank of the old factory building next door. The bamboos had grown to a height parallel with the apartment above ours, which also had a glass wall on that side, but no patio. So their view was of our bamboos, of the soft dense foliage of those enormous green plumes, shimmering or pulled sideways in the rain and wind, delicate long shoots protruding like praying mantises waving their legs in the air. I didn't know our upstairs neighbors, but I'm sure everybody in that building knew about the dead girl on the ground floor. I wonder if they ever thought of Aura when they contemplated our bamboos.

* * *

At Aura's funeral Mass, in the chapel of the funeral home, Katia stepped firmly into the sister role, at least for me. We practically clung to each other; or rather she let me cling to her. While the priest at the flower-heaped white coffin was rotely telling us how at peace and happy Aura was now that "her suffering has ended and she is finally at the side of the Lord," Katia stood beside me, her arm hooked tightly into mine. She led me into the line of people waiting to take communion and I knelt, opened my mouth, and let the priest drop the tasteless, airy wafer onto my tongue for the first time in decades. Later, I felt foolish about that, but it had hardly been an act of volition; I was led, had wanted to be led, could easily have been led off a cliff. When my mother, on the phone, also said that Aura was at peace and happy at the side of the Lord, it made me so angry I didn't speak to her again for months.

Two years before, after my mother had broken her hip, my sisters had sold the house in Namoset and my mother had moved to an assisted living residence in Florida, where she had her own little apartment. When we visited, my mother would rake her frail hand through Aura's mane—this was when she'd grown it long—and say, But why don't you ever comb your hair, Aura? Why do you like having it in your eyes? Here, give me a hairbrush. And my mother would make Aura lower her head, and with a look of almost baffled concentration and exertion would slowly pull the brush through Aura's hair. After a few strokes, she'd give up, as if exhausted, and hand the brush back to Aura and say, with a titter, Well, you can brush it, can't you? Or my mother would say, But why do you dress like that, Aura? Who has ever heard of wearing blue jeans under a dress?

Later, Aura would say, Ay, Francisco, your mother, she's not the dainty little dama everyone makes her out to be. Ohhh, she likes to *joder!*—*screw around with me,* more or less. Aura always called my mother "Señora." I'd tell her not to, that it made it sound like my mother was her boss. I don't call your mother Señora, do I? Call my mother Yolanda, or Yoly. Aura would promise to, but the next time she spoke to my mother, she'd go right back to "Señora."

When was Aura's hair long? When was it short? Why can't I remember this? That's something I ought to be able to track in my memory the way I can follow Aura's travels by looking through her passport at the stamps: June 2005, short; February 2007, long...

My plan was to be in Mazunte on the first anniversary and then, that same afternoon of the twenty-fourth, fly back to Mexico City. I'd paid for a memorial Mass to be said the next morning at a church in the Condesa. When Juanita and Leopoldo had begun to threaten me with lawyers right after Aura's death, some of my friends had set me up with a lawyer as well. His name was Saúl Libnic, and he had a practice, with another partner, near the U.S. embassy. They usually handled white-collar criminal cases, but also specialized in U.S. clients with legal problems in Mexico. For this summer of the first anniversary, I'd subletted a studio apartment in the Condesa. Libnic lived in the neighborhood, too, and whenever he wanted to talk to me, we'd meet for an early breakfast at a juice bar on Amsterdam. He was in his early thirties, about my height, trim, with a shaved head and earnest, watery eyes. That morning Libnic explained that as a case had been opened and I was going to the coast anyway, I should make an appointment to see the district prosecutor in Puerto Ángel. The case had originated in Mexico City, he said, but had then been sent to Puerto Ángel. What did that actually mean, I asked, that a case had been opened? It meant, he said, that it had fallen to the district prosecutor in Puerto Ángel to open an investigation into Aura's death. We could assume, of course, that no evidence had turned up against me. There was no outstanding warrant. As a formality, though, I should testify, because I never had. I did testify, I reminded him, it just wasn't accepted because I didn't have my passport. Yes, he said, but in order to get the case

closed, I should testify. Taking into account the prior behavior of
Aura's uncle and mother, said Libnic, I should want to get it closed.
He recommended that he come with me to Puerto Ángel. I would
have to pay all the expenses, along with the legal fees. When he told
me how much that would cost, I asked if it was absolutely necessary
that he come, and he said, No, not absolutely. I said that I couldn't
afford to bring him. Libnic said he'd make the appointment for me
and sound out the district prosecutor about where the case stood.
Also, he needed to be paid for his work so far, in cash. Of course,
I said. Saúl, I asked, do you think there's any chance of my falling
into a trap? Oaxaca State was governed by the PRI. Through the
influence of Aura's uncle or those university lawyers Juanita had
mentioned, might the district prosecutor be ordered or bribed to
arrest me? Could they plant false witnesses? Libnic said that he
doubted that would happen, though taking into account the reality
of Mexican justice, it wasn't impossible; that was why he'd suggested
that he come with me, as a precaution. I'll think it over, I said, but
I really can't afford that. He said that I shouldn't worry about it too
much; it did seem like the worst had blown over. I suppose I could
have afforded to bring him, but I didn't want a lawyer with me in
Mazunte on the first anniversary of Aura's death.

Fabis's parents arranged a dinner in their home and invited both
Rodrigo and I. We hadn't seen each other since the funeral though
we'd been in contact a bit by e-mail. We went into Fabis's father's
study to talk in private. Yes, Rodrigo told me, Juanita was still blam-
ing me for Aura's death. But, he said, she wasn't suggesting that
I'd committed a direct crime anymore. According to Juanita, said
Rodrigo, I'd failed to protect Aura from her own impulsiveness.
What she was accusing me of now was of a fatal irresponsibility.

I just nodded. I knew that Rodrigo didn't want to debate with
me whether or not that was true. Anyway, I thought, there's no way
to say that I *did* protect her. I certainly did not protect her. All of
Aura's life, her mother had worried about, had tried to protect Aura

from her impulsiveness. Had I ever thought of Aura as especially impulsive? Would I ever have described her as impulsive?

Juanita was no longer in touch with the tías or Vicky. The reason, Vicky had told me in an e-mail, was that Juanita had cut off communication with anybody who did not agree that I was to blame for Aura's death, or who dared to suggest, as Vicky put it, that I had been "the love of Aura's life." But Juanita, I thought, surely needs to regard our marriage as an insignificant episode in Aura's life; something like a back door carelessly left open, through which her killer entered. Juanita had more than twenty years of memories of Aura in which they'd been at the center of each other's lives. What was that compared to my and Aura's four years? I'd heard from an old friend of Aura's who was still at the UNAM that Juanita was now going around saying that Aura—rather her ghost or spirit I presume—was living with her in her apartment. There was nothing odd about that. For a few weeks, at least, I'd been convinced that Aura was in the tree at the end of our block, and ever since I hadn't been able to walk past that tree without feeling guilty, as if I'd betrayed Aura by not trying hard enough to keep that belief alive, and by no longer stopping to kiss the trunk, or even to whisper to it.

Juanita hadn't done anything with Aura's ashes yet, as far as Rodrigo knew.

I told him that if he ever thought my speaking to Juanita could in any way be of help to her, I would do it.

He said that he was sure Juanita did not want to speak to me. If I had a need to speak to her, then I could send her an e-mail and ask her, he suggested. He gave me Juanita's new e-mail address: it was Aura's name, with numbers. I was using a new e-mail address, too, AUFRA, with some numbers. How alike we are, I thought; in some ways, totally, pathetically alike.

I have no need to speak to Juanita, I said. If it would help her for me to speak with her, I will, that's all, because Aura would want me to.

But what would I say if I did speak to her? I didn't kill your daughter. She doesn't even want to hear that. I did kill your daughter,

I'm sorry. I'm to blame. You were right to accuse me. Would that lighten her suffering?

Is there anything I can say to you, Juanita, that will free you from having to think of me, and from your consuming blame, assuming that is what you do and that it is consuming, and that you do want to be freed from it? Maybe you don't. Some people need somebody else to blame, as if that's their one key to sanity, or an incitement to stay alive. But likewise, Juanita, is there anything that I can say that will free me from always having to think about you, that will stop you and your blame from getting between me and Aura, from invading every corner of my mourning?

Every night I go to bed hoping that this will be one of the nights when I dream about Aura, but sometimes I have nightmares about Juanita instead.

At dinner, Rodrigo let us pass around his cell phone so that we could see pictures of his new girlfriend. She was blonde, maybe a dyed blonde, and looked quite a bit younger than him; in one shot she was entwined in bedsheets, her shoulder bare. He watched us pass his phone around with an expression of priestly solemnity. Good for him, I thought. It's what a man should be doing after a divorce. He'd scanned and downloaded a few photographs of Aura as a little girl onto his telephone, too, and the next day he e-mailed them to me.

For three summers in a row, Aura and I had given a weekend barbecue on our patio for family and friends. About a hundred burgers each time, plus sausages, ribs, and hot dogs for kids. I did the barbecuing, and Aura and Fabis made everything else, the salads and the fideo seco. Three summers in a row—enough to have established a family tradition of our own, I think. Now, this summer, I would do it on Fabis's patio, after the memorial service. I invited Rodrigo and Katia. I actually told him to invite Juanita, too, knowing that there was no chance that she would come. He told me that Leopoldo was taking Juanita out of the city for those days.

At the memorial service, Fabis, her mother, and I sat in a pew behind Rodrigo, Katia, her husband, and their three children. The ponytailed baby girl kept leaving her mother's side to crawl along the back of the pew and climb onto Rodrigo's lap where she would grab his cheeks with her little hands. He beamed with the pride of a youthful grandfather. Katia's husband kept reaching out to take Katia's hand, and he snuck her quick pecks on the cheek. She looked beautiful. Though I rarely see Katia, I thought, whenever I do, I feel more fondness for her. She moves me. People do change, they grow, and it also helps to have a good-guy husband who adores you.

27

The summer before the last one, Aura and I had stayed with Jaime and Isabel and their little children for a few days at San Agustinillo, the beach adjacent to Mazunte. They, along with another couple—a poetry professor and his wife—and some friends from Madrid, had rented a row of bungalows on the beach. Aura had taken a few classes with the professor at the UNAM. He had a meek yet gallant demeanor. I guess it was no secret that he'd had a crush on Aura when she was his student ten years before—Aura had known it. I saw him squinting at her with a lingering, slightly befuddled expression, and knew he was thinking something like, Seems like just yesterday. Later, when we'd fallen silent listening to the surf, the professor spoke about his friend the poet Manuel Ulacia, who'd drowned one night, elsewhere on the Pacific coast, a few years before.

Down the beach, boulders and rocks jutted and hooked sharply into the ocean, barricading the waves in a way that, close to shore, created a shallow swathe that children could play in.

But out at the steep, jagged end of the promontory, currents swirled. That's where, the next day, the professor was swimming when we heard his panicked yelps for help, Auxilio, auxilio! Jaime and I scrambled along the rocks and clumsily plunged-flopped into the water, too far from the professor to help him, but Aura darted to the top of a high boulder and launched herself into the air and landed like a ray from the sky alongside the professor and swam him to safety, her arm around his chest. That the professor hadn't been in any danger of being pulled out to sea and had just lost his nerve in the current's pull and was very sheepish afterward didn't diminish Aura's heroism. Aura saved my life, the professor kept repeating, looking bewildered, as if he wanted to make light of it but couldn't. Aura saved your life! we all clamored. Mi amor, what were you thinking? I heard him shouting for help, she said, and I just reacted! Impulsive, yes, with no time for fantasy or reflection. The fast fearless impulsiveness of a superior human, is what I honestly thought. My Aura! What a mother she's going to be! We had hearty laughs, too, at my and Jaime's expense, how the professor would have drowned if saving him had been up to us. I was disappointed when everybody, within hours, after lunch and their siestas, no longer wanted to talk about how Aura had saved the professor's life, as if now it was more important to protect the professor's feelings, or maybe his wife and children's feelings, by not referring to the incident anymore.

But what if it really had been a riptide and it had swept the professor and Aura out into the ocean and drowned them both? What would we be saying about Aura's impulsiveness now?

Impulsiveness: an ungovernable excess bubbling up from within.

Originally we were going to go to Mexico in late May or June, but then Aura decided to teach a summer-semester Spanish class at Columbia. She was taking care of her CV again, the extra money would come in handy, and she was in no hurry to get to Mexico. Our apartment in Mexico needed some work, though, so it was agreed that I'd go down in early June for a week or so to get things ready. Aura made me a to-do list: I was to find a carpenter to build bookshelves; install some needed extra lighting; we needed stuff for the kitchen; she needed a desk. I was looking forward to being in Mexico on my own like in the old days. But a few reprobate nights in the cantinas and terrible hangovers later, I felt baffled by myself. What had I actually been hoping for? I missed Aura; she missed me. We were running up a huge bill with our cell phone calls and I complained about it in an e-mail. She wrote back, This is why we work and earn salaries, Francisco. I bought her a table-desk, with a dark reddish finish. I tracked down the carpenter who seemed the most esteemed, to build bookshelves, and flew home.

* * *

On July 3, 2007, at about half past two in the afternoon, Aura went out the door of our Brooklyn apartment for the last time, and I brought our luggage down to the waiting car. Her new multicolored quilt had been left behind, folded in the closet; her unseated bicycle was double-locked to the iron fence. By four, we were in the airline's lounge at Newark, having received one free upgrade thanks to my frequent flier status after decades of hoarding miles. I told Aura she could go first class, of course; I'd ride in economy. We drank champagne and toasted the summer.

By the end of our first week back in Mexico, Aura began to feel freer and to enjoy herself. We went out, saw our friends. She was reading Juan Carlos Onetti's novel *La Vida Breve*. She'd been devouring Onetti's writing all spring. The short story she was writing, in Spanish, was about a young man who drops out of a U.S. doctoral program to take a teaching job at a secondary school in a remote part of Mexico; the school and the faculty seem imagined by a Mexican Kafka—a reviewer later wrote precisely that, after it was published—as does the main character's fraught nighttime telephone conversations with his father in Mexico City. That story's title is "*La vida está en otra parte.*" She worked at her new desk downstairs, by the slid-open glass door to the patio. She loved her apartment. She was sure now that sometime in the near future we'd be spending more than just summers and school vacations here, and that was fine with me. If her writing career was primarily going to be in Spanish, as Aura had now decided it was going to be, it would make sense to live in Mexico for a while, and if we were going to have a baby, she wanted to be near her mother.

Just around the corner from where we lived, a brand-new shopping mall had opened on Patriotismo. Our neighborhood was about a half hour walk from the Condesa, and before it hadn't even had a convenience store or anywhere close by to eat except for a few small, very humble comida corrida places and sidewalk stands, but no place to get a decent cup of coffee. Now we had a Starbucks, a Sanborns, an Italianni's, and some of those other chain restaurants that Aura had childhood nostalgia for, all beneath one roof, along with the usual mall stores. A few times for lunch we went and rode the escalator up to the food court and, one time, stayed to watch some of the martial arts movie playing on the giant wall of video panels, starring the late Brandon Lee. One evening Aura bought a tube of Chinese pick-up sticks in Sanborns and we took it into the mall's T.G.I. Friday's where, over tequilas and beers, we played. It was surprisingly absorbing, requiring a pickpocket's deftness and steadiness of touch. Aura won every game, by a wide margin. That cardboard tube of pick-up sticks is on the altar now. But when I poured the sticks out onto the dining table, instead of the numinous glow that I seem to have expected to emerge from the uncapped tube, some surviving glimmer of that sweet hour or trace of Aura's featherlight touch and laughter, it brought back nothing. I was alone with a pile of plastic sticks.

Maybe memory is overrated. Maybe forgetting is better. (Show me the Proust of forgetting, and I'll read him tomorrow.) Sometimes it's like juggling a hundred thousand crystal balls in the air all at once, trying to keep all these memories going. Every time one falls to the floor and shatters into dust, another crevice cracks open inside me, through which another chunk of who we were disappears forever. I wouldn't sell that tube of sticks for a thousand dollars.

In Starbucks, Aura stopped at the shelves where retail goods were displayed, held up a turquoise coffee press, and gave me that smile, eyebrows entreatingly raised, that she'd use whenever she wanted me to buy something not very sensible. She already had a coffee press back in the apartment except it was black. I asked how much it cost. She told me. Now we were supposed to spend forty dollars just to bring this splash of shiny turquoise into our kitchen?

You already have one just like it, I said.

She made a disappointed face and put it back. That coffee press now looms like another uncanny sign or clue that I missed and can't decipher. Given the role her old coffee press was destined to play in our trip to Mazunte, it seems more like a clue, or evidence, though not in the ordinary forensic sense.

If I'd bought her the turquoise coffee press . . . ?

July 3, 2008, one year to the day after Aura and I flew from Newark Airport to Mexico, and I'm back: same evening flight to Mexico, same complimentary upgrade. On the flight to Mexico City, I have to fill in the immigration form, which requires that I identify myself as either married or single. I mark married, as I always do on such forms. Three weeks later, on July 22, I fly to Puerto Escondido and the next day take a taxi to the district prosecutor's office in Puerto Ángel, on a side street, back from the rancid harbor.

A sign on a closed door at the end of a short corridor off the front door reads, *Oficina de Investigación Criminal.* But the district prosecutor takes me into a small windowless office on the left, where there is a desk with the usual clunky, old desktop computer. The light in the room has a flickering, snippy quality, as if the air itself is rapidly blinking. There's a reason: the plastic blades of the revolving fan have been fastened *beneath* the two illuminated lightbulbs on the ceiling fixture they twirl from. The district prosecutor is a lanky young man with a nut-brown, chiseled face and shiny black hair, combed straight back. I will tell him my story that day as I haven't to anybody since hours after Aura's death, when I told it to that woman in the delegación who typed it all down and then couldn't use it as testimony because I didn't have my passport. That story has been running silently inside me ever since, but changing, too, seeking and finding its path, like a wild torrent narrowing into a stream: a story in which I assume what seems the proper amount of responsibility and blame, not as much as Juanita and Leopoldo assigned to me, probably not enough to send me to prison under any but corrupt circumstances, but enough to ensure that I'll never have a respite from self-condemnation, horror, and shame. But what the district prosecutor in Puerto Ángel will tell me that day when I'm done will alter that narrative again.

The house we'd rented in Mazunte was large enough to accommodate the several friends we hoped would come and spend at least part of the two weeks there with Aura and me and her cousin Fabiola and her boyfriend. Originally, Aura's friend Mariana was going to come, too. Mariana worked out of her own little apartment as a masseuse and mystic healer in the Hindu tradition; in university she'd studied to be a Lacanian psychoanalyst until one day, as she tells it, she admitted to herself that instead of sublimating the ego, she wanted to get rid of it. We were in Pata Negra when Mariana told us that she wasn't going to be able to come. She was having a hard time making ends meet and couldn't afford a vacation. She said she didn't want to go to Mazunte anyway, because the waves were too rough.

What? But Mazunte is a safe beach! That's how we—Aura and I, Fabis and Jaunca—unanimously answered Mariana. Because Mazunte is famously situated in a curving cove that impedes the waves rolling in from the ocean enough to diminish their size, momentum, and strength, it's considered safe for swimmers. Ventanilla, and even San Agustinillo, open to the ocean, are the dangerous beaches. You take your life into your hands when you swim at Ventanilla, to say nothing of Puerto Escondido or, farther down the coast, Zipolite, notorious for its riptides and known as la Playa de la Muerte because so many drown there every year, though people keep going, it being still the favored beach of hippies, druggie drifters, Euro nudists, and the like.

I know Mazunte may be safe compared to those other places, said Mariana. But you can't just have a peaceful swim there. Maybe I'm just getting old, but I don't like being knocked and rolled around in the waves and always having sand inside my bathing suit, in my hair, even in my teeth.

Aura said that if you swim out past where the waves break, the water is calm. That was where Aura always swam. Mariana said that she much preferred the Caribbean, especially Tulum with its placid sea, its yoga retreats. Yes, I like Tulum, too, I said. We all liked Tulum. But who could afford to rent a beach house in Tulum for two weeks? The airfare was more expensive, too, as much from Mexico City as from New York. But we all loved Mazunte. The waves could be rough, but they didn't scare me. Going into the water there, I never felt that trepidation in the pit of my stomach, like I did whenever I even thought about swimming at Puerto Escondido. The waves at Mazunte seemed about the same as at Wellfleet, on Cape Cod, where I'd learned to bodysurf as a teenager.

The first few times we went to that coast, Aura and I stayed in Puerto Escondido, for the hotels, but in the mornings we'd take a microbus to Mazunte and its beach, about a forty-five-minute drive, and a taxi back in the evening. A few years before I'd met Aura, I'd spent the millennial New Year in Puerto Escondido with Jaime and Isabel; when we arrived people were talking about the rogue wave that had dashed three surfers into the cliffs at the far end of the beach the day before, killing them. My first morning, I went swimming and then directly to breakfast at a café on the beach where the waiter, a scruffy Italian, said that the last time he'd gone into the ocean there, he'd come out bleeding from both ears. And Isabel told me about a high school teacher she'd had who was spending his vacation in Puerto Escondido and was out walking on the beach one night when a freakishly large wave crashed in and swept him out into the water and drowned him. At night, in my hotel room, I lay in bed listening to those waves, which now sounded to me as if they were grinding bones. I didn't go into the water again at Puerto Escondido until more than four years later, when Aura and I took a surfing lesson there during the three-day weekend trip when I proposed. A wave that caught me by surprise as I was on the board trying to push myself up onto my knees drove me off the front and my head struck the sandy bottom with a force that stunned me, sending a hard jolt through my spine; shaken and wobbly, I went and sat on the beach. The instructor laughed. He said that Aura was a more natural surfer than I was. She was stretched out upon and clinging to a board and the instructor, standing in the waist-high water, was pulling her around like a child on a sled and releasing her to ride in on the gliding foam of waves that had broken farther out. It turned out that he wasn't an authorized instructor. He'd lied to us and borrowed the surfboards without permission from the shop of a friend who ran a legitimate surfing school. Our lesson ended when the friend's mother ran onto the beach shouting at him that he was going to get us killed and to bring the boards back that instant.

We were staying at the Santa Fe, one of the nicest hotels on the beach. In the hotel's garden courtyard a ripe coconut plummeted from a tall palm and landed on the paved path just a few inches behind me with a hard splatter. We laughed about it, but if it had hit me on the head, I could easily have been killed.

In front of our hotel, across the road, there was a stone *mirador*, or lookout point, facing the ocean, and I had thought I might propose there, even if it did seem a little too picture-postcard. But the mirador wasn't so ideal after all, with its direct view of a rock formation topped by a grim statue depicting the hand of a drowning person thrust out of the water. The statue had been placed there by the families of swimmers and surfers, Mexican and foreign, who'd died in those waves.

I'd hidden the diamond engagement ring in our room's safety deposit box. I hadn't found the perfect moment or setting to propose in Puerto Escondido, and considered trying to do it in Mazunte when we went there during the day. But where could I safely hide the ring when I went swimming? I always worried about thieving druggies on that beach. By the last evening in Puerto Escondido I still hadn't proposed. My neck was stiff and aching from when I'd hit my head during our surfing lesson, I'd come down with a cold, and, worse, the bad shrimp I'd eaten the night before was giving me stomach cramps. For dinner all I had was a bowl of chicken soup and nursed just one margarita. Still, I had to do it. I couldn't go back to Mexico City not having proposed. I excused myself from the table and went to the room. A light rain was falling, one of those warm tropical drizzles that feel like the moisture-saturated air inside a cloud, soft as finest silk against your face. It might be even more romantic, I thought, to propose outside on the beach in this rain. I went into the bathroom and when I came out I took the little box with the ring out of the safe and put it into my pocket. Aura came into the room. Let's go out to the beach, I said. Why? she asked. I don't want to go out to the beach, it's raining. It's barely a drizzle, I said, come on, we have to go to the beach. I have to ask you something. She looked at my hand in my pocket and grinned. Ask me here, she said, laughing. Ay, mi amor, what do you have in your pocket? This is serious, I said, and I pulled out the box and dropped to one knee.

So Puerto Escondido, where we got engaged, in retrospect, might seem to have been sending us signs that suggested a warning that went unheeded. But it didn't go unheeded. Except for that one surfing lesson, we didn't swim there. We swam at Mazunte, which we believed to be safe. And what about Mazunte, were there episodes and premonitory signs there as well? The relation of premonitions and signs to evidence—how do you assign what wasn't correctly interpreted or heeded and should have been? A chain of evidence like footsteps in melting snow.

On one of those mornings when Aura and I took the microbus to Mazunte, we met two other passengers who got on at Puerto Escondido. He was a Mexican who'd studied in Sweden and settled there, but now he'd returned with his Swedish wife for a vacation. He was a computer programmer or technician or something like that. He sat across the aisle from Aura and, during the half hour or so drive to Mazunte, kept up an ebullient monologue about Mexico and its beaches. Sweden has a lot going for it but no beaches like Mazunte! He even chanted a long list of tropical fruits grown on that coast, including, he emphasized, five different kinds of bananas. He'd never actually been to Mazunte. He and his wife were both wearing straw cowboy hats that looked brand-new. We were let off at the intersection where you catch another camioneta into Mazunte, San Agustinillo, or Ventanilla; they got off a little before us, to visit Mazunte's little sea-turtle museum and hatchery before they went to the beach. The Mexican's nerdy, unjaded bumpkin quality delighted Aura—*The best beaches in the world! Five different kinds of bananas!* Several jungle-lined dirt roads led from the village to the curving cove of the beach. Thatched-roof palapas, restaurants, cheap rustic hotels, and hammock places lined the back of the beach; in front were beach chairs and tables with umbrellas that rent for the day— that's where Aura and I were sitting when a commotion broke out, shouts for help and swimmers running to the aid of someone who'd had an accident. We went, too, and saw the Mexican from Sweden at the edge of the shore, lying facedown in only a few inches of pooled water, flailing and kicking as if he were drowning. He was carried up onto the beach and set down on the sand, where he lay coughing, sputtering, and gasping, his wife crouched alongside. People stood around watching. Some had seen what had happened. He'd been knocked over by a wave, had apparently been disoriented by the rush of surf, swallowed some water, and totally panicked, even as the wave receded, having practically deposited him on the beach. He was fine. We went back to our chairs. Later we saw him and his wife trudge past us, sun hats back on, carrying their things. We said good-bye but only the wife replied; he stared morosely down at the sand. Over the next few years, we occasionally recalled the Mexican-Swede—a funny-sad story about the danger implicit in a certain kind of touchingly naive enthusiasm, rather than one about danger itself—and we'd always laugh.

We'd reserved and paid for tickets on the Monday night, July 23, first-class night bus to Puerto Escondido, which had seats that converted almost into beds. We decided not to fly because Fabis needed to save money; anyway, she and Aura had always traveled to the beach by bus. That was pretty novel, this frugal planning

ahead, and I was glad to be spared the price of airfares. Juanca had
to work that first week and would join us the next weekend. About
a week before we were supposed to leave, I went to Aura's family
doctor for a checkup and had my first ever blood tests for choles-
terol and the like. Aura had been hectoring me to do it throughout
the past year but I'd always said I didn't have the time. I was to
pick up the lab results on Saturday and bring them to the doctor
on Monday. Meanwhile, we were monitoring the weather in Puerto
Escondido online—we couldn't get the weather for Mazunte—it
was showing clouds and rain every day. That morning Aura gave
me a draft of her story about the wayward teacher, "*La vida está
en otra parte,*" to read. I found lots to praise, but I also told her
that I thought she'd rushed the ending. The next day, Saturday,
the twenty-first, a bit past one in the afternoon, I was just leaving
the gym, where I'd gone to a spinning class, when I got a message
from Aura on my BlackBerry:

> fabiola is here making a phone call and I made her eggs and
> coffee for breakfast. I'm still drinking coffee and working on
> my story which has already changed a lot. Did you really mean
> it last night when you said that I'm an artist? Or were you just
> flirting and working me up???? ... when are you coming back,
> you have to go and pick up your lab results.

> I wrote back: Claro que eres una artista, mi amor, de maxima
> sensibilidad e inteligencia. (Of course you're an artist my love,
> of maximum sensibility and intelligence.)

> She wrote back: Gracias mi amor, ¿pero a qué hora regresas?
> (... but what time are you coming back?)

> I wrote back: Ya en un ratito, mi amor (Right away ...)

> At 1:29, she wrote back: Ya ven estamos viendo de irnos hoy!
> (Come now, we're seeing if we can go today!) We're missing
> all the good weather.

That's the last e-mail I ever received from Aura.

When I got home, Aura and Fabis were in a state of high excitement. Fabis had been on the phone to a friend who'd just returned from Mazunte and who said the weather was great—our online weather reports had been all wrong. But we'd better go today because, according to the friend, it was definitely going to rain later in the week. They couldn't change our bus reservation because all the buses were fully booked, but Aura and Fabis had concocted a circuitous plan. We'd take a bus to the city of Oaxaca, stay over-night, and fly to Puerto Escondido, a short hop over the cordillera, in the morning, on a small airline called Aerovega. We'd lose our bus tickets, but we had to get to the beach while the weather was still good. I could go to the doctor with my lab results when we got back. Hurry up and pack!

Should I have fought against this new plan? No, *Ow-rra*, we already paid for bus tickets, we need to stop throwing money away! What about my doctor's appointment? I could and should have said that; I did, actually, but not very forcefully. (Juanita used to criticize me for always giving in too easily to Aura.) The woman from whom we were renting the beach house had already given me keys. We were on our way out the door when Aura remembered she'd forgotten to pack her coffee press. We'd need it, right? It wouldn't fit in her suit-case so she put it in a black plastic bag and we went out to the taxi.

At El Tapo, the bus terminal, we had enough time before our bus left to eat in the diner downstairs, delicious greasy tortas. It was supposed to be about a five-hour drive to Oaxaca. When we got there we'd still have time to go to El Central for a drink. But the trip took much longer than five hours. When we pulled into Oaxaca, its streets and plazas were deserted and dark, and we had to be up at five-thirty to go to the airport. We were carrying our bags from the taxi into the hostel when Aura realized that she'd left her cof-fee press on the bus. Back at El Tapo, when she'd placed the coffee press in the rack over our seat, where it was quickly hidden behind our other bags, I'd thought that it could easily be forgotten there and had made a mental note to remember; then I hadn't.

Well, now we can buy the turquoise one, I said.

But I've had that coffee press since Austin, Aura sighed sadly.

I wasn't happy about sleeping in a hostel. In my male dorm, a few other travelers were already asleep in their bunks, and I moved about as quietly as I could without turning on any light. Was this a *youth* hostel, I wondered, or just a hostel? I had only one thin blanket, and slept in T-shirt and jeans. I lay in the hard narrow bed and was angry with myself for giving in so easily to this roundabout and wasteful rush to the beach. Why was Aura so impatient?

That night, as we slept, where was Aura's wave in its long journey to Mazunte? Having done some research on waves since, I'm certain that that wave already existed. Most surface waves of any decent size, even the moderate-sized waves that reach Mazunte on a normal day, have come thousands of miles. A wind blows ripples across a calm sea and those ripples, providing the wind with something to get traction on, are blown into waves, and as the waves grow in height, the wind pushes them along with more force, speeding them up, building them higher. It's not the water itself that travels, of course, but the wind's energy; in the turbulent medium between air and ocean, water particles move in circles something like bicycle pedals, constantly transferring their energy forward, from swell to crest and back into the trough and forward again. Short choppy waves, like the ones you see on lakes, come from nearby. Large waves charge steadily along on high-velocity winds that have been traveling across the open ocean for many thousands of miles and for days; those are the waves you watch from a Pacific beach, forming into swells that, as they near the shore, rear into high curving crests that finally peak and break. Aura's wave might easily have gotten its start a week or more before, during a storm in the warm seas of the Indian Ocean, where strong winds consistently blow in one direction. The older a wave is, the more dangerous it is; the height of a wave, its steepness, I read, is related to its age: "As a wave ages, it gradually grows higher, longer and consequently faster." Where was Aura's wave that night, as we slept in our bunks in the hostel in Oaxaca? Was it already a murderous old wave, or still a relatively young one, born only the night before in a tropical storm maybe only a thousand miles out to sea? There's a Borges poem that ends with the lines:

> ¿Quién es el mar, quién soy? Lo sabré el día
> Ulterior que sucede a la agonía.

Who is the sea, who am I? I'll know the day that follows the agony—*agonía*, in this context, could be even more accurately translated as "death throes."
Am I the wave?

We reached the house in Mazunte at about noon the next morning. I had a hand-drawn map that the taxi driver had trouble deciphering, but finally we found the callejón we were looking for: a jungle-lined alley running below a restaurant that was perched on the steep slope above; at its end was a gate that we unlocked, and then we climbed several levels of stairs to the house, which was like a Swiss Family Robinson tree house nestled amid sprawling branches in a tropical forest. There were a few roofed patio areas, and Aura chose the largest, pushing furniture around to quickly create a self-contained writing studio. I took a smaller, shaded little deck, one level lower. Fabis, a graphic designer, was adamantly on vacation and didn't need a work area. There were bedrooms, with screened windows and beds covered by mosquito netting, and hammocks all around, but the best place to sleep was up on the roof platform, from which you could see out over the jungle to the bay and the ocean. We wrestled two thin futon mattresses up the ladder. Fabis would sleep with us up there, too, until Juanca came.
We swam in the ocean that afternoon. It was overcast, and there'd been a rainstorm the night before—the first rain in weeks. Nobody we spoke to had heard that more rain was forecast for the

coming days, but the storm was why the water was cloudy and full of plant debris, twiggy and grassy little clusters. Though she'd so often been to these beaches, and loved going into the water, Aura was always afraid of the waves; that day they were not very big. Aura would cling to my arm and make me wait with her at the water's edge, studying wave sets, timing them, and then we'd go running in. Afloat in the water she'd throw her arms around my neck and hold on until she felt ready to swim out, diving beneath waves until she was past where they broke, where the water was smoother, the swells gently rocking her as they passed before cresting. Aura loved to stay out there, tirelessly swimming back and forth, I always thought, like a friendly seal.

El agua está picada hoy, Aura said. Between swells were many smaller waves, little splashing bursts, as if stones were being dropped from the sky all around us. There were other swimmers in the waves bodysurfing, young men, mostly, adolescents and boys. I swam in closer to catch a wave. I missed a few and then timed one well, launching forward and swimming hard ahead of the wave's cresting curl, letting it catch and carry me, body and arms extended, head up and out of the water just ahead of its roaring break, finally engulfed by it, thrilled by the force and speed with which it propelled me almost onto the beach. As I swam back out to Aura, I wore a proud grin.

Is it dangerous? Aura asked. She definitely asked me that. Her curiosity about bodysurfing had been aroused. She was a much better swimmer than her fifty-year-old husband. If he could bodysurf, why couldn't she?

It is dangerous, I said, if your head gets driven into the sand. You always have to keep your head up. That's how I answered Aura's question, I'm sure of it, saying no less, but no more.

Getting out of the water, she'd hold on to me, too, until the smaller wave she'd been waiting for shoved her forward and she'd let go and scamper up onto the beach through the churning foam. It was sometimes a struggle to get out of the water as it flooded back. You'd get pushed back down, but then you'd let the next wave pitch you forward.

We had dinner that night in the Armadillo restaurant, perched just above the callejón leading to our house. Having hardly slept the night before, we went to bed early, climbing up onto our sleeping platform, where we put on insect repellent. The way the breeze off the ocean rustled the leaves in the trees all around us made the sound of a young restless sea. We woke in the morning to a cacophony of birdsong and squawks and to a view of the bay's rounded arc—enclosed on one side by Punta Cometa, and on the other by the far bend of hills separating Mazunte from San Agustinillo—and the Pacific Ocean spread out beyond, merging with the blue haze of the sky. We could see fishing boats and a freighter. We climbed down, leaving Fabis still sleeping. Aura was eager to get to work at her computer. There was a coffeemaker in the kitchen; we'd bought coffee, with our groceries, the previous afternoon. Aura cut up some papaya. When I remember that day, the only entire one we'd have at the beach, it feels like two days, or even three, because it seemed to last so long and pass so slowly, the way time is supposed to pass at the beach.

What did I work on that morning? I don't even remember. Maybe the novel I'd been trying to get started. I also had a book to review, a new translation from the Portuguese of a six-hundred-page nineteenth-century novel by Eça de Queirós, *The Maias*. I'd read up to the part where the indolent but intelligent young Carlos Maia is beginning his romantic love affair with Madame Gomes in a decadent, enervated Lisbon. I sat at a crudely carpentered wooden desk in the shade listening to the birds, watching hummingbirds buzz around flowers, getting up and walking around, sitting down again, feeling a little envious of the concentration with which Aura was already working, and how much nicer the work area she'd set up for herself was than mine. At about ten-thirty we all went for breakfast at the Armadillo. Then we went to the beach. Aura had an old boyfriend, J., who now owned a popular bar in

Mazunte that often had live music at night. This boyfriend was
a murky legend to me. All I knew was that when Aura was eighteen or nineteen, he'd broken her heart. He'd dropped out of the
UNAM and come to live the hippie life in Mazunte. The summer
before, we'd watched the France-Italy World Cup championship
match on the widescreen television in his bar and I'd met him, a
young man with a compact build, a short haircut, and a soldierly
bearing, who'd clearly cleaned up his act. He was married now
and had a child. He and Aura had talked that afternoon for the
first time in years.

At some point, while I sat reading *The Maias*, Aura and Fabis
went for a walk, probably to the village's Internet café. But when
Aura came back, she looked upset. You won't believe it, she said,
sinking down onto her beach towel. This is the last thing I needed.
She told me that when they'd stopped into J.'s bar to say hello, J.'s
wife had told them that J. was in the DF. And guess what he's doing
there? asked Aura. When I said I had no idea what he was doing
there, Aura said that J. had gone to the city to look at the artwork
for his book jacket. J. was having a book published. A book of short
stories about Mazunte.

So even my dropout hippie bar-owner ex-boyfriend, said Aura,
is getting a book published before I am.

Well, I said, it's not like his book is going to win the Juan Rulfo
Prize or anything. Stories about Italian hippies and potheads in
Mazunte? Who's going to want to read about that?

That isn't the point, said Aura. Anyway, maybe it's great. It
doesn't matter what it's about. I'm such a loser.

Oh, Aura, come on, you're not a loser. You're writing a great
story right now. Off I went, into my usual pep spiel. But I felt irritated
by this routine. Don't go and spoil the day, I thought, after you've
been looking forward to this for so long. But it did seem like weird
luck that her ex-boyfriend was publishing a book and that she had
to find out about it on her first day at the beach. Of course I've kept
an eye out for that book ever since, and have never seen it in any
bookstore, or been able to find any mention of it anywhere.

One thing about Aura, though, she could always rebound
quickly from these little crises and defeats. We went for a swim. She
never stayed out of the water for long. Pretty soon we were playing around and kissing in the ocean. I don't recall bodysurfing that
day; if I did, I didn't get a good ride. Mazunte wasn't a big surfer's
beach but there were almost always people bodysurfing and riding
boogie boards. The few surfers usually went out near evening. The
red cloth banner warning against swimming would have been up on
its pole, because it always was, every day. But not even the beach
waiter I would eventually ask about it knew why that was, or even
who was in charge of it.

That night we had dinner on the beach. Out of habit I took
out my BlackBerry; all day it hadn't worked but now, at night, it
had a weak signal. There was an e-mail from my friend Barbara
who works at a publishing house. She wrote to tell me that my
nonfiction book on the murder had received a starred review in
one of the prepubs. Well, yay! That was a wonderful night: the
deep blue phosphorescent evening, the brightly glimmering strings
of lights around the outdoor restaurants, the butane torches flar-
ing an incandescent orange. The night darkened to purple and
finally hid the ocean. Rock music on the restaurant speakers mixed
with the steady percussion of the waves, much softer here than at
Puerto Escondido. We shared two mediocre pizzas, two pitchers of
watery margaritas, and were very happy. It felt as if we possessed
a kind of wealth, a small fortune in saved-up nights on the beach
like this one.

In the morning Fabis went off to do some errand, leaving us alone
for a while, and Aura and I got to make love, though not for long,
sweetly but anxiously—Aura was nervous about Fabis coming back.
When we were dressed and had climbed down the ladder and were
in the kitchen, she grabbed my crotch and put her lips to my ear and
told me that soon we were going to be making love all the time to
make our baby. Ay, ya quiero un bebí! she exclaimed. And all that

made me feel so charged up and optimistic. Soon, for the first time in either of our lives, we'd be having sex to procreate!

Aura was working well that morning. I came upstairs and saw her at her laptop typing, headphones on. Later, around ten, we went to breakfast at the Armadillo again, sat at a table covered with a blue-and-white checked tablecloth, in front of the painted wooden statue of the Virgin of Guadalupe and another, unpainted, of a gryphon's head. I had enchiladas in a bright red sauce, fried eggs, and black beans. Aura ordered fruit and yogurt, like the day before, and split an order of enchiladas with Fabis. We each had big glasses of the orange juice mixed with carrot and beet juices they served there, mugs of strong coffee, and also, because it was so good, we all shared an order of toasted homemade bread, served with local honey.

We were walking to the beach when Aura said, I'm writing a really great story.

Of course, it was unlike Aura, and maybe unprecedented, for her to speak that way, but she'd spoken with shy conviction. Sure, the next day she might have felt discouraged again. But something was definitely happening for Aura. This seemed obvious to me later, when I realized how much her story about the teacher had changed and improved in only a few days; that last morning, she'd left it nearly finished—close enough, in fact, that it was eventually published, after a bit of editing. She'd been working so hard all year, why shouldn't it have arrived around then: that "click" when it feels as if a previously locked door has opened and words and sentences suddenly seem to exist in a new dimension located somewhere between your brain and the screen or page, leading you through an infinite house whose rooms have strange geometric shapes you've never seen before, yet you always somehow know where you are. We'd had a fumbling conversation like that recently, trying to describe that.

And to think, she still had two weeks left of those gloriously long beach days! Probably, she said, there'd even be days when she'd spend the afternoon working instead of at the beach.

Makes sense to me, I said. I was glad we'd decided to come a few days early after all. If we'd taken the Monday night bus, we might just be arriving in Mazunte now, wiped out and only wanting a cold beer and a nap.

An unforgettable aspect of that sunny, nearly cloudless day was the surprisingly large number of people at the beach and how many of them were in the water, including small children—swimming but also bodysurfing. The waves, I assume, must have seemed inviting that day. Moderate waves, maybe not so *old* after all. But waves travel across the ocean in sets, or trains, and it's never just one train that arrives at a beach, because along the way wave-trains meet or converge or overtake one another and mix, older waves with somewhat younger ones. But even a moderate wave, I've since learned, breaks and surges toward the shore with the innate force of a small automobile going at full throttle.

Sitting in our chairs, we watched the bodysurfers. Aura seemed especially interested, and kept commenting on their skills. I remember a pair of young guys in particular, light-skinned, well built, who I thought must be brothers and who were the best out there, skimming over the ocean surface expertly poised on the edge of their waves, arms out, looking like flying superheroes. We'd been into the water at least twice already and each time we'd all tried to catch waves. I don't think Aura and Fabis had caught any, though; mostly they'd tried to get in position and then, as a wave loomed over them, ducked under. I had one short ride. I rarely timed it just right.

I didn't like the skanky look of the young guy—long-haired, whippet thin, crudely tattooed, a piercing beneath his lower lip— who took the chair right next to ours. Why sit so close? Then his friend came and laid out a towel in front of him. Aura said she wanted to go back into the water. Again? That would be the third time already! I wanted to read. *The Maias* was getting interesting, the reader realizing, long before the characters do, that Carlos Maia has fallen in adulterous love with his long-lost sister, Madame Gomes—a great beach read, after all. Aura had finished reading a Fabio Morabito collection of stories the day before—she loved it—and was now restlessly switching between Silvina Ocampo and Bruno Schulz, and talking to Fabis.

But look how crowded the water is, I said. It still surprises me that Aura wasn't repulsed by all the people in the water. The water actually looked stippled with the heads of swimmers and Aura was usually, and oddly, hypersensitive to that—she could rarely even look at any surface that was densely patterned in that way, stippled, daubed, striated, without a shiver of revulsion going through her, goose bumps breaking out on her arms, which she'd always show me, grimacing. That's what the water looked like to me that day, like just the kind of pimpled surface that Aura couldn't stand!

I whispered to her that I didn't want to go into the water and leave all our things within easy reach of the creepy guys alongside us. Aura whispered back that she was sure they wouldn't steal anything. They were just beach hippies.

You two go in, I said.

Come on, both Aura and Fabis pleaded. The water's great today. Come with us!

No, I said, I'm going to skip this one. I want to read.

Aura was wearing the wet-suit booties she'd bought for this trip, which gave her a slightly waddling gait, making it harder for her to keep up with Fabis, much taller and voluptuous, as they walked down to the water's edge, Aura swinging her arms a bit to speed herself along, her head lifted and tilted up at Fabis while she talked, happily, excitedly, to her cousin. In her blue one-piece bathing suit, from behind, she looked just a little egg-shaped, much more so than she actually was. What an adorable, funny, beautiful person my Aura is, I thought to myself. This is the moment that decided everything: if I'm the wave, this is when I begin to crest, with an aching surge of love inside my chest; even if it had been only the prelude to just an inconsequential swim, I'm sure I would still remember it. I thought: I promise to stop feeling annoyed with Aura, with her insecurities, with her constant need for reassurance, who gives a fuck, my God, I'm going to love her more than ever and of course I'll go swim with her right now. Next, I turned my attention to securing my things against thievery without being too obvious or insulting about it. I put my wallet, T-shirt, sandals, and that book that I would (will) never again open into my cloth Gandhi bookstore bag, and looped the bag's handles around a chair leg that I lifted and firmly planted in the sand. I could see Aura and Fabis up to their shoulders in the water, facing each other, still talking, ducking waves, bobbing back up. I got up and ran down the beach, over the searing sand, and into the ocean.

If you go to YouTube and type in Mazunte and waves, you'll find a number of brief videos of that beach. The waves in those traveler's videos aren't much different than the ones we were swimming in, though probably ours, given the number of people who were in the water that day, were calmer. If you type in Zipolite, you'll see that the waves there are much wilder, more forbidding. I didn't know, before, about the different classifications of waves, that there are so-called spilling waves, considered the safest upon which to surf, found in "relatively sheltered areas"; or "plunging" or "dumping" waves, which occur when there is a rise in the ocean floor right before the beach, or in strong winds, and that are considered more dangerous than spilling waves; and there are "surging" waves, the most dangerous of all. Once I learned about these, I still wasn't sure which kind Mazunte had. The beach was relatively sheltered, but there was also a rise in the ocean floor that extended into the slope of the beach. A Web site run by the Seafriends Marine Conservation Center, in New Zealand, had good information on waves, so I sent them an e-mail with links to two YouTube videos of Mazunte's waves, asking for an opinion on what kind they were. The center's director answered:

The two videos definitely show "dumpers" even while the sea is still reasonably calm. Dumpers are indeed dangerous because they create a very steep beach of loose sand, from where it is difficult to exit. The waves also suddenly, over a short distance, dissipate all their energy in a violent mix of water velocities. I think Aura has been most unfortunate, and may have landed on her head. She may have tried hard to get out and become desperate. Who knows? I'm sorry to hear of this sad fate. But we can still warn people of the treacherous nature of dumping waves.

The director apparently thought that maybe Aura had drowned, though that is not what happened. The waves *were* reasonably calm. Swimmers, even little children, were not having any noticeable difficulty exiting the water that day, or at least not that I noticed. Waves violently dissipating—that seemed exactly right, as did "landed on her head."

As soon as I reached Aura and Fabis in the water, we all seemed to decide at once that now we were going to try to bodysurf. I quickly caught a wave about as well as I ever catch one, and came up about twenty or fifteen yards away, exhilarated, thrusting my arms in the air. Wasn't I the equal, or near equal, in bold and playful energy, of any far younger man on that beach? Fabis tried to catch the next wave but missed it. The next wave rose toward us as if pushed from behind by an invisible bulldozer, and I heard Aura shout:

¡Esta es mía!—This one's mine!

¡Esta es mía!—her cheerful-plucky voice suffused with her last ever impulse of delight.

I was out of position to catch it but I saw her launch herself and thought, as I dove under, that this wave seemed bigger, heavier, somehow more sluggish than the others, and I felt a twinge of fear (or is that just a trick of memory?). I came up amid a wide swathe of seething foam—the water looked like it was boiling. Fabis was next to me. Did you catch it? I asked her, and she said, No, did you? but I was already looking around for Aura. Where's Aura? I didn't see Aura. I swept my gaze back and forth over the teeming surface, waiting for her head to pop back up, gasping, her hands brushing hair and water out of her eyes. The most extraordinary bafflement, fear . . . She wasn't in the water. Then I saw her. The withdrawing foam uncovered her like a white blanket slowly being pulled back: her smooth round back and shoulders floating; she was floating, utterly motionless, facedown in the water. I reached Aura an instant or two ahead of three or four other swimmers and we hoisted and carried her onto the beach. How heavy she was. We set her down on the sand. She was unconscious, water dribbling from her nostrils. But then she opened her eyes. People were shouting, Don't move her! She gasped that she couldn't breathe. Someone shouted, Give her mouth to mouth, and I brought my lips to hers. I blew in and felt the hot breath slowly push back into me. I was surprised at the steepness of the beach; it was as if we were in a gulley. (Had it been like that earlier? Did it have something to do with the tide?) A wave came in and almost covered her. Several pairs of hands picked her up, and she slipped from all our grasps, and we grasped her again and carried her up onto the hot dry sand. A doctor, an ambulance, I was pleading. I had to stay by her. She said, Help me breathe, and I put my lips against hers. She whispered, That was too hard, and after the next breath, Like that. Somebody, maybe Fabis, said that it was *susto*, fright, that was making it hard for her to breathe, that once she calmed down she'd be able to breathe, and I repeated to her, Aura, you've had a terrible fright, that's why you can't breathe, when you calm down you'll be able to. I thought Fabis had gone to phone an ambulance and found out later she'd actually left to find a doctor. Just before she took off was when Aura said to me, Quiéreme mucho, mi amor. Love me a lot, my love. She couldn't move her limbs, nor did she have any feeling in them. She told me that with utmost composure, as if she believed that by keeping very calm and still, this horror might decide to abandon her and move on to some other prey. I told her that it was only temporary, that soon the feeling would start coming back. I was holding her hand, squeezing it, but she couldn't feel my squeezes. She was caked in sand. One of the other people kneeling around her prodded her leg and asked her if she could feel it. Where the fuck was the ambulance? Somebody, a German he sounded like, kept stating with authority that she shouldn't be moved. *Aire*, said Aura, whenever she needed me to help her breathe. The word came off her lips like a bubble quietly popping.

No quiero morir, she said. I don't want to die.

Of course you're not going to die, my love, don't be silly. Squeezing her hand, stroking hair off her forehead. My lips to hers, in, out, wait, in, out, wait . . .

Fabis never found the doctor. Somehow the doctor found us first. He was a wiry young Mexican who looked like a surfer. Maybe he was a medical student, not a doctor. By now Fabis was trying to call an ambulance but was having a difficult time. At first the restaurant owners didn't want to let her use their phone, or couldn't tell her who it was she should call for an ambulance. Finally she came back with the news that there was no ambulance. There was only one ambulance on that whole stretch of coast, she reported, and it was currently two hours away. So, no ambulance.

Aire, whispered Aura.

The young doctor took control. We couldn't afford to wait two hours, we had to get Aura to the nearest hospital, in Pochutla, about twenty miles away inland. Somebody volunteered to drive Aura to the hospital in his SUV. We would use a surfboard as a stretcher and load Aura into the back. When the doctor asked for help, some of the young men standing around moved away as if a blowtorch was being held to their feet, but others came forward to kneel around Aura and they carefully lifted her as a surfboard was slid beneath her and we carried her to the SUV. I was holding the board under her head. In the back of the SUV, I crouched behind her head, holding it with both hands, trying to keep her head and neck from moving, while continuously bending forward to give her breath. The SUV lurched slowly from side to side on the rough dirt road, every rut like a mountain or a deep ditch, and it was impossible to keep her completely still. Another youth was crouched at the end of the surfboard, as much to keep it from sliding out onto the road as to hold Aura's legs steady. Somehow he had a green feather in his hand, and he was stroking it against the bottom of Aura's feet and asking if she felt anything. She whispered that she did, and I kept telling her that being able to feel the feather meant that everything was going to be okay. The youth with the feather was praying over Aura. You're like an angel, I told him. Finally we hit paved road. About forty-five minutes after leaving the beach at Mazunte we reached the hospital in Pochutla. It was about three in the afternoon.

Pochutla is a small busy commercial town. The hospital was on the town's outskirts, a flimsy-looking, one-story construction that resembled a rural elementary school. They allowed me into their emergency care area with Aura. It was small and extremely spartan. They kept her on the surfboard, which they laid atop a bed. They put a neck brace on her. But that hospital didn't even have a respirator. I still had to help her breathe.

The first doctor who came to look at Aura was clearly an alcoholic: disheveled, bleary, and utterly indifferent. Outside the emergency room there was a little waiting area with screen windows and plastic chairs. Fabis was out there, making a last few calls on her cell phone before its battery ran out. She tried to call Aura's mother but got her answering service. She couldn't reach Rodrigo, either. At the end of that long day, Fabis would record forty-one unanswered calls to Juanita and Rodrigo. Her cell phone charger was back at the house in Mazunte. She asked the SUV's owner if he could go and get it for her, and he said that he would. She drew him a map and gave him the keys. He came back with the charger in not much more than an hour. He'd driven much faster than he'd been able to with Aura in the back.

Aura asked me, Am I going to die?

No, my love, of course you're not going to die. You're going to
be okay, I promise. This happens to football players sometimes, I
told her. They carry them off the field just like we carried you and
then, bit by bit, the feeling in their arms and legs comes back. Don't
you have a little feeling in your limbs already?

Sí, mi amor.

Finally they brought a hand-operated respirator and a nurse
held the mouthpiece over Aura's lips while I, with both hands,
rhythmically pressed the ovoid white plastic balloon that pumped
air. When I was told I had to fill out forms, another nurse took
over the balloon, and I was led into a tiny cubicle that had a
desk with a manual typewriter to wait for the doctor. I got out
my BlackBerry and it had a signal. I phoned Juanita and got no
answer so I sent an e-mail telling her that Aura had had a swimming accident, was in the hospital, and to please phone me or
Fabiola immediately. My phone's battery was also very nearly
gone. I e-mailed Silverman, my editor in New York, Gus, Saqui,
and I don't remember who else, to ask for help in getting Aura
medevaced to the United States. I was in my bathing trunks and
a T-shirt and was barefoot. Fabis had handed me the T-shirt.
She'd had the presence of mind to run and collect all of our
things where we'd left them on the beach.

The doctor who finally came into the cubicle where I was
waiting was an old man with white hair and a mustache. He would
make the diagnosis that Aura didn't have ocean water in her
lungs—good news, except it would turn out that he was wrong.
He asked me questions for his forms and slowly typed my answers;
the process seemed interminable. I thought I heard Aura calling
for me and abruptly got up and left. When I got back to Aura
there was a new doctor there, a husky young man with chubby
cheeks and an air of benevolent intelligence. He was working the
manual respirator now, calmly squeezing it between his hands and
looking intently from Aura's face to the monitor attached to her.
I asked if Aura had been calling for me and the nurses said no,

that she was tranquila. The young doctor handed the balloon off to a nurse and we went out into the corridor; there he, Fabiola, and I discussed what to do. We made the decision to get Aura as quickly as possible, by air ambulance, to a hospital in Mexico City, not to the hospital in the city of Oaxaca, which had been mentioned as a possibility. Aura needed to go that very day, the young doctor told us. When I got back the nurses asked me to pull Aura's blue bathing suit off of her, as if that was an act, even in a hospital, that could only be performed by a husband. They lifted her a bit, and I rolled the sandy bathing suit off her shoulders, down her body, and off her legs, and they pulled a bedsheet over her. With a wire cutter they snipped Juanita's old charm bracelet off of Aura's wrist. I took over the manual respirator and kissed her forehead and her cheek and she opened her eyes and closed them. The young doctor told me that her pulse and heartbeat had slowed considerably, but that they'd given her a shot of epinephrine and restored them to nearly normal. I was told to keep an eye on the monitor and that if her heartbeat sank below forty, to say something. The old doctor picked up Aura's hand and let go, and it flopped down limply. When he hammered under her knees there was a tiny reflex movement. He ran the reflex hammer down the sole of her foot and asked if she felt anything, and she said that she had. The nurses and I smiled at each other.

The doctor pretended to do it again, swiping the hammer downward but without actually touching her skin, and when he asked Aura if she'd felt something, she again said that she had.

My memories of all that happened that endless day will always be clouded and uncertain. I do know that Fabiola was constantly working her telephone. The tías were trying to track down Juanita and Rodrigo, though they wouldn't succeed until hours later, finding Rodrigo first. The plan now was to arrange for an air ambulance to fly Aura back to the DF from either Puerto Escondido or Huatulco, but we also needed to find an ambulance to bring Aura to either of those two airports. Both were proving to be difficult tasks. I went out to the corridor, where I'd left my book bag under a chair, to get my sandals and wallet, and that's when I discovered that somebody, probably back at the beach, had stolen all the cash in my wallet and then put the wallet back into the bag. I had one credit card, which the thief had left alone—an AmEx card, useless in any Mexican ATM. My other cards were back at the house in Mazunte. I heard Fabis on her cell phone say plaintively but urgently, But Ma, imagine if it was me—Odette had asked Fabis if we couldn't wait until tomorrow for an air ambulance. Fabis said, But Ma, she might not make it until tomorrow, the doctor says she has to go today. Just then a nurse popped out and told me that Aura was asking for me, and I went back inside.

Odette and Fabis's sister found an air ambulance service in Toluca, just outside Mexico City, that would fly to Huatulco. Time was short, it was already late afternoon, and the two of them were rushing to a bank branch that was still open to withdraw the twelve thousand dollars in cash that the ambulance service was demanding.

Inside, Aura said that her *nalgas*, her ass, hurt from lying on the surfboard. Clearly, that meant that she wasn't going to be paralyzed. I whispered passionately into her ear that she was going to be okay and kissed her face until a nurse told me to step aside. It was strange to observe the nurses standing over Aura, working the manual respirator, watching the monitor, chatting away to each other about their everyday lives. But we were all cheered up now, because if Aura was complaining that her ass hurt, surely the sensation in her limbs must be returning—it was unthinkable that she wouldn't recover. An air ambulance was coming for her. It was already past dusk. Supposedly a Red Cross ambulance was finally on its way, too. In Mexico City, Fabiola's sister had found a spinal cord specialist, the father of a friend, who was one of the very best in Mexico City and who was waiting for Aura at the Hospital Ángeles, in Pedregal, one of the city's wealthiest areas.

But there was a new problem: the air ambulance couldn't take off from Toluca because the Huatulco airport was denying permission to land—they were closing for the night.

The young doctor said that if Aura spent the night in Pochutla, she wouldn't live.

The Huatulco airport official was named Fabiola, too. On her phone Fabis told her, If my cousin dies you're going to have that on your conscience the rest of your life. Johnny Silverman, my lawyer friend in New York, was now applying pressure, too. His law firm had worked on corporate cases with one of the most powerful and connected lawyers in all Mexico, and he convinced this lawyer to call the Huatulco airport. After his call, the Huatulco Fabiola relented and said the airport would stay open until midnight.

The ambulance came at about nine, two hours later than arranged. The Pochutla hospital couldn't relinquish its only neck brace so Fabis and I dashed out to a pharmacy to buy one. The Red Cross ambulance didn't have a working respirator, either. The young doctor, who was actually an intern from Guadalajara recently assigned to the hospital, volunteered to accompany us, with the manual respirator. Finally Aura, wrapped in a bedsheet, was lifted off the surfboard onto the ambulance gurney. Whoever owned that surfboard had apparently given it up for Aura.

The airport at Huatulco was about twenty miles away on a slow, winding road. It took us nearly an hour. We came into the airport through a back entrance, amid vapor lamps and steamy tropical air, and I heard the whine of an idling jet engine. We were back in the twenty-first century, or had even leapt ahead to the next one, because the air ambulance looked to me like something out of a sci-fi movie; in my memory its crew of young medics wore shiny flight suits, though I doubt that's true. The lead doctor was a beautiful young woman with the cheerfully reassuring manner of the Good Witch of the North. The young doctor from Pochutla wouldn't even accept money from Fabis for a taxi back to Mazunte; off he went, after a round of heartfelt and hopeful good-byes, carrying the manual respirator, to stay at the house of a friend. Aura was transferred to a new stretcher and covered snugly in a silvery thermal blanket. The beautiful doctor said that Aura's vital signs were good and that she was sure she was going to be fine. Once we were in the air, she said that Aura didn't even need a respirator. It was true: she was managing to breathe on her own. Aura looked at me and asked:

Mi amor, ¿me puedo dormir un poquito? Can I sleep a little bit?

That might be the last full sentence Aura ever addressed to me; I don't remember any other. She slept awhile. So as not to wake her, I restrained myself from pouring whispered words of love and reassurance into her ear.

The last ambulance took us from Toluca all the way across Mexico City to Pedregal in the south. I rode in back with Aura, and Fabis sat up front with the driver. That last ambulance was austere and basic, with a metallic interior. Aura was back on a respirator. With us in back was a doctor who looked barely into his twenties, quick and sure in his movements; he seemed alert, serious and capable, pale, with delicate sharp features and glasses, Jewish probably. He was intently watching the monitor, reading Aura's vital signs. Then he said, his voice abrupt and tense, I don't like how this looks. The optimism of the air ambulance—such a mystery to me now—was gone. Now I can't say whether I am grateful for those last moments of hope and relief, or feel that we were cruelly deceived. Neither, I suppose.

Juanita and Rodrigo were waiting for us outside the hospital emergency entrance. Some of the tías were there, too. It was about two in the morning. Juanita, arms folded, glaring at me, spoke her accusation. This was how I'd brought her daughter back to her, the daughter she'd given away to me to protect in marriage, as I'd vowed to do. This was how I'd returned Aura to her mother.

Aura was awake. It was as if she'd saved up all her energy to be able to give her mother this last cheerful-plucky declaration: Fue una tontería, Mami. It was a stupidity, Mami.

I think the renowned surgeon-specialist and his team of

doctors knew almost right away. I don't remember how long it took before they came out to speak with us in the waiting room. The surgeon-specialist was a tall, corpulent man. He told us that Aura had broken and dislocated the second, third, and fourth vertebrae of her spinal column, and that they had pressed into her spinal column and severed the nerves that controlled her breathing and her torso and limbs. It was probable that she was going to be completely paralyzed for life. They were trying to stabilize her spinal cord so that its swelling might go down. Then they would decide if there was any way to operate. She'd ingested ocean water, too, and they were working to clear it from her lungs. I pleaded with the doctor. I told him that Aura had had sensation in her limbs off and on throughout the day, that in the air ambulance her vital signs had been fine and that she'd even breathed on her own. I told the doctor that she was going to be fine, and that he had to believe me, and I remember his stricken eyes helplessly observing me—me in my dirty, sweaty T-shirt and bathing suit.

None of us were allowed into the intensive care unit to see Aura. The medical teams needed to work without interruption. Fabis went home with Juanca to sleep. I don't remember anyone else in the waiting room other than Juanita and Rodrigo. They weren't speaking to me. They sat on one side of the waiting room, on the vinyl couches, and I sat alone on the other. The light in the room was very dim. We were on an upper floor. I couldn't phone anyone because I had no charger. Juanca had promised to bring me one in the morning. At one point I went out and walked in the long empty corridors and stopped into a little chapel to pray. I swore that if Aura survived I would live a religiously devout life and show my gratitude to God every day. Besides noticing it, I don't remember having any thought about Juanita and Rodrigo keeping their distance from me. My thoughts were only about Aura. If she was going to be paralyzed for some time, I would find a way to get her into the best rehab facility in the United States. I would read to her every day and get her to dictate her writing to me; those were the kinds of thoughts I was having. Now and then I got up and went to the shuttered window of the intensive care unit, picked up the receiver, pressed the button, and asked if I could come inside to see my wife, and every time I was told that visitors weren't allowed until the morning.

28

What did you think about that long night, my love, as you lay there dying, as horribly wounded as any soldier in war, and alone?

Did you blame me? Did you think of me with love even once? Did you see or hear or feel me loving you?

29

It wouldn't be until the next morning, when Aura was in a coma, that I was finally let in to see her. The eminent surgeon's assistant, a bulldoggish woman, told me that during the night Aura had had two heart attacks. I finally had a chance to press my lips to Aura's beautiful ear to thank her for the happiest years of my life, and to tell her that I would never stop loving her. Then the assistant surgeon brusquely ordered me out again. Ten or fifteen minutes later, stepping back in through the white curtain, I instantly sensed a vacuumed-out stillness around Aura's bed, a nuclear-blast brightness, and the assistant surgeon told me that Aura had died minutes before. I went to her. Her lightless eyes. I kissed her cheeks that were already like cool clay. My sobs must have been heard throughout the hospital.

30

Juanca missed the funeral because he went with a friend out to Mazunte to bring back our things. They found the house just as we'd left it. They packed up everything, even Aura's shampoo. Aura always just closed the lid of her laptop when she was done working for the day, so when I opened it later, I found the screen as she'd left it. There were two open documents, the latest version of her story about the schoolteacher, and something new, probably the start of yet another short story, titled "*¿Hay señales en la vida?*" or Does Life Give Us Signs?

31

At first the district prosecutor seems to misunderstand why I've come, and why my lawyer made this appointment. He seems determined to defend himself against, I realize, accusations of a negligent or mishandled investigation. In his little office, in the gnashing light caused by that maladroitly hung fan, he insists that he and his assistants have thoroughly investigated Aura's fatal injury at Mazunte. They've interviewed witnesses—the owners and employees of restaurants on the beach, the medical staff at the hospital in Pochutla—and have found nothing to indicate that it was anything but an accident. I tell him that I know it was an accident but that I'm here to give my required legal statement. I want to tell him my story, the one that, over the last year, I've ceaselessly refined into a narrative in which my own actions and lack of action, too passive, too assertive, too intrinsic to my character, all weigh as evidence. There is much else that I don't tell him about—the premonitory signs, the adolescent and later fixations on death in Aura's diaries, the mysterious pull that that stretch of beaches on the Oaxacan coast exerted on Aura as if her destiny were somehow foretold in its geography. What was I doing, at my age, bodysurfing in those waves? I should have known how dangerous it was. I knew the counterarguments to this, that had I been the kind of man who "acted his age," then I would have been a different person, one Aura wouldn't have fallen in love with. True enough. She'd broken her neck in the waves as a direct result of my being myself. In that sense, I *was* the wave.

But what about free will? Aura was a better swimmer than me, she chose to bodysurf, she chose to try to ride that wave; it was *her* impulse. Her whole adult life and even earlier she had struggled against the attempts of other people to control and to define her. So do you or I have any right to try to control her in death? All of that is true, but the fact remains, if I hadn't joined her in the water when I did, if I hadn't surfed a wave first, if I hadn't been there being myself, she wouldn't have flung herself into that wave.

There are dangerous beaches on this coast, says the district prosecutor. Zipolite is called la Playa de la Muerte because every year there are so many fatalities there. Puerto Escondido, Ventanilla, even San Agustinillo can be dangerous. But not Mazunte. Oh sure, you can get rolled and banged up in the waves and get hurt. But Aura is the first fatality at Mazunte in years. It was incredibly bad luck, what happened to your wife, says the prosecutor, well, that's how it seems to me.

He has the numbers. The district prosecutor goes down the list of beaches and notes how many have died at each one in recent years—I don't remember the figures, except that at Zipolite there'd been a lot, and at least a couple fatalities at every other beach, except Mazunte, where there were none, until Aura.

An accident so freakish it has happened to only one person, Aura, and to not one other of the countless swimmers who've bodysurfed at Mazunte for years and years, day after day. Aura has been most unfortunate. She died because I was being myself, an eternal adolescent, a *niñote*. She died because, bursting with love, I decided to join her in the water. But all of that is also an evasion of the TRUTH, against which my diligently constructed narrative collapses like a huge wave of nothing. My being myself shouldn't have been enough to kill Aura. Aura's being herself, launching herself into that wave for *whatever reason*, also should not have been enough to kill her. The utter freakishness and meaninglessness of it—there is the TRUTH. That day, after I leave the district prosecutor's office, that seems even harder to bear than my own responsibility.

It turns Aura's death into something that will never stop happening, as if the ludicrous fan in the district prosecutor's office is always blowing her death out into the universe, as if the sun and light of the world are now like the light in that office, frenetically gnashing at the earth, at the night, at my sight whether my eyes are open or shut.

32

The front steps of our building in Brooklyn were unusually steep, and because I have a gimpy knee from an old high school football injury, I'd take every step going down with that leg first, keeping it stiff, lowering it like a crutch. Descending at my side, Aura would imitate me, exaggerating, lurching like a cripple, her face turned up at me with a funny look of strained concentration. On cold damp days, when my knee ached, I'd limp a bit, and Aura, walking next to me, would imitate my limp, matching her steps precisely to mine. To people behind us on the sidewalk we must have looked pretty comical.

All my life I've been a tripper and stumbler. Frankie, lift your feet when you walk, don't drag your feet—when I was a boy, my father was always on me about that. But Aura thought it was hilarious whenever I stumbled against a curb or a raised crack in the sidewalk; she'd laugh like I'd performed a clown pratfall just for her. One reason she found it so funny, I thought, was because she never tripped. She was so light on her feet. Icy sidewalks did give her trouble, though, and then it would be my turn to giggle. I tripped and stumbled but I never fell: I always quickly regained my footing, like a halfback bouncing off a tackle, I was at least still limber enough for that.

Back in Brooklyn after Aura's death, only a week or two after that first return without her, coming up the stairs from the reeking summer furnace of the Broadway-Lafayette subway station, I tripped and fell as I never had before, facedown, astonishingly hard—my whole body slammed the stairs and I slid down several steps, my knees and torso and hands banging against the hard filthy iron. Mostly people kept on charging up and down, ignoring me, but a

few bent to help, holding out their hands, asking if I was okay. A
man in a suit actually knelt by me with his hand on my shoulder,
and asked, Are you hurt? Should we get help? I'm fine, I said. Please,
thank you, leave me alone, I'm okay. I pushed myself up onto my
feet and resumed climbing the stairs. My knees and hands ached as
if they'd been sledgehammered and I felt blood trickling down my
shin. There was a small tear in my jeans over my knee. My face was
burning and there were tears in my eyes, of humiliation as much
as anything else.

  What did it mean? Did that hard fall on the stairs mark the start,
finally, of being old? Maybe, but that's not the lesson I decided to
take. Later it seemed a lesson about grief. One of the most common
tropes and complaints in the grief books I've read is about the loneliness of the deep griever, because people and society seem unable,
for the various reasons always listed in those books, to accommodate such pain. But what could anybody possibly do or say to help?
Inconsolable doesn't mean that you are sometimes consolable. The
way things are has seemed right to me; it's all been as it should be,
or as if it could not be any other way. I even feel grateful for some
of the appalling things that have been said to me—Why can't you
go back to being the way you were before you met Aura?—because
they starkly demarcate a border, showing you a truth about where
you are now, whereas a supposedly sensitive comment might only
soften that border a little, but never make it less impenetrable. You
have to, can only, live this on your own.

33

When I spoke to Rodrigo at Fabiola's after the memorial service one year after, I found out for the first time that he and Juanita *were* let into the intensive care unit to see Aura that last night. Now Rodrigo thanked me. He thanked me for all that Fabiola and I had done, throughout that last day and night, to bring Aura home to Mexico City so that her mother could say good-bye to her.

When they were let in to see Aura, she was still conscious.

What did she say? I asked him.

Rodrigo told me:

Aura said, I don't want to die. She said, There's so much I want to do. *No quiero morir.*

34

I don't know how Juanita endures. I worry about her, and I don't say that to make myself seem less cold. I try to picture Juanita in her apartment, where she lives with Aura's ashes, try to follow her through her day, and I feel frightened. I worry about carrying the blame for another death. She no longer even speaks to the tías. If she were grieving in some other way, some way that appeared more positive at least to others, would it make a difference in how she feels? Maybe she survives with superhuman strength. She believes she will be reunited with her daughter in the afterlife. I hope she has found a new, very close friend to whom she can speak as she never could even to the tías, who can even make her laugh, who makes her feel loved and forgiven or understood, and who will always be there for her no matter what, who somehow always knows how to pull her back from the abyss.

Of course it was Aura, only Aura, with whom Juanita had a relationship like that.

35

A woman friend of mine—a bit older than me and the mother of a recently married young daughter—said that Aura had still belonged more to her mother than to me, that Juanita had still been Aura's "rightful caretaker." She meant no unkindness, and was only expressing what seemed obvious to her.

You hadn't had time yet to make Aura all your own, she said. Once you'd had a child and started a family of your own, that metamorphosis would have been complete.

Aura's closest friends, especially Lola and Fabiola, close observers over the years of Aura's relationship with her mother, themselves the daughters of mothers with strong personalities and careers of their own—Mexican mothers if that makes any difference—didn't agree.

Aura didn't think of her mother as her caretaker anymore, said Lola. If anything, it was the other way around. Aura had already taken her steps away and made her decisions, and she'd already started her own family, with you.

Will Lola still see it that way when, years from now, her own daughter, baby Aura, is taking *her* first seemingly decisive but perhaps only defiant steps away?

If she wanted to, would Juanita win this argument?

36

However you try to justify it, I thought, it's not right to keep a wife's mortal remains from her husband. Surely, most religions would forbid that. Even leaving religion out of it, a husband has a sacred right and duty to bury his wife's body, bones, ashes. I should have gone and taken the ashes, just like Juanita was afraid I was going to. What's wrong with me, why didn't I, why am I so cowardly?

But I also thought what I usually think: Poor woman, let her have the ashes, Aura is not her ashes, I'll keep the Aura I have.

Confusion, I don't know how to resolve this question, am not sure where the right or the wrong lies, but I look for answers where I usually do, in books. Ralph Waldo Emerson's first wife died at a young age after a long struggle with tuberculosis; for two years he was despondent and people feared for his sanity and health. Finally he had his wife's coffin dug up and opened so that he could confront the physical fact of her death and decay. Then he went to Europe. I haven't been able to confront that truth, but do I need to? I usually picture myself scooping Aura's ashes up in my hands and rubbing them all over my face, into my eyes, nose, even into my mouth.

I went to Europe too, using the insurance money from being hit by that car. And inside a church, I had a sort of revelation. The church was in a medieval fortress town about two hours by train outside of Paris. In the oldest part of its nave, high up in the walls, were two intact stained-glass windows from the fourteenth century. During World War II, townspeople had taken the windows down, carefully disassembled them, and stored them in a safe place, and that's how the windows had survived the bombs that later destroyed a large part of the church. Mass was over and

I was wandering around the restored nave, reading the pamphlet that told the history of the windows in English, and remembering the times Aura and I had visited old churches and cathedrals in Paris. Aura described herself as a believing Catholic, though she never went to Mass or performed any observances in her daily life. She always lit candles, though, when she visited these churches, and would cross herself and sometimes pray silently. I stopped at a little side chapel to the Virgin, dropped a euro in the tin box, lit a candle, and thought my own silent prayer, Virgin, if you exist, please take good care of Aura, while at the same instant, in harmony, another inner voice mocked me.

Then I stood under one of those ancient windows and tried to imagine the townspeople holding those seven-hundred-year-old pieces of colored glass in their hands, so fragile and precious, and carefully folding them away inside—inside of what? For a moment I got stuck on that. Old newspapers, old clothes, tablecloths, rags, maybe priests' vestments and the like? Purple, red, blue, yellow, green, the window was a translucent circle of those colors packed into a complex geometrical pattern that also gave the impression of a joyous simplicity. Seven hundred years, the window seemed to say, that's nothing, probably I'll still be here in a thousand years, looking just like I do now. In the expanse of time that the window and the dusky interior of that church suggested, I was just a speck, one more human who'd lost someone, among the thousands upon thousands of humans who over seven hundred years had sat or stood in this church staring up at those same windows while thinking of loved ones lost. I really don't have much time left, I thought. It'll all be over in a blink. I thought of Juanita and Leopoldo and their hatred of me, and their determination to erase from Aura's history our love and marriage. In a way, I thought, it's as if they took those windows down and instead of putting them away and keeping them safe, they stole and hid them. These words came to me: Your hatred can save me. Your hatred can even free me. Because it leaves behind an emptiness that I have an obligation to fill in for Aura and me. Those are the words that came to me in that church.

I walked to the other window. The sky must have been a little less overcast on that side of the church, because it was as if a finger had pressed down on a computer keyboard's sun-icon key, infusing that stained-glass window with just a little more light. It was easier to distinguish the ancient kaleidoscopic patterns, the colored circles inside of circles and other shapes, images of plants and tiny human and animal figures. That yellow oblong shape down near the bottom, I thought, looks like a drumstick.

I left the church and walked down through the streets toward the river, marking my steps with *frond, rings, marooned, barreling up, lewd, skein, squall, crevice, drumstick* . . . in 2009 Aura Estrada is thirty-two. Her birthday was a little more than a month away. I was in my down jacket and was wearing a new Chinatown aviator's hat, fake-fur earflaps down. Stairs led from the sidewalk down to the river. Long wild grass grew along the bank, and I walked on some large smooth stones out amid reeds and stood there with the shallow water flowing around me. The bridges that spanned the river, the long uniform row of black-roofed, dun-colored houses on the opposite bank, smoke from the chimneys, gray sky, ducks.

37

I'd flown to Paris. I wanted to stand outside the amphibian house in the Jardin des Plantes, go to the Cité Universitaire where Aura and I had once stayed in a windowless basement room of the Maison du Mexique, and to 15 rue Violet, where we'd subletted a small apartment for a month during the holidays of 2004–'05. I wanted to go to the neighborhood market where we'd bought the capon she cooked for our Christmas dinner and to the little laundromat where we'd washed, dried, and folded our own clothes, something we'd never done even once in New York or Mexico because there we always dropped our laundry off. I retraced the long walk—which Aura described in one of the completed chapters of her novel—that Marcelo Díaz Michaux, the future psycho-analyst, then a Mexican student at the Sorbonne, takes on that snowy afternoon in 1972 when he receives a letter from Julieta, his sweetheart, Alicia's future mother, telling him that she's marrying another man—starting at Rue du Bac, going down to the Boulevard Saint-Germain, across the Seine at the Pont de Sully, up through the Place des Vosges, and all the way to Boulevard Voltaire in the Oberkampf, where Marcelo stops at Le Bataclan to buy a ticket for that night's Velvet Underground concert.

I wanted to go to one of those small musty cinemas where we used to see movies in languages that neither of us spoke—Arabic, Thai—though Aura had no problem following the French subtitles. I loved sitting close to Aura in the dark, not understanding what the characters were saying, trying to decipher and piece the story together like something I'd give to her later, like a gift I'd made myself. One movie was about a Lebanese family in war-torn Beirut. Out on the sidewalk, I said:

Well, obviously, that girl had really cruel parents and brothers, the way they wouldn't even let her out of the house. No wonder it ended like that, poor girl.

Frank, she was a *slave*! said Aura. That's the whole point! She's a Lebanese Christian slave, and the family that owns her is Muslim. ¡Ay, mi amor!

I went into one of those cinemas without Aura, saw a movie in Finnish, crushingly tedious, and fell asleep about a third of the way through. I was staying alone in the same fleabag hotel near Les Gobelins that Aura and I had once stayed in. A friend had recommended the Jeanne d'Arc to us but later we discovered that multiple hotels had that name and this was not the one my friend had meant. We were about to board our flight back to New York when Aura, at the ticket counter, was informed that her student visa was expired. In the freezing cold, near the Arc de Triomphe, I waited outside the U.S. consulate while Aura was inside. French police kept telling me I couldn't stand there with our possibly bomb-packed luggage, but I kept refusing to move. There were more suitcases than I could carry and then how would Aura find me? Go ahead and arrest me, I said heatedly, I'm not moving, I'm waiting for my wife—I pulled out my U.S. passport and waved it in their faces—and nobody's going to tell me I can't wait for my wife outside my own country's consulate! I'd said wife though Aura wasn't yet my wife. But the police did leave me alone after that. Because of the visa screwup we had three extra days in Paris, which we spent in the Jeanne d'Arc our friend had recommended, in the Marais.

Of course there's a nice Paris and a supremely nasty Paris; people get consigned to one or the other, and that's the Paris they know. That's how it seemed to me, but going to Paris with Aura was like stepping through the Looking Glass. Now waiters stood over our tables making wiggly cat's cradles with their hands and struggling with their terrible Spanish, trying to translate obscure French menu items for Aura. If we asked directions, the French practically turned into cordial Mexicans, *Paris es tu casa*. They were delighted to take our cameras and snap pictures of us. The French really liked Aura, though a disconcerting number thought she resembled Amelie, that pretty but annoying Parisian movie character.

Now I was back in pre-Aura Paris. Youngish French goons in tracksuits trailed me off a Metro train, taunting me by mimicking stereotypical Egyptian music—*dada-dah-dah-dahhh*. Oh, and so on. The world, not just Paris, is too idiotic and hateful to be left alone in. I'm remembering that New York wedding we went to, where Aura found herself seated next to a glamorous rich white writer. In the middle of a conversation they were having, he exclaimed, You're Mexican? Then how come you speak English? Aura was beginning to realize what it was going to mean to be a Mexican writer in the United States. That was one reason she'd decided to make her career mostly in Spanish.

Just as had been happening all winter in New York, I kept finding myself trapped in a silent movie, everything black and white and jittery. I went into a bar, Le Sully, that some of the Mexicans I knew in Paris used to hang out in, but didn't recognize anybody and sat alone in a corner and ordered a drink, and then another. Everything flickery. Everyone's skin, face, and hands like candy canes with the stripes licked off. Radioactive eyes. Rat-like scheming in every facial expression. People rubbing their hands together under their chins, pursing their lips, and trading glances. A man crying into his hands like a Rodin sculpture. Flames in the mirrors, and the whole bar looks like it's melting or like celluloid film about to combust, and I paid and headed outside to walk.

The main reason I'd come to Paris, though, was that I wanted to visit La Ferte, the asylum clinic that was the model for the asylum in Aura's unfinished novel. So that Aura could research La Ferte, our plan had been to go there in the spring of 2008. Now it was nearly a year after. I felt I owed it to Aura to fulfill that ambition. What I'd known before about La Ferte, from Aura, I'd since supplemented with some research of my own. I knew that it was an experimental utopian asylum clinic of a very French kind where, in Aura's novel, the psychoanalyst Marcelo Díaz Michaux was going to work. La Ferte is housed in a seventeenth-century château where patients, mental health professionals, nurses, and other staff are all supposed to live side by side as equals, running the clinic together. In the kitchen, psychoanalysts chop parsley alongside psychotics chopping onions. In theory, the patients at La Ferte aren't supposed to always know who among the other patients is a psychoanalyst, and so on. Even a psychoanalyst, I read somewhere, might not always know if he's speaking to a patient or to another incognito psychoanalyst.

Late that last fall, her first semester in the MFA program, Aura wrote a letter to La Ferte, addressed to the clinic's longtime director, the eighty-seven-year-old Dr. Olivier Arnaux, asking if she could visit. About two months later she received a reply in the mail: a plain brown envelope with our Brooklyn address hand-printed in green ink, and inside, on a sheet of paper without a letterhead, in the same handwriting and with the same green pen, a few lines inviting Aura to visit La Ferte. But instead of being from Dr. Arnaux, the letter was signed by Sophie Deonarine. Was that Dr. Arnaux's secretary? No title, professional or otherwise, identified her. The handwriting looked as if a trembling grip had painstakingly traced each letter from an alphabet of crudely shaped thin wires. Was Sophie Deonarine just a patient who, with or without permission, answered Dr. Arnaux's mail? That possibility had kind of thrilled us.

The time Aura and I had stayed in the Cité Universitaire was because I'd been invited by my friend Juan Ríos to talk to the evening writing workshop he ran at the Mexican Cultural Institute. One of the students was a young Frenchwoman, Pauline, who'd lived in Ecuador a few years working for an organization that was trying to save an endangered species of Andean bear. She was a PhD student, too, but was enrolled in the workshop to keep up her Spanish writing. After the workshop, we all went out for dinner, and Aura and Pauline were talking when one of those coincidences occurred that can make a writer, especially a young writer like Aura, feel as if the cosmos is aligning to help bring her book into being. It turned out that when Pauline was a very small child, some twenty-five years before, her mother had worked at La Ferte. Some of Pauline's earliest memories were of being a little girl at La Ferte.

Later I found notes of that conversation with Pauline in one of Aura's notebooks. Psychotics can seem pretty normal, Aura had recorded, until they don't. Like the patient who used to give Pauline's mother a shopping list of things he wanted when she went into town. She'd saved one of these lists as a souvenir and Pauline saw it: *Le Monde*, pipe tobacco, batteries, cherry preserves, semen . . .

I took a Sunday morning train to the town nearest La Ferte. In the seat across from me sat a little boy dressed in a Spider-Man costume, traveling with his parents. I should dress like that, I thought. Maybe tomorrow I will. For a moment it seemed so plausible and even reasonable that tomorrow I might dress as Spider-Man that I felt a little scared.

In the train station I stopped at the newsstand and with my third-grade French tried to ask the elderly woman working there where I could get a taxi to La Ferte. Her answer was improbably long, and I didn't understand it. A tall, young black man buying a newspaper turned and said, in Caribbean-accented English, She says that you do not need a taxi. There is a van that will come from La Ferte. You only need to telephone. You are going to the clinic, correct?

The newsstand woman had a card with La Ferte's telephone number printed on it, and after the Caribbean fellow had done me the favor of phoning La Ferte on my cell, he said, They will come for you at one in the afternoon. You are to wait in front of the station. It is a blue van.

It was a little before eleven in the morning. I wandered the town, stopping into the church, and then went down to the river.

A psychoanalyst, seated in his chair, sees a new patient come into his office for the first time, observes him for a moment, and says, Oh, you aren't here, are you? You are still outside in the garden.

I read that anecdote in an essay by Dr. Olivier Arnaux that had been published in English. Most personalities, wrote Arnaux, are organized around a single point that holds the self together. But schizophrenics have many such points that are all over the place and that's why their selves aren't limited only to their bodies or even to the same enclosed space that their bodies happen to be in. The psychiatrists and psychoanalysts at La Ferte, with their famous method of Intuitive Poetic Diagnosis, are trained to recognize such conditions at first sight. That's how the psychoanalyst could tell that even though the patient was there in his office, he was really in the garden, or at the beach, or somewhere else a century ago, or a few years ago.

At La Ferte, the method is to treat psychotics, schizophrenics, and severe melancholics like normal people who, however medicated, can still respond to talking therapies and participate in a community and have chores and take classes and so on. The goal, I read, is to be able to *graft* into that patient just enough of one of those self-anchoring points that, amid the chaos of all those other points, the patient will be able to reach for the grafted one, or at least have a chance to. It's not a cure but can lessen suffering and provide a patient with unprecedented, if fleeting, instances of repose and even human connection. Cobweb thin, I pictured it, or delicate as an eardrum, a peaceful prosthetic soul, artfully grafted into the middle of swirling delusion, pain, lostness, terror. I liked that idea, like something out of a fairy tale, the elf cobblers who come out at night to make, instead of magical new shoes, a self or a soul. What had Aura made of that idea when she came across it? When Marcelo Díaz Michaux saw Irma—Julieta and little Alicia's housekeeper—for the first time, what did he see that made him want to take Irma back to France and put her in La Ferte? Could a shadowy facsimile of Aura's soul or self be grafted onto mine? Was it maybe already there and would they see it?

A large blue van pulled up. There were two people in front and a few passengers scattered among three rows in back, including a man in the very back staring out the window at me, long pale face, thin mouth, a dark fedora, a resemblance to William Burroughs. Patients on a Sunday outing into the city, I thought. But maybe that man in the fedora isn't a patient.

The front window came down. A woman with thick curly black hair, vivid eyebrows, and brown skin, a striking woman somewhere in her thirties, wearing a down vest over a sweater, said my name. I shook her delicate hand through the window, pulled the van door open, and got in. An elderly woman next to me, in a crumpled wool coat, sat slumped forward, looking resolutely out the window; on the seat between us was a plastic shopping bag with some items in it. The driver, a ruddy man in a watch cap, asked me something, and it was instantly established that I didn't speak French. The woman in front, however, turned out to be a visiting intern from Brazil who could speak Spanish. Her name was Luiza. We were driving out of the town when Luiza asked, And which patient are you coming to visit? I answered that I wasn't coming to visit any patient. She translated that for the driver, who glanced at her questioningly, but neither of them said anything. We were driving along a woods-lined road, bare skinny trees flashing past like obelisks. I was sure that Luiza was silently rehearsing how to tell me that I wasn't going to be allowed into La Ferte. I hope I at least get to see it, I thought. I turned and looked at the pale man in the fedora, who stared back at me with the sad quivering gaze of a dog in the rain.

And what is the motive for your visit? Luiza asked me.

I told her about Aura, her incomplete novel, and our correspondence with Dr. Arnaux. Aura had received an invitation to visit, I said, from Dr. Arnaux's secretary.

But Dr. Arnaux doesn't work on Sundays, said Luiza, and neither does his secretary. There's hardly any staff today.

If I could just have a look around, I said. I paused and added, So that when I do get a chance to speak to Dr. Arnaux, I'll have a better idea what to ask.

The château was like a castle in a forest, with sandstone walls, gables, dark slate roofing, a pillared portico, long rows of windows, and a tower topped by a conical roof on each side.

The person in charge that Sunday, Luiza told me, was Catherine, and I would have to speak to her. Catherine was a slight woman with gray-yellow hair and a lined face, dressed in sweater and jeans, wearing a dark red lipstick. We found her smoking a cigarette at the back of the main hall, by a bay window through which I could see some of the other buildings on the property, a few with smoke pouring from their chimneys, and the winter woods and fields beyond. Catherine, who did speak English, quizzed me about my visit. I repeated what I'd told Luiza in the van. The whole time, I felt her smallish blue eyes observing me. What did she see? It couldn't have been so terrible, could it have? She gave me permission to spend the day. The van, she said, would bring me back to the town in time for the last evening train to Paris.

And so my love, that's how I managed to get us into La Ferte. What I saw there is what I imagine you expected or hoped to see. I think it would have lived up to your expectations. They have their own little bakery, where the patients crowd inside, standing close together in the warmth from the wood-burning oven and that damp yeasty smell, singing children's songs while they wait for the cheesecloth-covered loaves to rise; and they have a goat barn, and horses, and all kinds of classes, art, music, even creative writing classes in the old stone chapel. Do you know what the château reminded of? Mohonk Mountain House, though without hunting trophies on the walls, and shabbier, the furniture more worn out, it being an asylum, of course, and not a spa-hotel. But there was a fire in the stone fireplace. There was a bar—with dark wood-paneled walls and a domed, painted ceiling unlike anything at Mohonk— serving soft drinks, fruit syrups, cookies and candies, and where every Saturday, Luiza told me, Marie, a folksinger from the town, comes to perform from two in the morning until just before dawn. The patients themselves chose those hours. Those are the hours when they are up and awake and in the mood to listen and sing along. If I asked Marie to sing "Stephanie Says," would she? I felt a strong longing to be there with them, singing, thinking that maybe I would find something out, something important, if only I could do that. The patients, of course, were nothing like the guests at Mohonk. But I will spare you descriptions of the colorful mad.

Luiza, in the first room she took me into, unlocked a cabinet and began dispensing medicines to the horde of patients crowded in there. Among them was a man who would not get off the floor. He was lying prostrate on his stomach with his head turned to the side, occasionally even conversing, though barely, and in a tortured voice, with the other patients who were stepping and milling around him.

I am not like that man after all, I thought. I've come all the way here for you, and for me.

So what *would* Aura have made of La Ferte? Why *was* Marcelo Díaz Michaux going to bring Irma back here with him?

When I was climbing the curving wooden staircase to the second floor of the château, I noticed dust on all the steps, and spiderwebs in the corners and on the banisters. Such a pity that Irma isn't here anymore, I thought, she'd never let this place get so dirty. That wasn't my voice. It was Marcelo's. I was Marcelo, the psychoanalyst, climbing the stairs, on my way to work with some patients. Isn't my young wife waiting for me at home? Doesn't she love me? Then why do I feel so bereft? Is it because Irma isn't at La Ferte anymore? But she still lives in France, doesn't she? Where is Alicia? She's not here anymore, either, is she? Where has she gone? Où sont les axolotls?

How can I ever know or imagine what Aura would have made of La Ferte? Do with La Ferte what you will, my love. I know it will be great. I kept my promise, and brought you here.